Praise for *The Widow's House* 6/28

"Carol Goodman hits it out of the scary, crumbling, haunted ballpark with *The Widow's House*, a tale that blends a perfect gothic premise—an old mansion, a long-dead baby's cries, madness, and betrayal—with modern, mysterious twists and turns that will keep the reader guessing until the last page. I couldn't put it down but I didn't want it to end."

—Wendy Webb, bestselling and award-winning author of *The Vanishing*

"*The Widow's House* is foreboding and moody, haunted by the long dead—and by long-dead dreams. As you're pulled deeper into its crumbling corridors and gothic history, you'll never guess where its true threats lie, or who will survive to break its decades-old curse."

—Miranda Beverly-Whittemore, *New York Times* bestselling author of *Bittersweet* and *June*

"Carol Goodman is, simply put, a stellar writer. She doesn't tell a story as much as she weaves a dream. I sank right into *The Widow's House*—a rich, complex, scary, and utterly compelling novel about the layers of love, the tangle of marriage, and the ghosts that haunt us. This is the very best kind of read—the one you want never to end even as you can't stop yourself from turning the pages."

—Lisa Unger, *New York Times* bestselling author of *The Red Hunter*

"Evocative and resonant references to local folklore and to literature such as Charlotte Perkins Gilman's 'The Yellow Wallpaper' and Edgar Allen Poe's 'The Fall of the House of Usher' combine with influences from both classic gothic works and domestic suspense novels. . . . Gripping readers with its fast pace, supernatural elements, and a conclusion that will have them questioning what really happened here, this psychological thriller is for admirers of Barbara Michaels, Kate Morton, or Daphne Du Maurier."   —*Library Journal*

Praise for Carol Goodman's Other Novels

"Voluptuous. . . . Goodman has a flair for the stylistic flourishes of romantic suspense."   —*New York Times Book Review*

"Goodman takes crime fiction to another level with her complex plots and lyrical prose."   —*Globe and Mail*

"A gothic and elegant page-turner."   —*Boston Globe*

"Goodman expertly melds the psychological thriller and academic mystery into a compelling story of revenge and grief."
—Associated Press

"Gives her many fans a dose of what she does best: good storytelling, with velvet swaths of gothic mist and fairy-tale eeriness."
—*Plain Dealer*

THE
WIDOW'S
HOUSE

Also by Carol Goodman

The Lake of Dead Languages
The Seduction of Water
The Drowning Tree
The Ghost Orchid
The Sonnet Lover
The Night Villa
Arcadia Falls
River Road

THE BLYTHEWOOD SERIES
Blythewood
Ravencliffe
Hawthorn

THE
WIDOW'S
HOUSE

CAROL GOODMAN

wm

WILLIAM MORROW
An Imprint of HarperCollinsPublishers

HarperCollins
PUBLISHERS
— Since 1817 —

P.S.™ is a trademark of HarperCollinsPublishers.

HarperCollins books may be purchased for educational, business, or sales promotional use. For information, please email the Special Markets Department at SPsales@harpercollins.com.

FIRST EDITION

Designed by Diahann Sturge

Library of Congress Cataloging-in-Publication Data has been applied for.

ISBN 978-0-06-256262-3

17 18 19 20 21   RRD   10 9 8 7 6 5 4 3 2 1

For Lee

And now the flight
of sea hawks hints at pterodactyl blood
while ancient sunlight shimmers on the bay,
and our thoughts turn to love, which if it lasts
a year will flirt with immortality.

Vesuvius has nothing new to say,
haze-shrouded, calm. This all goes by so fast.

There's more than one kind of catastrophe.
—LEE SLONIMSKY, "SEASIDE BENCH, SORRENTO"

Chapter One

When I picture the house I see it in the late afternoon, the golden river light filling the windows and gilding the two-hundred-year-old brick. That's how we came upon it, Jess and I, at the end of a long day looking at houses we couldn't afford.

"It's the color of old money," Jess said, his voice full of longing. He was standing in the weed-choked driveway, his fingers twined through the ornate loops of the rusted iron gate. "But I think it's a little over our 'price bracket.'"

I could hear the invisible quotes around the phrase, one the Realtor had used half a dozen times that day. Jess was always a wicked mimic and Katrine Vanderberg, with her faux country quilted jacket and English rubber boots and bright yellow Suburban, was an easy target. *All she needs is a hunting rifle to look like she strode out of Downton Abbey,* he'd whispered in my ear when she'd come out of the realty office to greet us. You'd have to know Jess as well as I did to know it was himself he was mocking for dreaming of a mansion when it was clear we could hardly afford a hovel.

It had seemed like a good idea. Go someplace new. Start over. Sell the (already second-mortgaged) Brooklyn loft, pay back the (maxed-out) credit cards, and buy something cheap in the country while Jess finished his book. By country, Jess meant the Hudson Valley, where we had both gone to college, and where he had begun his first novel. He'd developed the superstition over the last winter that if he returned to the site where the muses had first spoken to him he would finally be able to write his long-awaited second novel. And how much could houses up there cost? We both remembered the area as rustic: Jess because he'd seen it through the eyes of a Long Island kid and me because I'd grown up in the nearby village of Concord and couldn't wait to get out and live in the city.

Since we'd graduated, though, 9/11 had happened and property values in exurbia had soared. The rustic farmhouses and shabby chic Victorian cottages we'd looked at today cost more than we'd get for the sale of our Brooklyn loft and Jess had immediately rejected the more affordable split-levels and sixties suburban ranches Katrine showed us.

"They remind me of my dismal childhood," he said, staring woefully at the avocado linoleum of a Red Hook faux Colonial.

"There's one more place I think you should see," Katrine had said after Jess refused to get out of the car at a modular home. She'd turned the Suburban off Route 9G toward River Road. For a second I thought she was driving us toward the college and I tensed in the backseat. Jess might want to live in the area where we had gone to school, but he didn't want to *see* those young hopeful college students loping along the shaded paths of Bailey College. At least not until he'd finished the second novel and he was invited back to do a reading.

But Katrine turned south, away from the college, and I heard Jess in the front seat sigh as we entered the curving tree-lined road. *This* was what I knew he had in mind when he talked about moving to the country: dry-laid stone walls covered with moss, ancient sycamores with bark peeling off like old wallpaper, apple orchards, clapboard Victorian farmhouses, and, through the gaps in the trees, glimpses of stately mansions and the blue ridges of the Catskills beyond the river. The road itself was filled with the light of a Hudson River school painting. I could see it reflected in Jess's face, replacing the sallow cast it had taken on this winter as he'd labored over his long-unfinished work. Or the "unborn monster," as he'd christened it. If only there were something we could afford on this road, but even the dreary farmhouse I'd grown up in was surely out of our price range.

When we pulled into a weed-choked driveway and parked outside a rusted gate, though, I immediately recognized where we were and thought Katrine had misunderstood our situation. Lots of people did. Jess was, after all, a *famous* writer. The first book had done well enough—and he'd been young and photogenic enough—to get his picture in *Granta* and *Vanity Fair*. He'd gotten a high-six-figure advance for the second novel—but that was ten years ago. The advance was long gone; the second novel was still incomplete.

But Jess had already gotten out, drawn by that golden river light, and gone to stand at the iron gate to gaze up at the house. Silhouetted against the afternoon light, so thin and wiry in his black jeans and leather jacket, he looked like part of the iron scrollwork. *How thin he's grown this winter,* I thought. The late afternoon sun turned Jess's hair the red gold it had been when we first met in college, banishing the silver that had begun, not unattractively, to limn his temples. His eyes were hidden behind dark sunglasses, but I could still read the longing in his face as he gazed up at the house. And who wouldn't long for such a house?

It stood on a rise above a curve in the river like a medieval watchtower. The old brick was mellowed with age and warmed from centuries of river light, the windows made from wavy cockled glass with tiny bubbles in it that held the light like good champagne. The sunken gardens surrounding an ornamental pond were already cool and dark, promising a dusky retreat even on the hottest summer day. For a moment I thought I heard the sound of glasses clinking and laughter from a long-ago summer party, but then I realized it was just some old wind chimes hanging from the gatehouse. There hadn't been any parties here for a while. When the sun went behind a cloud and the golden glow disappeared my eyes lingered more on the missing slate tiles in the roof, the weeds growing up between the paving stones of the front flagstones, the paint peeling off the porch columns, and the cracked and crumbling front steps. I even thought I could detect on the river breeze the smell of rot and mildew. And when Jess turned, his fingers still gripping the gate, I saw that without that light his face had turned sallow again and the look of longing was replaced with the certainty that he would always be on the wrong side of that gate. That's how he had become such a good mimic, by watching and listening from the other side. It made my heart ache for him.

"No, not in our 'price bracket' I think."

If Katrine noticed his mocking tone she didn't let on. "It isn't for sale," she said. "But the owner's looking for a caretaker."

If I could have tackled her before the words were out of her mouth, I would have, but the damage was already done. Jess's face had the stony look it got when he was getting ready to demolish someone, but as he often did these days he turned the rancor on himself. "I've always fancied myself a bit of a Mellors."

I was about to jump in and tell Katrine that Mellors was

the caretaker in a D. H. Lawrence novel but she was laughing as if she'd gotten the reference. "That's just the sort of thing Mr. Montague would say. That's why I thought you two might get along."

"Montague? Not Alden Montague, the writer? This is his house?" Jess looked at me questioningly to see if I'd known it was the old Montague place, but Katrine, ignoring—or perhaps not noticing—Jess's appalled tone, saved me.

"I thought you might know him, Jess being a writer and since you both went to Bailey. He's looking for a caretaker for the estate. A couple, preferably. He's not paying much, but it's free rent and I'd think it would be a wonderful place to write. It could be just the thing for your . . . circumstances."

I glanced at Katrine, reassessing her. Beneath the highlighted blond hair and fake English country getup and plastered-on Realtor's smile she was smart, smart enough to see through our dithering over the aluminum siding and cracked linoleum to realize we couldn't afford even the cheapest houses she'd shown us today.

"But you wouldn't get a commission on that," I pointed out, half to give Jess a chance to get ahold of himself. The last person who'd mentioned Alden Montague around him had gotten a black eye for his trouble.

"No," she admitted, "but if someone was on the grounds fixing up the place it would sell for a lot more when the time came—and if that someone planted a bug in Mr. Montague's ear to use a certain Realtor . . ."

She let her voice trail off with a flip of her blond hair and a sly we're-all-in-this-together smile that I was sure Jess would roll his eyes at, but instead he smiled back, some of that golden light returning to his face.

"In other words," he said in the silky drawl he used for inter-

views, "you don't give the old man much longer to live and you
want an accomplice on the inside."

To her credit, Katrine didn't even sham surprise.

"I wouldn't put it quite like that. But the word around town
is that Mr. Montague is a pretty sick man. I have no intention
of taking advantage of that, but I did think the situation might
be mutually beneficial . . ."

Jess grinned. "Why then, by all means, set up the interview.
I'd give good money to see Old Monty on his deathbed."

THE ARRANGEMENTS WERE made so quickly—Katrine purring
into her cell phone by the side of the road while Jess and I
stood at the gate—that I suspected the "interview" had been
set up beforehand. Katrine must have known we'd be interested, which meant we must have smelled as desperate as we
really were.

"You're not seriously thinking of doing this," I said to Jess
when Katrine excused herself to make another call to change
"a few previous engagements." "After what Monty did—"

Jess winced. He hated any reference to "the review" but
then he turned that look of pain on me and I knew that wasn't
what he was thinking about. "I thought *you'd* want to see him.
He always liked your stories."

Now it was my turn to wince. It was true that Alden
Montague—or Old Monty as he had been called around the
college by both his friends and enemies—had said a few nice
things about my stories, but I had come to suspect that he
had singled me out because my sophomoric attempts hadn't
threatened him as much as Jess's writing had. A point borne
out when Alden Montague wrote a damning review of Jess's
first book.

"He felt sorry for me," I told Jess, not for the first time. "The local girl surrounded by all you big city sharks. I'm sorry to hear he's sick, though. It's kind of sad to think of him all alone up there in that moldering pile."

"Are you kidding?" Jess snorted. "He's become a character in one of those dreadful Gothic novels he so admires. I just want to see him. Maybe he'll be in a wheelchair with a moth-eaten afghan over his lap . . . Ooh! Maybe he's on an oxygen machine."

I swatted his arm. "That's awful, Jess." There wasn't much conviction in my voice, though. The review had been damning and, coming from his former teacher, had crippled Jess's attempts to write for years. *Not bad, but not all that good either,* was one phrase I often heard Jess repeating in a perfect imitation of Alden Montague's patrician drawl.

This past winter, though, just when things had seemed the worst and after two aborted drafts that he'd literally burned, Jess had started working in earnest, and I didn't want a reminder of Alden Montague to derail him. I was going to suggest that we simply leave—we could look elsewhere for a less expensive house, further west in the Catskills, perhaps—but just then Katrine came toward us.

"He says the keys to the gate are in the third mailbox to the right." She pointed to a row of warped and listing metal mailboxes to the right of the gate pillar.

"Why so many mailboxes?" I asked, as I struggled to open the rusted metal flap.

"Over the years Mr. Montague has rented out some of the outbuildings, to Bailey students, a new-agey type who makes puppets for the Halloween parade and tells fortunes, a metal artist who works in the south barn—"

The flap came suddenly loose and something long and black slithered out of the mailbox. I screamed and jumped back as the snake fell inches from my foot. It wound itself into a figure eight and drew back its wedge-shaped head. Before it could strike, Jess brought down the heel of his heavy boot onto its head.

I screamed again, more from surprise at Jess's violent and swift response. When he lifted his boot I could see that the snake's head had been crushed.

"Quick thinking," Katrine said, peering over my shoulder, apparently unruffled by the appearance of the snake or Jess's action—which still had my heart racing. "It's a rattler."

"*Was* a rattler," Jess said, kneeling to examine his kill.

"I'd forgotten there were snakes up here," I said, thinking that here was another reason to turn around and head back to the city. "We got them at our farmhouse—"

"The old Jackson place, right?" Katrine asked. "I thought I recognized you."

I smiled, trying to recall her face, but drawing a blank. "I'm sorry . . ."

"Oh, you wouldn't remember me. I was a year behind you and not in honors classes like you were. I went to Dutchess Community for two years and then SUNY Potsdam. By the time I got back you had already graduated from Bailey and gone to live in the city. Married to that famous writer"—she turned toward Jess and smiled—"and valiant snake killer. Do you think you could get those keys now?"

Jess looked skeptically at the mailbox but under Katrine's bright smile—the same bright smile she'd used when assuring us that the watermarks in the last basement we'd seen had come from a broken boiler and not habitual flooding—gamely stuck his hand in to retrieve the keys. As he pulled his hand out he jarred a vine hanging over the gate pillar, uncovering a marble plaque with the words "River House" carved on it—

only the last letter had been defaced. It looked as if someone had taken a chisel to it and crudely carved in an "n." I peered closer and heard Jess, reading over my shoulder, bark a dry laugh as he read the reconfigured name.

"Oh," Katrine said, looking more uncomfortable about this than the venomous snake. "Some vandal's idea of a joke— unfortunately one that's stuck. People in the village call it that because of . . . well, you've probably heard the stories, Clare." With that she passed through the gate.

Jess was still staring at the plaque. "Riven House," he said aloud. It might as well be called Broken House." Then he grinned. "Perfect place for a broken-down writer, eh?"

Now that Katrine had mentioned it, I did remember hearing some locals call the old Montague place "Riven House" because of its unhappy history, but I'd also heard people call it the widow's house. Sometime back in the thirties the owner of the house had been killed in a shooting accident. His grieving widow was said to have wandered the house and grounds, crying inconsolably and finally killing herself. Even then, the townspeople said, she was seen walking the grounds or appearing at windows, a specter of grief and remorse. The house had slid into decay after that, but that wasn't uncommon for these old Hudson River mansions, which often enough had their stories of scandal, financial ruin, madness, ghosts, and declining maintenance. As we got closer to the house it became even more apparent what truly bad condition it was in. Chunks of the sandstone trim had fallen clean off the brick façade. The bricks were pitted and pockmarked, as if the house had at one time had a case of smallpox. A swath of ivy hung over half the façade like a veil the house had donned to hide its marred face. *A widow's veil,* I found myself thinking. The whole house looked as if it had gone into mourning.

As we walked up the hill we passed an old apple orchard that looked like it was suffering from fire blight. I had the feeling that all the surrounding vegetation was creeping toward the house. Even one of the apple trees had broken free from the ranks of the orchard and was listing against the side of a clapboard addition built onto the north side of the house. We were walking through knee-high grass—remembering the snake, Katrine's boots no longer seemed like an affectation—which surrounded the house like a green whispering sea. The front door hung marooned over a flight of demolished stairs, giving the house the look of a stranded ship wrecked on a coral reef. I wouldn't have been surprised to see crabs crawling out of its blind eye-socket windows; I did notice swallows darting in and out of the attic windows.

"It looks like a medieval tower," Jess remarked.

"It's an octagonal house," Katrine replied. "They were quite a fad in the mid-nineteenth century. People believed they generated some kind of *vital energy*." Katrine laughed to show she didn't hold with such new-age nonsense but would happily use it to sell a house. "This is one of the most famous examples. You can see the glass skylight in the central dome . . ."

"It looks like the House of Usher," I said to Jess as Katrine stomped on ahead.

"Yes!" he said, his face shining with a thin sheen of sweat and unmistakable excitement. "It's wonderful!"

For not the first time in our marriage I noticed that for all Jess's writerly powers of observation he tended to overlook some things—little things like the trail of bread crumbs he left on the kitchen counter after making his toast in the morning; bigger things like our mounting credit card debt. Right now he was clearly seeing a magical fairy-tale castle while I saw a large crumbling bio-habitat for mice and bats. Or perhaps he saw the big picture—the possibilities—while my eye was drawn to the imperfections, the flaws.

"Would the caretakers *live* in the house?" I asked Katrine when we caught up to her at a side door.

"Oh no!" Katrine said. "Mr. Montague likes his privacy. There's a caretaker's cottage down by the river. It's quite cozy—and in much better shape than the main house," she added in a lower voice.

"What were you thinking, Clare," Jess muttered in my ear. "Us field hands don't live in the big house."

I suppressed a giggle as Katrine led us around to the addition on the north side. We passed under the old apple tree to a heavy oak door. She pushed it open and we stepped down into a dim, cool space. It was what my mother would have called the mudroom—which shared space with the washer and dryer in my childhood home—but which Katrine referred to as the boot hall. An assortment of boots and shoes that looked like they dated back to the mid-fifties lined the cocoa-matted floor. The walls were thatched so thickly with jackets, coats, dog leashes, canvas bags, leather satchels, and various gardening tools that the room had narrowed to a clogged corridor.

"Should we take off our shoes?" I asked, doubtfully looking down at the grimy matting, caked with what looked like decades' worth of mud.

Katrine laughed. "Gawd no! You'll step on a nail and need a tetanus shot. That's all Mr. Montague needs. He can barely afford to heat this big place. He lives downstairs in a basement apartment"—she pointed to a doorway half hidden between the hanging coats—"but in honor of you two he's opened up the library for us today. He's waiting there."

The Library, Jess mouthed as we followed Katrine out of the boot hall and into an equally dark and cluttered corridor

(this one lined with stacks of newspapers and empty bottles).
"Where we shall take some more tea."

"I've had nothing yet," I answered, recognizing Jess's prompt
from *Alice in Wonderland*, "so I can't take more."

"You mean you can't take *less*," Jess finished in his Mad
Hatter's voice, "it's very easy to take more than nothing."

I smiled and relaxed a bit. Quoting from *Alice in Wonderland* was always a sign that Jess was in a good mood. This
was a game to him, an adventure. He was already turning it
into a story to tell our Williamsburg friends at dinner. *Our visit
to the famous writer in his decaying mansion.* I could see his
eyes, hungrily scanning the dim hallway for details, cataloging
the stuffed deer heads and peeling wallpaper and age-mottled
prints of family ancestors. I paused in front of one sepia-tinted
photograph of a young girl in a flimsy white dress crowned with
a wreath of blossoms, wearing a sash that read "Apple Blossom
Queen 192-," the last digit obscured by the curve of her waist,
and remembered that the town still crowned an Apple Blossom
Queen each spring when I was in grade school. The Montagues
owned orchards, which might explain the floral pattern of
apple blossoms on the sliding pocket doors in front of which
Katrine and Jess were waiting.

Katrine knocked briskly on the doors and then slid them
open to some inaudible summons within. As the doors opened
onto the sun-filled room I caught, for a moment, the scent of
apple blossoms on a spring breeze, a smell completely at odds
with the damp, mildewed corridors through which we'd just
passed.

But then so was this room. When my eyes adjusted to the
light I saw that we were in an octagonal room. Glass doors
opened onto a stone terrace and a view of the sunken gardens
bathed in the late afternoon light. Was the scent coming from

those gardens? Only it was far too late in the season for apple blossoms and the apple orchards were on the other side of the house. I sniffed the air again, but the scent was gone. I must have imagined it because of the painted blossoms on the door, a motif that was echoed in the painted fire screen and plaster frieze on the high domed ceiling.

"I see you're admiring the room," a man's voice said.

He was seated in a wing-backed chair behind a desk, the chair partly turned toward the glass doors so that I hadn't seen him at first. He leaned into the slanted sunlight and motioned for us to come forward. As I walked across the room my feet sank into the thick carpet. Looking down, I saw that it was an oriental rug figured in the same pattern of apple blossoms.

When I looked up I discovered that the man behind the desk was staring at me. "It's Clare, isn't it?" he asked, holding out a thin, trembling hand. "Clare Jackson. You were in my fiction workshop the last year I taught over at Bailey."

I took his hand, which felt like dry paper, and looked down at the man in the chair. My surprise at his recognizing me was nothing to my surprise at *not* recognizing him. Thirteen years ago, Alden Montague had been a hearty bear of a man. True, his hair had been white then, but he'd looked like Ernest Hemingway about to set off on a safari. This man had shrunk to half his former size and the full white hair was reduced to a wispy aureole around a sunken yellowish face. He really *was* ill. Still, his grip on my hand was strong and his eyes were the same icicle-sharp blue that I remembered skewering a hapless student who had uttered some foolish, ill-considered remark.

"It's Clare Martin now," I said, stepping a little to the side so he'd see Jess. "You remember Jess, don't you? He was in your class too."

For a moment I was afraid he didn't. That would be the

worst thing, I realized. Jess could tolerate disdain, criticism, even a vitriolic attack, but to be *forgotten* was Jess's biggest fear. He once confided in me that he had a recurring nightmare of wandering through an empty house that was full of mirrors, but that when he looked in them they were blank. He cast no reflection.

But then Alden Montague's cavernous face split open into a wolfish grin. "Jess Martin! I'd hardly forget my most famous student. Come here, boy. Let me see you. You're even more dashing than your author photo."

I felt, as Jess brushed past me to clasp Monty's outstretched hand, how tense his muscles were and I recalled the way he'd struck out at the snake. For a moment I had the wild idea that he was going to strike Monty, but he took his hand instead.

"Hardly the most famous student, sir, and perhaps mostly famous for a certain review in the *Times*."

"Heh, heh," Monty laughed as he pulled Jess into a tenuous embrace. Jess still hovered a good six inches above the chair, his back tensed. "I believe I said you had the promise to write the best novel of your generation, son. I just didn't think you'd done it yet. But you will. I feel it in my bones."

With that I saw Jess's back muscles relax and he folded himself into the old man's embrace. When he stood back up I saw that his face, washed in the golden light of the setting sun, was full of joy. *This* was why we were here—not because of any caretaker's job—but because Jess had been waiting all these years for his mentor's approval.

"Well then," Monty said, slapping his thin knees. "What do you say you finish your magnum opus here? I think that would be poetic justice, don't you? I'd like to see my legacy confirmed before I die."

I turned away from them and went to look at the view as

Jess half sat on the edge of the desk and they began working out the details of "the arrangement." I knew there was nothing I could do or say to stop it, nor would I want to. To see that look on Jess's face again was worth living with snakes and bats. It *was* the perfect solution, I thought, as I watched the sun begin to set over the Catskills, the river turning bloodred as it sank, to all our problems.

Chapter Two

Before we left that day Monty took us for a tour of the house—a shadowy, dusk-lit tour because most of the rooms no longer had working lights.

"I'm afraid the river damp plays havoc with the old copper wiring," he said, chuckling amiably as if the climate were a worthy and entertaining adversary.

The rooms were arranged in a circle, each room connected to the next as well as opening onto a central rotunda. "My great-grandfather subscribed to the theory that the octagonal shape magnified vital energy," Monty lectured. "I know it sounds like hogwash but I've gotten some good writing done in this house."

After the library, though, the state of upkeep declined as though whatever "vital energy" generated by the house's octagonal shape had withered and died. The parlor to the south of the library was papered in the same apple blossom print ("Designed by Candace Wheeler," Monty told us proudly) but there were extra blooms in the pattern that I suspected were mold. At least it was furnished. Other rooms had furniture *in* them but not arranged to make the space livable. One room contained nothing but straight-backed chairs ("We had a girl from the college once who was going to upholster them but then she got an internship at Sotheby's . . ."), one had an array of rocking horses lined up as though at a starting gate, their eyes milky in the dim light. Another room held boxes of papers that Monty airily referred to as "the family archives."

"I'm working on a book about the family," he said as he took us up the grand staircase that now seemed to float in the murk of the central rotunda. The domed skylight that once lit the space was covered with a layer of green pollen, giving the stairwell a subaqueous pallor, an impression reinforced by the coralline configurations of mildew on the plaster moldings and the cobwebs that hung from the ceiling like seaweed.

"So you've given up fiction?" Jess asked.

I tensed, knowing what Jess thought of novelists who turned to memoir, but Monty only laughed and replied good-naturedly, "Yes, the last resort of the failing imagination, I'm afraid. But if you knew my family's history you wouldn't say I'd given up on *fiction*, lad. Untangling the layers of lies and omissions is like deconstructing a Henry James novel. But then you probably know something about it, Clare, seeing as you're a local girl."

I was looking away at a portrait so dark I couldn't make out the subject, so Monty didn't see me wince. *Local.* It had been a while since anyone had called me that—or since it had meant anything negative. *Buy Local,* bumper stickers exhorted now. *Think global, act local.* It didn't mean rube, charity case, or dimwit, I reminded myself, turning to Monty with a frown that he could interpret as polite embarrassment.

"My father always said the villagers made up stories about the river folk because they were bored with their own lives." I didn't mention that he'd say it when my mother and her sisters were sitting around the kitchen table telling those stories.

Or that his grandmother had been *in service* in one of the old houses.

"Your family had that little orchard on Apple Ring Road, didn't they?" Monty asked.

"Yes," I answered, supposing that fifty acres was little to a man who lived on five hundred. "They sold it in the Depression, but my grandfather stayed on as manager and my father after him."

"I don't imagine he had much time or use for the foolish goings-on of the *river folk*, as you called us."

"No," Jess answered for me. "Clare's too high-minded for gossip. I'm always trying to explain that's how we writers make our livelihood. Gossip and lies."

"Well, you'll find plenty of both here," Monty said, gesturing to the oil portrait I'd been trying to make out. "That's my father, Alden Bayard Montague. Bay, as he was called. You may have heard of him—"

"Didn't he die in a shooting accident?" Katrine asked, peering at the murky portrait.

"You're being polite, Miss Vanderberg. It was ruled an accident by the police, but everyone knows it was the curse that killed him."

"Curse?" we all obligingly echoed. Although we were on the landing of a decaying mansion we might as well have been back in Monty's Senior Fiction Seminar. He'd always been able to command the attention of his audience.

"Ah, the curse, you have to hear about the curse, but first . . ." He was already striding around to the other side of the circular gallery, surprisingly fast for a man who'd looked at death's door downstairs. Perhaps the house still had some pockets of "vital energy" after all.

"Don't let Mr. Montague scare you with his talk of ghosts," Katrine said, lingering behind. "These old river families all lay claim to ghosts right along with their membership in the DAR and Colonial Dames."

I laughed. Of all the things I'd had to worry about lately—unpaid bills, finding affordable health insurance, bolstering Jess's mood—ghosts seemed quaint. "I just don't want him to get Jess going," I said. "He's got such a vivid imagination."

"Oh, he'd have to, wouldn't he?" Katrine said, widening her blue eyes at me. "It must be pretty exciting living with a writer. Do you ever worry he'll put you in his books?"

She obviously hadn't read Jess's work.

"Jess would tell you he doesn't borrow from reality; he remakes it," I said, parroting one of his interviews.

"Oh," Katrine said, "like God." Then she turned to follow the men. She *was* smarter than she looked. Before I left the landing, I spared one last look for Alden Bayard Montague. It had grown even darker under the dirty skylight, but Bayard's face loomed out of the gloom like a bloated fish belly bobbing to the surface of a pond. He had the bland, broad features of a Dutch patroon (despite the Frenchified name, the Montagues, like most of the old families around here, were mostly Dutch). Only the wide sensual mouth suggested his French lineage. His eyes, though, were cold as the ice floes that jammed the river in winter. I found myself shivering as if an icy breeze had blown in off the river and found its way onto the airless rotunda. The cobwebs and strips of wallpaper hanging from the ceiling, though, were still and limp. There was no draft, just the chill of those dead eyes. I turned and walked away from them to find Jess and the others.

They were in a room on the west side of the octagon—a room that caught the last bit of evening light, perhaps because it was papered in a pale parched yellow that seemed to drink the light thirstily. The paper was unfigured except for white dots and a frieze that ran waist-high around the room. It made me think of that awful story Monty had had us read in his class about the woman who goes crazy from seeing figures in her wallpaper and ends up creeping around the floor trying to get inside the pattern. Looking closer, I saw that this pattern was an innocent parade of clowns and circus animals.

"It's a nursery," I said.

"My nursery, as it so happens," Monty said, "only I didn't use it past infancy. You see, Bayard married my mother, Minerva Delano Noyes—a second cousin of the Roosevelt Delanos—in the summer of 1929. She was soon—some would say suspiciously soon—with child. Old Bay was . . . well, let's just say he had a way with the ladies."

He smirked at Jess, who flicked his eyes toward me, but answered accommodatingly. "A ladies' man, got it."

"In fact," Monty continued, standing with his back to the windows, his hands clasped behind him, so that he was silhouetted against the deepening indigo in the west, "he rather had an eye for the *village* ladies. He especially liked to judge the May Fair competition in which the daughters of the local farmers competed to be crowned Apple Blossom Queen. Perhaps one of your ancestors competed, Clare."

"My mother never said," I lied. What she'd said was that it was a barbaric ritual that paraded farmers' daughters like livestock in front of the local gentry. But then my mother was plain and probably had never even been asked to compete. "But I've seen pictures in the library and I noticed one in your hallway as we came through."

"Ah," he crooned. "Always the keen observer, Clare. I'm surprised with your beauty you aren't descended from a former Apple Blossom Queen—"

"Clare's adopted," Jess said. "So she got her beauty on her own."

I rolled my eyes like any good wife indulgent of her husband's flattery, afraid to show how pleased I was. It had been a while since Jess had called me beautiful. It made up for his mentioning that I was adopted, which I didn't like to tell people, but I knew it was one of Jess's favorite facts about me. He said it made me like a character out of Dickens.

"Oh!" Monty said, momentarily thrown, then quickly recovering himself. "But you see my point remains. You *might* be the descendant of one of the local Apple Blossom Queens and not know it. At any rate, Bay came down from Harvard in May of '29 to crown the Apple Blossom Queen. After the crowning, the girl was lifted into a wagon, bestrewn with apple blossoms, toasted by the local populace and the river folk with apple cider, and paraded through town in a gay procession."

"Sounds positively medieval," Jess remarked. "Let me guess, did they end the ceremony by burning her in a wicker basket along with a goat and corn sheaves to assure the fertility of the community?"

"No," Monty said gravely, "but that spring my father, having had a bit too much hard cider, took it into his head to drive off with the cart—and the Apple Blossom Queen. They disappeared in a cloud of dust on the Old Post Road and weren't seen again for a week."

"Like Tess of the D'Urbervilles," I said, thinking that I had heard this story before. Or read it. "Only with apples instead of strawberries."

"Exactly." Monty beamed at me. "And with, I'm afraid, the same outcome."

"She got pregnant," I said. Yes, I must have read it. It had the feel of a story out of one of those tourist books they sold in the town drugstore: *Legends of the Catskills* or *Haunted Hudson Valley*.

"Yes, and her dear old dad came to Riven House with his disgraced daughter, demanding restitution. To give my father credit, he always claimed afterward that he was willing to marry the girl, but his father, Birdsill Alden Montague, said he'd cut him off without a penny. Old Birdie sent the farmer packing with a deed for a hundred acres of apple trees and shipped my father off to New York, where he was paraded in front of that year's crop of debutantes. He was soon married to his second cousin twice removed, little Minnie Noyes, my mother."

"What happened to the apple blossom girl?" I asked even though I thought I remembered the end of this story.

"Her father married her off to the son of the farmer who owned the adjoining farm. Not a bad settlement for the time, considering he could have washed his hands of her."

"I suppose it depends how she liked the farmer's son," I said, thinking of my mother's bitterness at being married to a farmer. She would have loved to have gotten out of the old farmhouse I grew up in and moved to that split-level faux Colonial Jess had stuck his nose up at. "Not everyone takes to farming."

"Events would suggest she did not," Monty said. "It's hard once you've tasted champagne to go back to beer and I imagine my father gave her plenty of champagne that week they spent together. But what choice did she have? An unmarried mother today has it hard enough. Imagine what it would have been like in 1930."

I caught Jess's eye but then looked away. We both knew we were thinking of the fight we'd had in college.

"She could have given the baby up for adoption," Katrine

said. "There was an orphanage and home for wayward girls right here in Concord. St. Anne's—"

"Ah, imagine knowing you had a child in this world but not being able to hold it and watch it grow up," Monty said, shaking his head and looking so sad that I wondered if he regretted never having children. I looked at Jess, but this time he was the one to look away as Monty went on with his story. "In the end she might have been better off giving the baby to St. Anne's. She married the farmer's son and had the baby on a cold night in February in the middle of an ice storm. The roads were so bad the midwife couldn't get to her. Her husband helped her best as he could I suppose, poor fellow, but must have fallen asleep after the baby was born. When he woke up she and the baby were gone. She must have been half out of her mind. She took the baby, wrapped in a blanket, and carried it to the steps of this house where she laid it down and left it. Maybe she thought someone would hear it cry, but the night was loud with the crack of trees breaking under the weight of the ice. As for the girl, she walked around the back of the house and out onto the frozen pond. Halfway across, the ice broke and she went down under it. They found her in the morning, frozen under the ice, her eyes staring up at the sky."

Monty shook his head. It had grown so dark in the room that I couldn't see his expression.

"And the baby?" I asked.

"The kitchen maid found it in the morning," he said, looking up, no smile on his face now. "Her scream so shocked my mother, who was pregnant with me at the time, that she went into premature labor. Luckily, the housekeeper was trained as a midwife, or no doubt I would have suffered the same fate as the apple blossom girl's baby. I survived . . . but the experience changed my mother. She'd sustained an injury to her back during childbirth and was given laudanum for the pain. She began having delusions that the apple blossom girl haunted the house and was jealous of her and her baby. She said she saw the girl's ghost standing above the weir at the end of the pond and standing on the terrace looking up at the nursery window. Then she refused to take care of me because she said I wasn't hers. She thought her real baby had been taken away and I was a fairy changeling. She became so agitated that my father feared she'd hurt me. She must have been suffering from postpartum psychosis, but of course no one knew about that then. They sent her away for a rest to the Hudson River Mental Hospital."

"I wouldn't call that a restful place," I said, rubbing my arms to banish a sudden chill.

"Neither would Minnie, I'm afraid. When she came back she shot my father with his own revolver. It was ruled an accident, but everyone knew by then that Minnie was mad. The villagers saw her wandering the house and grounds in her widow's weeds—even after she was found dead in the bathtub, her wrists slit."

"How dreadful!" Katrine said.

"Yes. That's when the locals started calling the place Riven House. I was shipped off to live with cousins in Hartford. The old place was left to molder and decay. Technically it belonged to me, but I didn't have much interest in it. After college I went to Europe and started writing. It was only when I got the position at Bailey College that I decided to live here again. Since my retirement I've been hoping to put the place to rights . . ."

He looked around the darkening room and then at us as if he'd forgotten for a moment to whom he'd been telling this story. I'd seen that look in class sometimes. It had always made me nervous that he had lost the thread of his lesson, but he always found it again and he did now. "That must seem crazy, eh? To come back to a house where so much bad has happened. But a place like this . . . once it gets into your blood, you're never free of it."

Chapter Three

In the weeks that followed I thought about what Alden Montague had said about places getting into the blood. Was Concord in my blood? I had done everything I could to get away from the small town where I'd grown up. Sure, the view from those river mansions was beautiful, but the view from the tiny farmhouse where I'd grown up was mostly of mud, ice, and snow. Monty's story had brought back memories, though, of apple blossoms in the spring and apple picking in the fall. I was sure that I'd heard it before and thought that I had even written something about it at some time—back when I was still writing. Maybe moving back upstate would reignite that creative spark.

I was sorry, though, to be leaving our Brooklyn apartment. It was the first floor of a Williamsburg loft that Jess and I had bought with the money from his first advance. We'd considered ourselves modest not buying a whole brownstone in Brooklyn Heights with what seemed like a huge amount of money at the time, but Jess had fallen in love with the high ceilings, vast space, and arched windows, as well as its proximity to the burgeoning café and art scene in Williamsburg.

"We'll just wait out the old folks on the second floor and buy them out when I sell the second book."

Now the "old folks"—a CUNY professor and his psychologist wife—bought *us* out for their son and his wife, who had recently graduated from Bennington. We were lucky to sell so quickly and smoothly in the current market—our friends told us horror stories of buyers demanding extensive work before signing—but I had a hard time watching the Bennington couple measuring our living room for their Ikea bookcases and West Elm coffee tables.

"I wish we could afford something like this," the wife, a design student at Pratt, said, running her hand over our dining room table. "It's a Bend Becker, isn't it?"

"It is," I admitted, stroking the reclaimed barn oak that had been polished to a satiny sheen. "But he wasn't so well known when he made this for us."

"It's a custom piece!" she exclaimed, her voice warbling with excitement. "Copper, did you hear that? Bend Becker made their dining room table."

Copper, who'd cornered Jess into a discussion about the current state of publishing, said, "Shit, man, a Bend Becker. I bet you write on that table for inspiration. I don't suppose you'd want to sell it? I mean, it does kind of go with the space."

I was sure that Jess would say something about inspiration coming from the head, not a block of insensate wood, but I was surprised to hear him ask instead, "How much would you give me for it?"

The wife—whose name, unbelievably enough, was Penny ("We knew we were, like, meant for each other because of our names, although of course his real name's Copernicus and mine's Penelope")—had gotten up to whisper in her husband's ear. He had then, in a cracking voice, offered us five times what we'd paid for the table. I still thought Jess would turn it down—he *had* written the last (burned) draft of the second novel on it—but instead he said, "Wow. I wish my career were doing as well as old Bend's. You have yourself a deal."

When they had gone I asked him why he hadn't asked me if I wanted to sell the table. He blinked, surprised at the question, then said, "I thought you hated that table. You were furious at me for spending so much on it. We had a terrible fight and then . . . oh . . ."

I tilted my head and looked up at him sideways, fingering the wood.

". . . and then we made up on it," he finished with a crooked grin. He ducked his head and burrowed it in my neck. "Whoops. I'm sorry, Clare. Do you want me to tell them we changed our minds? Shall we tell them . . ." he said, nibbling on my ear, "that we can't get rid of the Bend Becker because it's where we always have our makeup sex?"

I slid onto the table and tugged his head up by his hair. He gasped at how hard I pulled.

"Are you kidding?" I asked. "We can have sex for a week at the Mercer for what they're paying for this table."

He grinned back at me, my coconspirator, and pulled my hips toward him over the slick surface. "Then let's say we give the Bend Becker a proper send-off."

I WOULD HAVE sold the Bend Becker, which really was a monstrosity and would have cost a fortune to move, and every other stick of furniture we owned to get Jess back in my bed. We'd barely made love for months—practically a year, if I were being completely honest. At first I'd attributed the drop in his libido to writer's block and then, when he started writing, to his preoccupation with the new book. Then I wondered if he was having an affair. He disappeared sometimes for hours—seeking the muse, he'd say, not giving any more specifics.

"Is the muse that tattooed barista at Sweetleaf's?" I'd asked nastily when he came back late one night smelling of clove cigarettes and dark roast coffee.

He'd slept in his study after that.

Now, though, our tryst on the table (as Jess dubbed it) lit a match to our dry spell. We made love in our bed again that night and in the morning he slipped into the shower with me and slid inside me from behind as suddenly as he'd struck that snake. If I hadn't had to deliver a galley in Manhattan we might have stayed in bed all day. When I got home he'd set the table with candles and the white Jasper Conran china that his editor had given us as a housewarming present, and takeout from Samurai Mama. We didn't make it past the kuro edamame. We made love more times in twenty-four hours than we had in a year.

It had been the anxiety over money, I saw now, even though Jess had pretended not to be worried. That had been my job: fretting over the diminishing savings account, taking more freelance editorial jobs to pay the bills. Jess always said he'd be happy to live in a shack. Now he seemed almost gleeful to see our possessions go in boxes to the vintage stores on Wythe Avenue and the Salvation Army. Even our books he tossed eagerly into cardboard boxes bound for the Strand—the signed ones from the dozens of readings we'd attended over the years, the review copies publishers sent him, the expensive art tomes he'd bought when, for a year, he'd thought his protagonist was a painter. The only books he kept were the classics—mostly what he'd read in Monty's class—and the remaining copies of his first novel, which he'd bought up rather than see them pulped. The shaking off of possessions and debt made him a new man. He even suggested we have a dinner party—something we hadn't done in longer than we hadn't had sex.

I invited Jess's agent, Ansel, his Dutch animal rights activist wife, Hanneke, my old publishing friend Marika, her partner, Duma, and our poet friends Abe and Yuriko, who both taught at Brooklyn College.

"Quite the literary salon," Jess said when I listed the guests. "What does Duma do?"

"She's in PR at Hachette and writes YA."

"Why A?" Jess asked. "Why not B?"

I swatted him with a dishcloth and went back to marinating tofu. Because of Hanneke the meal would have to be vegan, but I wanted Jess to see Ansel before we left—or rather, wanted Ansel to see how good Jess was looking and hear how well the book was coming along. When I'd gone to drop off the galley at Broadway Books I had stopped by Marika's office and heard that there was a rumor going around that Jess had shown Ansel his latest book and Ansel had told him he couldn't sell it.

"That's completely untrue," I said. "Jess didn't even show *me* the book before burning it."

Marika lifted an elegant eyebrow. "Do you want me to spread *that* story around instead?"

No, I didn't. I thanked Marika for telling me—and for sending so much work my way over the last two years—and walked back to the elevators, passing through the beehive cubicles where I'd started as an assistant thirteen years ago and worked for five years until Jess had fallen out with his editor. It had been too uncomfortable to stay, but Marika had steered enough freelance work my way to make looking for another job unnecessary. Which was for the best anyway now that we were moving. I could keep up the freelance copyediting remotely.

I didn't miss working in an office, I told myself, even though I'd enjoyed the camaraderie at first—all the underpaid college graduates working long hours and hanging out at each other's cramped and overpriced apartments as if they were a continuation of our college dorm rooms, drinking at bars, telling each other after enough drinks what novels *we* planned to write like it was a dirty secret you were supposed to keep to yourself. But then Jess had published his book and *that* had made a difference—but not as much of a difference as when Jess had a loud fight with his editor at Craft and lobbed a cast iron terrine of creamed spinach at him. After the Craft incident ("The closest he'll come to actually working in the craft," Jess had gotten fond of saying) I'd pass these same cubicles and hear them whispering—or hear a sudden silence—as I went by. Even now I could hear it—the story of Jess's rejected book passing from cubicle to cubicle all around the city. No, I didn't miss it. I'd FedEx the next set of galleys "from the country," as the editor I'd worked for used to say when she was at her Litchfield house.

But first I had to put a stop to the rumors. So I invited Ansel and vegan Hanneke and Abe and Yuriko, who would tweet about it (poets *loved* Twitter), and Marika so she'd see I'd been telling the truth and Duma—well, Duma because she came with Marika and a YA author wouldn't bother Jess like a *real* novelist might.

At first it went well. Everyone wanted to hear about Old Monty and his decaying mansion and Jess reveled in the story. "He's like Miss Havisham up there. I swear all the clocks are stopped at the exact hour his last book was published."

"Is he still writing?" Ansel asked.

"He mentioned some kind of memoir about his family and went on about the magical properties of the octagonal house,"

Jess said. "Even his desk is shaped like an octagon. Monty claims the shape generates energy that has a positive influence on the brain."

"In other words, he's gone completely bonkers," Marika said, spearing an artichoke leaf left-handed and gesturing with it. "Are you sure it's a good idea to put yourself and Clare at the mercy of this monomaniac's whims?"

"Oh, he loves Clare," Jess replied, beaming at me. "He's always maintained that Clare's the one with the real talent in this family."

I felt myself grow warm under the lamp of Jess's praise.

"Well, I've always said that too," Marika replied tartly.

"Do you write?" Duma asked me.

"Not anymore," I said quickly. "I prefer to edit other people's work."

"And she does so brilliantly," Marika said.

"It's a waste," Jess said, oblivious to the fact that he was talking about Marika's profession. "I think living in Riven House is going to have a galvanizing effect on Clare."

"We're not actually *living* in the main house," I explained to the table, hoping to change the subject. It was one thing for me to dream of apple blossoms and writing again and another to voice that hope. "We're going to live in the caretaker's cottage by the river."

"How bucolic!" Ansel said. "Is it in better repair than the main house?"

"We didn't actually get to see it," I admitted, sorry now I'd brought it up after all.

"Yeah," Jess said, saving me from explaining. "By the time Old Monty was done scaring Clare half to death with a preposterous ghost story it was too dark to go look at it."

"It didn't scare me," I lied. I'd been dreaming about the story and those dreams *were* scary. "It was just sad."

"Of course sad," Yuriko, who'd been quiet all night, said. "Ghosts are always sad. That's why they're ghosts. They come back because they were wronged."

"Don't get Yuriko started on ghosts," Abe said, smiling fondly at his wife. "Japanese ghost stories are all about wronged women seeking revenge. I think she tells them to me to keep me in line."

"Then you'll love this one—" Jess began.

"Let Clare tell it," Hanneke said. "I can see she was the one most affected by it."

"By all means," Jess said, emptying the dregs of a wine bottle into his glass and then getting up to get another one. "Go ahead, Clare. I've heard it."

"Oh, it's probably just something Monty made up," I said, hoping to deflect the table's interest. "It has all the earmarks of the Gothic stories we read in his class. A local village girl seduced by a rakish millionaire, she gets pregnant—"

"Poor thing," Hanneke interjected. "Of course there was no birth control or abortion."

"Don't get Hanneke started on health care," Ansel sighed.

"She *could* have put it up for adoption," Duma pointed out with a sideways glance toward Marika that made me wonder if they were thinking of adopting.

"But she didn't," I said. "She had the baby in the middle of an ice storm. The midwife wasn't able to come because the roads were impassable. All through the night she could hear the apple branches breaking and falling on her roof. She thought the whole house would come crashing down around her. She thought she would break in two . . ."

I could almost feel the cold and the terror and the aloneness. I felt the ice under the girl's bare feet as she walked through the storm-wrecked world to her lover's house and laid the baby on his doorstep wrapped in a pale pink blanket, the same color as the apple blossoms she'd worn in her hair when he crowned her queen and carried her away. She'd embroidered the blanket with apple blossoms so *he* would remember. She wore a nightgown with the same pattern embroidered on the hem, which trailed over the ice as she walked out onto the frozen pond. When the ice cracked beneath her she thought it was her heart breaking . . .

I looked up at the end of the story to see all the faces at the table staring at me in the flickering candlelight. The candles had all burned down. How long had I been speaking?

"Wow," Duma said. "That crazy old man's right. You *are* quite the storyteller."

"Of silly melodramatic legends," I said, getting up to clear the dishes. "Your art department would have to put a woman in a white nightgown fleeing from a looming castle on the cover."

"*The Apple Blossom Ghost*, you could call it," Jess said. "That was good, though, about the blanket embroidered with apple blossoms. I don't remember Monty mentioning that."

"I'm sure he did," I said, shouldering my way through the swinging door into the kitchen with a stack of plates. Duma and Abe brought some too, but they went back to the table while Yuriko and I washed up and started the coffee. I could hear Ansel asking Jess to "tell me about this book you're working on" as the door swung open.

"You go back too," I told Yuriko. "I asked Ansel earlier about publishers for your chapbook. He knows someone who'd be perfect for you."

"That's sweet of you, Clare," she said, drying a plate with a dish towel. "You're always looking out for other people. I hope you'll look out for yourself up there."

"It's not the wilds of Alaska," I said. "Remember I come from there. Or do you really think I'm going to be attacked by a vengeance-seeking ghost?"

"Why would anyone seek vengeance on you?" she asked with only a hint of a smile. "I just wondered if it will be good for you to be so . . . *isolated.* I wish you could have stayed here where you have friends. If Jess had only taken the job at Brooklyn College . . . but I suppose that he thought teaching would interfere with his writing."

"Yes," I said, scrubbing at a bit of dried kale on the rim of a plate. "I think he does. That was kind of you, though, to think of Jess. I haven't had a chance to thank you—"

"Oh, it was all Abe. He spoke to the department chair and they would have been thrilled to have Jess. But of course it was three classes—more than Jess would want to do. We just thought . . . well, I don't know what we would do without our salaries and health insurance benefits. But then we're poets and Jess will write a big book that makes you both rich. It just would have been nice." She smiled. "I would have had company at all those boring faculty parties."

"It *would* have been nice," I said, handing a plate of fruit to Yuriko. "Would you take this out? I'm going to pour the coffee. This damned Italian espresso machine is so temperamental it might scald you."

Yuriko squeezed my arm before leaving with the fruit plate. I watched her rearranging a slice of melon as she backed through the door. Then I turned and rinsed the last plate, letting the cold water run over my wrists to calm myself down. Jess hadn't told me about the job—a job with insurance benefits and a fifteen-minute commute from our beautiful apartment filled with all our smart, witty friends and our enviable Bend Becker dining room table . . .

The plate slipped from my soapy hands and fell into the sink. I heard a crack and cursed, but when I fished it out of the sink I saw it was unbroken. I took a deep breath and put my hands back under the cold water to make them stop shaking. Jess knew how I felt about honesty. He knew I considered an omission as good as a lie. My parents hadn't told me I was adopted until I was twelve. When they told me I felt as if my entire life had been a lie. Didn't this omission make our entire marriage a lie?

When my hands were so numb they no longer shook, I dried them and arranged the little blue and yellow espresso cups we'd bought on our trip to Italy (during the year that Jess had thought his second novel might take place in Rome) on a tray, filling each one with a perfect dollop of black aromatic coffee from the temperamental La Spaziale espresso machine Jess had bought for two thousand dollars because he couldn't write without a "decent" cup of coffee. (Another reason I'd been suspicious of the tattooed barista: why did he have to spend all that time in a coffeehouse with a two thousand dollar coffee machine at home?)

As I came back into the dining room I was afraid they'd all look up at me and see the hurt and shame on my face but they were all staring at something on the table. Only Jess looked up and he was too excited to notice my expression.

"Clare! Do you think Hopper and Benny will want their money back? Bend Becker's work isn't indestructible after all."

I looked down to see what he meant. Running from one end of the table to the other was a narrow but deep crack that I could have sworn hadn't been there when I set the table.

Chapter Four

Copper and Penny didn't want their money back. "Dude," Copper said when I showed him the crack, "that's what Bend's all about. Imperfection. History. He makes one table that's got glass rings, spilled wine, and a bullet hole all embedded in the finish. Like, shit happens."

Really? I wanted to say to his pudding-bland face. *What shit's happened in your life other than your parents giving you a million dollar apartment in the trendiest neighborhood in Brooklyn as a graduation present?*

But I was glad of the check. Even though we'd sold the loft for way more than we'd paid for it, we were so over-mortgaged that most of what was left would go to paying off bills and credit card debts. Copper's check would pay for the moving van and the first three months of rent on a storage unit in Poughkeepsie. We'd decided to store most of our stuff because the caretaker's cottage was furnished.

"It makes it more of a fresh start," Jess said. "When I sell the book we'll buy our own place."

We packed the stuff into a rented U-Haul van in a torrential downpour the weekend after Labor Day. "Have you ever noticed that it always rains when you move?" I asked.

"Not before I met you," he said without smiling.

Our sex idyll had come to an abrupt end when I questioned him about the teaching job. "If you'd wanted a nine-to-fiver with a steady paycheck and benefits you should have married that guy you were dating before me—Dusty? Wasn't it? Didn't he become a fireman or something?"

"Dunstan," I corrected. "And he's a policeman."

He'd shrugged and then retreated into a stony silence for the rest of the packing, becoming even more ruthless in the winnowing of our possessions. Each item he rejected seemed to be a piece of our past he was throwing out—the thrift shop mugs we'd bought on a camping trip to Vermont, a Bailey College sweatshirt I'd borrowed from him our first night together and worn ever since ("It was mine in the first place," he'd said when I complained about him throwing it out), all the birthday and anniversary and Valentine's Day cards I'd given him over the last thirteen years. As with his library, he threw out all but the "classics" and I was beginning to think that I wouldn't make the cut.

Because Jess's Saab was a manual, which I didn't know how to drive, I got stuck driving the U-Haul, following Jess on winding back roads as far as Poughkeepsie. "The main road is safer in this weather," I'd pointed out.

"Isn't the whole point of this move to take the road less traveled?" he'd asked, slamming the Saab's door.

Despite the rain he drove fast on the slick, winding roads, taking every curve like an angry flip-off to me trying to keep up.

Fine, I thought, gripping the steering wheel so hard my knuckles turned white. Let him be angry. I was angry too. I'd been the one supporting us for the last three years since the advance money and home equity had run out. I'd had no problem putting aside my writing when I took the publishing job (who could write when you were faced day in, day out with *thousands* of would-be writers trying to hawk their manuscripts?). Why couldn't it be *his* turn to take the practical job so I could write?

Or have a baby, I thought, fishtailing around a tight curve.

Not that we could ever even talk about that. We hadn't talked about having children since spring of our senior year, when I'd gotten pregnant.

"It will be the end of both our writing careers," he'd said then. "Every decision we make will have to be about what's good for the kid, not what's good for the writing. We'll take awful jobs or write crap to pay the bills. Look around at the writers who have made it. How many have kids?"

There were plenty I could point to, but most were either men or had someone to support them, or ended up being crap parents. There was Muriel Spark, who'd had a baby around my age, but she'd left him with her parents to raise. There was Shirley Jackson, who delighted in having four children and whose work Jess admired, but I didn't think a woman who had grown enormously fat and died of a heart attack at forty-eight was the best example to offer.

In the end I hadn't had to make the choice; I miscarried.

"See," Jess had said, "even your body knew it wasn't the right time."

But it had never been the right time again. Now I was thirty-five. Sure, I still had time—but not endless time. And Jess hadn't shown any sign of changing his attitude toward children. If I really wanted to have a baby maybe I'd need to do it without Jess.

The thought nearly sent me off the road. This would be the time to make a break. There'd be no assets to split up. We'd paid off our debts and split the meager profits from the apartment into our two separate accounts (Jess had never wanted a joint account). I could leave Jess in Monty's caretaker's cottage and go back to the city. Marika would let me sleep on her couch until I found a place and she'd help me look for an editorial job. Better to do it now while I was still young enough to start over and have a baby than to wait another decade for Jess to finish his second novel and be ready. Because, really, would he *ever* be ready?

I spent the rest of the drive planning my new life. I could get a cat (Jess was allergic), a television (Jess thought watching television was a waste of time), and hang out with friends from work without Jess's voice in my head judging them as vacuous and shallow. There were a lot of people who would welcome me back into the fold if only to finally tell me what they really thought about Jess.

I might even start writing. I *had* been thinking about writing something about the apple blossom girl ever since Monty had told the story. In fact, I was sure now that I'd started a story about it back in college. I could write that. *Nothing* would make Jess sorrier to have lost me than if I published a successful book.

And if I hadn't met someone in five years I'd adopt—another option Jess had rejected.

"You always say how you grew up feeling like an outsider," he'd once said when I brought it up, turning all my confidences back on me. "Would you want that for *our* child?"

By the time we reached the U-Haul drop-off and storage unit I had planned out my novel and named my future Siamese cats. Franny and Zooey—names Jess would abhor. My anger had not so much dissipated as frozen into an icy shaft at my core. I had to peel my fingers off the steering wheel. We unpacked in silence. I made sure my stuff was all together near the front and asked for two keys at the desk. I put the deposit for the storage unit on *my* credit card and I took the key so I could come back and get my stuff when I needed it. We didn't talk on the rest of the drive. I considered asking him to drop me off at the train station in Rhinecliff but I was afraid that once I broke the dam of silence Jess's voice would flood over me. I was afraid he'd try to talk me out of it. Or maybe I was afraid he wouldn't. Better to call a taxi after we got there.

When we turned onto River Road I felt a momentary pang. Even in the rain River Road was beautiful, the ancient syca- mores forming a canopy, fog lying along the old stone walls and apple trees like a sheen of ice—

Which reminded me of the apple blossom girl story again.

Had Jess not thought for one minute that I might not want to live next to a house where a baby had died?

I refrained from pointing out the gate and Jess nearly went past it, swerving at the last minute and missing the mailboxes by inches. He revved angrily, scraping the undercarriage of the Saab on the rutted driveway. I registered every dent and ping with satisfaction. Let him see how long he lasted up here with this impractical car. *City boy.* Dunstan Corbett had driven a pickup. Maybe I'd look him up on Facebook.

I looked toward the house but it was shrouded in fog, as if it had closed its doors to visitors today and was making clear we were only welcome in the servants' quarters of the estate. At the turn to the caretaker's cottage someone had posted a hand- painted plywood sign that read: "Rivendell this way."

"Great," Jess muttered. "LO-TOR fans."

"I like Tolkien," I informed him.

He turned to gape at me, and so didn't see the deer stand- ing in the middle of the road. I screamed and he slammed on the brakes, swiveling the Saab sharply to the right toward a stone wall. We screeched to a halt millimeters from the wall, the engine dying. When he tried to start it the car made a grinding sound.

"Don't bother," I said. "We're here."

I pointed past the stone wall to a brown single-storied house. I think when Jess had heard "caretaker's cottage" he'd pictured a thatched cottage like the one on his copy of *Sons and Lovers*, not a sixties-era modular home with aluminum siding. I almost felt sorry for him, but then I remembered that he'd scoffed at my request to see the house—and that we could have stayed in Brooklyn if he'd taken the teaching job.

I got out of the car, stepping into three inches of water. The house was poorly situated in a shallow depression. I could hear rushing water as soon as I got out. I recalled the ornamental pond in the garden and realized that the stream that flowed out of it ran right beside the cottage. It would flood easily and be prone to mildew and mold. *And mice,* I thought, catching a shadowy movement in the overgrown grass as I walked up the slick, mossy path to the front door. Jess would be sorry he didn't have a cat.

I was almost disappointed not to unleash a deluge when I opened the front door. The interior was dry and smelled of onions and cumin—the previous caretaker must have liked Indian takeout. I heard Jess behind me flick on a wall switch but the room remained dark, as murky on this rainy afternoon as if it had been night already.

"The electricity is probably down," I said. "I wonder if there's a generator—or candles and a woodstove at least."

I felt my way forward gingerly and bumped into a table. Someone had put out a battery-operated lantern. I switched it on and found an assortment of candles, flashlights, and matches in the bluish glow. And a note. Jess snatched it up before I could read it and snorted.

"His highness says we should let him know when we get in. In person. He switches off his cell phone while writing—"

"I'll go," I said before Jess could launch into a tirade against "the great writer." I'd have to point out that he always turned off his phone when he wrote and I didn't want to argue. The cold shaft of ice was already splintering inside of me. It was one thing to leave Jess and another to leave him in this miserable place.

I put up my hood and pulled on a pair of rubber boots that were standing by the door. They fit perfectly and reminded me of the ones Katrine had worn. Maybe I'd keep them.

"Clare—" Jess began as I opened the door. I didn't turn around. If he said he was sorry now the ice would crack inside me and I was pretty sure it was the only thing holding me up.

"I'll be back soon," I said. "See if you can get a fire started in the stove." And then I left, letting the screen door bang shut behind me.

The rain came down harder the minute I stepped away from shelter. It wasn't so bad under the trees, but when I struck out across the open field it came down in unrelenting sheets. I looked up only long enough to sight the house—still shrouded in fog but identifiable by a cluster of blurry lights on the hill (Monty would have a generator)—and then I pulled my hood over my head and took off in that direction. I only knew I had passed from open field into the gardens by the texture of the ground beneath my feet—from stubby hay to once-manicured grass. The hay held off the water better; the grass was sodden. My boots sank inches into the mud.

It was typical of Monty not to consider the inconvenience

of asking one of us to slog through the rain and mud to "check in" when he could have just turned on his goddamned cell phone and called us. But no, mustn't disturb the muse. Let Clare slog through the mud instead and drown out here in the rain—

The ground gave way beneath my feet and I slid in mud so slick it felt like ice. When I put my hand down to brace myself I felt that it *was* ice. The rain had turned to sleet—a freak hail storm—and I had wandered off course into a bog.

I looked up and saw that I was standing at the edge of the pond. Tall reeds and cattails rimmed the dark, rain-dimpled surface. Across the water stood a figure, watching me.

The ice on the ground seemed to have crept up my arm into my heart. I was sure I hadn't seen anyone when I started across the field. Where had she come from?

"Hello?" My voice sounded small and frightened. As if in answer, the icy rain came down harder, falling in a silvery sheet that obscured my vision of the other side of the pond. When it let up the figure was gone. As if the rain had washed her away . . . or as if the black water had swallowed her up. But the surface of the pond was undisturbed. Could someone have disappeared beneath it so quickly? My heart pounding, I made my way around the edge of the pond to where I'd seen—*thought I'd seen?*—the figure. In the spot where it had stood was a narrow wooden walkway spanning a spillway—a weir, my father would call it—from the pond into a stream that led to the river. There were no footprints on the walkway, or in the mud on either side of it. There were cypresses, though, just beyond the pond at the edge of the garden. I must have mistaken one of the tall wavy trees for a person. An easy mistake to make, especially after that story Monty told about the girl drowning herself in the pond.

I turned to walk up the hill to the house through the heavy, but no longer ice-laden, rain. As the adrenaline rush of fear receded the icy core of anger inside me also melted. I felt leaden, weighed down by my wet clothes and the glowering storm clouds over the bloodred bricks of Riven House. *You'll never have the courage to leave,* they seemed to say, like Monty, who'd thought he'd gotten out of Riven House but had ended up back here.

I saw a light in the library and decided to approach from the back terrace rather than trudge around to the boot hall. When he looked up from his desk, Monty startled at the sight of me. I must look like a specter, hooded and dripping in the rain, I thought, feeling a perverse spark of satisfaction for giving him the same fright I'd just had on the lawn. Then he smiled and I felt guilty for scaring an old man.

"Clare, you're soaked," he said, pulling me inside. I only thought of the mud as I stepped over the lintel. I stopped and tried to take off my boots.

"Don't worry about it," he said. "These old floors have seen worse . . . but you do look like you went *into* the pond in those."

"I practically did. I couldn't really see where I was going through the rain and then it started hailing."

"Hailing? Really? I must have missed that. I've been immersed in my writing—" He gestured toward the octagonal desk, which was covered with old books, marbled folios, notebooks, and photographs. A photograph of a girl in a white dress with an apple blossom wreath—the same photo I'd seen framed in the hallway—was propped up against the base of a bronze Tiffany lamp.

"I didn't mean to disturb you—" I began.

"Oh, please, I'm happy to see you. I was worried about you driving up in this. Did you say there was hail?" He shook his head and chuckled. "The weather in this valley sure plays its tricks. Is Jess all right?"

"Jess is fine," I bit off. "He's back at the house trying to light a fire. I suppose I ought to get back there before he burns down the house."

Monty chuckled again, as though not in the least disturbed at the idea of his new caretakers burning down his property. "I'm glad you came up. I especially wanted to give you this—Jess mentioned you might want it back . . . now let's see, where is it . . . ?" He shuffled the papers around on his desk and finally retrieved an old, dog-eared composition book, the kind with a black-and-white marbled cover. I looked down at it, wondering why Monty would be giving me an old notebook, and was startled to see that my name was on the cover—or rather my maiden name, Clare Jackson, written in my own handwriting.

"My old notebook," I said. "From college. You collected them at the end of the semester . . ."

"And then due to my unfortunate run-in with the administration I was unable to ever return them. Jess told me that you always regretted not getting yours back. He seemed to think its restitution might inspire you."

"When did he say that?" I asked, running my hand over the worn surface of the book.

"When you were both here," Monty said. "I think, well, if I'm not being too forward, I think Jess feels bad that you gave up writing, that perhaps you have felt overshadowed by him. I've seen it happen myself with many writing couples—why look at poor Zelda! Not that you're as fragile as her. Jess said he hoped that coming here would inspire you to write again."

"He told you that?" I asked, looking up from the notebook.

"Yes, Clare. Why are you so surprised? You were easily the best writer in my class that year—the best I'd seen during my time at Bailey—and Jess had the wit to see that and fall in love with you. Although I can't swear that was his primary reason for falling for you," he added with a sly smile that reminded me of his reputation with the female students back at Bailey.

"Then he must be disappointed," I said, looking back down at the notebook. Beneath my own name I had written "Senior Fiction Seminar—Professor Alden Montague" in careful schoolgirl script. How young I'd been! How proud of getting into Old Monty's elite circle.

"He did not sound like a man disappointed with love when I spoke with him," Monty said gravely. "Only a man disappointed with himself and worried about his wife—if it's not intrusive of me to say so. He said you hadn't been well this winter. I think he hoped that being up here would be good for both of you—and that is my hope as well. This place . . ." He looked over my shoulder, past me and out the window. "It has its *moods*, but sometimes it still has the power to surprise me."

I turned, following his gaze out the window, half afraid that I'd see that figure standing on the weir again. Across the river the sun appeared wedged between a bank of storm-gray clouds and indigo mountains. It cast a low beam of light across the river, skating over the lawn and pouring through the glass doors.

"Oh!" I said, awestruck by the power of light to utterly transform the landscape. Even the gloomy pond glowed now like a copper plate in a jewel-green lawn. An empty lawn, of course; there was no figure on the weir.

"Go on," Monty said, waving me away. "Take your time settling in. Let me know if you need anything . . ." He was already moving back to his desk, which now lay in the sunlight as though preserved in amber. I had the feeling he was rushing back to his work while the desk, and the room around it, held the charge of that electric light.

I left without saying good-bye and walked quickly down the hill, leaping over puddles and steering well clear of the boggy area around the pond, keeping my eyes on the ground. Not looking at the weir. I wanted to get back before the light faded, wanting above all to share it with Jess.

Jess had given up the Brooklyn job so that I could come here and start writing again because he thought that's what I needed. It was true that I hadn't been well this winter. All the worrying about money had taken a toll on me. I needed to get away as much as Jess did. No wonder he'd been angry when I questioned him about it. He wouldn't want to tell me that he was hoping I'd start writing again. He always said that other people's expectations could kill the muse quicker than a bullet to the head. But he'd feel—irrationally, of course—that he was being criticized while he'd only been trying to do something nice for me. It had been one of those inevitable mis-understandings that crop up in marriages—like something out of an O. Henry story—but it didn't have to be the end of the marriage. Of course I should talk to him about telling me what was going on. I knew that Jess believed that it was good to have some mystery in a marriage, but keeping a job offer secret was really too much.

When I cut through the field it whispered silkily at my pass-ing. I arrived breathless at the house just as the sun slipped down beneath the mountains on the other side of the river. But the light was not entirely gone. When I opened the door Jess was standing at the window watching the sun set. As he turned I saw the light reflected in his face from the fire in the stove and a dozen candles. He'd laid the white china plates out on the kitchen table. There was wine and bread and cheese and apples and grapes. There were even flowers—a damp fistful of late summer wildflowers in a Mason jar. I pictured him gathering those flowers in the rain and forgave him everything.

"There you are," he said. "I thought you'd gotten lost."

"A little," I admitted, going to him. "But I found my way back."

Chapter Five

We had left the city sweltering in summer, but awoke the next morning, twined inside Jess's old camp sleeping bag, to cool air that smelled like apples. My thoughts of leaving Jess had evaporated with the rain. He'd turned down the teaching job because he thought coming here would be good for me and he was worried about me. And maybe he was right, I thought, putting away the notebook in a bureau drawer. I hadn't been myself this winter—maybe not since our last year of college. Jess had seen something in me in Monty's class—he'd seen me like no one ever before or since had seen me—maybe better than I saw myself.

We spent the morning unpacking and cleaning together. I expected Jess to complain about the house—it was worse than the ranches and split-levels he'd turned his nose up at—but he seemed amused by its seediness and evidence of former tenants—empty Southern Comfort bottles, Mickey Spillane novels, and a stack of racing forms that revealed a former care-taker who'd thought his ticket out of here was the trifecta at Monticello.

"Let's hope our writing has better odds," Jess said.

Our writing.

Our nearest neighbor, the puppet maker Katrine had mentioned, drifted up from the barn, the roof of which we could just glimpse through the trees, in a cloud of gauze and patchouli to give us a loaf of zucchini bread and offer to do our "charts" for half price. She had a Dutch accent like Hanneke's and said she'd been born Sanne, a Dutch version of Susanna, but had been reborn as "Su-sun" to celebrate her kinship with the stars and added that everyone just called her Sunny (which sounded so close to her Dutch name that I was unsure why she bothered with the lengthy explanation).

"She looks like she spent the last thirty years baking in the sun," Jess said when she'd gone, referring to Sunny's lined, leathery face. "Did you notice she said she used to live up at the big house? Do you think she was one of Monty's early conquests? Exchange student circa class of '78?"

I swatted him with a dust cloth. "It was sweet of her to bring us something to eat."

The zucchini bread had a weird taste, though, and we'd eaten all the food from last night, so around midday I suggested we go to the store to buy groceries. Just then Monty showed up in his Subaru station wagon offering to lend it to me for the duration of "our stay"—as if we were guests instead of employees—in exchange for picking up his groceries and running a few errands.

"Sure," I said, wanting to give Monty and Jess some time alone. I left them ambling off toward one of the barns, like two old farmers talking about their crops, and drove into town.

I approached the IGA on Route 9 with trepidation—a lot of the kids I'd grown up with had worked there after school—but I found it transformed into a shiny new health food store called Eden that rivaled Whole Foods at half the price. The checkers and baggers *did* bear a familial resemblance to the kids I'd grown up with, but they were younger, and if any of the older staff recognized me they didn't say. I'd never looked like I belonged here and in my Brooklynite uniform of skinny black jeans, hand-printed T-shirt, and slouchy sweater, I must have looked even more out of place.

The town of Concord itself was largely unchanged, a corner crossroads on Route 9 anchored by Dietz's, a family-owned pharmacy still hanging in there despite a new CVS down the road, a gas station, an empty storefront that once held the Concord Department Store, and a college hangout that had changed its name since my day from Pete's to Cassie's but, I discovered when I went in, still had the same purple trim, broken-down couches, and, seemingly, the same stoned wait-staff. My server, a skinny boy with a scraggly goatee, gave me a flier for a Harvest Moon festival. "It's going to be held in an orchard," Scraggly Goatee told me in an awed whisper. "Those old trees have a lot of earth energy."

I tried not to smirk as I slid my change in the tips jar. When had the town gotten so new-agey? It had always had the hokey apple stuff. I'd grown up eating Sunday dinners at the Apple-a-Day Diner and had gone to Lil' Blossoms Preschool. The high school mascot was Johnny Appleseed and our football team had been called the Redskins until it was changed in the seventies, but I didn't remember any of this hooey about moonlight festi-vals and earth energy. I *did* remember stealing into the Corbett orchards at night to meet Dunstan and how eerie the apple trees looked in the moonlight, like bony witches reaching their arms out to grab me, and how Dunstan had slipped his jacket over my shoulders because I was shaking and I hadn't told him it wasn't from the cold.

When I gave Jess his latte he told me he'd "given up such citified confections in favor of black joe *berled* on the stove with a couple-a eggshells tossed in." By which he meant coffee cone-dripped in the Braun coffeemaker left behind by the previous caretaker. So much for the La Spaziale espresso machine and, I thought with a little guilty pleasure, the tattooed barista at Sweetleaf's. Even if he wandered into Cassie's he was unlikely to be charmed by Scraggly Goatee.

Nor did Jess seem tempted to go into town in our first few weeks. While I spent the mornings grocery shopping and running Monty's errands, Jess stayed in the house writing. When I came home he would rise from his desk, slipping pages from the printer into a drawer, stretch, and say he'd go see what Monty was up to.

Monty was showing him around the place, teaching him the outdoor chores that involved, mostly, mowing and fixing broken things. Sometimes they ended up at the South Barn, where the men would drink beers with Dale the Welder (as Jess called him, eschewing the phrase "Metal Artist"), a Vietnam vet who'd followed a Bailey girl from California in the seventies and had made his home here. I spent the afternoons cleaning the new house, unpacking, and copyediting. Sometimes Sunny would come by with some late-season tomatoes or a Mason jar full of murky green tea that smelled and looked like pond water. She wouldn't stay long though, always saying she had to get back to her children. She looked too old to have kids, so I guessed they must be her grandchildren. One sounded like a baby from the crying I heard sometimes at night.

At five I'd head up to "the house" as we'd come to call Riven House, as if there were no other, to meet Monty and Jess for drinks in the library. When I realized these drinking sessions could go on all night while Monty and Jess *talked writing*, with only a box of saltines and a tin of sardines to sustain us, I offered to whip us up some dinner. First, though, I had to clean the kitchen. It took me nearly a week to clean decades' worth of bachelor neglect but then Monty and Jess oohed and aahed over the simple salads, grilled fish, and pasta dishes I added to our evening drinking sessions, all garnished by the early fall produce I found at the nearby farm stands.

At first I'd avoided the Corbett stand, afraid that a vestige of my childhood was still lurking amidst the barrels of apples and crates of gourds and squashes where I had worked in the summers and after school. But the girls who worked there now—girls with tanned, toned arms and flowered aprons like rustic milkmaids—were clearly Bailey girls. Only the smell of apples was the same—the cotton candy scent of Northern Spys that instantly took me back to autumn afternoons picking in the orchards and riding back in the wagons loaded down with twenty bushel bins with the three Corbett boys—Dunstan, Derrick, and Devon. Lifting a knobby, firm Northern Spy to my nose I recalled Dunstan's hard, muscular arms pulling me in for my first kiss among the barrels and bins, his lips tasting tart and sweet as cider . . .

"Those are an heirloom variety called Northern Spy." When I looked up I saw a pretty, dark-haired girl in a yellow flowered apron. She was holding an apple, a paring knife poised against its dark red skin. In her flowered dress and old-fashioned apron, she might have drifted out of the last century. She could have been that girl in the picture—the Apple Blossom Queen of nineteen-twenty-something, come to offer me a taste of the forbidden apple. "They're especially good for—"

"Pies," I said. I must have startled her because her knife slipped and sliced into her thumb. She yelped and dropped the apple, which rolled under a bin leaving a trail of blood on the dusty boards and a coppery tang in the air.

"Are you all right?" I asked looking back at the girl. She was sucking on the injured thumb. A drop of blood had landed on the collar of her dress, a new blossom in the floral print.

"Yeah," she said. "Occupational hazard." She held up a hand that was nicked and scratched. I remembered my mother's worn and scarred hands.

This is what a farmer's wife's hands look like, my mother had said to me once when she caught me looking at them. *Remember that when you're kissing Dunstan Corbett out behind the hay barn.*

Dunstan's going to be a policeman, I'd countered.

She had laughed, wiping down the counter with a dismissive gesture. *That won't stop them Corbetts from putting you to work. How do you think they took over all the orchards in these parts? Don't let Dunstan's soft smile fool you; he comes from hard people.*

I looked around at the fruit of all those orchards—fifty acres of which had once belonged to my family—and then back at the girl, who was still nursing her finger.

"At least you made a sale," I told her. "I'll take two bushels."

THE SMELL OF blood stayed with me the rest of the afternoon as I peeled and cored apples in the kitchen of the main house. I made two pies, one a Dutch apple with a cinnamon and brown sugar crumb topping and one plain apple in a fluted crust with an apple leaf design cut out of pastry scraps. When I was done the odor of blood had been banished by the scent of apples. I opened all the windows in the kitchen to let the steam out and a crisp breeze blew in, rattling the glass in the cabinet doors, shivering the china cups in the cupboards. As I passed one closed cupboard I could hear a sound like a bell ringing. I put down the tray of cheese and crackers I was carrying and

pressed my ear to it. Yes, there was a bell ringing—a faint
faraway sound, like those wind chimes I'd heard on the first
day. I tried to open the cabinet but found that it was sealed,
painted shut. What could be in there making that sound? Some
ancient kitchen timer jarred into life? Mice playing "Chop-
sticks" on the family crystal?

If it was mice I should find out and put out traps. I took
out a flat-edged screwdriver from the tool drawer and began
chipping away at the paint. As I worked the bell seemed to
ring louder, frantic, as if whatever was trapped inside sensed
its chance for freedom. When I'd cleared the paint around the
edges I saw that the cabinet opened from the bottom. I dug my
fingernails under the bottom ridge and pulled, but it wouldn't
budge. For a moment I pictured someone on the other side,
holding the door down—a thought so horrible I started to back
away—but then it flew open so suddenly I tore a fingernail
and stumbled backward. A gust of air wafted against my face,
so foul it felt like a solid presence, a hand brushing against
my face. But there was nothing there except an empty space
and a brick wall. I stepped closer and leaned into the opening,
angling my head to look up . . . into blackness. The cabinet
went up and up into the house. Of course, I realized, it was
the dumbwaiter. Lots of old houses had them, to save the servants carrying trays upstairs or, more likely, so the master and
mistress didn't have to *see* their servants carrying the trays upstairs. They had another name, I remembered from some old
book I'd read: *The Silent Servant.*

But this dumbwaiter wasn't silent. That bell was still ringing. And it was coming from up above.

As if someone was summoning a servant.

All those old houses are wired with bells, my father once told
me, *so those rich people don't need but to lift a finger to have*

their every need and whim attended to. My grandmother turned into a bitter old shrew working for those people.

Being summoned by such a sound would grate on your nerves, I thought as I followed the imperious ringing into the rotunda and up the stairs. It must be one of the old servant's bells set off by the wind. *I'll put a stop to that,* I mentally told Old Bay at the top of the stairs. He seemed to retreat further into his chiaroscuro gloom, as if afraid to meet my eye. I followed the sound around the gallery and into the yellow room. The nursery. Of course, it made sense to have a dumbwaiter in the nursery, but where was it? I stood in the doorway, listening and looking around the room, the parade of circus animals looking back at me with feigned innocence, as if they were hiding something. The only break I saw as the little door that led to the back of the closet in Jess's study. But the sound wasn't coming from there; it was coming from the closet on the other side of the room.

I crossed the room and opened the closet door, but I didn't see a dumbwaiter, only a bulge in the plaster, like a tumor grow-ing from the inner organs of the house. The bell was coming from there.

I knelt down on the dusty floor, and pressed my ear to the bulge. At first all I heard was a dull roar, as if the house with its convolutions of interlocking rooms and spiral stairs was a hollow conch shell that mimicked the sound of the ocean. But then I made out something else beneath the roar. A baby crying . . . a bell ringing . . . and then even more horribly, my own name.

I was so startled I rocked back on my heels. And heard my name again. Only it wasn't coming from the bulge. It was coming from behind me. I turned around quickly, my skin prickling with the sense of being watched . . . of being *touched*, as the dirty air from the dumbwaiter had seemed to touch me—

But there was no one in the room. I heard my name again and realized it was coming from the open window. *Had it been open when I came in here?* It must have been. Maybe that's where the ringing was coming from. The breeze had set the old glass in the window chiming. I looked back at the bulge in the plaster but no sound was coming from it now. It must have something to do with the house's acoustics, I thought, getting up and walking toward the window. One of its *tricks*, as Monty had put it.

The window was in a deep eave that had been fitted out with a cupboard and window seat. As I leaned over the window seat I saw Monty and Jess sitting on the terrace in the coppery autumnal light. *The old venerable professor shares his wisdom with the young disciple.* Monty sat back in his Adirondack chair, at ease; Jess leaned forward, elbows on knees. He laughed at something Monty said and leaned back, taking a sip of amber-colored scotch (with the fall Monty had switched from Beefeater to twelve-year-old Macallan), his forearms bared by rolled shirtsleeves. I hadn't seen Jess look this happy and healthy in years. We'd made the right choice coming up here. This place was good for Jess.

I knelt down on the dusty floor, tucking my apron under my knees, and rested my arms on the window seat to look out across the gardens to the river and the Catskills, blue in the distance. Of course if it was good for Jess it was good for me, but when I breathed in the smell of apples I felt a restlessness tugging at me, an undercurrent like that smell of blood, like a bell ringing deep inside the house. What was I here for besides cleaning and cooking? I might as well have been a servant.

But I had chosen those chores, I reminded myself. Jess had

wanted to come here to inspire me to write again, and Monty had given me my notebook, which I had put away unopened in a drawer.

And set about scouring the kitchen and baking pies. Because cleaning—or any mindless physical labor like picking apples or peeling two bushels of them—emptied my mind.

What did I need emptied from my mind?

Clare.

The sound of my own name in my husband's voice drew my attention to the terrace. A trick of the breeze had carried his voice up to the window where I sat. I leaned forward to hear what he was saying, feeling both a pang of guilt at the idea of eavesdropping and a queasy thrill at the prospect of hearing my husband's unguarded thoughts. But I'd missed whatever Jess had said about me. Instead I heard Monty ask, "Where has she gotten to?"

"From the intoxicating aromas I'd say she's in the kitchen," Jess said.

Were they only talking about me because they were wanting their dinner?

"I do hope she isn't working herself too hard," Monty said. "Perhaps I shouldn't have encouraged her to start on cleaning the kitchen. Once you start working on this house it's hard to stop."

"It's not the house," Jess said. "Clare likes to keep herself busy. It's how she was raised."

"Ah, that's right, her parents were farmers—"

"They were sadists," Jess said savagely. "Her mother used to put tacks in the tablecloth to keep her from putting her elbows on the table."

I felt the blood rush to my cheeks. I'd told Jess that story in the first year we knew each other, but it wasn't something I liked other people to know. The blood was rushing so loudly in my ears I missed what Jess said next. All I heard was a shocked murmur from Monty.

"Of course they didn't understand her." Jess's voice, raised in outrage, lifted clear up to the second-story window. "She was smarter than them so they thought she was a freak."

Had I ever said that? It was true that Bill and Trudy Jackson hadn't known what to do with a shy, bookish child. Trudy would have liked a pretty blond doll she could dress up in frilly dresses and ribbons. Bill would have liked a boy. But a freak?

"They burned her books . . ."

Now he was really exaggerating. Trudy *had* thrown out my copy of *The Bell Jar* in eighth grade because she'd heard that Sylvia Plath had killed herself and she thought that reading her was making me morbid and moody. The book just happened to end up on the fire because we burned our trash.

". . . and forbade her to write."

Only because it was taking time from my chores. Jess had grown up in a suburban neighborhood in Massapequa. His "chores" had consisted of taking out the garbage and mowing a lawn the size of a New York studio apartment. Mine had included milking two dozen cows, mucking out the barn, picking apples in the fall, hauling firewood in the winter, working at the farm stand, watering and weeding three acres of vegetables, then picking and canning bushels of tomatoes, cucumbers, peaches, and raspberries. If I holed myself up in the barn loft to scribble in my notebook that meant more work for my father, whose heart was bad. When my father had a fatal heart attack in my senior year of college my mother didn't exactly *say* it was my fault, but she did forbid me to read a poem at his funeral because "he might be alive if I had spent more time helping and less time foolin' around with books." When I told Jess all this he had actually seemed *jealous*.

"It's like Dickens and the blacking factory," he'd said. "What great material!"

So I shouldn't have been surprised when he said to Monty now, "Writing about all that is what kept her together in college. It worried me when she stopped. Now I wonder if it's not my fault."

I heard Monty's murmured echo of his last two words. "Your fault?"

The rattle of ice told me Jess was taking a long drink before answering. (At some point I'd closed my eyes to concentrate.) I could hear the whisky in his voice when he continued. "When I started working on my book senior year I gave Clare chapters to read. She urged me on. I don't think I would have been able to write it without her—without her faith in me."

"Ah," Monty said. "It's a gift to have a reader like that."

"Yes. She always asked the right questions to get me to the next chapter. I sometimes felt like she was reading my mind, that she understood the characters better than I did myself, especially the girl . . ."

"Rachel Bartley."

Jess laughed and took another drink. "Of course you remember. In your review you said she was the only lifelike character in the book."

"The *most* true to life," Monty gently corrected. He was right. I knew the line by heart because I'd had to correct Jess myself in the months after the review came out. More than the damning last line it was the part that bothered him the most because—

"You were right, though, because Rachel was Clare. I stole her from Clare."

Monty made a tsking sound. I heard the clink of glass and the splash of liquid as he refilled their glasses. "It's what writers do. We borrow from the people around us. We can't help it. Clare of all people must understand."

"Clare has never complained," Jess said quickly, but with a sharpness that made it sound like a failing on my part. "But she stopped writing after that. Don't you see? I stole her childhood. I sucked it out of her. Like a vampire. I did more harm to her than her parents did."

Monty murmured something conciliatory that I couldn't make out. It didn't matter. When Jess decided to take himself to task for some imagined fault no one could talk him out of it. It was why I always forgave him for being so hard on other people; he was hardest on himself.

But I'd never known he blamed himself for my not writing. He was, of course, completely wrong. I'd loved the year that Jess was writing his first book, handing me pages as soon as he wrote them. I'd never felt closer to him. And yes, I'd recognized myself in the character Rachel and felt a queasy pang when she'd died at the end of the book—as if Jess had killed a part of me. But I saw that it was the right artistic choice and I'd been flattered—no, more than flattered; I'd felt *seen* for the first time in my life. I hadn't stopped writing because he'd stolen my material. I'd stopped because I didn't need to write anymore. Ushering Rachel into life had made me feel whole.

Did that make *me* the vampire?

No wonder Jess had stopped writing. He blamed himself for my stopping. Well, I could change that, couldn't I? I could write . . . *something*. Anything. There were a dozen unfinished stories in that notebook Monty had given back to me. I would start there. It didn't have to be any good—a little voice whispered that it might be better if it wasn't *too* good—all I had to do was convince Jess that I was writing again.

I opened my eyes, blinking at the darkening view. The sun had dipped beneath the line of mountains across the river. The cypresses that edged the garden cast long shadows over the lawn like accusatory fingers pointing at me. How long had I been lingering here (lollygagging, my mother would say) while dinner got cold and the men sat hungry on the terrace? I could hear the sound of their voices, but not what they were saying. The wind had shifted, carrying their voices out into the twilight garden and the river beyond, where they would flow down to the sea.

I rubbed at my face and was surprised to find that it was wet and covered with a white chalky substance. Flour from the pies? I wondered. But I'd washed my hands before leaving the kitchen. I looked around the window seat and saw what had happened. While I'd been eavesdropping I'd picked at the loose wallpaper. It was a bad habit I had, which was the real reason my mother had put tacks in the tablecloth—to keep me from unraveling the fabric while I ate. Here I had peeled loose a whole patch of the yellow wallpaper, covering my hands with the dried paste.

I wiped my hands on my apron and tried to pat the paper back, but it only came loose in my hands, exposing the bare plaster wall beneath—but not entirely bare. There were long scratches in the plaster. Had I made those? But then there would be plaster under my fingernails if I had. These scratches were deep. They looked like they had been made by someone trying to dig herself out of the room.

Chapter Six

I didn't sleep well that night. It didn't help that Sunny's crying baby woke me in the middle of the night—at 3:36 according to the digital alarm clock—and went on for hours, filtering into my dreams whenever I drifted off along with the sound of that invisible bell chiming in the dumbwaiter and images of those scratches in the plaster. The bell must have been some trick of the wind. As for the scratches . . . they must have been made by Monty's mother, Minnie. No wonder they'd sent her to a mental hospital.

When I fell back asleep I dreamed that I was in the nursery closet scratching at the lump of plaster because a baby was trapped inside the walls. I had to reach it before it suffocated. I woke in a sweat, my hands beating against the pillow as if I were the child trapped in wet plaster.

Jess caught my hands and held them against his chest. "Clare, it's all right—you were dreaming—Clare . . ." He said my name over and over, holding my hands against his chest with one hand and stroking my face with the other until my breathing steadied and I came out of the dream.

"It was an *awful* dream," I told him.

"Tell me," he said.

So I did. I told him about the scratches in the nursery and then the dream. How a baby was trapped in the wall and I had to get it out . . .

He gathered me into his arms and pressed my face against his chest. His skin was warm and moist, even though the night had turned cool. "That *was* an awful dream. Monty's mother must have made those marks. She was nuts, remember? You came up with the part about the baby trapped in the wall because you have such a powerful imagination. You have to use it, Clare. If you don't use it, it uses *you*."

He held me until I fell back to sleep and, mercifully, slept until morning without dreams. When I woke up I could tell by the light that it was late. Jess had gotten up already and left a note on my pillow.

Thought you could use the extra sleep, he'd written, *there's coffee in the pot. I promise I, not the ghost baby, made it.*

He'd drawn little handprints on the paper.

Ha, I thought, getting up, *very funny.* But truthfully it made me feel better to have him make fun of it. In the morning light the whole thing *did* seem silly. A ghost baby caught in the wall—what a horror movie cliché! But he was right about one thing. If I didn't use my imagination, it would use me. And the thought of being used by *anything* made me feel queasy.

After I showered I poured myself the coffee Jess had left in the Braun and took my notebook out of the drawer where I'd hidden it (*from whom?*). But where should I read it? I'd gotten into the habit of leaving the house in the morning so Jess could write. He'd gone out for a walk now, but he'd probably be back, and I knew he didn't like anyone around when he was work-ing. I could go to the gardens, but there was a chill in the air and I'd had a creeping dislike of the gardens since that first day when I'd seen the mirage of the figure standing beside the pond. Those cypresses looked funereal and the boxwood maze smelled like cat pee. I was sure that Monty wouldn't mind me using a room in the house, but I didn't like the idea of reading my old notebook where he might see me. What if it was terrible? What if he had written something in it that upset me? I knew it was foolish, but I felt self-conscious about having him witness my reading the notebook.

My first sip of the reheated stale coffee decided me. I'd go to Cassie's. It was an oddly public choice given my reluctance to have a witness, but I'd noticed when I went in there for coffee that it was the sort of place where students and professors sat for hours with their laptops and notebooks. It was a congenial working environment that would be a safe place in which to read the notebook. And neither Monty nor Jess ever went there.

I brought a manuscript I was copyediting and the Muriel Spark biography I was reading, the notebook sandwiched between them in a canvas book bag as if camouflaged. I got a large pumpkin spice latte and an apple cider donut from Scraggly Goatee—who told me when I asked that the Harvest Moon festival had been "awesome"—and staked out a big upholstered chair in the corner. On the couch across from me a heavily tattooed girl was tapping on her laptop, nodding her head in time to the music coming from her iPod. A fiftyish woman with gray-blond hair was correcting a stack of papers while sipping jasmine-scented tea. Everyone seemed to be in their own worlds. I took a bite of the apple cider donut, which I'd bought more out of nostalgia than anything else, and was disappointed that it didn't taste anything like the ones my mother used to make for the farm stand—or anything like apples, either—and slid the notebook out of the bag.

I sat for another moment staring at my own name on the

cover as if examining it for signs of forgery. It was clearly my own handwriting—funny how that stayed the same, like a fingerprint—only a bit larger than the cramped script I used now. Hardly surprising, I supposed; a decade of writing notes in the margins of other people's manuscripts would lead to writing smaller. Or perhaps I'd only written larger on the outside of the notebook, as if it were a title that called for a larger font. Clare Jackson! Starring in Professor Montague's Senior Seminar! I had been pretty full of myself getting picked for the class, like I was the shiniest apple on the highest bough.

You had to get picked for Monty's class, though; you couldn't even apply for it. Only a handful of senior English majors were chosen, no one knew exactly how. It was unlikely that he consulted the other creative writing faculty. He didn't mingle much, never kept office hours in the department, and seemed to despise most of his colleagues. If they had recommended a student it might be reason enough for Monty *not* to admit them. Perhaps he read the submissions to the campus literary magazine, *Hesperian,* but the year I was a junior, Amy Feinstein, who'd never submitted to *Hesperian,* had gotten in.

There were rumors, unsurprisingly, that he picked girls for their looks and potential bed-ability, and certainly there'd been a fair amount of attractive women in Monty's classes (and rumors that after graduation they had wound up in Monty's bed), but that didn't explain how he chose the guys (although some tried to posit bisexuality, those rumors were squashed by Monty's ferocious Hemingwayesque heterosexuality) or why he sometimes picked aggressively plain girls.

Camouflage, I overheard Jess say to someone on our first day of class, *for the really good-looking girls.* And then he'd looked at me and I had blushed. Did he mean I was beautiful? Or that I was the camouflage? His smile seemed to indicate the former.

I'd looked down and busied myself writing my name on the notebook—

That had been the moment I'd written these words, with Jess looking at me. It hadn't been the first time I'd seen him. Jess Martin was a legend on campus. There was a rumor that he'd already written a novel and burned it on a bonfire in the woods that had gotten him kicked out of the dorms sophomore year. He'd lived off campus since then and dated local girls. I'd seen him at the farm stand with a tall blonde in cowboy boots. He was already publishing short stories in real literary magazines. But it was, I was pretty sure, the first time he had really seen me.

Not many students had. I still lived off campus (my scholarship did not cover room and board) and worked at the farm stand in the afternoons and I hardly ever spoke in class. It wasn't so much that I didn't have anything to say as that Bailey students had so *much* to say. I'd never encountered a group with so many opinions and so much faith that the world was waiting to hear them. But on that first day of Monty's Senior Fiction Seminar, Jess had looked across the broad oak conference table and smiled at me as if we'd known each other for years and were sharing a private joke. Under that regard I'd written my name with such verve and flourish. Because being chosen by Monty (I didn't think it was for my looks) had made me suddenly *visible*. In turn, it had been Jess's smile that gave me confidence. When Monty had appeared—fifteen minutes late, in a rumpled white linen jacket and with a Mason jar full of iced tea, like a plantation owner who'd just wandered in off his veranda to find unexpected guests—and barked "Why are you all just sitting here like bumps on a log? Write something for God's sake!" I had opened my notebook and begun a story that had been rattling around in my head all summer. I hadn't even *thought* about it. It came pouring out. I'd gotten so immersed that I'd forgotten the class around me, the intimidating cool poses of the Bailey students, Monty sipping from his Mason jar (which smelled suspiciously of bourbon), and the light breeze coming in from the open window carrying with it the early autumn scent of cut hay and ripening apples—or perhaps the apples had been in my mind because that's what I wrote about.

At some point I became aware that the sound of my pen moving across the paper was the only sound in the room. I looked up and saw, to my horror, that the other students had stopped writing and were all looking at me.

"Now *that*," Monty said, wafting his nearly empty Mason jar in the air, dispersing the incense of Lipton and Jack Daniel's, "is writing. Care to share a few lines, Miss . . ." He'd squinted down at a crumpled sheet of paper—a class list, I supposed. ". . . er, Jackson, isn't it?"

I think now that I would have refused if I could have formed the words to do so, but I'd spent all my words. The only ones I had left were those on the page in front of me. So I'd read—

I opened the notebook now and read the first line of the story I'd started fourteen years ago. It was called "The Apples of Discord."

> Every year when the apple blossoms bloom the town council of Discord selects a Queen of the Apple Blossom Festival . . .

I felt an icy prickle at the nape of my neck, as if someone had laid a cold hand on my back. This was why I'd remembered the apple blossom girl story. I *had* written a story about her and here it was!

I read through the next few pages, the chill spreading from the nape of my neck to the base of my spine, like cold water pouring down my back. The details were eerily similar to the story Monty had told us, from the seduced girl carried off in the apple blossom laden cart to the girl drowning herself in the pond. *When the ice broke,* I'd written, *she thought it was her heart breaking.* No wonder I'd been able to recite it at our dinner party—I'd been quoting myself! Clearly the story had been inspired by the history of Riven House. I must have over-heard it listening to my mother and her friends gossiping in the kitchen and assimilated their stories into my own version over the long summer working in the orchards. I must not have known the story had anything to do with Monty's family—or else I'd never have read it aloud. What must he have thought? I remembered that when I had finished reading he'd been star-ing at me. I'd been terrified of what he'd say. He was famous for making withering comments that sent students running from the class in tears. But what he'd said was, "Well, class, Miss Jackson has set the bar exceedingly high. Go home and endeavor to write something worthy. Class dismissed."

Funny how I had remembered his comment all these years better than the story that had prompted it. Had I ever finished it? I began flipping through the pages to see, but the sound of my own name made me look up.

"Clare! It *is* you. Hi!"

I stared at the pretty blonde for a full ten seconds before recognizing her.

"Katrine," I said, quickly enough that I hoped she didn't see that I hadn't recognized her at first. Her wide, friendly smile gave nothing away. She was wearing a burgundy wrap dress and teetering on high heels, clasping a travel mug. Of course, I realized, her real estate office was practically across the street.

She must come in here all the time. She didn't look dressed for tromping through snake-ridden fields today, though. "How nice to see you. Do you want to . . ." I gestured to the seat across from me.

"Oh, I wouldn't want to disturb your writing," she said, looking down then at the notebook, which I'd closed and drawn protectively against my chest. "I didn't know you wrote too."

"I don't," I said. "At least not anymore. I was just reading over something . . ."

"Is it one of Jess's books?" she asked, perching on the arm of the couch across from me. The tattooed girl looked up and scooted a few inches away, giving Katrine room to sit, but she remained perched, as if she was really too busy to commit to sitting or she was worried that she might pick up something from the ratty old upholstery. "It must be so exciting to see a writer as talented as him at work. Is he finding the atmosphere at Riven House inspiring?"

"He's been writing," I said, not liking to admit I hadn't read anything. "But I don't know if he finds the atmosphere inspiring. Jess doesn't really believe in those things."

Katrine tilted her head, a perplexed look creasing her smooth forehead. "And what about you? How are you settling in?"

"Oh, I'm fine," I said quickly. "The caretaker's cottage is . . . *okay*. Once I got it cleaned out."

She clucked her tongue. "I asked Sunny Gruenwald to straighten up, but she must have forgotten. Did you get the welcome basket I sent?"

I looked at her blankly. "The basket . . . ?"

"With bread and cheese and wine. I thought it would make a nice romantic dinner for you guys on your first night."

I recalled the picnic dinner spread out in the candlelight. "Oh, yes, of course," I said. "That was so thoughtful of you. I should have thanked you for it"—*only my husband never mentioned where the food came from*—"I was just so busy unpacking."

"No worries," she said with a smile that suggested otherwise. "Jess thanked me."

He had?

"Of course, that's right, he told me he was going to take care of that, but still . . . It was all delicious."

"Oh, it all came from the new wine bar on the corner, Bread & Bottle—except for the grapes, which I got from the Corbett stand. In fact, one of the Corbett brothers mentioned he knew you from high school."

"Dunstan?" I asked, my voice high and shrill as a teenager's.

"No, I think it was Devon . . . or Derrick?" She laughed. "I never can tell those Corbett boys apart, one's more handsome than the next. But then you know that." She smiled coyly and waggled a finger at me. "You dated one of them in high school, didn't you?"

"I . . ."

"Don't look so surprised," she said, getting up and adjusting her slinky dress over her long legs. "It's a small town. You'll get used to it again. If you like, we could have a glass of wine at the Bread & Bottle and I'll fill you in on all the gossip."

For a moment I almost told her I couldn't—that I was needed at the house. But for what? To make Monty and Jess dinner? To listen to them trade literary gossip into the night?

"That would be great," I said. "I haven't had much female companionship up here."

"You mean you haven't been hanging out with Sunny and her *children*?" she asked coyly.

I smiled. "She's actually been very nice. She dropped off some dandelion greens and raspberry tea—to strengthen my uterus," I added a bit wickedly.

Katrine snorted coffee through her nose. "You *definitely* have to come for a drink at the B&B. We don't want your uterus getting too toned."

I laughed and said I'd love to. Then, feeling bad about making fun of Sunny, I added, "She must have her hands full taking care of her grandkids. I sometimes hear the baby crying late at night."

Katrine shook her head. "Grandkids?"

"Yes, at least I assumed they were her grandchildren. She just calls them her children—"

"Oh," Katrine said, a sly smile curling her lipsticked mouth. "That's what she calls her puppets. Sad, huh? You must be hearing something else at night. Foxes, maybe. They can sound like babies."

"Oh," I said, my skin prickling. "That must be it."

There was an uncomfortable silence and then Katrine glanced down at her watch and pretended to be surprised at the time. "I've got to go. I'm catching a train into the city."

"Oh," I said, wistfully. "Do you go in often?"

"As often as I can. I was a theater major in college and you can't really see anything worthwhile up here. You should come in with me sometime. I've got a girlfriend with an apartment who lets me stay there and a friend who gets me discounted theater tickets."

I told her I'd love to go in with her sometime although I was thinking that I had friends of my own in the city I could visit, like Marika, who'd called only a few days ago to ask me to come down for drinks.

After she left, I went back to my coffee and notebook but the pumpkin spice latte had grown cold and cloyingly sweet. I opened the notebook back to where I'd stopped reading and read the last line of the story I'd begun fourteen years ago.

And ever after the inhabitants of Discord House were haunted by the smell of apple blossoms and the sound of a baby crying in the night.

No wonder I heard a baby crying in the night. I'd scared myself with my own ghost story.

Chapter Seven

I drove back from town, clutching the steering wheel to keep my hands from shaking. I wasn't sure what had rattled me more—Jess not telling me where the food had come from (*he hadn't, had he?*) or the news that Sunny didn't have any children—at least not the kind that cried at night. I must have imagined it; it wouldn't be the first time.

Merging onto River Road I nearly ran into a speeding Audi. It honked and swerved past me—Bailey students driving too fast—and I pulled into the dirt parking lot of the Corbett farm stand to catch my breath. Taking deep breaths to steady myself, I glimpsed a plaid flannel–shirted man hauling a crate of apples off a flatbed. The contours of that broad back reminded me of Dunstan, but his face was hidden by a canvas baseball cap. Besides, it wouldn't be Dunstan—he was a policeman. It would be one of his brothers, Derrick or Devon. One of whom had asked after me. Maybe seeing a friendly face would calm me down.

I got out of the car and walked across the dusty lot, the sun hot on my back, and under the striped canvas awning into cool, raftered shadows. My father had built the open-air building and the slatted tables now laden with baskets of apples. They were in full apple season now—Jonagolds, Cox's Pippins, Blue Permains, Honeycrisps, Sweet Sixteens, Macouns, Sommerfelds. I saw the dark-haired girl in the yellow apron weaving in and out of the tables with a paring knife, slicing apples into the china saucers laid out in front of each basket, and hoped she'd be more careful with her knife than last time. I didn't think I could stomach the smell of blood right now. I walked around for a few minutes, sampling apples, their scent, the lazy drone of bees, and the pale yellow light of sun filtered through canvas, soothing. I wasn't entirely sure that Jess hadn't said where the food had come from—and even if he hadn't, it didn't mean anything. Things were going well. Jess was writing. We were happy up here. Waking up in the middle of the night (*at 3:36, it was always at 3:36*) wasn't a big deal. I could always nap later.

I tried a Sommerfeld, an apple I hadn't tasted since college, and nearly swooned at the rich caramel flavor. I bought a dozen, but I didn't see either of the Corbett boys at the register, only another flash of plaid flannel out in the back.

"Tell Devon that Clare Jackson said hello," I told the yellow-aproned girl.

I drove back crunching on a Sommerfeld, feeling better. When I pulled into the drive a fox streaked across the road, a red blur like a smear of blood. There was probably a den nearby. That's what I had been hearing in the night. A little further up the drive I had to pull over to let Sunny's pickup truck pass by. When she was parallel to me she leaned out her window and said she was going down to Beacon for some supplies for "the children." I wished her luck and drove on, feeling sorry for her. She must be pretty lonely to think of her puppets as children. Then again, papier-mâché and wire never broke your heart.

When I came into the house and found Jess at his desk, head bent over his laptop, my voice was casual, as if I always interrupted him when he was writing.

"I just saw Katrine at Cassie's."

Jess looked up from his laptop, his eyes soft and vague, a look he often had when he was writing, as if he were hearing a voice call his name and he'd forgotten whose voice it was. Or maybe even forgotten his own name. After a moment he said, "Oh, the Realtor," and closed his laptop. He must have been done for the day. "Did she try to sell you a split-level in MY-lan?"

Ever since Jess had discovered how the locals pronounced the neighboring town of Milan he'd taken any excuse to use its name.

"No, but she did ask me if I liked the welcome basket she sent. Why didn't you tell me she sent that food?"

He scratched his head. His hair was standing up in peaks, the way it did when he'd been writing all day. I'd seen him pulling at it, as if he were trying to tear the words out by the roots. He smiled a boyish smile to go with his boyishly tousled locks. "Didn't I? I guess I thought you saw the card."

I rolled my eyes. "Well at least you sent a thank-you."

He lifted both eyebrows in an expression of comic surprise. "Jeez, Clare, didya think you married Emily Post?"

"Crap. She must think we're barbarians."

"City slicker barbarians." Jess grunted and pulled me into his lap.

I squealed, not at all angry anymore. Not mentioning the card was no big deal—not like keeping the Brooklyn job from me and I'd all but forgotten about that already—and Jess's arms felt warm around me. The fall was still mild, but it would be getting cold soon. We had the whole winter to hunker down together in our cozy little house like the foxes in their den. Soon we'd sleep with the windows closed and I wouldn't hear them anymore.

WE DIDN'T GO up to the house for drinks or dinner that night. We stayed in and I made grilled cheese sandwiches and sliced the Sommerfelds. I made Jess taste them with his eyes closed.

"What do you taste?" I asked.

"Caramel. You've dipped them in caramel." But when he opened his eyes he saw the apple slices were bare.

"Witch," he accused.

"Barbarian," I countered.

When he kissed me, his mouth tasted fleetingly of caramel. That was the secret of the Sommerfelds. The first time you bit into one your mouth was flooded with caramel, but when you took another bite, looking for that taste again, you got plain apple. You had to sneak up on it, Dunstan Corbett had told me the first time he'd fed me the apples with my eyes closed. The taste was elusive, but when you caught it you wanted to suck that sticky sweetness right out of its flesh. That's how Jess kissed me that night. Like I'd surprised him. Like he was looking for something he'd lost.

Later, lying in bed, moonlight paring the room into white crescents, I watched Jess sleep, his face half in moonlight, half in shadow, and thought love was like those apples. You had to sneak up on it. And just when you thought it was gone— there it was again. I drifted in and out of sleep on this thought, each time I opened my eyes finding Jess's face a quarter inch more in darkness, as if he were slowly vanishing before my eyes, until only a sliver of cheekbone remained and I fell into a deeper sleep.

I WAS AWOKEN to the sound of someone crying. I looked at the clock and saw, surprise, that it was 3:36 A.M. The time the crying started. Those foxes must be able to tell time, I told myself, turning over and spooning myself against Jess's back. He groaned and moved away and I knew if I woke him he'd be angry.

I won't be able to write in the morning if I don't get a good night's sleep, he'd say.

So I lay on my back listening to the warbly wail carried on the wind through our open bedroom window. It didn't *sound* like a fox. And it couldn't be coming from Sunny's barn since Sunny was gone for the night. I rose up on one elbow and listened *harder*, but it was like the taste of the Sommerfelds—the harder you tried to pin it down, the more it eluded you. The sound was growing weaker—like a baby that'd worn itself out—

I sat up and swung my legs over the side of the bed. The floor was cold against my bare feet, the breeze coming through the open window chilly. I pulled on a sweatshirt—a new Bailey's one Jess had surprised me with last week to make up for the one he'd given away—and crept out of the room softly so as not to wake him. I pulled on rubber boots and opened the front door slowly so it wouldn't creak.

Once I knew where the sound was coming from it wouldn't trouble me any longer. My father had taught me that. *Face your fears,* he had said, when he made me go up into the attic to see it wasn't inhabited by Great-Granny Jackson's ghost thump-dragging her feet across the floor, only a family of mice that had taken up residence in an old trunk. When he saw the trunk was full of old women's shoes—the left ones each with a built-up heel to correct an uneven gait—he had looked at me a little funny. Still, once he'd thrown out the trunk and drowned the mice I never heard the shuffling limp overhead or glimpsed the lopsided shadow on the walls of my bedroom again.

I stepped outside into the night. A cloud cover had rolled in, muting the moonlight but also taking the bite out of the cold. Overcast nights and clear days make for a good apple harvest, my father would say. Now that I was outside I could hear that the night was full of sounds—the faint buzz of the last crickets still hanging on until the first hard frost—the whistle of the Amtrak train, the hum of the river flowing south, and, as if in answer to my waiting, the hoot of a barred owl.

Who who who waits for you?

Maybe it had been the owl I'd heard before. I'd heard barred owls cough and growl, and the babies screeched like hyenas, but when the owl paused in its endless question (who, indeed, I always wondered, waits for me?) I heard it. A baby crying, weak now, but all the more insistent as if it didn't have much time left. It definitely wasn't coming from Sunny's barn, though. It was coming from the gardens.

I headed out across the mown hay field, wading through ankle-deep fog that looked like curdled milk in the muted moonlight, the plaintive cry growing louder in my ears until it blocked out all the other sounds of the night.

After that visit to the attic I'd heard my father ask my mother if I might have overheard that Great-Granny Jackson had one leg shorter than the other, but she'd scoffed at the notion that she'd waste her breath talking about that crazy old woman. *But what can you expect from the girl?* she had asked. *Given where she was born.* That's when I found out that I'd been born in the Hudson River Mental Hospital, where my birth mother had been an inmate—and when I learned that Trudy Jackson didn't love me. Something I should have cottoned on to years before, only I'd held on to the idea that all the strictness—the thumbtacks in the tablecloth, the mouth washing with soap, the times she locked me in the closet for lying—were signs of love. They weren't. What I realized after the attic was that Trudy was afraid of me and I soon learned to use that to my advantage. If I wanted something—piano lessons, books, new shoes, things Trudy considered frivolous—I'd only have to look over her shoulder as if I'd just glimpsed the ghost of lame, crazy Great-Granny Jackson hovering in the air and she'd agree just to get away from me. It wasn't love, but in some ways it made my life easier. My father was right. It was better to face up to things. Just as it was better, I thought, wiping the dampness from my face, to know where this damned sound was coming from.

When I reached the edge of the field I got my answer. The sound was coming from the pond. I could hear mucusy hiccups coming from the far shore where the fog was thickest and where, I recalled, there was a walkway over the weir. Where I'd seen the figure standing the day we moved up.

But that had only been a tree, I reminded myself as I walked cautiously around the pond, going around the west side to avoid the bog I'd stepped in that first day. As for the weeping sound . . .

As I came around the west side of the pond I made out the wooden bridge emerging from the fog. The crying sound came from the other side of the weir where the fog was billowing upward, roiling the air like cream in a churn, thickening . . .

Into a shape . . . a figure . . .

I froze, my feet sinking into the cold mud, and stared, willing the figure to vanish, to dispel into mist and air.

But instead it thickened—the way pudding thickens as you stir it, quickening under the spoon into something gleaming and firm—into a woman in a long dress, her head covered, clutching something to her chest.

I only made out the shape for an instant, but in that short moment the woman looked at me out of the hollow spaces in the fog where the black of night pressed through. I could feel that darkness bearing down on me with the weight of cold stone, holding me motionless even as I wanted to run from the horror of that ravaged, empty face.

But that was what she wanted me to feel. Horror that she'd been driven to this moment, standing on the edge of the weir, with her child in her arms, ready to take its life and her own. *They have driven me to it.* I heard the words in my head as though they had been spoken aloud. They filled me with ice water, as if the contents of the pond had been poured into my body.

And then she was gone. The image dispelled into the air as if it had turned to water and been poured over the weir and washed out to sea. And with it the icy hold on me melted and I fell to my knees in the mud, my legs weak as water, the only sound left in the night my own heart pounding.

When I was able to get up I walked up onto the bridge, but of course it was empty. *You imagined it,* I told myself, *a trick of fog and moonlight.* The weeping had been the sound of the water moving over the weir. As I turned to go back to the cottage, I slipped, nearly falling over the weir, and landing hard on my knee. As I braced myself to get up I saw what had made me slip. Although the night was warm, the boards under me were coated with ice.

Chapter Eight

The first thing I did the next morning was check the overnight temperatures on the Weather Channel. There was a cold front coming in the wake of a tropical storm that was supposed to just miss our area, but it had only gone down to the fifties in Poughkeepsie, high forties in Albany. Across the river, west in the Catskills, it had gone below freezing, but not here in the sheltered river valley of the Hudson.

That was why the area was ideal for growing apples, my father had explained to me more than once. The river—and the fog that came off the river and covered the orchards like a warm blanket—kept the temperatures temperate, giving the apples time to ripen. But then, as Monty had said, the climate up here *played its tricks.* I knew from my father that there were dozens of microclimates folded into the hills and dales of the valley, so that a killing frost might leave one orchard unscathed while destroying another man's harvest.

That's what had happened in the winter of 1930. An ice storm had destroyed half the trees in the Jackson orchards, but had spared the Corbetts. That's why the Corbetts had been able to buy us out.

They took our luck, my father said once, looking after Dunstan and his brothers when they roared by on their tractor. *And then they took our land.*

When I asked my mother why he resented the Corbetts so much she'd said his grandmother had filled him with some nonsense about a curse on the family. *She was a bitter, crazy old lady,* Trudy had told me. *She worked as a servant in one of the big houses and it turned her head. Made her think she was better than other folks. She told me when I couldn't have babies that it was the curse. When I told her we'd adopt instead she said I was crazy bringing a stranger into the house. That no good ever came of that.*

No wonder I had imagined Great-Granny Jackson thump-dragging her uneven feet across the attic floor, down the attic stairs, and into my bedroom, where her lopsided shadow told me I didn't belong in *her* house.

As Jess said, if I didn't use my imagination, it would use me.

Jess came into the house from his morning walk while I was checking the Weather Channel. I switched it off quickly because I knew he hated the sound of television in the morning when he was getting ready to write—hated the sound of *any* voices other than the ones inside his own head—so I was surprised when he spoke to me.

"Did you get up in the middle of the night?" he asked.

"I didn't mean to wake you—"

"You didn't," he said absently, already moving to his desk and flipping open his laptop. "I just woke up and noticed you were gone. Bad dream?"

"No, I . . ." If I told him that I'd woken to the sound of a baby crying—that I'd been waking at 3:36 every morning to a baby crying—he'd only worry. If I told him I'd followed it out into the night and seen a figure standing on the weir he might do more than worry. "I had an idea—something I wanted to get down," I said instead.

He looked up from his laptop. "A writing idea?"

"Yeah," I said. "I mean, nothing big, just an inkling—" I snatched my old notebook out of my bag. "I've been going through my old stories and one of them sparked something."

"That's great," he said, getting up from his desk. He put his arms around me and pressed me to his chest. His flannel shirt smelled like cut hay. He must have been walking across the field. I wondered if he'd noticed my footprints . . . "I'm really glad you're writing again. You always seemed . . . *happier* when you were writing."

Had I?

"Do you want to write here today?" he asked, gesturing toward his desk. "Monty said I could use one of the rooms in the house if I needed it."

"No!" I said, shocked that he'd offered to give up his desk. "I mean . . . I have some stuff to look up. I thought I'd go to the town library and work there."

"Good," he said, giving me another hug, his eyes already straying back to his laptop. "Lucky you can write in public places like that."

"Yeah," I agreed. "Lucky."

JESS HAD ALWAYS marveled at my ability to write in public places. The truth was they were the only places in which I felt safe writing. I'd found that out in high school when I tried to write a story about Great-Granny Jackson in my bedroom and conjured up the *thump-drag* footsteps overhead. Better to write in the school cafeteria or Cassie's (Pete's, back then) or the library.

And I *did* have some things to look up in their historical

records archives. I could see if there was something about the apple blossom girl in there that I could use if I rewrote the story I'd started writing fourteen years ago. Jess was right. I was happier when I was writing. I needed something to keep my mind busy, to keep me from conjuring up ghostly cries and figures in the night.

I looked up at Riven House as I drove past. The morning mist was burning off, rising in smoky vapors from the grass as though from scorched earth. The house rose from the last remains of the fog as though rising out of a dream, the bricks on the east side turning a warm red in the sun. Like the mist burning off the fields, the memory of that figure I'd seen last night was already dissipating. It slipped further away as I made the drive into town. The morning bustle of Concord—the yellow buses stopping ahead of me to take on children in warm jackets and teenagers underdressed in sweatshirts and skimpy dresses, the farm stand putting out a sign for apples, pumpkins, and a "haunted orchard," hunters in camo-wear filling their thermoses at the Stewart's, Katrine putting out an open house sign in front of her office, Bailey students waiting for the shuttle—all of it felt too normal to occupy the same world as that ghostly apparition standing above the weir.

It had been an illusion born of fog and sleep deprivation, a vivid, powerful dream—I could still feel the grief and horror radiating out of those black-hole eyes—but a dream nonetheless. And a dream didn't mean I was crazy. It had come out of re-reading my own story just as my childhood illusion of Great-Granny Jackson had no doubt come from overhearing my parents talk about how she had warned them against adopting me. Instead of cowering in fear I could write the apple blossom girl's story. As Jess said, I could either use my imagination or it would use me. I'd write a story about the apple blossom girl—*maybe even a novel,* a little voice whispered—and then she would stop haunting my dreams.

I stopped at Cassie's for a coffee to go and drank it walking the two blocks to the town library. I sat on a bench outside finishing my coffee, enjoying the Indian summer weather (freakish after that frost last night) and bracing myself to go inside. The library was another relic of my past to face. I'd spent hours in the town library in my childhood and adolescence, tucked away in a back corner reading everything I could. Old Mrs. Trowbridge, head librarian throughout my childhood, had gotten to know me well enough to put aside books she thought I'd like, classics like *Jane Eyre* and *Rebecca*, but also surprises like the short stories of Lorrie Moore, who, she told me, had grown up not far from here and whose success showed that a girl from a small town in upstate New York could become a famous writer.

Of course Mrs. Trowbridge was long gone. Retired if not dead. The woman behind the desk was around my age and, with her retro black-framed square glasses, heavy black bangs, and vintage-y cardigan, tweed skirt, and bright yellow tights, looked more like she hailed from Brooklyn than Concord. She was clearly one of the new breed of hipster librarians that had come out of my cohort. In fact, my guess was that she was a Bailey student who'd gone up to SUNY Albany for her library degree and then come back to the area to work. She was shelving books when I came in, but stopped to ask if she could help me. I noticed her nametag read CJ BRENNAN.

"There used to be a local history section . . ." I began, peering through the stacks to the alcove where I remembered the archives had been kept. Where there had been a dark corner was now a cheerful nook full of children's books and a bronze plaque reading THE ELIZABETH TROWBRIDGE MEMORIAL CHILDREN'S READING CORNER. Next to it was a sign with a picture of a cell phone and a line drawn through it. I reached into my bag and thumbed the ringer off on my phone as the librarian replied.

"Yeah, there still is but I moved it to another room when we got the funding for the children's section. It's in here now."

She opened a door to what I expected would be a dusty closet crammed with old newspapers but which turned out to be a clean and orderly room lined with file cabinets, well-polished glass bookcases, and a reading table, above which the apple blossom girl looked out at me with eyes as dark and deep as the black holes I'd met last night.

"Was there something in particular you were looking for?" CJ Brennan asked me.

"Yes," I said, feeling cold as I stepped closer to the picture. "Her."

CJ BRENNAN SHOWED me where the old issues of the *Concord Gazette* were kept. "They're on microfilm too, but I've filed all the print issues in acid-free binders if you'd rather look through them. They're your best source for local history. The crowning of the Apple Blossom Queen was a big event, so you'll just have to look through all the May issues in the twenties to find her."

Monty had said his father had come down from Harvard in the spring of 1929, so I started there. I found the article in the May 2 issue, along with a larger version of the same picture that hung in the library. "Local beauty is pick of the crop," the headline read. And then below in smaller print: "Mary Foley, age seventeen, named Apple Blossom Queen at annual May Fair."

Mary Foley. The name didn't sound familiar, but then it was such an ordinary name—there had been many Foleys in my school—that it wouldn't.

I looked closer at the picture. Next to Mary was a young man in a striped suit, his face shaded by a straw boater, only his even white teeth catching the flash of the camera. He had the same wicked grin as Monty when he told us an off-color story about some literary luminary he'd rubbed up against. The man in the picture was looking at Mary Foley as if he'd like to gobble her up. Bayard Montague looked years younger than his portrait hanging in the rotunda, even though the portrait couldn't have been done more than a year later, since he hadn't lived much longer than that.

I scanned the line of farmers and small town businessmen and found one other familiar person in the photograph, her uneven shoulders giving her away: my great-grandmother, Mildred Jackson, in a high-necked black dress and white apron. It gave me a chill to see her there, as if the ghost of my childhood had found its way into my present. But it wasn't surprising for her to be in the picture. The Jacksons were prosperous orchard owners back then. Mildred was probably on the pie baking contest committee or some such thing.

I looked back at Mary Foley. She was glowing. She looked like she'd been dipped in dew and polished. Even in the black-and-white photograph you knew her cheeks were as pink as the blossoms that crowned her head and her lips, which were slightly parted, would be as red and glossy as a candy apple. You could practically smell the apple blossoms.

For a moment I thought I did, a scent so heady and sweet it made me dizzy. I had to put my head down on the table to steady myself. When the scent was replaced by the maple syrupy smell of old paper, I opened my eyes. I read the short article through and found that Mary Foley was engaged to one Ernst Jackson.

Oh, I thought with a shiver, we were almost related. Only Mary was never going to bear any Jackson children and even if she had they wouldn't be my blood relations. I looked through the faces again and found a bashful looking young man, looking uncomfortable in a plaid suit, who had the same square jaw and wide-set eyes as my father. Ernst Jackson was Mildred's son. My father's father. I remembered Monty's story. Mary's father had married her off to the neighboring farmer's son—to my grandfather. He must have remarried eventually and had my father, but surely the story of his first wife, who killed herself and abandoned her child, would have been passed down in the family. I must have heard it when I was little and hiding under the kitchen table eavesdropping on my mother and her sisters talking.

I put the newspaper aside, meaning to make a copy of it before I left, and picked up the file for 1929–30, counting nine months in my head as I did. January 1930—unless the baby had come early . . . I flipped through stories about the local quilting bee and church socials and advertisements for farms for sale and used farm equipment until I found the story in the January 13 issue of the *Gazette*. No picture this time. Just two inches of newsprint.

> Tragedy struck last night as a local farmer's wife and infant fell victim to the worst ice storm of the decade. Mrs. Mary Jackson, formerly Foley, was found frozen to death on the Montague estate, River House, by the estate caretaker, Albert Finley. Mr. Finley, who has worked for the estate since he was a boy, said he found her when he came out in the morning to check on the damage caused by the storm.
>
> "She looks to have slipped off the spillway bridge,"

Mr. Finley told this reporter. "But I don't know what she was doing out in such a storm. The poor girl must have been mad."

An even more gruesome and tragic discovery was made by the housekeeper when she opened the front door. An infant, presumed to be the child of Mrs. Foley, was found frozen to death on the doorstep. Dr. Herbert Melchior, who was at River House attending the confinement of Mrs. Montague, examined the mother and child, but declared that they were both beyond his help. "One can only hope they are in heaven together, the poor souls," the housekeeper averred.

I was surprised to find tears in my eyes, as if I'd been standing on the steps with the housekeeper waiting for the doctor, hoping he might perform a miracle. How on earth could she have thought the frozen child could be revived? And hadn't Monty said his mother had found the child on the doorstep? I read on—

Mr. Montague was not available for comment as his own wife was in confinement, but he sent a message through the estate caretaker expressing the family's deepest sympathies at the regrettable accident. "In the future," he wrote, "the estate will be gated off to avoid any further misfortunes."

The horror I'd felt last night rose up again, replacing my tears, but now the horror was laced with anger. As if that had been all that was needed to avert the tragedy of Mary Foley killing herself and her newborn child! I flipped through the rest of the paper looking for some other mention of Mary Foley, perhaps some public outcry at her death. But who would speak up for her? Her father, who had bartered her for a hundred acres of apple trees? Her lover, Bayard Montague, who had seduced and abandoned her to marry another woman? Her husband . . . ?

What about her husband?

I looked back at the awkward figure in the May Fair photograph. Although twice her size, he looked like he was cowering in Mildred Jackson's shadow. He'd married a girl who had run off with another man and who was carrying that man's child. Had he gone along with the marriage because it had been arranged—a deal between neighboring farmers to merge resources and land? Or because he still loved Mary?

I looked through the next few days of the *Concord Gazette*. Three issues later I found a two-line notice announcing a memorial service for "Mary Foley Jackson, who left behind her husband, Ernst Jackson." There was nothing else.

I remembered that in my junior year of high school one of my classmates, Tracy Van Dyke, had died of leukemia. Her picture had been plastered around the town for months. The *Gazette* had run a full-color spread on her short life, featuring baby pictures, shots of Tracy in the school production of *Our Town*, playing lacrosse, at the junior prom. Local merchants had kept a can with her face on it to collect for the Leukemia Fund. Her class had planted a tree in her honor in front of the high school and a big poster with her picture hung in the front lobby next to our trophy for winning the basketball championship in 1984. Girls would lay down teddy bears and cards that read "Love you Forever, Trace!" under it. I remember getting almost *tired* of seeing her face everywhere, her dead girl's eyes watching reproachfully as the rest of us went on with our lives—went to prom, made out with our boyfriends, graduated—did all the things she would never get to do.

But now I wondered if the town of Concord had done anything to remember Mary Foley.

I looked up from the reading table, now strewn with issues of the *Concord Gazette*, to the glass bookcases and spied the familiar gold apple logo on the spines of row after row of tall red volumes of the *Concordian*—Concord High School's yearbook. I got up and knelt in front of one of the cases. They were arranged by year, from a spindly 1901 edition to last year's much thicker tome. I plucked 1929 from the shelf and—unable to resist—1995. I put the newer yearbook on the edge of the table and sat back down to look at Mary Foley's senior year. The cover of the book was stamped with a picture of the old high school building framed by apple blossoms. Underneath was a quote from Ralph Waldo Emerson: "We are born believing. A man bears beliefs as a tree bears apples." The same quote that they still put on the yearbook in my year.

I began paging toward the class pictures, but I didn't have to go that far to find Mary Foley. She was in the Latin club and the glee club, the 4-H club and the debating society. It was clear that she was a star student even before I got to the picture showing her receiving the award for class valedictorian. She was glowing even more than in the Apple Blossom Queen crowning. It was hard to believe that in less than a year she would be dead.

My eyes burning, I pushed the 1929 yearbook away and pulled the 1995 one to me. I opened it to near the end, half surprised it didn't fall open to the page my own copy always opened to, but soon found the picture of my own valedictorian award. It had been announced at the end of the year award assembly after all the other awards. I could still remember the buzzing in my ears when my name was called and how for half a second I wondered if I'd imagined it. But then Dunstan was nudging me, his own face beaming with pride, and telling me to "get on up there, Clary, before Charity Jane takes it from you." Charity Jane Pratt had been the girl whose grade point average had hovered next to mine since the eighth grade.

I looked back at the picture of Mary Foley. Did she have someone in the audience cheering for her the way Dunstan had for me? Ernst Jackson, perhaps?

I flipped forward to the senior class pictures and looked under the J's, but didn't find him. Maybe he was older—or maybe he'd left school early to help with the farm like a lot of farmers' sons.

I went back to the *Gazette* issues, shuffling through them for the last week of May. The *Gazette* always dedicated a whole issue to the high school graduation. I scanned the pages quickly for the valedictorian, but found another name listed, a boy named Edmund Hilary Canning. Mary must have lost the valedictorian award after she ran off with Bayard Montague. In fact . . . I looked through the whole list of graduates. Mary wasn't on it. So she hadn't even been allowed to graduate!

I turned the page, wondering if any mention had been made of her, and found a short sidebar with a photograph of a young man, hair parted on the side and slicked back, heavy glasses dwarfing his narrow face and close-set eyes. "Mr. Edmund Hilary Canning to receive scholarship to Bailey College," the caption read, and then below: "Mr. Canning will take the place formerly awarded to Miss Mary Foley since the young lady has decided to marry instead of attending college. Mr. Canning intends to study religion . . ."

I had to resist tearing the page to shreds. Poor Mary Foley! Not only had she lost her place as valedictorian and her high school diploma, she had lost her scholarship to Bailey. And all because Bayard Montague had taken a fancy to carry her off for a brief dalliance! And all that happened to him was to be shipped off to New York City to be paraded in front of a bunch of debutantes—

Well, that might have been pretty awful too. Especially if he had cared for Mary—and who wouldn't? She hadn't just been beautiful; she'd been smart and hardworking. Who knew what she would have made of herself if she had gone to Bailey?

I pulled the 1929 yearbook to me again and stared at Mary Foley's face as she received the award for valedictorian. I was still staring at it when the door cracked open and I heard someone behind me. I wheeled around, half expecting Mary Foley herself come back from the grave to command me to right the wrongs committed against her, but it was only the librarian, fiddling with her geek-girl glasses.

"Hey," she said with a strained smile. "Sorry to disturb your research, but we're closing early because of the storm."

"The storm?" I repeated, staring at her blankly. I could see my own reflection in her glasses. At some point I'd screwed my hair up into a sloppy knot that listed to one side of my head, giving me a slightly off-kilter manic look.

"Can't you hear it?" Her eyes rolled upward. At first I thought she was actually rolling her eyes at me and the anger I'd felt simmering all morning nearly erupted, but then I realized she was only looking toward the ceiling, against which rain was pattering. I could also hear now the low moan and shriek of the wind.

"Oh wow," I said. "I was so immersed I didn't notice."

She cast her eyes down on the scattered *Gazette* issues and yearbooks. For a moment I thought she *would* roll her eyes at me. Who got so caught up in old local newspapers and yearbooks that they failed to notice the roof was rattling like it was about to be torn off? But she only picked up the 1995 yearbook and smiled. "Yeah, sure, that happens to me all the time. But you'd better get on home. The weather service has issued a flood warning and the bridge over the Saw Kill could wash out."

How did she know I had to cross the Saw Kill to get home? I wondered, starting to neaten up the newspapers.

"Leave those," she said sharply. Then in a more modulated voice, "I'll put them back in the morning. Let's get out of here."

I closed the 1929 *Concordian*, sorry to lower the cover over Mary Foley's hopeful face, and got up. My legs felt stiff. "How long *have* I been in here?" I asked, looking at my watch. It read 3:36, but that couldn't be right.

"Six hours," she said. "I peeked in to make sure you hadn't, like, gone to sleep. But you were so engrossed you didn't even notice me."

"Crap, I'm sorry," I said, shaken. How had that much time passed?

"It's all right," CJ Brennan said, flicking off the light switches as we crossed the main lobby to the front door. Now that we were in the front of the library I could see the rain lashing the windows, the sky outside dark as night. I didn't have a raincoat, just the Bailey sweatshirt. I pulled up the hood and strapped my bag crossways over my chest, making sure it was closed securely to keep my notebook from getting wet. "No one expected the storm would be so bad. It was supposed to pass us, but a change of wind drove it right into the Hudson Valley instead. The weather here—"

"Plays its tricks," I finished for her.

She gave me her first genuine smile. "Yeah, my dad always said that . . ." And then, tilting her head to one side, "You don't remember me, do you?"

Crap. "You look familiar," I said, feeling awful. "Were you at Bailey?"

"No," she said, turning away from me to take her raincoat down from a hook by the door. "We were in high school together, but I don't blame you for not recognizing me. I had braces, weighed fifty pounds more, and went by my maiden name, Pratt."

"Charity?" I said tentatively. "Charity Jane Pratt?"

"Yeah," she said, flipping her hair over the collar of her bright yellow slicker. "I married Dean Brennan. I know it's pretty retro to change your name but I always hated Pratt." She blushed and I remembered that kids had called her "Charity Twat." I also remembered how crushed she had been when I won the Bailey scholarship and not her.

"Well, you look great!" I said sincerely. "I'm sorry I didn't recognize you. We were in Honors English together."

"And AP History and—well, all the APs."

"You were salutatorian," I said. And only one-tenth of a point away from being valedictorian and winning the Bailey scholarship for herself. We were standing in the doorway. Outside the sky was dark as night, the rain coming down in sheets. I could only make out the shimmer of CJ's glasses and the yellow glow of her coat. Her expression was unreadable, but I guessed she was thinking about the same thing. "I remember how much you loved books," I said to make up for not recognizing her earlier. "Wasn't *Wuthering Heights* your favorite?"

"Yeah," she said, "And yours was *Jane Eyre*."

Had it been? My Freshman Lit professor had convinced me that *Wuthering Heights* was the superior book.

"Well, it's great you've become a librarian!"

"Yes," she said. "When I didn't get the Bailey scholarship I went to SUNY Albany. They have a good library program. And you . . . I guess going to Bailey worked out for you. You ended up working as an editor in New York, right? And of course, you married that writer."

I was glad the doorway where we stood was dark so she couldn't see my face.

"Yeah," I said, "but I've been working on a book. That's why we're back up here." It wasn't exactly a lie, I told myself. Jess had turned down the Brooklyn College job because he thought I'd go back to writing up here—and I *was* working on a book now. "That's what I was researching today."

"Ah," CJ said, "no wonder you lost track of time. Well, I'm glad things worked out for both of us . . ." She hesitated, biting her lip, then went on. "You know I hated you for a while, right? I mean, I was so sure I was going to win that scholarship. I even had the principal retally our averages. But it turned out that I'd messed up the final exam in English. I must have gotten the order of the questions wrong, because I remember *knowing* all the answers, but when Mrs. Ramsey fed the test into the Scantron my answers were all wrong. Anyway." She turned away and punched in a code on the alarm pad. "I got over it. SUNY Albany was fine, probably better than being with all those snobs at Bailey."

"Yeah," I agreed, wondering if she meant that *I* was a snob, "those kids were pretty pretentious. Sometimes I wonder if I wouldn't have been better off going somewhere else too."

She gave me a peculiar look. "But then you wouldn't have married Jess Martin and come back here to live at Riven House—which clearly has inspired you . . . only . . ." She hesitated.

"Only what?" I asked.

"You're a braver woman than me. All those stories about the house . . ."

"You mean those things they print up in the local haunted legends books?" I asked. "I don't think you can put much stock in those."

"No," she admitted, "but my aunt worked for Mr. Montague when he first came back and she told some stories that would raise the hair on the back of your neck. She said she used to find wet footprints on the steps of the main staircase every morning. She thought it was one of Monty's hippie girlfriends traipsing up and down after skinny-dipping in the pond, but then she opened up the house one morning after it had been closed for a week and the footprints were still there. Wet footprints going all the way up the stairs and into the old nursery. She said that's when she knew it was the ghost of that girl come back to find her baby. She quit that day. Didn't even go back to collect her pay. Said she'd never set foot in that house again. Mr. Montague never could get anyone from the village to work there after that. Word travels fast around here."

I thought of the accumulated grime in the kitchen that I'd scrubbed away. I thought of the cries I'd heard in the night, that bell ringing in the dumbwaiter, the figure on the weir. "My father always said the villagers made up stories about the river folk because they were bored with their own lives."

Charity turned to me, the overhead lights reflecting off her glasses, lips thinned. "Sure, that must be it. Us poor village folk, we've got nothing better to do with ourselves." She switched off the lights and opened the door.

"I didn't mean—" The slap of rain and shriek of the wind cut off the rest of what I was going to say. Which was just as well because I wasn't sure what I *had* meant.

Chapter Nine

I replayed CJ's remarks while I dashed through the pouring rain and flung myself, drenched and shaking, my bag still strapped across my chest, into the car. As I thought of those wet footprints leading to the nursery a drop of cold water dripped down my neck and I shuddered. It was only a story town folk made up because they were jealous of the rich people who lived in the big houses on the river, I told myself as I drove back. Charity Jane had told it to me because she was jealous of me, always had been. She'd always been high-strung and sensitive about her name. Everyone got called names ("Jack-off," Ryan Moser had called me until he fell flat on his face one day when he was doing it and everyone had laughed at him). I'd always been nice to Charity Jane, never calling her "Charity Case" or "Charity Twat." It wasn't my fault she'd screwed up her final exam. Imagine asking the principal to retally our GPAs! I remembered her bent over her test, penciling in the circles so hard she kept breaking the tip of her pencil. No wonder she'd lost track of the order when she had to keep resharpening her pencil. And no wonder she'd told me that awful story—wet footprints on the stairs, the ghost of that drowned girl come back to find her baby—

I swerved, nearly hitting a yellow-coated policeman who loomed out of the rain to wave me past a downed tree, and put CJ Brennan firmly out of my mind to concentrate on driving. The world had been utterly transformed from the autumnal idyll I'd passed through this morning. The streets were deserted except for policemen and emergency workers. Wind and rain had stripped the leaves from the trees, splattering the ground with a slick red mat that proved as slippery as ice. Turning onto River Road I skidded and almost plummeted into the Saw Kill, which had risen above its banks and was lapping at the road like a hungry animal. My heart pounding, I wrenched the car back onto the road and drove blindly. The gate to Riven House suddenly lurched out of the murk like a black-toothed mouth and I fishtailed the car through them, narrowly missing the high, spiked gate.

In the future, Bayard Montague had written, *the estate will be gated off to avoid any further misfortunes.*

As if the villagers were clumsy children who had to be kept from the risky grown-up world of their betters. When really what the Montagues had done was draw back into their world of wealth and privilege, barricading themselves behind their high gate and solid brick walls. No wonder the townies told stories about them.

I could glimpse the house now, standing on the hill like a child playing king of the mountain. Without the sun, the windows looked like cataract-covered eyes. Even the cries of a dying baby could not penetrate those thick walls, which in the rain looked as though they had been soaked in blood. How could they go on standing after what they'd seen—

A sharp crack cleaved through the thunderous rain. The world shook. I was staring into a frozen lake splintered into a spiderweb, my ragged breath steaming the air, my hands still

clutching on to the steering wheel as though it were a life preserver and I was about to be sucked under.

A gust of rain-soaked air slapped against my face and I realized what had happened. A bough had split, landed across the
hood of the Subaru, and crashed through the windshield. One
long branch pointed a bony finger just inches from my face.
Another few inches closer and I would have been skewered.
Instead I was stranded in the rutted drive in a wrecked car that
was taking on water.

I undid my seat belt with numb fingers, wrenched open
the door, and stepped out into ankle-deep water. The icy water
woke me up—and frightened me. I was in the low part of the
drive, not far from where the Saw Kill flowed into the river. I
could hear the rush of the water above the sound of the rain.
The cottage was still a good half mile down the road. Was Jess
there? I could picture him at his desk, writing obliviously while
the creek rose and lapped over the doorstep. Monty wouldn't
think to come help him, Dale was probably too stoned, and
Sunny was away.

I fished my cell phone out of my bag, still strapped across
my chest, and hit the first number on speed dial—Jess's cell—
but it went instantly to voice mail. Of course he turned it off
when he was writing and we hadn't bothered to get a landline.
Again I pictured him at his desk, tapping away at his laptop,
hair standing on end, while water lapped at his ankles.

Or maybe he'd gone up to the house.

I tried Monty's cell but it too went straight to voice mail.
Fucking writers. Not that I was one to talk. I had sat in the
library while the worst storm of the season—of the century
for all I knew—roared into town. I looked back up the hill
toward Riven House. A moment ago the house had looked like

a forbidding fortress but now it looked like a safe haven on high ground above the floodwaters—

I looked toward the pond. The Saw Kill had been rushing into it all day, gathering up against the ancient stone weir that regulated the flow of the stream past the cottage. Where the pond should be was a lake, swollen as a blister, ready to burst. And when it did, all that water would rush downstream over the cottage. *Our cottage.* I had to make sure Jess got out of there.

Getting around the downed tree wasn't easy, though. It blocked not only the road but a good ten feet on either side. On one side the Saw Kill rushed past, too deep and treacherous to go near, and on the other a steep embankment that the rain had turned into a mudslide. I had to climb over the tree itself, through a thicket of prickly pine branches, dense with needles, dried sap, and birds' nests. By the time I emerged on the other side I was scratched and bleeding, the salt of my tears stinging the scratches on my face. I was picturing Jess looking up from his desk and noticing the water. He'd try to save his books and notebooks and the boxes of files he hadn't unpacked yet that contained drafts of his first novel, the copyedit, and galley—what we called "dead matter" in the trade. Jess had hung on to all of it and he wouldn't leave it. I pictured him trying to stack the file boxes up high, the boxes spilling, the papers falling like dead leaves to be washed away in the floodwater while Jess was caught up in the rushing water, swept away with all the dead matter, drowned in his own words.

I waded through the now calf-deep water and driving rain to the cottage. So vivid was my image of its destruction I was surprised to see it still standing. But it wouldn't be for long. The Saw Kill rushing down the slope from the weir had divided into two streams that swarmed around the cottage and lapped at the front door like an angry bill collector. I waded up the front path and opened the door, letting the tide seep in across the cracked green linoleum and the stained carpet. What did I care if it ruined it all? I just wanted Jess.

But he wasn't there. Not at his desk—empty of his laptop—or in the bedroom. Nor were the file boxes of notebooks and dead matter. He must have evacuated it all hours ago and gone up to the house to wait for me. The only paper I found was a sticky note stuck to the refrigerator. *Clare, went up to the house to wait out the storm.*

I could almost hear his voice. *I thought you'd go straight there,* he'd say. *Why would you go to the flooded cottage?*

Why indeed? I looked around. What was there to save here? What had it ever been but a temporary way station between our old life and the murky future?

I walked out without shutting the door behind me. Let the waters come. I walked uphill with my head down, watching the water swirl around my feet, but when I got to the top of the hill I looked back down toward the pond. For a moment the rain coalesced into a figure standing above the weir, rain sodden, clothes dark and plastered to her skin. *Not from the rain,* I thought, *but because she drowned.* She looked up at me as if to say, *If I drowned, why shouldn't the whole world drown?*

At the thought the rock wall of the weir gave way to the force of the water and tumbled into the rushing stream like it was made of toy blocks. The water leaped over the lip of the pond and ran toward the river—and the caretaker's cottage that lay in its way. The dark figure hovered in the air for a moment and then turned into a black crow that flapped noiselessly toward the tree line.

She was gone.

I turned around—and there she was. Standing on the terrace facing me, a drowned revenant risen out of the flood-waters to wreak her vengeance on the house.

I blinked rainwater out of my eyes and she was gone again. I was staring at my own reflection in the glass library doors. *I was the drowned revenant standing outside in the cold, looking in at the warm glowing room beyond*—at the two men sitting beside the fire drinking glasses of scotch that looked like liquid firelight in their crystal tumblers. Monty saw me first. He lifted his head and a look of terror washed over his face, draining the warmth of the firelight from his skin. He looked like a ghost himself. That's what I must have looked like to him. The ghost of Mary Foley come to take her vengeance on the last of the Montagues. I saw his lips part, but instead of a scream he must have said my name. Jess bolted out of his chair, dropping his glass, and lunged for the glass doors. For a moment I had the strangest feeling he was rushing to lock me out, but of course that was nonsense. He flung both doors wide open, with that flair for the dramatic I'd always admired, and grabbed me by the shoulders.

"Clare! My God! We looked all over for you! Where have you been?" He was pulling me into the room as he shouted, not giving me time to answer. Monty, still looking pale and shaken from his first glimpse of me, was struggling up from his chair, feebly plucking an afghan from the back of it and tottering forward.

I could have killed him, I thought. *I might have given him a heart attack appearing like that in the window.*

Jess drew me toward the fire and planted me in the chair he'd been sitting in. He tore the afghan out of Monty's hands so violently that Monty stumbled.

Be careful, I tried to say, but found that my teeth were chattering. Jess wrapped the throw around me and Monty poured a glass of scotch with shaking hands and thrust it at me. My hands were shaking even harder than his, so Jess held the glass to my lips and tipped it down my throat. I spluttered and coughed like a drowning woman spitting seawater.

Or pond water.

I took a long swallow of the whisky. It burned through the layer of ice that had settled in my stomach. Jess knelt down in front of me and chafed my hands, and then, slipping my mud-soaked loafers off, my feet. His hair in the firelight was a beautiful russet color.

"The cottage," I managed to say after another swallow, "it's flooding."

"You went there?" Jess asked, looking up from my feet. "I left you a message on your phone telling you not to go there. Your phone's been off all day!"

He sounded so aggrieved I nearly laughed. *See how it feels!* I almost said. But he looked so worried I didn't do either.

"I guess I turned it off in the library," I said instead. "There was a sign telling me to."

Now he laughed. "That's you all over," he said, hugging me hard against his chest. "Conscientious Clare. Always following the rules." He pulled back and held me by the shoulders at arm's length. "I was worried sick about you!"

"We both were," Monty said. He'd taken his seat and was holding his glass of scotch, hands steady now, color coming back to his face. "The storm hit so unexpectedly. We thought you'd head back hours ago."

"I was in the archives room looking through old news-papers and yearbooks—there aren't any windows in there so I didn't notice the rain. To be honest . . ." I took another sip of scotch. "I don't know that I'd have noticed if there were. I found out all sorts of things about the apple blossom girl. Her name was Mary Foley. She was actually married to my grandfather! But she never had his children—and oh! She won the locals' scholarship to Bailey but it went to someone else when she got pregnant."

"Well, well," Monty said, grinning wolfishly. "It looks like Clare's found her subject."

"Yes," Jess said, still gripping my shoulders tightly, "that is if she doesn't die of hypothermia before she gets a chance to write it. You've got to get out of these wet clothes."

"But everything is at the cottage," I objected. "And the cottage is flooding." Suddenly I was on the verge of tears at the thought of our little cottage—the only home we had—floating away on the Saw Kill. How could I have been so callous about it before? I'd even left the door open!

"I brought our stuff up earlier," Jess said. "Monty insisted when he saw how bad the rain was. We're all set up in a room upstairs. I brought your clothes and some of your things. I couldn't get everything . . ."

He let go of my shoulders and I threw my arms around his neck. "It's okay," I said. "As long as we're both safe."

I felt a tremor go through him as if he'd been tensed and only now let go. *He really had been afraid for me!* I burrowed my face into his neck and felt him shiver.

"I've gotten your clothes all wet," I said, pulling back. "I'll go change. Maybe you should too."

"I'm all right," he said, helping me up to my feet. "I'll go warm us dinner. There's that soup you made last night—and some bread. You need something warm inside you."

I gaped at him, about to joke that I hadn't realized he knew how to work the stove, but seeing the stricken look on his face thought better of it. I left them in the library and hurried upstairs, only remembering on the top of the rotunda that I didn't know what room we were staying in.

I turned around to go back down—and saw the wet footprints on the stairs. Just like in Charity Jane's story about the drowned girl come back to find her baby. *They're your footprints,* I told myself, but then why did I still hear the patter of bare feet? The sound seemed to be coming from everywhere, even from above me. I looked up. Water was beading on the murky glass dome, reflecting splattered handprints on the curved walls . . . as if someone was beating at the walls, trying to get *in*. The patter of wet feet was loudest, though, further along the gallery. I walked toward it, wondering if there was a leak somewhere. Instead I found the half-opened door to the room just before the nursery. *The nursemaid's room,* I thought as I pushed open the door. But it was too big to belong to a servant. This must have been Monty's mother's room. It was papered in the same apple blossom print as the downstairs parlors and breakfast room—*designed by Candace Wheeler,* Monty had told us that first day. It was hardly faded at all, probably because the shutters of this room had been closed for many years.

The shutters and windows were open now to air out the room. That was why I'd heard the pattering. Jess had spread his sleeping bag over the (no-doubt) musty bedding. A duffel bag with my clothes was on top of the sleeping bag. I stripped off my sodden clothes and dumped them into the big claw-foot tub in the adjoining bathroom and filled the tub to soak the mud out of them. I toweled off and pulled on dry jeans and a loose oxford cloth button-down shirt that had once belonged to Jess but which I'd co-opted when he renounced his preppy phase.

I stood at the window, rolling up the French cuffs, looking out over the deluged landscape. The rain looked like it was finally letting up. Across the river a sliver of sun appeared, wedged between ink blue clouds and indigo mountains. It burned fiercely for a moment, blazing a path across the river and over the flooded lawns, and the swollen pond, turning the wreckage into something beautiful.

"That's what art does," Monty had told us once in class. "It turns the catastrophes of our lives into something glorious."

I looked for the dark figure standing on the weir, but she wasn't there—or anywhere outside. She was back where she came from, inside my head where I intended to keep her. As Monty had said, I'd found my subject.

Chapter Ten

The caretaker's cottage was completely destroyed. Jess and I went down the morning after the storm to see what could be salvaged and found a pile of broken wood sticking out of the swamp where our home had been. It looked like a beaver lodge that had been ravaged by a bear. Wading through the debris, we found artifacts—wads of paper clinging to branches, broken bits of white china like seashells littering a beach after a monsoon, bloated books floating on the surface like dead fish.

"It's a good thing most of our stuff was in storage," Jess said, poking a swollen copy of *The Paris Review* with a sharp stick. "I only had time to save our laptops and a few boxes of papers." He looked at me guiltily. "I'm sorry I couldn't save the china."

"I always thought that plain white china was kind of . . . *unimaginative.*"

Jess grinned, delighted, as I knew he would be, to hear that I'd never really liked his editor's housewarming gift. Standing knee deep in water surrounded by the wreckage of our home, he looked like Huck Finn ready to ride his raft down the Mississippi. "Yeah, like a pattern would've cluttered up the narrative flow."

Jess went back to happily poking at the wreckage. Truthfully, I had liked the china, but I didn't care that it was gone. Each object I unearthed—the broken glass carafe of the Braun, plastic bottles of the Kiehl's shaving cream Jess used, reusable shopping bags from Trader Joe's—seemed like a relic of a lost civilization. When I'd woken this morning in Riven House, a fresh breeze rustling yellowed lace curtains, I'd felt like I was finally in the right place. I had Jess and I had a story to tell. Mary Foley's story.

The sound of a woman crying reproached my good humor. It was coming through the trees, from the direction of Sunny's barn. I waded through the muck toward the sound and came out by the old barn, which stood square and solid in the middle of a lake. *Of course,* I thought, *the Montagues built their barns to last, not like their caretaker's cottages.* But as I rounded the barn and looked through the wide double doors I saw that the contents of the barn had not weathered the storm so well. Bundles of tangled limbs and hair swayed from the rafters like gallows' corpses. Sunny was standing in the middle of the barn, her long madras skirt trailing in standing water, holding one of the broken figures to her breast and wailing.

"Oh, Sunny!" I said as I approached her. "I'm so sorry! I didn't think . . . I knew you were safe in Beacon . . ." When I laid my hand on her shoulder she flinched and raised her tearstained, ravaged face to me. Her eyes were rimmed with mascara and purple eye shadow, her silver hair as wild as a fright wig. She looked like a vengeful Japanese ghost out of one of Yuriko's stories. Her eyes glittered with such malice that I thought she was going to lash out at me and blame me for the destruction of her *children*. I *should* have done something, I rebuked myself, only the damage must have happened when I was in the library before I even knew about the storm.

"It's not your fault," she said, wiping at her eyes and leaving a purple streak across her cheek. "You had your own house to worry about. I saw what the storm did to it . . . I'm sorry . . ." Her voice warbled, making me feel guilty that I didn't care more about the ruined cottage.

"We didn't have anything of value there," I told her. "Not like your puppets. Will you be able to fix them in time for the Halloween parade?"

She shook her head. "I don't know—it's less than two weeks away and the papier-mâché is soaked. I left the barn doors closed, but they somehow got opened during the storm."

"Maybe the wind blew them open." I looked doubtfully at the heavy wooden doors with their thick iron latches. Sunny followed my gaze toward the doors and gasped. Jess had appeared, looking like one of the scarecrow puppets with his hair standing up in tufts and his long stick brandished like a spear.

"You might have forgotten to latch them," he said, inspecting the doors.

"I *always* latch the doors when I'm going away," she spit back. "I'd never leave my children alone at the mercy of the elements."

I saw Jess's lip twitch at *children* and glared at him over Sunny's head.

"No, of course you wouldn't," I soothed, stroking her arm. "Could someone have come over to work on the puppets when you were gone? One of your volunteers from the college maybe?"

"That girl Noelle maybe," Sunny said, darting her raccoon eyes back at me. As soon as her eyes were off him, Jess twirled his finger by his ear. "She means well but she's forgetful, like many artists."

"Well, what can we do to help?" I asked, shooting Jess another stern glance. "Should we untangle them?"

Sunny looked up at the puppet she was holding. There were

two puppets, actually, a skeleton and a blue-haired witch, their limbs intertwined as though they had held each other for comfort during the storm. She gingerly peeled a skeleton arm away from the witch's waist. A layer of silver and blue foil came with it, like sunburned skin peeling off. I winced as if it really were damaged skin.

"We can try," she said. "If we untangle them all now while they're still wet and let them dry I might be able to repair them." I could hear she was trying to keep from crying.

"Let's get to work, then," I said, giving Jess an imploring look when Sunny went to get a broom to sweep away the mud and water.

He crossed his eyes at me but said in his most charming voice, "I can't think of anything I'd rather do than spend the day disentangling zombies and witches. It will be just like my freshman dorm Halloween party."

WE SET TO work separating the puppets from one another. It *was* a little like a scene from one of the wilder Bailey parties (there had been one I chanced upon of drunk naked freshmen playing Twister), only here the limbs we pried apart might dissolve in our hands. It was excruciating to feel an arm coming loose from its wire socket or hear an ankle plop wetly to the barn floor. I had to keep reminding myself that they were not people, but Sunny had done such a good job painting their faces that, even damaged as they were, they felt like they had personalities. They certainly did to Sunny.

"Be careful of Griselda," Sunny told Jess as he wrestled a witch free of a zombie's embrace. "She's very delicate."

"I can see that," Jess said, holding up the puppet's hand as though he were admiring her manicure. "Do they all have names?"

"Yes," Sunny confided shyly. "It helps me when I work on them to give them a story. Griselda, for instance, escaped the Salem witch trials and lived by herself in a cranberry bog for two hundred years—see her cranberry wreath?—before coming back to civilization to share her herbcraft with select acolytes. I based her on one of my teachers at Bailey."

I was afraid that Jess would laugh but instead he said, "It's just like writing a book. Even the minor characters have to have their back stories."

"Yes," Sunny said gratefully. "There really aren't any minor characters, are there?"

"No," Jess concurred, "just minor writers."

I wasn't sure Sunny would get the joke but she surprised me by laying a damp, gluey hand on Jess's shoulder and replying, "No, my dear, we're all just vessels for the sacred muse. There's nothing *minor* about that."

I was afraid Jess would laugh or make another joke, but his face looked suddenly washed clean of levity. I knew that it was what he was most afraid of—that he was a *minor writer*, a one-hit wonder whose one hit hadn't even been quite a hit, a mid-list author.

"Wouldn't it be better to be a minor writer than not to be a writer at all?" I had asked him once.

"No," he had answered without hesitation. "I'd rather never have written a word than be second-rate."

Now he swallowed and replied hoarsely, "That's a good way of looking at it, Sunny. I think you may be right."

Sunny smiled back at him and turned around, leaving a gluey handprint on Jess's jacket. Jess ducked his head and went back to work, delicately lifting each finger of Griselda's hand from the boney arm of her zombie dance partner, his face as intent as when he wrote. I turned back to the wildman I was rescuing from the embrace of a lascivious scarecrow and said a little prayer of thanks. *This* was what Jess needed. To be out of the shark tank of New York and in an environment that valued process over product. It was worth losing the cottage to see Jess content.

By midmorning we were joined by Noelle, the Bailey intern, who also turned out to be the yellow-aproned girl from the farm stand. She wailed and berated herself for not coming during the storm.

"Don't be silly, dear," Sunny chided her. "I wouldn't have had you risk your life for some lifeless puppets."

I noticed she didn't accuse Noelle of leaving the doors open. Instead she asked her to get on the phone and call "the troops" to come help. By lunchtime we were joined by a dozen volunteers who came with hot coffee, food, and goodwill. Sunny marshaled them into order, explaining how to separate the puppets with the least damage and where to hang the recovered ones to dry. Even Monty came down for an hour to see what damage had been done and ask what he could do. He didn't help with the puppets himself, but I saw him handing Sunny a wad of cash, which she tearfully accepted by throwing her arms around Monty's neck and crying, "Bless you, Alden." He left, giving Dale, who'd wandered over around noon smelling like pot and looking like he'd slept through the storm, instructions to haul the drying racks over from the old tobacco barn.

When Dale came back with the drying racks Sunny ordered us to lay the broken limbs out on them and had Noelle start a system of identifying, labeling, and color coding the puppets and their lost parts.

"Looks like Nam," Dale croaked.

The barn *did* look like a gruesome triage center, but the

mood was cheerful and determined. I recognized a few people from town—CJ from the library (who smiled at me as if she hadn't tried to scare me half to death with that awful story), Katrine, and Devon Corbett. I said an awkward hello to Devon, holding up my mucky hands to show I couldn't hug him, but he hugged me anyway, crushing me against his broad chest. He was the youngest of the Corbetts but well over six feet tall. Being hugged by someone that tall reminded me of Dunstan, and when Devon held me out at arm's length to look at me, I felt the prick of tears in my eyes.

"Goddamn you look good, Clare! Mom's asked about you. You oughtta come by and see her."

She had? "She must hate me," I blurted out.

Devon looked appalled. "No one hates you, Clare! You were young. We all knew when you went to Bailey you'd probably give Dun the boot eventually. You were always too good for this town. We knew you'd go off to the city someday and Dun . . . well, you know Dun. He's a small-town boy. He'd never be happy anyplace but Concord."

I stared at Devon—little Devon whom I'd babysat and read *Goosebumps* to—amazed that the great drama of my life, leaving Dunstan Corbett for Jess Martin in my senior year of college, could be reduced to a question of geography. But he was right. Dunstan would have been miserable in New York City and moving to the city was all that I'd wanted back then.

"How is he?" I asked.

Devon twisted his mouth in a crooked smile and shrugged. "Practically running the town. Busy. You know he got divorced?"

"No," I said, furrowing my brow. I *had* tried to look Dunstan up on Facebook, but in his Luddite fashion, he didn't have a page. "That's too bad. What about you, Devon? You look great. Still playing football?"

He guffawed—something I hadn't seen anyone do in years. "*Fantasy* football. I blew out my knee sophomore year at Ohio State. I've got a tree removal business and I help out with the orchard—we all do." He gave me a sly look. "Noelle says you've been coming in for our Northern Spys. Your great-granddad planted those, you know . . ." His voice trailed off, probably embarrassed when he remembered that I was adopted—or that the Corbetts had bought the orchard from the Jacksons. "Anyway, I'd better get back to work before these things calcify." He nodded at the puppets. "It'd be a shame not to have the parade. My kids always look forward to it."

Kids? When had little Devon Corbett gotten old enough to have kids? Before I could ask, he whipped out a cell phone and showed me a picture of two blond boys, their broad, dimpled faces just how I remembered Devon and his brother Derrick. Strong stock, my father used to say of them. As if they were apple trees.

Then he gave me another crushing hug and shambled off to help Noelle bring in more drying racks. I wiped my face with the back of my hand, smearing glue across my cheek, and looked around the barn to see if Jess had witnessed my reunion with Devon. But Jess was gone. I asked Sunny if she'd seen him and she said he'd slipped away an hour ago.

"He had that look, like he had an inspiration and had to get it down on paper before it was gone. I told him to go, that I knew how he felt . . ." She smiled, her mascara and glue streaked face beaming. Her hair was speckled with bits of glitter (one of the main ingredients of the puppets, I'd learned) and shreds of paper. "When the muse calls, you must answer. Look at how she's graced me today!"

I looked around the barn at the wreckage, wondering what she could mean. The salvaged puppets hung in a row on one end of the barn, their faces as bloated as if they really had been garroted by the hangman's noose, their limbs and costumes a motley patchwork. The witches wore bits of scarecrow, the skeletons had acquired the ectoplasmic glow of ghosts, fairy princesses were whiskered with werewolves' fur. Only the zombies looked appropriately piecemeal. Even the volunteers were wearing bits and pieces of the puppets, their faces stained with glue and papier-mâché, their arms and clothes covered with paint and glitter and bits of paper. My own arms were so spackled with paper I could have written on them. It was as if we'd all become part of the parade—a great big installation art project. That's what Sunny was beaming about. This was what she loved—the process of making art even more than the final product. I hoped that Jess had brought some of this fairy dust back to his writing desk.

"I'm glad we could be a part of it," I said. "But I'd better be getting back to the house—"

"I didn't even think to ask," she cried, clamping a bony hand on my shoulder. "Where will you stay now that the cottage is gone? There's room here at the barn—"

"That's sweet of you, Sunny," I said, smiling to think how Jess would react to that. "But it's okay, we're staying up at the house."

"But just until you find someplace else, surely." She looked puzzled. "You could build something—a yurt, maybe!"

I laughed. "I don't think Jess would agree to living in a yurt. No, we're going to stay in Riven House. There's plenty of room. Monty says we can have the whole second floor . . ."

I stopped because her face had turned as white as paste. "You can't live there!" she croaked in a hoarse foreign voice. My skin prickled at the sound. It was like someone else's voice was coming out of Sunny's mouth. Like she'd become one of her own puppets and a ventriloquist was speaking through her.

"Yes, we can," I said slowly, as if explaining to a child. "Monty says we can."

"But he's never let anyone before." Her voice was her own again, high and agitated. I understood now. She was jealous. Monty hadn't asked *her* to stay in Riven House. She had stayed there once—back when she and Monty were lovers—but he'd banished her to the barn. He'd no doubt told her something about writers needing their own space.

"It's different, you see," I said patiently. Hadn't I been the victim of jealousy of the time Jess spent working, of the tattooed barista, of the newest fan? "With Jess and me being writers. We work the same, in quiet. It's not like . . . *this*." I gestured at the noisy, paper-spackled crowd in the barn. "It's great that you can do this big collaborative thing—I'm sure that's why Monty gave you all this space—but writers need quiet."

Sunny stared at me for a moment and then spoke slowly, as though *I* were one of her children—an insensate confabulation of paper and glue. "The reason you can't live in Riven House is because it's haunted. Why do you think I moved out? It was sucking the life force out of me. It's an unhappy place. There's a spirit there that begrudges the living their happiness. It will tear you and Jess apart. It will tear *you* apart."

Chapter Eleven

In the days and weeks to come I thought about what Sunny had said and the story CJ had told. That figure I'd seen on the weir and the sound of the baby crying in the night were no doubt products of my overactive imagination (*If you don't use it, it will use you*) but I did wonder whether some places were inherently *unhappy*. Riven House had surely been an unhappy place since Mary Foley had left her baby to die on its steps and Minnie Noyes had shot her husband. But maybe Jess and I could bring happiness back into it and in so doing, heal our marriage.

I thought so in those last golden days of autumn. As the leaves fell outside we made Riven House habitable again, like squirrels building our nests for winter. Jess still took his walk in the morning and when he came back he found some desk or perch to write at through the afternoon. I wanted him to have a permanent study, though, so when I'd finished cleaning our new bedroom, I explored the other rooms on the second floor. Not the nursery; I had my own plans for that and Jess hated the color yellow. And not the other master bedroom with its massive furniture standing around like sentinels. Instead I picked the room on the south side of the house that was lined with bookshelves and empty save for an elegant writing desk.

"Minnie's morning room," Monty told me when I asked. I thought he'd meant *mourning* room, imagining her in her widow's weeds, haunting the house and grounds. He explained that it was the room that his mother "repaired to" after breakfast to answer letters and plan "menus and floral arrangements."

"Poor Minnie," Monty said, as though she were a distant acquaintance and not his mother. "I don't think she had very much to occupy her when she moved up here from the city. God knows what she did in that room except drink laudanum and cut clippings from the magazines for her scrapbooks. For heaven's sake, put the place to some good use. Maybe Jess writing in it will shake out the cobwebs."

There was no lack of cobwebs in Minnie's Mourning Room, as I still thought of it, but I sucked them all up with the fancy new vacuum cleaner Monty bought for me at the Target in Kingston. It was harder to know what to do with the scrapbooks. The very idea of scrapbooking—a pastime made popular by Martha Stewart and indulged in by crafters like my mother and her sisters—repelled me. And there were dozens of them—portfolio-sized tomes with tooled leather covers decorated with forget-me-nots and sentimental quotes. I wondered at first how Minnie had justified their cost when her husband had lost all the family money, then I noticed shadowy marks on the backs of the pages, little triangles pressed into the paper like some ancient cuneiform, and realized that they were the marks from adhesive corners that had once held photographs. Minnie had ransacked the family's photo albums to make her scrapbooks. She had even used the photos themselves, severing heads from bodies and pasting them into fanciful collages. The hostility of the act piqued my interest. I knew Jess would be appalled by them, though, so I stashed them all in the closet, which I'd discovered had an adjoining door to the nursery so I could get to them when I was done converting the nursery into my study.

I'd found a small vanity table that fit into the window seat eave to use as my desk and a faience glass lamp painted with apple blossoms. I'd rescued one of the straight-backed chairs from the "chair room" and brought up one of the rocking horses so the room wouldn't feel so empty. As I cleaned out the closets and attic, I rescued small relics and brought them to the nursery, like offerings to an altar—a silver picture frame, which I polished and emptied of its whiskered Montague ancestor and replaced with a picture of Mary Foley; a wreath of paper apple blossoms, which I perched on top of a phrenology skull I'd found in the attic; a chipped china baby's cup painted with violets, which I filled with pens and pencils. Lugging a carton of paper into the closet I looked at the papered-over dumbwaiter, considering whether I could use it to transport heavy items, but something about that malignant lump in the wall made me reject the idea.

One night while we were sitting around the fireplace I asked Monty why it had been papered over.

He looked embarrassed for a moment and then said, "After Minnie had me she developed some strange ideas. The laudanum she took for her back only made her worse. We'd call it postpartum depression now, but they didn't know about that then. The cousin who took me in after she died told me that she had delusions that I wasn't really her baby, that I'd been stolen at birth and switched with an imposter." He tried to laugh, but it sounded forced. "She said that on the night I was born they took me from her and then later she heard crying coming from the dumbwaiter. Perhaps the housekeeper had taken me into the kitchen to wash me, but Minnie believed that the fairies had come into the house through the dumbwaiter to steal her baby. And so later . . . she thought to get her *real* baby back she had to put me in the dumbwaiter. My father had to take me away from her. He gave her a doll to hold instead but she shoved *that* into the dumbwaiter too."

"Oh!" I said, appalled. I wondered if I should tell him about the bell I'd heard coming from the dumbwaiter, but decided against it. "That's awful, Monty. I'm sorry I brought it up."

He smiled at me. "Not at all, my dear. Far better to clear the cobwebs—as you've been doing. I've been thinking about this house. You know that its octagonal design was inspired by Orson Squire Fowler."

"Wasn't he that phrenologist guy?" Jess asked, taking a sip of his scotch. He looked relieved that the subject had moved away from Minnie's postpartum delusions.

"Yes, he also wrote a book exhorting the adoption of the octagonal house. He believed that just as men's skulls correspond to their characters, so men's habitations correspond to their intellect. Which I suppose makes me an old ruin," he chuckled.

"This house isn't a ruin," I objected. "And neither are you. You both just need a little . . . *maintenance*."

Monty threw back his head and laughed heartily. "Thank you, Clare. I believe you're right—and that you are doing both the house and me a world of good."

I smiled back at him, his regard warming me even more than the fire or the scotch. But then Jess asked, "If a man's home is a reflection of his personality, what does that say about a homeless man?" and I felt cold, remembering Jess's dream of wandering through a house full of mirrors that didn't show his reflection.

"This is your home," Monty said, his voice hoarse with emotion. "I hope you both know that."

Jess was sitting far back in a wing-backed chair, his face in shadow, so I couldn't read his expression. But I felt his reluctance to take generosity at face value. His parents had been critical and unsupportive—suspicious of relying on something as ephemeral as writing for a living—which had only made it harder when we fell into financial trouble to keep in touch with them; Jess hated the thought that they had been right. Our loveless childhoods were something that Jess and I had in common. I knew what it was like not to trust love when it came along. I was afraid now that Jess would say something cruel to Monty's magnanimity, but after a moment he leaned forward into the firelight and held up his half-empty glass.

"Let's drink to second acts then, F. Scott be damned, for Riven House and its ragtag crew of writers."

We clinked glasses, the chime of the heavy Waterford crystal reverberating in the quiet room and, I imagined, spreading out into the house, banishing cobwebs and shadows.

For Mary, too, I thought to myself. I would give her a second act by telling her story. When I met Monty's eye he nodded and I felt sure he knew what I was thinking.

The next day, as I was gathering the empty tumblers from the library, Monty grabbed me by the hand and pulled out a chair beside his desk. "Let me show you what I've found about her," he said without preamble.

He didn't have to say her name. I knew he meant Mary Foley. He opened an old accounting ledger to a page on which the *Concord Gazette* article about her death had been neatly glued. There was also the article about her crowning as Apple Blossom Queen below it and, in elegant old-fashioned script, a notation.

Fifty acres, one hundred apple trees bearing, deeded to John Foley on May 12, 1929, by Birdsill Montague in exchange for the maidenhood of one Mary Foley.

The line made me feel cold despite the sun on my back and the fire in the grate.

"Who wrote this?"

"My father," Monty answered. "It's the only mention he makes of Mary Foley in all his correspondence and notebooks. Unless you count . . . well, turn the page."

I did, the old paper crackling like autumn leaves. The next page was an ordinary ledger with household expenditures and revenue from the orchards and hay fields arrayed in neat columns. Even at a cursory glance, it wasn't hard to see that the revenue was hardly enough to offset the lavish expenditures of the household. But more poignant than the faltering finances was the dried flower that had been pressed between the pages, an apple blossom, its petals faded to palest pink.

"He loved her," I said, looking up at Monty, whose eyes were glittering in the sunlight.

"I don't know about that," he replied, "but he certainly was haunted by her."

"Haunted?" I repeated in a whisper. Jess was upstairs writing in his new study, but he sometimes wandered around when he was writing—walking helped him think, he said— and I didn't want him to hear Monty and me talking about ghosts.

Monty smiled. I thought he was going to make fun of me the way he used to mock a student's naïve unreasoned remark, but instead he said, "You sense her here, don't you?"

A shiver passed through me, but I wasn't sure what I was afraid of more—that Monty had also sensed Mary Foley's ghost, or that Jess would hear us. "Jess thinks that it's crazy— ghosts, apparitions . . ."

"Jess has an admirably rational mind," Monty said. "It's why he writes so lucidly. But he doesn't see very far into the dark.

Not like you, Clare. It was your vision that gave his first book its heart—"

"No," I said automatically.

Monty held up his hands, palms out, as if I were about to tackle him. I hadn't meant to sound so angry. "Very well, we'll leave that. But you will admit that you see things that Jess does not."

"Jess misses things when he's writing," I began. "He can't be bothered with everyday details—"

"That's not what I meant," Monty said. "I mean things not of this world."

"Oh, well, there are things I've imagined . . ." I told him about the figure standing on the weir the first day and her re-appearance the night before the storm when the sound of a baby crying had woken me, and then how I'd seen her standing on the weir after the flood. "But those were just things I con-jured up out of mist and imagination."

"Uh-huh," he said. "And what time did you say the crying woke you up?"

"3:36," I said, wishing I'd never admitted to any of it.

He got up and snatched a book from a shelf and handed it to me, open to a page. I turned it over to read the title. *Ghosts Along the Hudson.* There was a picture of a ruined mansion on the cover, wreathed in fog, a double exposure "apparition" float-ing above an overgrown rose garden. I was surprised Monty owned such a book. I turned back to the page he'd opened it to and read a passage that had been underlined in blue ink. It was an account of "The Riven House Ghost" purported to have been related by a caretaker in the 1960s whose wife had been woken every night by the sound of a baby crying, always at the same time.

3:36

"Maybe I read this," I said, looking back at the cover. "I wrote a story about the apple blossom girl so I'd probably read something about her. This looks like a book the library would have had."

"And you think you remembered it so well you made yourself wake up every night at the same time?"

"It's possible . . ." I began, but the skeptical look in Monty's eyes stopped me.

"Is that really what you think, Clare?" he asked me gently, but firmly.

"I . . . don't know what I think," I said.

"Don't know or don't want to know?"

I remembered him doing this in class, challenging a student's assumptions until he proved his point.

"It's just that . . . if I thought what I saw was real . . . well, that would mean I was crazy, wouldn't it?"

"Isn't it crazier to deny the evidence of what you see with your own eyes?"

Instead of answering I asked him a question. "Have you seen . . . *her*?"

"No," he said. "But I've felt her. Felt her wanting someone to tell her story. I've been trying to do it myself . . ." He looked at the scattered papers on his desk and smiled ruefully. "But I'm afraid I'm not the right person for the job. I think you are and that's why you're here."

"I'm here because of Jess," I said, feeling a prickling of unease. "I thought you needed a caretaker. I thought you wanted Jess."

"It doesn't matter what I wanted," he said, dismissing my concerns as irrelevant. As if it wouldn't *kill* Jess to think it was me Monty wanted here instead of him. "It's Mary Foley who brought you here."

I thought of all the events that had led to Jess and me coming to Riven House two months ago—our failing finances, the crisis in our marriage, Jess's struggles with his second novel, the fights and tearful scenes we'd had last winter, the rising prices of real estate in the Hudson Valley, Jess's disdain of split-levels and aluminum siding. Could a disembodied ghost of a nineteen-year-old girl who had died over eighty years ago possibly engineer all that? But despite the outlandishness of the proposition, I felt that everything in my whole life—Great-Granny Jackson's nighttime visitations, my lonely childhood, that feeling of being an outsider, the sunlit days in the apple orchards, meeting Jess, leaving Dunstan for him as Mary had left her farmer fiancé to ride off with Bayard Montague . . . all of it had led to being here at Riven House.

"If Jess thinks I'm seeing things he'll worry," I said. "I had a breakdown . . . senior year . . ."

"Clare," Monty said, leaning forward and taking my hands. "I'm sorry. I didn't know."

"It was at the end of the year. You . . ." I faltered, not liking to bring up the scandal that had ended Monty's teaching career at Bailey when a student told the administration that Monty had made sexual advances toward her.

"I was having my own difficulties," he finished for me. "An unlucky year for us both, then. Was it . . . I don't mean to pry . . . Did it have to do with Jess?"

"It wasn't his fault," I said quickly. And then in a rush, "I'd gotten pregnant. Jess was upset of course. Neither of us was in any shape to be parents. It would have ruined Jess's chances to write . . ."

"Oh, my dear," Monty said, squeezing my hands. "I used to think the same thing myself, but now I see how foolish the notion is—as if a creation of paper could ever take the place of a flesh and blood child. Did you . . ."

"No," I said. "I lost the baby." *Even your body knew it wasn't the right time.* "It was probably for the best, only . . ."

"Of course it must have been a terrible experience for you! I hope Jess was supportive."

"Jess was wonderful! He took me to the hospital, he stayed with me, even when I started . . . raving. They said it was a kind of postpartum depression brought on by hormones and the pain pills they gave me. I don't do well with drugs—or being in a hospital; I've always been scared of them—but I got this terrible idea in my head that I had *made* it happen."

Monty nodded. "I'm sure it's quite normal to feel guilty in those circumstances. Especially if you had felt ambivalent about the pregnancy—"

"But you see," I interrupted him, "I'd made things happen before. Little things . . ." *Threads unraveling in the tablecloth, Charity Jane's pencil snapping during her exam.* "Usually when I was angry." *Plates flying from the china cabinet . . .*

"Doors slamming? Things breaking?"

"Yes," I said, looking up at Monty. His eyes were glittering feverishly and his color looked bad. I was afraid I was upsetting him, but it was such a relief to be taken seriously that I went on. "You must think I'm crazy."

"No," he said, "I think you're a *sensitive*, for lack of a better word. I know because I am too—or *was*. In my youth I saw things and *made things happen*, as you put it, but that gift—or curse—has faded with age. But you, I saw it in you right away that first day of class when you plucked the story of the apple blossom girl right out of my head."

"Plucked it out of *your* head?"

"I'd been thinking about the story when I came in and then you wrote about it. Oh, I'm not saying you *stole* it, Clare. Don't look at me as though I'd accused you of plagiarism. The words, the framing, were all your own. I suspect that the truly great writers all have a touch of the psychic about them. And you have more than a touch. That's why you will be able to tell her story."

"But don't you want to do it yourself? You said you've been working on it."

He shook his head. "I'm an old man, Clare. It's time I stepped aside and let youth step in. It will be enough for me to see my legacy continue in you. I would be honored to a part of the process, though, to hear your ideas, be a sounding board."

"I'd like that," I said, squeezing Monty's hands. "Only I'm afraid that Jess might not understand. That he might worry if he thought I was working on something that might trigger another episode." *And that he'd be jealous that Monty had chosen me and not him,* I thought but didn't say.

"He's so engrossed in his own work he'll never notice," Monty said. "It will be our little secret."

I hesitated. Jess would be angry if he knew I was entering into a secret pact with Monty, not to mention how hurt he would be if he knew Monty had chosen me as his legacy and not him. Which was exactly what I had to protect him from. Jess couldn't know that Monty regarded me as the better writer. And if I tried to explain that Mary Foley wanted me to tell her story he would think I was having another breakdown and I couldn't put him through that again. When I'd told him after the miscarriage that I had made it happen, just as I'd summoned Great-Granny Jackson's ghost and made all the plates break in the china cabinet, he had looked so frightened for me that he'd never left my side again. I sometimes wondered if he had married me because he felt responsible for my breakdown—as if I were a bit of bric-a-brac that he'd had to buy because he'd broken it.

It was better he didn't know.

"Yes," I told Monty. "It will be our secret."

Monty clinked the empty glass he held against the one in my hand. In the silence of the house I thought I heard an answering echo—a bell chiming, the shiver of glass in the windowpanes—as if the house had joined in our pact.

Chapter Twelve

It wasn't hard to keep our secret from Jess. He'd entered into the "deep stage" of writing that made him nearly oblivious to everything going on around him. He wouldn't say what he was working on. He believed, as Hemingway had, that talking about a book could kill it, but I could tell by his behavior that he was on to something. He stopped sleeping regularly, getting up in the middle of the night and sneaking out of our room to work in Minnie's Mourning Room—or work somewhere, I presumed. I heard him wandering around the gallery, down the stairs, and then in circles around the first floor, murmuring lines under his breath, his footsteps fading into the distance as if he were the ghost haunting Riven House, doomed to vanish at first light. He *was* often gone when I woke up, out walking, I presumed. He said that the sound of Monty's typewriter drove him crazy. I chided him that coming all the way from Monty's basement it wasn't really so loud.

"It's the idea of it," Jess shot back. "It's as if he uses a manual typewriter to make sure we can all hear that he's being productive."

In the past when Jess had gotten so engrossed in his writing I'd felt envious and abandoned, but now I was glad that he was so distracted. It meant I could work on my own research without him noticing how much time I'd started spending with Monty.

I usually started out in the morning reading aloud to him what I'd written the day before. He'd listen, make a comment or two, and ask a few questions. He was interested in what came from research and what came from my "own head." Not, I learned, because he held the latter in less regard.

"The trouble I've had writing about Mary over the years is that we know so little about her and I haven't been able to fill in those gaps with my imagination. But you seem to have a direct pipeline to her."

"I think it's because we have a lot in common," I said, feeling a little uncomfortable with Monty's assertion that I could do something he couldn't. "We both grew up on apple orchards, we both got the Bailey scholarship, only she couldn't go. I think of her life as what would have happened if I'd gotten pregnant in high school instead of college—and if Jess had left me the way Bayard left Mary."

"Yes, the similarities are interesting," Monty said, looking at me speculatively. "You even look a little like her."

"I don't know about that," I said, blushing. I'd thought the same thing myself, but hadn't wanted to admit it. It wasn't just that Mary Foley was beautiful, it was that as an adopted child I'd learned to guard myself against finding resemblances in strangers. It was too easy to convince myself that I was really some famous movie star's daughter whom she'd had to give up in order to pursue her career or the long-lost daughter of my eighth grade English teacher who'd taken the job at Concord High School just so she could be close to me and encourage me in my writing.

"In fact," Monty went on, "you might be related to her. Do you know anything about your birth mother?"

"No," I said. "My parents never told me anything about her. The only thing I ever overheard about her was . . ." I hesitated.

"Yes?" he asked.

I took a deep breath. "That she was in the Hudson Mental Hospital when she had me."

"Oh," Monty said, looking embarrassed. Finally I'd come up with a detail that shocked him.

"Besides, I don't want the story to be about me. It's about Mary. I'm going to the library today to read through the 1920s papers and to look at the school records to see if she's ever mentioned."

"Well, it pays to be thorough," Monty said, sliding my pages into a folder on his desk. He kept the pages I gave him each day to reread and gave them back to me the next day with notes. "But don't let the research slow you down. Research can be a trap, as I well know . . ." He looked ruefully at the piles of paper on his desk, then grinned at me. "Do you want to see my antidote to writer's block?"

I hesitated—the question sounded almost unsavory—but Monty was already opening his desk drawer and lifting something out of it, something heavy and metal.

"It was my grandfather's service revolver, a souvenir of the Mexican-American War."

I stared at the heavy revolver. I'd grown up with guns on the farm. My father wouldn't hesitate to shoot a fox or coyote menacing our chickens and he'd made me learn how to shoot. But I'd never liked them. I could smell the metal and oil from where I sat.

"Is it loaded?" I asked, noting the tremor in Monty's hand.

"Of course. It wouldn't do much good if it weren't. When I'm dithering over a passage I tell myself I can either get down to it or put an end to it. I find a loaded gun focuses the mind."

He looked up, saw the horrified expression on my face, and put the gun back in the drawer.

"Don't be so literal, Clare. It's a metaphor. Like Chekhov's gun."

"Oh," I said, trying to smile, "I see." But as I left the library I remembered what Chekhov had said about the gun: *If in the first act you have hung a pistol on the wall, then in the following one it should be fired.*

As I DROVE to the library that day I told myself that Monty had just been trying to get a rise out of me, the way he'd say provocative things in class to stimulate a lively discussion. Saying I looked like Mary Foley and suggesting I might be related to her was another way of "getting me going." If so, it had worked. At least on the subject of Mary Foley. (As for the gun, I'd already decided to sneak into the drawer when Monty wasn't around and unload it.) Was it really such a far-fetched idea that I was related to Mary? Concord was a small town made up of close-knit families. I'd noticed several Foleys in my school. Mary might have had a sister or brother who had a child who had landed in the nearby mental hospital—it wouldn't be such a big surprise given the family history—and given up their baby for adoption. I could check the census records to see what other siblings Mary had. I remembered from a report I'd done in high school that the Village Hall kept the local census records—and the Village Hall was right across the street from the library.

As I pulled into the Village Hall parking lot I realized there was another option. I could go to St. Anne's and ask to see my records. Trudy had told me that the records were sealed, but I'd often wondered if she hadn't lied about that. Besides, I knew there were ways to petition to have your records opened. I'd never tried. The truth was that since overhearing I'd been born

in a mental hospital I'd been afraid to learn how crazy my birth
mother had been.

But if I could find out first who she had been, if she had
been a descendant of Mary Foley's sibling, I didn't think I
would be as afraid.

The Village Hall was a two-story brick building with a relief
of golden apples over the door. Inside there was a mural depict-
ing the history of apple growing in New York State, from 1647
when Governor Peter Stuyvesant planted an apple tree from
Holland on the corner of Third Avenue and 13th Street (a spot
I'd pointed out to Jess once) to the introduction of apples to the
Hudson Valley and the famous varieties bred in the state. In
third grade we'd all had to do a report on the history of apple
growing and make dioramas based on the Village Hall mural.
I could still remember gluing cotton balls onto stick trees to
represent apple blossoms and tiny red gumballs for apples. I
remembered every detail of the mural—the coppery skin of the
half-naked Seneca Indians and the tiny frogs and birds hidden
in the reeds of the riverscape. So why had I forgotten the story
of the apple blossom girl? Could it be that the idea had entered
my head only when Monty came into the class that day—that
I had picked it up psychically from him? Maybe I had forgotten it so quickly because it wasn't my idea at all and now it
had come back to me only because I was in daily contact with
Monty.

I had heard a few writers over the years talk, as Sunny had,
about being the vessel for the muse or God or some other
spiritual force. They talked as if it was some kind of gift to be
the mouthpiece of an external force, but it had always sounded
to me like a curse. I didn't like the idea of being Monty's mouthpiece. But if I had some family connection to Mary, wouldn't
that mean the story was as much mine as his?

I turned away from the mural to the clerk's window where a middle-aged woman with tight gray curls and pale blue eyes sat crocheting a colorful afghan. When I asked if I could see the census records for 1930 she sighed, put down her wool regretfully, and eased herself out of her chair. I followed her to a small windowless room in the back of the building where the town's census records were kept in large bound volumes on tall metal shelves. She pointed vaguely toward the rear of the room and wheezed her way back to the front desk. Figuring that the older books would be in the rear of the room, I decided to start there. The dates on the bindings were so faded on these, though, that I had to take down each book to read the date, climbing onto a rickety stepladder to reach the ones on the top shelves, discovering as I did that they were out of order. It took me half an hour to find the 1930 census. By the time I found the Foleys of Concord I was wheezing just as heavily as the clerk had been. I found two Johns, one on Main Street whose profession was listed as "pharmacist" and one whose profession was listed as farmer and who lived on Apple Ring Road. The address startled me. There were only two farms on Apple Ring Road—the Jackson farm where I'd grown up and the Corbett farm. In 1930, though, the Corbett farm had belonged to a John Foley who lived there with his wife, Margaret, and one daughter, Elizabeth, age seventeen.

Of course Mary would have been dead by 1930. To be sure it was her family I went back to the 1920 census and—after much scrambling up and down the shelves—found her. Mary Foley, age nine, Elizabeth Foley, age seven.

So Mary did have a younger sister. Elizabeth could have had children and one of them could have had a daughter who ended up pregnant in the Hudson Mental Hospital. But how to find out who Elizabeth had married? By the 1940 census she would have been twenty-seven, probably married and listed under her husband's household. I looked back at the 1930 census and noticed that Elizabeth was the last entry on the page—but not necessarily the last in the Foley household. I turned the page and found three more listed: Sonia Larsson, cook, Betty Murfree, housemaid, and Kevin Corbett, apple picker.

That explained it.

Dunstan had once told me that his grandfather had started out a picker and married the orchard owner's daughter. Of course it made sense. The Corbett orchard was the one next to ours until the Corbetts bought my grandfather out in the Depression. So that meant Dunstan Corbett might actually be related to Mary Foley. Maybe that was the connection I had to Mary. I'd always found the Corbett family warm and open compared to mine. What if Mrs. Corbett had been so welcoming precisely because she knew of some connection?

I went back to the 1940 census and looked up Kevin Corbett. I found him listed on Apple Ring Road, only now he was listed as the head of household and John and Margaret Foley as father- and mother-in-law. At least he'd let them live there. Elizabeth Foley Corbett was listed as his wife and there were three sons: Daniel, Patrick, and John—Dunstan's father.

Those Corbetts are a fruitful family, my father used to say.

When I'd told Dunstan that he'd responded, *It sounds like he's calling us a bunch of fruits.*

I smiled at the memory of Dunstan's voice as I got up to put the books back on their shelf. Would it be so bad to find out I was related to him now? I wondered as I balanced precariously on the stepladder, clutching the two heavy census books. After all, it had been years since we dated, years since that first time he had put his arms on my waist to steady me on a ladder . . .

The memory was so vivid that the dusty shelves vanished and I was reaching instead through gnarled branches for a just-out-of-reach apple, the ladder shimmying under my feet and a voice calling out for me.

"Clary!"

The voice was so real I lost my balance and began to fall, but there were those hands again, so broad they encircled my waist, carrying me safely to the ground. I looked up into eyes that were still as blue as the sky glimpsed between apple boughs.

"You never did have much sense of balance," Dunstan Corbett said. "You almost broke your neck."

I swallowed, my throat tight from all the dust. "Maybe the Village Hall should invest in a sturdier ladder," I pointed out, stunned that Dunstan's first words to me in thirteen years were to call me unbalanced.

"I'll put it on the agenda next town meeting," he replied, his lips quirking. "Along with a suggestion that city folk be kept out of the records room."

"City folk?" I balked. "I'm just as much from here as you are, Dunstan Corbett."

"Is that what you're aiming to prove looking through the town records?"

"Actually," I said, "I was looking for someone else . . ."

"Mary Foley?"

"How . . . ?"

"It's a small town, Clary—or did you forget that too, living down in New York City?"

I wanted to tell him that I hadn't forgotten anything—not the way that one lock of blond hair fell over his eyes, or the way his hands had felt on my waist, or the crease in his left cheek when he was trying not to smile. But of course I couldn't say any of that because I was married to Jess Martin.

"Yeah," I said, "I guess I did. I've forgotten a lot of things."

He smiled then. "Let's get you a cup of coffee—you look like you could use one—and I'll tell you a few things about Mary Foley."

WE WALKED TO Cassie's through dead leaves swirling in the chilling air. I shivered in my too-light sweater and Dunstan handed me his denim jacket as automatically as when we were seventeen and he'd hand me his jacket on our walks home from school. It might even have been the same one with the frayed collar that used to brush against my face when he leaned in to kiss me . . .

"You're not wearing a uniform," I said.

"Day off," he said, holding the door of Cassie's for me.

"So why were you in the Village Hall?" I glanced around the coffee shop but didn't recognize anyone. Still, I felt half a dozen eyes snag on us as Dunstan led me to a back table by the window and pulled out a chair for me. Dunstan always drew attention when he entered a room. I'd always thought it was because he was so tall, but watching him now I realized it had more to do with the quietly self-possessed way he carried himself and those blue eyes that seemed to take in everything around him.

"Stop looking so nervous, Clare. You make it sound like I was stalking you."

"I didn't . . ." The crease on the left corner of his mouth deepened and I saw he was teasing me. "I'm sure you have plenty of reasons to go to the Village Hall on your day off."

"I do. But today my reason was you. Maureen phoned me to say you were in the records room so I came down to see you. Pumpkin spice latte and a cider donut?"

I nodded mutely to my usual order and watched Dunstan

walk up to the counter, glad for a moment to collect my thoughts. Not only wasn't meeting him an accident, he knew what I'd been ordering at Cassie's for the last two months. I looked around the café again, catching eyes just as they turned away. Dunstan was right; I'd forgotten what a small town Concord was. If you kissed a boy at the Lyceum Theater on Saturday night half the crowd at the Sunday farmer's market knew about it. How long before the town was talking about two old high school sweethearts having coffee together at Cassie's?

"Are you worried about your husband being jealous that we're talking?" he asked when he brought back my latte and his plain black coffee.

"No!" I said, taking a scalding sip. "Jess wouldn't . . ." I was about to say Jess wouldn't care but amended it to, "Jess won't mind. He's not the jealous type. At least not romantically. Now, if you were an editor offering me a six-figure advance for my new novel . . ."

Dunstan laughed and his shoulders relaxed. Mine did too, although I felt a little disloyal that I'd used Jess's literary envy to set Dunstan at ease.

"No fear of that. I always said you'd have to be the writer in the . . ." He grimaced. He'd been about to say *in the family*, the closest Dunstan and I had ever gotten to talking about getting married. He'd be the steady income provider with insurance— he'd always known he wanted to be a cop—and I'd make our fortune writing novels.

"You always believed in me," I said. "I hope you know how much that meant to me."

He raised his eyes from his coffee and looked at me, giving me the full force of those blue eyes. I was afraid he'd say that it clearly hadn't meant enough, but instead he said, "I still believe in you, Clare. I'm still expecting you to write the great American novel."

I could hear Jess's dismissive laugh in my head at the phrase, but ignored it. "I'd settle for something a whole lot slighter than that, but I do have an idea for a story."

"Mary Foley?"

"How do you know that? And don't say it's a small town again."

"CJ told me you've been researching her in the library and I remember you being interested in the story the summer before . . . before your senior year."

The words *before you broke up with me* hovered in the air, but I was too intrigued by what he had said to worry about that. "You do? I talked about her?"

"You don't remember? You told me you had a dream about her—a nightmare, really. Like one of those dreams you used to have about your great-grandmother." He shuddered. "Maybe that's why you forgot about her. Those dreams you had gave me the heebie-jeebies."

I smiled to think of Dunstan Corbett afraid of anything. He was the guy you'd call if a spider or wasp got stuck in the apple bins, the one who'd step into the middle of a fight if a smaller kid was getting bullied, the boy who dove under the Saw Kill waterfall when his brother slipped and fell into the water.

"Yeah," I said, "I think I tried to put those dreams out of my head. I don't remember dreaming about the apple blossom girl, though. But you must be right. I found a story I started senior year and thought I'd try writing something about her now."

"Farmer's daughter runs off with a rich guy from the city. I can see the appeal."

"Jess isn't rich," I said too quickly.

"No, I guess not if you had to come back here."

"You make it sound like I hated the place."

"God, Clare, you *have* forgotten a lot. You told me once you'd rather die than wind up growing old in Concord."

"I said I thought I *would* die if I stayed here. It wasn't Concord or you, it was living in my home after my father died. My mother . . ." I stopped, realizing my voice had risen and that the tables around us had gone quiet. There were prob-ably people in here who had known my mother. Only when Dunstan reached across the table and squeezed my hand did I realize how close I was to tears. That was another thing about Dunstan—he always knew what I was feeling before I knew myself. Like how he'd known I was leaving him for Jess before I knew it.

"I don't blame you for that, Clare. Hell, I don't blame you for any of it. I was a pretty big jerk that whole last year."

"No you weren't."

"I think you're doing that editing thing you do again. I *was* a jerk. I knew the minute you met Jess Martin that you'd leave me for him, so I started preemptively acting like an asshole. For Christ's sake, Clare, I dumped a truckload of manure on the lawn of that frat house he was living in."

"Bailey doesn't have fraternities," I said. "It was the Organic Cooperative Wellness House." Dunstan's lip twitched and I felt a tug at the corner of my mouth. "Which actually made the whole manure thing pretty funny."

"It *was* completely organic manure," Dunstan said with a straight face. Then we were both laughing so hard I got pump-kin spice latte up my nose.

Dunstan handed me a napkin. "It wasn't funny at the time, though. You broke up with me the next day. I've wondered since if I didn't drive you off, but then I figured that you were bound to go away after college anyway. You needed to get out of Concord to become the writer you wanted to be. I used to think I'd come to peace with it as long as I knew you were happy and that you'd done what you had set out to do."

"I guess you were disappointed then that I haven't."

He looked at me strangely. "Are *you* disappointed, Clare?"

For a moment I wasn't sure if he were asking me about writing or marrying Jess.

"I think I have been," I said, "but coming back here has changed that. Jess is writing again—and so am I."

He looked away from me and I noticed for the first time that there were fine lines around his eyes. "What about you?" I asked. "I heard you got married."

"And divorced," he said, without looking at me. Then he smiled. "I married a Bailey girl. I think I did it to get back at you, which isn't something I'm particularly proud of. It turned out she didn't much like living in Concord either."

"I'm sorry, Dun. I'm sure you'll find someone else."

He smiled. "I didn't say I hadn't." Before I could react to that he said, "Look in your pocket."

"My pocket?" Then I remembered I was still wearing his denim jacket. I reached inside the right-hand pocket and pulled out a slim leather-bound book. It felt warm, as if it still held the heat of his body. I laid it on the table between us.

"Don't you want to know what's in it?"

"Yes," I said, my voice hoarse.

"It's my grandmother Lizzie's diary. She was Mary Foley's sister . . ."

"Elizabeth Foley. I just came across her name in the records. Did she ever talk about her sister?"

"She died before I was born," Dunstan said. "And my father never talked about her. There was something about that side of the family that was . . . *haunted*."

"What do you mean *haunted*?" I asked, feeling a chill move up my spine.

"I meant *gloomy*. John Foley was a hard-assed businessman who bought up failing orchards in the Depression." He looked at me warily. "What did *you* mean, Clare?"

"Nothing . . . just there are stories . . ."

"Maybe Riven House isn't the best place for you to live. You always had a pretty wild imagination. Have you seen anything there?"

"No," I said, gulping down the rest of my lukewarm latte. I reached for the book at the same time he did and our hands touched. He covered my hand with his.

"If you do, if you see anything that frightens you, Clare, let me know."

I started to laugh, but Dunstan's blue eyes pinned me with a look so grave I didn't. He was, once again, the nineteen-year-old boy who would kill wasps for me and defend me against all danger, real or imagined. It had been a while since anyone had made me feel so protected. No wonder he'd become a cop.

"Of course, Dunstan. First sign of trouble, I'll call 911 and ask for you."

I'd meant to lighten the gravity just a little but he didn't smile as he took out a card, put it inside the book, and pushed it toward me.

"Call my cell first," he said, "and I'll be there before you hang up the phone."

Chapter Thirteen

Driving back to Riven House I thought of what Dunstan had said—not the part about him rushing to Riven House, sirens blaring (although I *did* find that oddly reassuring)—but the part about how he was afraid he'd driven me away because he'd already decided I wasn't going to stay.

He *had* acted like a jerk that year. Not just when he dumped the manure on the Wellness House, but all year, making fun of the writing class (*What do you need it for, Clary, you already know how to write*), and complaining when I couldn't do something with him because I had to work. But had he started acting that way before or after I fell in love with Jess? Would it have made a difference if he hadn't acted like a jerk? Although I'd made a joke of it, I remembered how embarrassed I'd been when he dumped that load of manure on the lawn of the Wellness House. As if everyone would know it had been the *local*'s crude boyfriend who'd done it. I walked around for weeks feeling like the smell of manure still clung to me. No wonder I was grateful to retreat into a fantasy of apple blossoms. I'd accused Dunstan of trying to pull me down in the shit with him and I'd seen in his face a confirmation of something. I'd thought at the time that it was a confirmation of his worst suspicions about me: I was a snob, thought I was better than everybody else, the adopted girl who thought she was smarter than her plain, hardworking parents, but now I saw that what I'd confirmed were his fears that I would leave him.

Hadn't I done the same thing with Jess when I accused him of sleeping with the tattooed barista? And hadn't I allowed myself to grow distant from him because of my jealousy? There'd come a point when it had been too painful to imagine him with other women and so I had tried to make myself love him less. I'd even tried to think about other men (and who had I daydreamed about but Dunstan Corbett?) so that I wouldn't think about him with someone else. The result, I hated to admit, was that I loved him a little less and maybe, just maybe, I'd *wanted* to come back here to see Dunstan again.

I'd come to the fork in the drive, marked now by a stack of neat firewood where Jess and Dale had cut up the tree that had fallen on the Subaru. When I stopped the car I could hear the buzz of a chain saw coming from the field beyond the trees. Jess and Dale had repaired the weir and were working now on rebuilding the bridge that went over it. If I went back to the house now and went up to the nursery I could sit at my desk and watch them working—or I could walk across the field and join them. I had brought back a bag of cider donuts and a latte that I'd planned to drink at my desk, but I could bring it to Jess instead. In fact, I had an extra to-go cup in the car. I could divide the coffee between two cups and bring coffee and donuts to both men. I could reassure Jess—and maybe myself—that I wanted him and not Dunstan.

I pulled the car past the fork so Sunny and her volunteers could get by—no one else used the drive to the house—split the coffee between the two cups, and got out. The day had warmed and the sun felt good on my face as I came out of the trees and crossed the field. It was already low in the sky over the Catskills to the west, turning the river into a wide band of glitter. Dale and Jess were silhouetted against that brilliant backdrop, their long shadows painted on the lawn as they worked on the bridge. Dale was on the ground below the weir, sawing the thick, twisting branches they were using to make the new rustic railing, and then handing them up to Jess on the bridge. They looked like figures in a Millet painting: Dale, with his weathered features, slouchy posture, and loose shirt would be the hoary old peasant and Jess his youthful apprentice. When Jess leaned down to take a branch from Dale his face was ruddy and healthy looking in the sun. I tried to lift my hand to wave to him, but it was awkward while holding two cups of coffee and a bag of donuts—and he had turned away to hammer in the rail while Dale sawed another one. He wouldn't hear me over the buzz of the chain saw, so I put my arm down and then my head, to navigate across the muddy field.

I wasn't wearing the right shoes for it. When the weir broke the Saw Kill flooded the lower part of the lawn, turning the fields and gardens into a marsh. Although the weir was mended, water still stood in irregular patches and pools that reflected the glare of the sun back into my eyes, half blinding me. When I glanced up from the ground toward the weir the figures of the two men shimmered and blurred like a mirage, thin and insubstantial as wraiths in the bright autumn air. Something about the sight made me sad, as if I'd been given a presentiment of Jess's death.

Or maybe, I admitted to myself, it was my talk with Dunstan that had left me feeling sad. For years I had felt guilty for leaving Dunstan for Jess, so Dunstan's confession that he'd been at least partly at fault should have made me feel better. Instead, it made me sad to realize how careless we'd both been of our feelings for each other. How easily Dunstan's love for me had turned to resentment and jealousy and how easily I, blind to what he was going through, ran to Jess. Dunstan had driven me into Jess's arms *because* he loved me too much. If I had known, would it have made any difference? Would I have stayed with Dunstan?

It shouldn't matter, I told myself. I'd wound up where I wanted to be, with Jess, and I was happy with that.

Right?

I stopped in the middle of the field, my eyes blurring with tears, stunned by the conviction that I had made a terrible mistake thirteen years ago leaving Dunstan, that I would have been happier with him. I would have written my books, maybe taught at the high school, while he made sure we had everything we needed. I wouldn't have spent the last five years worrying about money and fighting with Jess about how much he was spending or carping at him about tattooed baristas. I wouldn't have gotten sick this past winter. And who knows? By now we might even have a baby—a towheaded Corbett boy with chubby pink cheeks . . .

The image of the baby was so real that I felt a cramp in my insides that made me double over. I looked up, as if looking at Jess could make up for the sheer disloyalty of the thought, and fixed my eyes on the figures on the weir . . .

Only instead of the two men I saw a different tableau. A shawled figure stood on the bridge, holding a bundle in her arms. A second figure standing below it reached for the bundle. As I watched, the higher figure passed the bundle to the lower one over water that now had the gloss of ice. I held my breath, terrified that it would fall. I stepped forward, arms out, as if I could bridge the distance between us and catch the baby—because I was sure that's what the bundle was—and stumbled in the mud. I looked down to steady my footing and when I looked up again the women on the weir were gone. The shawled woman was Jess in a hooded sweatshirt and the woman reaching for the baby was Dale taking a piece of wood from him. Jess was looking toward me, his eyes narrowed, his brow creased with worry. I lifted a coffee cup in greeting and he smiled at me.

It was all right, I told myself, skirting the pond to reach the men. It hadn't been a ghost or a delusion, just a trick of the light brought on by my mourning an imaginary child. Which was ridiculous. Who knew how things would have turned out between Dunstan and me? Besides, Jess and I had plenty of time to have children. I just had to quit mooning over my high school boyfriend and stop this cycle of jealousy and suspicion. Then Jess and I would be fine.

As I approached I held out the two cups of coffee and bag of donuts. An offering.

"I thought you guys could use something hot out here."

"Cool," Dale said, taking the cup and inhaling the steam from it. "Mmm, I love Cassie's pumpkin spice latte."

I smiled to think of grizzled Dale imbibing fancy coffee drinks and looked to see if Jess found it funny too, but he was wiping the sweat off his brow with the sleeve of his flannel shirt so I couldn't see his expression.

"Have mine," he said, lowering his arm. "It's too sweet for me."

I knew Jess preferred plain coffee, but would it have killed him to pretend—or at least say thank you—in front of Dale?

"Your loss, man. Are those cider donuts?"

I handed Dale a donut and walked up onto the bridge to give one to Jess. He was still frowning at me.

"Is that a new jacket?" he asked.

I looked down and saw that I was still wearing Dunstan's denim jacket. I was surprised Jess had noticed. It was just an ordinary denim jacket, although it was too big on me. I could say I'd picked it up from the mudroom, but then Dale said, "Yeah, and since when did you join the police auxiliary?"

He was pointing a half-eaten donut at the right sleeve. I pulled it around to see the patch. "Oh," I said, inwardly cursing Dale. For a stoner Vietnam vet he'd become suddenly sharp-eyed and observant. "I met a friend in town for coffee and he lent me his jacket. I didn't realize how cold it had gotten when I went out. They're saying there'll be a hard frost tonight."

"A friend?" Jess asked, undeflected by my weather report.

Dale looked from Jess to me and widened his eyes in comic alarm. "Uh-oh, your old lady's out gallivanting with the Man." Then he turned away and fired up his chain saw.

"Dunstan Corbett," I shouted over the roar of the chain saw. "I was doing some research in the Village Hall and ran into him. We went for coffee at Cassie's and he gave me his jacket when he saw how cold I was."

"What a gentleman," Jess remarked dryly. "Has he gotten enormously fat? That jacket is *huge* on you."

"What? No! He's just got broad shoulders . . . Why are you being so awful, Jess? It was just coffee with an old friend."

"An old boyfriend. I can't imagine you'd be so casual if the situation was reversed. Didn't you accuse me of hooking up with an old girlfriend when I came home a few hours late from my high school reunion? You were hysterical—"

"You're right," I cut in. "I was just thinking today that jealousy has hurt us too much already and it's time to move past it."

"Convenient thinking now that you're back in your hometown with your old boyfriend and I'm stranded out here in the sticks sawing wood, for Christ's sake."

"It was your idea that we move to the country," I objected. "And there's nothing to be jealous about."

"I'm not jealous," Jess hissed. "I'm just beginning to wonder how much us being here has to do with you wanting to be back with your boyfriend Dusty—"

"Dunstan," I said. "And that's ridiculous. We've been here two months and this was the first time I've seen him. We just ran into each other."

"And you immediately went for coffee and he gave you his letter jacket just like in high school—"

"It was *cold*! And we went for coffee because he had some research material he thought would help me." I took out Elizabeth Corbett's diary from my pocket and thrust it at Jess as if it proved the innocence of my meeting with Dunstan.

Jess stared at it and then asked me coldly, "If you *just ran into each other* how come he had the book on him? And if this is the first time you met how'd he know what you were writing about?"

I knew that if I told Jess that Dunstan had heard about my research through town gossip he would be skeptical. And if I explained that Dunstan had come into the Village Hall on his day off because he knew I was there it would just confirm his suspicions that Dunstan was interested in me. I knew from my own jealous tirades that the more I tried to defend myself the more he'd be convinced I was guilty. It wouldn't matter that I had done nothing wrong. Knowing how he would twist the argument made me angrier. I had lost half my friends in New York to Jess's sophistry; I didn't want to lose Dunstan.

So instead I asked, "Are you really jealous of Dunstan? Or

are you jealous that I may actually finish my book and you know you won't finish yours?"

It was the meanest thing I could say—I'd even shouted it to be heard over Dale's chain saw—and I was instantly sorry. If I could have plucked the words out of the air and stuffed them back in my mouth I would have, but Jess was already turning away from me, his face white with rage. I reached for his arm to stop him, but he shook me off. It was the motion of shaking me off that upset his balance—that and the fact that the railing on the bridge was unfinished. His foot caught on an uneven plank and his arms pinwheeled to regain his balance. I screamed and reached for him, but my fingers only grazed the rough wool of his shirt as he fell over the edge of the bridge—straight toward Dale and his chain saw. I saw Dale lift his head—he wouldn't have heard my scream over the sound of the chain saw—and the expression on his face as he looked up, the surprise turning to horror as Jess hurtled toward him. Did he even know it was Jess? The horror seemed to be for something else, as if the thing coming at him was a monster out of his worst nightmare. Something so frightening that he raised the saw to ward it off, at the same time stepping back into slick mud and losing his balance. He went down and the chain saw came down with him.

I scrambled down off the bridge as fast as I could. There was so much blood on the ground that it was as if the weir had broken again and let loose a tide of blood over both men.

"Are you all right?" I screamed at Jess.

He nodded, his face white beneath blood splatter. He was kneeling beside Dale. The chain saw was lying over Dale's right shoulder. Jess pulled it off and threw it to the side where it sputtered and whined in the mud like a dying animal. Dale screamed and blood spurted from his shoulder and it occurred to me that maybe moving the chain saw had not been the best idea. But Jess wouldn't have known that. He'd never had to deal with something like this. Growing up on a farm I'd witnessed some horrible accidents—an apple picker who'd gotten his hand stuck in a thresher, Derrick Corbett getting his foot run over by a truck, my own father catching a splintered ax blade in his face while chopping wood . . . I could hear my dad's voice now.

Stop the bleeding. Apply pressure. Call for help.

I stripped my jacket off (*Dunstan's jacket* that had started all the trouble), wadded it into a ball and, shouldering Jess aside, pressed it into Dale's shoulder. He let out another wail and looked at me with eyes that rolled like a spooked horse's.

"You're okay," I told him, although I was far from sure that was true. "It missed the carotid artery. I've stopped the bleeding."

But not for long. I could already feel the thick denim moistening under my hands.

"Call 911," I yelled at Jess.

I saw Jess patting his pockets and knew already he didn't have his phone. *I can't think if it's even near me,* he had said once when I complained about not being able to reach him.

I didn't have mine either. I had left it in my pocketbook in the car.

"You have to go to the car—it's parked at the fork—get my phone from my bag and call 911, then go to Sunny's barn and get help." Hopefully there'd be a crowd of volunteers so close to the Halloween parade. *Hopefully* they wouldn't all be stoned. "Tell them to bring one of the drying racks. We have to get Dale out of here and the ambulance won't be able to get close enough in this mud."

Jess nodded at me but remained kneeling. He was staring

at the reddening jacket in my hands, his face the sickly white of curdled milk.

"Go!" I screamed to break his trance.

He lurched unsteadily to his feet and stumbled away like one of Sunny's puppets with a string broken. How badly had *he* hurt himself in the fall? But he was running now and I had to worry about Dale first. I turned back to him and found his bloodshot eyes fixed on mine.

"It's okay," I said, "Jess has gone to get help. We'll get you out of here."

He said something I couldn't make out. I lowered my head closer to his lips and smelled beer and pot on his breath as he rasped something that sounded like *chop*. I thought he was talking about the chain saw chopping into his arm but when he tried again I made out *choppers*.

I pulled back to look into his face—at the web of lines creasing his leathery skin around once clear blue eyes. It had been over forty years since Dale Cartwright had served in Vietnam, but that's where he'd gone. Maybe we all went to our worst place when we were scared.

"Yeah," I said, "they're on their way."

He jerked his chin to show he'd heard me. The motion must have jarred his injured shoulder. His lips drew back over yellowed teeth in a grimace of pain. I pressed down harder on the jacket and blood oozed through the denim onto my hands.

"Aanggg . . ." he groaned.

"I'm sorry," I said. "I have to keep the pressure on."

"Aangg . . ." he groaned again, and then, gritting his teeth, "aangg-ul."

"Angel?" I asked. "Don't start seeing angels on me, Dale. You're going to make it."

"Saw . . ." he said.

"Yeah," I told him. "You fell with your chain saw in your hands and hurt your shoulder. But you'll be okay—"

"Saw aangg-ul," he bit out, "when . . . fell . . ."

"Oh," I said, remembering the look of horror on Dale's face when Jess fell on him. He hadn't looked like he was seeing an angel.

"Aangg-ul," Dale sputtered, and then, fixing me with a suddenly lucid stare, he spoke clearly. "I saw the angel of death."

Then his eyes rolled up in their sockets and I was left looking into their whites.

Chapter Fourteen

⁓

It felt like an hour before help arrived but it was probably only ten or fifteen minutes. Noelle came running with four burley guys in Bailey sweatshirts carrying a wooden drying rack. Sunny was next with a roll of cloth that she wrapped around Dale's shoulder with surprising speed and dexterity. We got Dale onto the drying rack and carried him off the field. By the time we reached the drive an ambulance had arrived. We handed Dale over to the EMTs, who lifted him from the drying rack onto the stretcher. I heard one of them ask Sunny what the rack was for originally and when she said it had been a drying rack for tobacco he made a bad joke about Dale being nine-tenths tobacco anyway.

"THE MAN'S A WAR VETERAN!" someone roared.

I turned and saw Monty, his white hair flying around his face, which was an alarming shade of red as he yelled at the young EMT. "He served his country for two tours in Vietnam. You goddamned better make sure he's treated right."

The EMT muttered a yessir and hurried into the back of the ambulance. Monty wanted to go in the ambulance, but Sunny convinced him it was better to follow in the car. Looking at Monty's color I wondered if he might not need an EMT soon himself, but all I said was that I would drive the Subaru. At which point I looked around. Noelle and the Bailey boys were standing in a knot smoking cigarettes.

"Where's Jess?" I asked.

Noelle answered. "He hurt his foot in the fall so Katrine took him to the hospital."

"That was nice of her," I said, thinking spitefully that if it weren't for Katrine bringing us here none of this would have happened. Of course I didn't say that. I already knew it wasn't true. This wasn't Katrine's fault. It was Mary Foley's.

I DROVE MONTY and Sunny to the hospital. They both sat in the back talking in hushed whispers to each other. I wasn't listening to what they were saying; I was thinking about what Dale had said about seeing the angel of death.

True, Dale had probably been high enough to see leprechauns and unicorns (*too high to be operating a chain saw*) but hadn't I seen Mary Foley on the weir too, standing just where Jess fell? I'd dismissed it as I'd dismissed all the visions I'd had as my imagination. But what if there really was a remnant of Mary Foley's spirit left behind in the place where she had suffered and died? A malevolent spirit that *pushed* Jess. But why would the ghost of Mary Foley want to harm Jess?

I was no further along in my reasoning (if you could call parsing the behavior of a ghost *reasoning*; if just thinking the ghost was real didn't mean I'd left *reason* behind) when we got to the Northern Dutchess Hospital in Rhinebeck. We all crowded around the desk to ask about Dale. The young male nurse told us that he was being stitched up and that he'd lost a lot of blood but was stable.

"What about Jess Martin?" I demanded.

I saw the nurse's eyes widen at the sight of me. "Are you okay, ma'am?"

I wasn't sure what bothered me more—being called ma'am or the assumption that something was wrong with me—then I realized he was staring at my shirt, which was stained with blood.

"I'm fine," I answered, willing calmness into my voice. "This is Dale Cartwright's blood. I stanched the wound—"

"And saved his life, I warrant." Monty put his arm around me. "Her husband, Jess Martin, hurt himself aiding Cartwright as well. Would you kindly take this young woman to him immediately?"

The nurse blinked at Monty's imperious tone, but he must have encountered much worse. "Of course," he said, "he's right through here."

I left Monty and Sunny in the waiting room and followed the nurse through heavy automatic doors into a fluorescent-lit linoleum-tiled hallway with fever-yellow walls. The light and the smell of disinfectant merging with the metallic tang of blood on my shirt and the sickly shade of yellow all suddenly transported me back to the last time I had been in this hospital. I felt my stomach lurch. This was where Jess had brought me when I miscarried—

"Whoa, there!" The male nurse—CLAUDE, his nametag read—had his arm around me. We'd somehow ended up slumped against the yellow wall. My ears were ringing and I was covered with clammy sweat.

"Sorry," I said, "I don't know what came over me."

"Delayed shock," Claude said, "after the adrenaline rush to your system. Do you want a wheelchair?"

"No, I'm okay now. I just want to see my husband—"

Through the buzzing in my ears I heard angry voices, one of which I recognized as Jess's. I struggled to my feet, Claude helping me, and stumbled toward the voices into an open examining room. The doorway was partly blocked by a man wearing a police jacket. Had something more happened to Jess when he left the weir? Had there been another accident?

"There's my wife now," Jess said, angling his head to see around the police officer. "Maybe you'll listen to her."

The police officer turned and I recognized Dunstan. I felt that lurching sensation in my stomach again, but this time because I was unprepared to see his face. He looked different from this afternoon. In the harsh fluorescent glare his blond hair was streaked with silver and the lines around his mouth and eyes were deeper, his features harder. They softened for a moment at the sight of me, then his gaze fixed on my blood-soaked shirt.

"Are you hurt?" he barked first at me and then, wheeling on Claude, "Why isn't she being treated?"

"I'm not hurt," I said, "Jess is the one who fell—" I tried to look around Dunstan to see Jess but he was firmly planted in front of me. I noticed that Katrine was sitting in a corner, but she was watching Dunstan instead of making eye contact with me.

"Causing injury to Mr. Cartwright," he said. "I'm trying to explain to Mr. Martin that we need him to take a blood alcohol test to rule out the possibility that he was intoxicated while using dangerous equipment."

"But Jess wasn't using the chain saw when Dale got hurt. And it was an accident . . ." My glance wavered under the blue glare of Dunstan's eyes. *I can tell when you're lying,* Dunstan had once said to me, *you look off to the left.* I *was* lying. I knew it wasn't an accident, but I could hardly explain to Dunstan that the ghost of Mary Foley had pushed Jess. At least I couldn't explain it to *this* Dunstan, the cold-eyed police sergeant. All trace of the boy I'd known and glimpsed this afternoon was gone. And I certainly couldn't tell Jess that I'd seen a ghost. He would think I was crazy.

"It was my fault," I said. "Jess and I were arguing. I took a step toward him and he stepped back and fell." I held Dunstan's eyes through this speech, watching them grow colder.

"What were you arguing about?"

"How's that any of your business?" Jess asked.

Dunstan half turned to glare at him, giving me a better view of Jess. He was sitting on an examination table, his foot propped up on a bag of ice. His ankle was swollen and discolored and his face was bloodless.

"You," I said. "We were fighting about me having coffee with you. Do you want me to put that in a statement?"

Dunstan turned back to me. He examined my face for a long moment, his eyes looking for something. It was the same searching look he'd given me thirteen years ago when I broke up with him and it had ended then with the same disappointment that crept over his face now.

"That won't be necessary, Mrs. Martin. If you can attest that your husband fell because he was backing away from you on the bridge that should be sufficient." He turned back to Jess. "A blood test shouldn't be necessary. But I should tell you that Mr. Cartwright's blood alcohol level was way too high to have been handling a chain saw. He's lucky to be alive. Perhaps you'll keep that in mind the next time you're conducting maintenance on Mr. Montague's property."

I saw the blood rush into Jess's pale face and knew he was about to say something that he'd regret—or at least that I'd regret. I opened my mouth to head him off, but Katrine got there first.

"I think Jess will be concentrating on his writing for the present; he's got a broken ankle. He won't be doing any maintenance work for a while. Why don't I walk you out, Dun," she added, getting up and looping her arm in Dunstan's.

I should have been grateful to her for diverting Dunstan from Jess, but I felt irritated.

"Why'd you tell him we were arguing about him?" Jess demanded as soon as Dunstan and Katrine were gone.

"I was trying to keep you from being arrested."

"For operating a chain saw under the influence? Please. Officer Dusty was just trying to throw his considerable weight around. He had no legal right to ask me to submit to a blood test."

"Still, it's better he knows it wasn't your fault."

"Why? So he can think I was jealous that you and he were having coffee together?"

I was about to point out that Jess *had* been jealous, but thought better of it. Clearly Jess was going to argue with anything I said right now. He was acting like a cornered and injured animal.

"No, because it was my fault you got hurt. Are you in pain? Is it really broken?"

He looked down at his ankle as if it belonged to someone else. "Katrine gave me a Vicodin on the way over here, which is why I didn't want to take the damned blood test." He looked like he was going to start in again, but instead his shoulders slumped. "It hurt like hell before."

"Oh, Jess." I stepped closer and started to put my arms around his shoulders but he flinched at the sight of the blood on my clothes. "Fucking Dale," he said. "The way he looked at me when I was falling, I thought he was going to swing that chain saw at me and take my head off."

Chapter Fifteen

It was a couple more hours before we got out of the hospital. Jess had to have his ankle set in a cast, which took a couple of sleep-deprived interns two tries to get right. Sunny came in to tell us Dale was going to be all right and that she was taking Monty back to the house in a taxi. Monty told me that if Jess couldn't get up the stairs we should bed down in the library. Which is what I decided to do after struggling up the terrace steps. Before we had left the hospital a nurse had given Jess a Vicodin that he swallowed before I could remind him he'd already taken one earlier. By the time we got back to Riven House he was groggy and delirious. Leaning heavily on me as we hobbled up to the terrace through a gusty wind he kept going over what had happened on the weir.

". . . thought he was going to take my head off . . . so much blood . . . like a geyser shooting out of the ground . . ."

I shivered in the wind recalling the image I'd had of the weir breaking and releasing a tide of blood, but all I said to Jess was, "It's okay now."

I got him into the library and settled him on the couch near the fireplace. The room was cold—that wind was carrying arctic air—so I made a fire and pulled a ratty old afghan over

Jess. The afghan smelled like Monty's cigars and the ointment he used on his arthritic hands and it barely covered Jess.

"I'm going upstairs to get you more blankets," I told Jess.

"So much blood," Jess murmured.

The rotunda was awash in moonlight and shadow. The wind was blowing leaves over the oculus, splattering their shadows down the broad marble steps. The house felt restless tonight, as if it was excited by what had happened out on the weir. It seemed to have taken up Jess's delirious mutterings. *So much blood.*

Moonlight splashed over the portrait of Bayard Montague at the top of the stairs, dredging his fish-belly face out of the shadows, his cold eyes staring at me askance. I'd brought the reek and stain of blood into his house, defiling the pristine marble steps. I looked down the stairs and saw bloody foot-prints . . . which shifted at the next stir of leaves over the oculus and became leaf shadow. The blood on my clothes was dry.

Still, the reek of it, now that I was away from the hospital disinfectant smell, was unbearable. I'd take a bath after taking the blankets down to Jess.

In the bedroom I tore my bloodstained shirt off and put on one of Jess's flannel shirts. As I was buttoning it, I heard a rustling sound coming from the bathroom. I opened the door and saw that the blind was rattling in the open window. I closed the window so that it wouldn't be so cold when I came back up, and gave the big claw-foot tub a longing look.

I grabbed Jess's sleeping bag from the floor and ran down the stairs, shadow leaves scuttling at my feet as if my motion was scattering them. Jess was soundly asleep when I reached him, his face bathed red in the firelight.

So much blood, so much blood, the house murmured.

I covered him with the sleeping bag, making sure his injured foot was elevated. After my bath I'd come back down and sleep on Monty's chair. I'd watch over him in case he woke in the night and needed to go to the bathroom. I'd take such good care of him that he'd see that I loved *him*, not Dunstan Corbett, and that there was no earthly reason for him to be jealous. We'd put this behind us just as we'd put the miscarriage behind us—

So much blood . . .

By the time Jess had found me in the bathroom the tub and floor were covered with blood. If he hadn't found me, the doctor told us later, I would have bled to death. And if he hadn't found me, no one would have. It was spring break and all his housemates were gone. We'd been fighting. Jess had told me that if I didn't have an abortion he would leave me. "I won't be blackmailed into marriage," he had told me.

I'd left his room, crying, and gone into the bathroom at the end of the hall. The old house had a big old-fashioned tub. I'd decided to take a bath to ease the cramps that were knotting my insides. Only the cramps had grown worse, twisting into barbed wire knots, and I'd passed out from the pain. If Jess hadn't found me I might have drowned as well as bled to death.

But he *had* found me, and wrapped me in his old flannel robe and carried me to his car and driven me to the hospital, where he'd stayed with me and taken care of me . . .

Just as I would take care of him now.

I pulled the sleeping bag over his chest, stood up, and startled at the sight of my reflection in the glass doors. Only it wasn't my reflection. The figure on the terrace was splattered with blood too, but she was wearing a long dress and a shawl covering her head and shoulders and she clutched a bundle to her chest. I stood frozen, waiting for the image to dissipate into something else—as it always had before—into a scrap of fog, a trick of moonlight, a shift of shadow. But it didn't. Instead it—*she*—turned and vanished into the darkness of the lawn.

It took me a few moments to break the icy hold of fear and then I ran to the doors. I fumbled with the latches, the wind outside pushing against the doors as if to keep them closed, and then, when I got the latch turned, flinging them open. A pane of glass broke with a sound like ice shattering. I was halfway across the terrace before I realized that if I left the doors open Jess would freeze. I wrangled them closed and then ran back across the terrace, sure the apparition would have vanished.

But it hadn't. Just as I reached the edge of the terrace the wind ripped the clouds away from the moon and I caught a glimpse of white gown on the lawn below me. She was walking toward the pond.

I ran after her. She *was* real. I hadn't imagined her the other times. The ghost of Mary Foley had shown herself to me. I still felt the prickle of fear on my skin but I felt something else too. *Excitement*. She had something to show me—why else had she come back tonight? She had appeared to Dale on the weir—his angel of death—and now she had come back to tell me something—something about the baby she had left on the doorstep of Riven House. Only she hadn't left it on the doorstep. She was still carrying it. Was that what she was trying to tell me?

There was no fog tonight to mask the figure's progress, only fitful moonlight and shadow as the wind blew the clouds across the moon. I lost her when the clouds blocked the moonlight and caught sight of her again when the sky cleared. It made her look like an actress in a silent black-and-white film, her movement jerky, her shape insubstantial. But when she reached the weir, she turned to face me. *See me,* she seemed to be saying, *be my witness.* Then she spread out her arms—

Where was the baby?

—and vanished over the edge of the weir.

I cried out and ran to reach her. I had to skirt the pond to reach the weir and then be careful climbing up to the bridge not to fall over the pieces of wood Jess and Dale had left there. When I looked over the edge of the weir she was gone. There was only the rushing water and to the side of the stream, Dale's chain saw, the moonlight glinting off the bloodstained metal. Was *this* the gruesome sight she wanted me to see? But then I saw something else—a book lying in the blood. Elizabeth Foley's diary. I must have dropped it when Jess fell. I'd forgotten all about it.

I climbed down the steps and made my way gingerly across the damp ground. The diary was lying facedown in the mud, splayed out like roadkill. I picked it up, cringing at the mud and blood splattered across the cover. What would Dunstan think if I returned his grandmother's diary like this? But then, Dunstan hadn't said he wanted the diary back and after today I didn't think it was likely we'd be seeing each other again soon.

I closed the book, and looked around one more time. The moon was shining full on the weir, turning the water cascading over it to silver. I could see where Jess and Dale had repaired the stone wall, which angled out in graduated steps. Jess had been proud of his stonework, quoting Robert Frost's "Something there is that doesn't love a wall" often. Watching the water riffling over the rough, irregular rocks I thought of another line from the same poem, something about gaps that no one had seen or heard made.

Is that why the ghost appeared on top of the weir? Because there was a gap here between this world and the next? What would it take to close it again? I wondered as I made my way back up the hill.

In the library Jess was still sleeping. I sat down in the chair by the fire and listened to the house, but the creaks and groans had ceased as the wind had died down. I heard a murmuring noise, but that was coming from below me, from Monty's apartment. It was a woman's voice and I guessed that Sunny had decided to spend the night to watch over Monty. She must have really been worried about him to stay in the house.

I opened Elizabeth Foley's diary and it fell open automatically to the pages that had lain in the mud and blood. The entry was dated January 12, 1930.

Mary died last night. It happened in the ice storm. I wanted to go to her because I had one of my "feelings" that something was wrong, but Father forbade me to because the storm was so bad. I lay awake listening to branches breaking in the orchard and I knew something was wrong. Sometime in the middle of the night I just knew I had to look out my window. The storm had passed and the moon had come out, lighting up the ice-covered trees so that they looked like the Christmas decorations in the Woolworth's windows. I knew I shouldn't find it pretty because we'd likely lost a lot of trees, but I couldn't help it.

"It looks like an enchanted fairy land," Mary would say when she took me to see the Christmas windows in Kingston. I hoped that if Mary was looking out her window she would see how pretty it was and it would take away the black cloud she'd lived under all this winter. I looked toward the Jackson farm to see if I could make out a light in her window, but instead I saw someone walking through the orchard. I thought for a moment I was seeing a ghost because the woman

walking between the trees wasn't dressed for a night like this. She was wearing a long flowered nightdress with only a shawl over her head. Then I knew that it was Mary.

I still thought it might have been a ghost. Mary used to read to me from a book about people who saw visions of their loved ones at the moment of their deaths even if they were thousands of miles apart. Mary only lived across the orchards at the next farm. If she had died having her baby she'd come to say good-bye. But then I saw her trip on the ice and knew a ghost wouldn't trip. I ran downstairs as quietly as I could and pulled on boots and a coat and held my breath as I lifted the latch and tried to keep the door from creaking. I wonder now why I didn't wake Father, but I think I already knew that if Mary was out wandering in her nightdress something had come unhinged inside her head and seeing Father wouldn't help any. She hadn't spoken to him since he fetched her back from River House and told her she'd be marrying Ernst Jackson just as they'd planned. She hadn't spoken much to anyone, even me. All winter she'd grown quieter and heavier until it seemed like my sister had been swallowed up by the baby growing inside her. "She'll feel different when the baby comes," Mother said, but now I thought she might be like these apple trees that had grown so heavy with ice through the night that the weight broke them in two. Something had broken inside my sister.

I couldn't see her in the orchard now but I guessed where she was heading—to River House. I crossed River Road and went through the gap in the wall near

the gate where Mary and I had snuck through when
we were little to go skating on the pond. I caught a
glimpse of Mary on the drive and called her name but
if she heard me she gave no sign. She had taken the
lower fork in the drive, the one that led to the gardens
and the pond—

Which is when I knew what she meant to do. I
tried to run, but the drive was slick with ice and I fell
twice so I had to settle for walking fast. The branches
of the tall sycamores that lined the drive were cracking
under the weight of the ice. It sounded like gunshots.
Twice a branch fell almost right on top of me. It's a
wonder one didn't hit Mary or me. I was glad when I
came out into the open. I could see Mary at the edge
of the pond. She was walking around it, heading to
the wooden walkway that went over the weir. I thought
maybe it would be all right then. Maybe she was meeting Mr. Montague here. Maybe she'd just come to say
good-bye to him. I saw she was carrying something in
her arms. I knew it had to be the baby and I wondered
if it had been born dead and that's what had unhinged
her mind, but then I heard it crying, a thin piteous
wail. Poor thing, I thought, he must be cold. I ran
faster then, calling Mary's name. She must have heard
me because she turned around and waited. I was so
out of breath when I reached her that I couldn't speak.

"Lizzie," she said, as if she wasn't surprised at all to
see me there, "I should have known you'd come. Remember how we used to skate on this pond?"

She didn't speak as if she were out in an ice storm
in her nightdress. Something had broken in her mind.

I tried to talk to her the way Father would talk to a spooked mare.

"I do, Mary. We'll take your little one skating when it's old enough. Is it a boy or a girl?"

"A boy," she said, looking down at the bundle in her arms. "That's why Ernst's mother wanted to drown it. 'A bastard girl would have been all right, but we can't have a bastard inheriting the farm.'"

Mary always had been good at voices, but it gave me a chill to hear Mary saying such awful things in Mrs. Jackson's voice.

"She's a spiteful old shrew," I said. "Working at those big houses has made her think she's better than everyone else. Ernst won't let her hurt the baby."

"Ernst is weak," Mary said. "And Mildred is crafty. She'll bide her time and find a way to do him harm."

"Then you'll come back and live with us," I said, but Mary shook her head.

"You know Father would never have me back. No, you have to take him for me, Lizzie, and bring him to Bayard. He won't let his son die. Those Montagues care too much about their own precious blood."

She handed the bundle over to me. I was surprised at how warm it was—no wonder Mary hadn't minded the cold walking here.

"Maybe that's for the best," I said. "At least for now. Are you sure Bayard will take good care of him?"

I looked up at Mary, but she wasn't looking at me. She was looking at the house. All the windows were lit up by the moonlight. The house looked like it was made of ice—beautiful but fragile too.

"He had better or I'll make them sorry," I heard her say and then I heard a loud crack. I almost thought it was the house itself breaking in two at the force of Mary's curse, but then I looked back at Mary. She wasn't on the bridge. A crack had opened up in the ice below the bridge. She had stepped onto the pond in just the spot near the weir where the ice is weakest. I screamed and reached for her but I was holding the baby. Could I put him down safely? And if I did what would I do? Dive into the water myself? Run for help?

I know that I will always blame myself for not saving Mary. I knelt on the bridge above the weir crying her name but when I knew she was gone for good I walked up to the house. Mary had entrusted her child to me and if I couldn't save her at least I could save him. I would give him to Bayard Montague and I'd tell him what Mary had said. That if he didn't take care of the child he'd answer to Mary—and to me. I was prepared to pound on the front doors but when I came to the top of the hill I saw there was a light in the room at the back of the house. It was a room lined with books and glowing with firelight. Bayard Montague was sitting there beside the fire drinking a glass of something that looked like liquid gold. As he lifted his hand I noticed that his shirt cuffs were pink and I marveled at a man who would wear a pink shirt. When I knocked on the glass he startled and looked up and his face turned as white as though I were a ghost.

Good, I thought, let him feel haunted from this day on.

He opened the glass doors and tried to draw me inside but I wouldn't step over the threshold. I handed him the baby. As he took him I noticed that his shirt *wasn't pink, it was just that his cuffs were damp and stained with something pink, as if he'd been peeling beets, although I knew that was pretty unlikely. When I told him what had happened to Mary he cried out and said he would go down to the pond, but I told him it was too late. Then he asked me how he should explain how the baby came to him and I told him he should tell everyone that he'd found it on his doorstep. Everyone would think Mary had left it there for him to find. Then I turned and left before he could ask me any more questions or I could change my mind about leaving the baby—my nephew!—in that house. I could feel that there was something wrong with it, just standing on the threshold, but it was what Mary had wanted me to do.*

I have waited all morning to hear news from the Jackson farm and River House but the roads are still covered with ice and Father has spent the morning counting broken tree branches. If only he knew that wasn't all that was lost in the storm. But now I see old Mrs. Jackson coming up the drive from River Road in her halting gait like a beetle scuttling across the floor. She has come to tell us the bad news—I can see her eagerness. I'll go down and see if I can hear it without spitting in her face—

Later—I don't know how to write this. Mrs. Jackson says that Mary laid her baby on the steps of River House and then drowned herself in the pond. All that I knew of course, but then she said that the baby had frozen to death before it was found. Did Bayard leave that poor baby on the steps to freeze to death? I will never forgive myself—or him—if that's what he's done

I turned the page, but found that the next few pages had been torn out and the rest of the diary was blank.

I closed the book and sat looking into the fire. As sad as the original story had been, this was worse. To have entrusted the baby to Bayard Montague only to have him betray her . . . no wonder the ghost of Mary Foley haunted this house! Had she wreaked her vengeance by driving Minnie to shoot her husband and then, months later, kill herself? Feeling weary, I laid the book aside on the armrest . . . and a slip of paper fell out from between the pages. It fluttered in a draft and nearly flew into the fire, but I caught it before it did. It was a newspaper clipping, yellow and brittle as a butterfly's wing. I carefully unfolded it and read it. It was the notice of Minerva's death. "Widow of River House drowns herself in blood bath . . ." it read. This must have come from a racier paper than the account I had read. Then I noticed a faint note penciled below the printed line, written in the same handwriting as the diary.

The second bloody bath, it read.

What on earth did that mean? I wondered. I was staring at the bit of newsprint, hoping for some detail to make clear what Elizabeth meant, when a drop of water splashed onto it. I startled, convinced I'd summoned the blood bath of the story, and then looked up. On the ceiling was a jagged line extending from the pocket doors on the south end of the room to just above my head. As I watched the crooked line swelled and grew and another drop landed in my lap. A broken pipe? I wondered, getting slowly to my feet. I looked up at the ceiling with dread, expecting at any moment that it would split open . . .

Unleashing a tide of blood.

I rubbed the paper. It left a red smear on my finger. But then, I still had blood on my hands from Dale. I hadn't had a chance to take a bath yet . . .

The bath. The spot where the line started was not far from the bathroom in our room. I had wanted to turn the bath on but I hadn't. Or had I? Had someone—or *something*—turned it on? Had I forgotten that I had?

I wasn't sure which I was more afraid of: that I had turned on the bath and forgotten or that something had turned it on for me. I ran out of the library into the rotunda and up the marble stairs. The moonlight was still casting leaf shadows on the steps, but now they looked like splatters of blood. I imagined the whole house dripping with blood. I could hear it, hear the drip drip drip . . .

I ran into our bedroom but paused in front of the bathroom door. The closed bathroom door. I didn't remember closing it. But then I didn't remember leaving the water on either and there was water seeping under the door. Red water.

What would be in the bathtub when I opened the door? Minnie with her wrists slit? If that was what was behind the door I wasn't sure that my mind wouldn't crack in two at the sight. But I had to know.

I opened the door.

Water lapped over the rim of the tub. Red water. It pooled under my feet as I stepped into the room and looked over the edge of the tub . . .

Something was floating in the water. Something white and streaked with blood.

Chapter Sixteen

I reached into the water and lifted out my own shirt. The one soaked with Dale's blood. Had I put it in the tub to soak and forgotten about it?

Whether I'd forgotten turning on the tub and leaving Dale's bloodstained shirt in it or someone—or something—else had done it, I knew I wasn't going to sleep that night. I mopped up all the water with towels and then washed and bleached the towels in Monty's ancient washing machine. I was doing the last load when Sunny came up to the kitchen. I noticed that *she* looked oddly rested and happy. She was wearing one of Monty's beautiful old monogrammed shirts over leggings, her frizzy white hair billowing around her face like a halo. She was smiling to herself and humming as she put the coffee on. Then she turned and saw me standing by the washing machine and her smile vanished.

"Clare, darling! You look like death! Have you been up all night? Is Jess very bad?"

"Jess is fine," I said. "Still sleeping. But I . . ." I hesitated. Would she think I was crazy if I told her about the tub? But I had to tell someone. "I think you were right about the house. It *is* haunted."

I told her about the figure on the weir and the book and the bath. I showed her the diary and the newspaper clipping with the penciled note from Elizabeth.

"And then I went upstairs and found the bathtub full of blood."

She turned as white as Monty's shirt and looked like she wanted to run as far away as she could from me and from the house, but she firmed her jaw and asked me to take her upstairs to show her the bathroom. I almost wished then that I hadn't cleaned up the blood so she could see it as I had seen it, but even though I had scrubbed the whole room with bleach, it still smelled like blood and it still felt . . .

"Bad," Sunny said, standing in the doorway as if she were afraid of entering the room. "This is a bad place."

"I suppose I could have forgotten I left the bath on—" I began.

"No," she said, "don't start doubting yourself. That's what *she* wants. To drive you crazy. She was here. I can feel her—" She shuddered so violently I thought she might be having a seizure.

I didn't have to ask her whom she meant.

"Let's get out of here," she said.

We went back down to the kitchen where we were greeted by the comforting smell of freshly brewed coffee. I poured us two cups and was surprised when Sunny added two teaspoons of sugar to hers. She struck me as a sugar-is-white-death-I-only-use-organic-honey sort of person.

"For shock," she explained. "You should have some too."

Without waiting for me to agree, she spooned two teaspoons of sugar into my cup and sat down at the kitchen table, motioning me to join her.

"I told you that I lived in the house with Monty when I first came to Riven House, yes?"

I nodded, grimacing at the taste of the coffee.

"What I didn't tell you was that I had a child—a little girl. She wasn't Monty's; he had made it very clear that he didn't want any children. To tell you the truth, I was never sure who the father was. It was back in the sixties, the time of 'free love' as we called it then . . ." She laughed, the sound coming out like a hoarse bark. ". . . as if love ever came without a price. We were all high most of the time. Living here, we didn't have to work at regular jobs. Monty supported us in exchange for chores around the place or just for our company or . . . well, I knew I wasn't the only one sharing his bed and I didn't mind—or I pretended not to mind because it wasn't cool to be jealous or possessive in those days and I liked living here. I had Anya in the bedroom where you and Jess are staying, with a midwife and a doula. She was a beautiful baby and a beautiful little girl—an angel . . ." Sunny's voice trailed off, her face soft and unfocused. She wrapped her fingers around her coffee mug and looked into it as though looking into her daughter's face. "When she was five we had a big party at the barn. It was my first 'opening' for the puppets. There was music, food, dancing . . . and of course drinking and pot and someone brought peyote. I remember Anya dancing like a little firefly, darting in and out of the crowds . . . and then it was morning and I was waking up on the barn floor in a tangle of bodies. I didn't even realize Anya was gone for a few hours. I figured she had gone up to the big house to go to bed—and she had. Only she had also decided to give herself a bath . . ." Sunny laughed again, but this time the sound was like something breaking. "Imagine the five-year-old who would give herself a bath. Imagine how much she had to take care of herself! When I found her clothes on the floor I saw someone must have spilled beer on her. That's why she had taken a bath, because she hated the smell of beer. The medical examiner said she must have fallen asleep . . ."

"Oh, Sunny," I said, reaching across the table to take her hand. "I'm so sorry."

"But now," Sunny said, squeezing my hand, "I wonder if the ghost drowned my little girl because she was jealous of her."

I looked into Sunny's eyes. I'd never seen them before without the protective circles of kohl and mascara. She looked both older and younger without them.

"Because her own baby died?" I asked.

Sunny shook her head and released my hand. She picked up the newspaper clipping and held it out to me, her hand trembling. "Maybe not. Elizabeth wrote on this 'the second bloody bath.' And remember how Elizabeth described Bayard as he took the baby from her—his shirt cuffs were pink and damp. I think he must have found Minnie in the bathtub earlier that night . . . Maybe she tried to kill herself that night . . . or she had a miscarriage . . . don't you see? It wasn't Mary's baby who died that night; it was Minnie's. And when Elizabeth handed Bayard a healthy baby boy—"

"He claimed it for his own," I said. "And put Minnie's baby on the doorstep." I shuddered. Even if the baby was already dead it was a horrible picture. "But then that means that Monty is—"

"Mary Foley's child," Sunny whispered.

"Maybe that's what Mary wants," I said, "for Monty to know that she was his mother."

Sunny sighed. "Yes, that's what Mary wants. But what do you think Minnie wants?"

"Minnie?" I asked, feeling chilled.

"Yes, Minnie. She lost her own baby and then she was given another woman's child as if she wouldn't know the difference.

When she told people it wasn't her baby they told her she was crazy."

I thought of Minnie hearing a baby crying from downstairs, the sound traveling up the dumbwaiter. And then they'd placed another woman's baby in her arms and she'd known it wasn't hers. In her delirium she'd conceived the idea of putting the baby back where she thought it came from: the dumbwaiter.

"It would have driven any woman crazy," I said.

"Yes," Sunny said, "especially right after giving birth, which is such a vulnerable time. It made her so crazy she shot her husband. Then she was all alone in this house with a baby she didn't think was hers. No wonder she took her life in the same bathtub where she miscarried. She certainly has as much reason to curse this house as Mary did—and as much reason to haunt it."

"But why is she haunting me?" I asked.

Sunny didn't answer. She was looking over my shoulder. Following her gaze out the window I saw that someone had come to the kitchen door. "It's just Katrine," I said, getting up to let her in.

"I came by to see how you were doing," Katrine said to me, and then, eyeing Sunny in Monty's shirt, "but I see Sunny's beaten me to it."

"I stayed last night to make sure Monty was all right," Sunny said defensively.

"How considerate of you," Katrine said. "It must have been a terrible shock for him—and for you, Clare, being there when it happened. I'm afraid you haven't had much luck since coming here. I confess I feel guilty since I was the one who suggested you and Jess move here."

"I told Clare I didn't like the idea of her and Jess living in the house," Sunny said.

"Did you have a presentiment?" Katrine asked, her face so serious that if I hadn't recalled her making fun of Sunny I wouldn't have guessed she was doing so now.

"I did," Sunny said. "I don't think it's a good place for her or Jess."

"Perhaps you should do Clare's chart," Katrine suggested with only the slightest twitch in her mouth.

Although I'd mocked Sunny myself, I didn't like hearing Katrine do it after what I'd just learned. "That's really not necessary," I said.

"I suppose it wouldn't be a bad idea," Sunny said, turning to me, "only I'd need the date and time of your birth."

"I don't know the time," I said. "It's not on the copy of my birth certificate."

"Didn't your mother ever tell you?" Sunny asked.

"No," I explained. "I was adopted."

"Oh," Sunny said, "I'm sorry. I didn't know."

I was surprised at how awkward she looked. And then a little angry. I'd just listened sympathetically to her story of letting her five-year-old daughter wander off and drown herself and she was looking at me as if there was something wrong with me because I was adopted. It was why I hated telling people.

"You might be able to get your original birth certificate from the agency where you were adopted," Katrine said. At least *she* wasn't acting like being adopted was a disease. "Do you know where you were adopted from?"

"St. Anne's right here in Concord. But I've never asked for my records . . ."

"I can see why you might not want to . . ." Sunny said, looking away uncomfortably. Then she looked alarmed at the time on the oven clock even though it was broken. "Oh my . . . I should bring Monty his coffee before it gets cold . . ." She hesitated, looking from me to Katrine. I had the feeling she wanted to say something more about what we had spoken about but didn't want to mention it in front of Katrine. But then she said, "I told you that this house wasn't good for you. Perhaps it would be better if you left." With that Sunny hurried out of the kitchen with Monty's coffee.

I watched her go, shocked and baffled. Maybe telling the story of Anya's death had unhinged her. No wonder she'd grown so strangely attached to her puppets. *Her children.* It was sad, really.

"*That* was weird," Katrine said. "She acted like there was something wrong with you being adopted."

"I'm used to it," I said, "but I don't know if that's why she was acting so strangely. She'd just told me this awful story." I leaned closer to Katrine and lowered my voice. "Did you know Sunny had a little girl who drowned here?"

Katrine's eyes widened. "No! I'd heard that a little girl had died during one of those sixties parties but I didn't know it was Sunny's. Hell, no wonder she's so loopy about her puppets. I'd go out of my mind, wouldn't you?"

"I might," I admitted.

Katrine shook her head. "Some children are better off being adopted than getting stuck with their birth parents." She paused and took a sip of her coffee. "Have you really never tried to find out who they were?"

"My mother told me the records were sealed."

"I've heard it's easier now to have those records opened," she said, getting up. "And St. Anne's is so close. But perhaps I'm being a noodge. I'm sure you've got enough on your mind with the book you're writing—and taking care of Jess. Tell him I hope his ankle's better—and that he owes me a Vicodin." She winked, and then squeezed my shoulder. "Remember, if you ever want to go have that glass of wine, I'm available."

I told her I'd like that and then, when she'd gone, I poured two cups of coffee—dumping the sweetened coffee down the drain—and brought them into the library, thinking as I went that I really should take Katrine up on going out. She was the closest I'd found to a sensible, levelheaded friend up here and I could use one.

I found Jess awake, sitting at Monty's desk.

"How's your ankle?" I asked.

"Hurts like a motherfucker," he swore. "And my head feels like it's stuffed with cotton."

"That's the Vicodin," I said. "You took two last night. You'd better—"

But he was already swallowing one of the pills with a swig of black coffee. He grimaced at the taste.

"You really shouldn't be taking that on an empty stomach."

"You've become quite the authority, haven't you?" he snapped. "Is it because Monty's taken you under his wing?"

I looked down at the desk and saw that he had the folder where Monty kept my pages. I was shocked that Jess would read someone's work in progress without their permission. I could have pointed out that he would be appalled if I had done the same to him, but instead I said, "We've been working on this together because we're both interested in the same story. I didn't tell you because I know what you think about collaborations."

"Is that what you call this . . . *historical romance?*" He spit out the last words as if they were the most damning epithet he could come up with, which they were probably for Jess. I felt the blood rush to my cheeks.

"Monty thinks it's good," I said.

"Then he truly is losing his mind. Really, Clare, you can do better than this. 'His kisses tasted like apples,'" he read in a falsetto imitation of my voice. "Were you thinking of Dusty when you wrote this?"

I snatched the page out of his hand. "I thought you wanted me to write again. I thought that's why we came here."

He looked up at me, his eyes blank and unfocused. "What are you talking about, Clare?"

Too late I realized I would have to admit to eavesdropping, but that seemed minor considering he'd been rifling through Monty's desk. "I heard you tell Monty that you thought I might start writing again here. I thought it was why you turned down the Brooklyn job."

Jess was staring at me as if I'd sprouted horns. "You must have imagined that little bit of conversation. First of all, why should I feel bad that you stopped writing? That was your choice. I always told you that editing other people's work would kill the writer in you—just as teaching would kill the writer in me. *That's* why I turned down the Brooklyn job and accepted Monty's charity so I could finish my book. I see now, though, that he only wanted you to finish his for him."

"That's not what I'm doing . . ." I began, but then realized I'd fallen into one of Jess's traps of changing the argument. I was stung to realize that Jess hadn't come here so I could write again. *Had* I misheard him? Or had he been lying to Monty? But I also recognized that Jess was in pain and high from the Vicodin.

"I'm sorry you don't like what I'm working on, but I don't need your approval. I suggest you focus on your own work." I plucked the folder out of his hands. "I'm going to drive over to the hospital to see how Dale is doing. Do you need anything before I go?"

Jess shook his head and got up from the desk, intending, I was sure, to stomp out of the room. The effect was ruined, though, by his hobbling gait. Watching him leave, I almost felt sorry for him.

As I DROVE out the front gate I thought about what Katrine had said about it being easier to open adoption records now. St. Anne's was just across from the hospital. I could easily go there and ask to see my records. I didn't care about Sunny doing my chart, but I was tired of all the things I didn't know about myself, down to something as simple as the hour of my birth. Other people knew where their blue eyes or their artistic talent or propensity for alcoholism or high blood pressure came from. All I knew was that my mother had been in a mental hospital when she had me. Perhaps that's what had kept me from wanting to know more. I didn't want to find out more about a mother who had been crazy. But now it occurred to me that maybe she hadn't been crazy. Maybe she, like me, *saw things* and that had been enough to get her locked up. Maybe if I could find her I could let her know that she wasn't crazy.

I didn't know if I could just show up at St. Anne's and demand to see my records, but at least I could get the ball rolling.

The orphanage had originally been located in an Italianate mansion on the edge of Concord, founded in the late nineteenth century by Anne Montague as St. Anne's Asylum for Young Orphaned and Otherwise Neglected Girls. "Otherwise neglected" was often a euphemism for unwed mother. It had been Anne Montague's aim to provide these young girls with the domestic skills that they would need to find a husband or employment at the River Road mansions. Although I didn't doubt that Anne Montague's heart had been in the right place it always seemed to me as though she had founded a training academy for her own future housemaids.

The orphanage had closed in 1934 and was subsumed into St. Anne's Home for Children, later St. Anne's Services when orphanages had gone out of style and were replaced by the foster care system. I was lucky, Trudy often explained to me when we passed the old crumbling edifice of St. Anne's, that I'd been adopted so quickly. I might have spent my life shuttled from foster home to foster home or, if I'd been born in an earlier era, reared up to be a rich woman's slave.

St. Anne's Services was in a clean, antiseptic steel and concrete building across from the hospital. An improvement over the old orphanage, I supposed, but it had always looked to me far colder and more frightening, more like an institution where you would be locked up. When I pulled up in the parking lot I saw that at least the bars had been removed from the windows and orange and red chrysanthemums planted on either side of the driveway. There were Halloween decorations that reminded me that the Halloween parade was tomorrow and made me wonder if Sunny would be up to ushering "her children" through it. The thought of those papier-mâché substitutes for poor drowned Anya struck a chill in my heart as I pressed the handicap button to open the wheezing automatic doors. I remembered what Katrine had said. Perhaps some children were better off in orphanages.

I asked at the front desk where the adoption records were kept and was told by a woman who looked up from her needlepoint to go down the stairs, turn left, and keep on to the last door on the right.

Perhaps they were kept in a dungeon, I thought, descending the stairs. I was beginning to feel like the heroine of one of those Gothic romances we read in Brit Lit, wandering through catacombs and underground passages to unveil the secret of the cursed mansion where she was imprisoned.

The records office, though, was a brightly lit room with vinyl couches and inspirational posters featuring sunsets and mothers and children playing in meadows. The woman behind the counter was—big surprise—knitting a scarf. Were all the office workers in Dutchess County engaged in some kind of fiber craft? She had short choppy highlighted blond hair and huge enamel cat earrings and was wearing an artful lavender tunic that matched the scarf she was knitting. Her blue eyes looked familiar, but I'd already begun to guess that all the office workers were related. Perhaps there was someplace like St. Anne's that trained homeless women to knit and file.

I told her I wanted to find out if my adoption records were sealed.

"You'll have to fill out these forms," she said, licking her finger and peeling off half a dozen Easter egg–hued pages from the wire baskets lined up on the counter. "Do you know if you were adopted from St. Anne's?"

"My parents—my *adoptive* parents—told me so. Do you know how long it will take to find out?"

"Well, even if your records aren't sealed you're supposed to make an appointment . . . but let's see . . ." She snatched the robin egg blue sheet I'd started filling out and read my name. Her blue eyes flicked up at me and she pursed her lips. "Give me just a minute," she said. "Why don't you have a seat?"

She gestured with a hand jangling with silver bracelets and vanished into an inner office. Had my name set off some automatic alarm system? For children of mental patients, perhaps? I sat reading a poster that listed twenty-six (one for each letter of the alphabet) reasons for happiness while I waited for men in white suits to take me away. I had just gotten to "You have permission to be who you are" when the woman in lavender came back carrying a thin manila folder.

"This isn't how we're supposed to do it," she said, "but your records aren't sealed and I sense you need answers. Here." She handed me the folder, gave me a pat on the back, and went back behind the desk. I felt her eyes on me as I gripped the folder and wished that I hadn't come, but how could I not look with all the posters around me telling me to Dare, Dream, and Aim High?

I opened the file. There was the adoption form signed by Trudy and Bill Jackson. Seeing their signatures on the yellowed page gave me a pang. What a big leap it must have been for them to take in a stranger's baby! It must not have been easy to raise a child who was so different from them. I felt suddenly disloyal looking for my birth mother, but then Trudy and Bill were dead. And although I'd come to believe in ghosts I didn't think they were spending their afterlife thinking about me.

I turned the page and found my original birth certificate. I suppose I was expecting to feel some frisson of recognition at the sight of my mother's name but I didn't. Amy Louise Birnbach. The name meant nothing to me. But then I looked down to the next line and felt a tremor that shook me by the roots. Under NAME OF FATHER Amy Birnbach had written Alden Montague III.

Chapter Seventeen

She could have lied, I thought as I drove home. Amy Birnbach, who listed her occupation on another form as "English Major, Bailey College," could have written the name of her favorite teacher on her baby's birth certificate because she wanted it to be true. How much grander to write "Alden Montague III" than the name of some pimply boy she'd hooked up with after too many beers at a dorm kegger or "I don't know." Maybe she had planned to extort money from Monty.

But if that were true—if she had told Monty that she'd had a baby—why hadn't Monty *done* something? Had he really known that he had a child left at St. Anne's?

The thought that Monty had known about me and let me be adopted by the Jacksons made me so angry I had to pull the car over to the side of the road and catch my breath. I sat in the parking lot of Del's Dairy Dream staring at the THANKS FOR A GREAT SEASON—SEE YOU IN SPRING! sign swinging in the wind until my vision cleared.

I didn't know for sure that Monty had known about me—or even that he really was my father. But I was pretty sure one person knew that Amy Birnbach had had a baby.

When I reached the fork in the road I turned toward Sunny's barn. She was sure to be there with only one day left before the Halloween parade. I found her supervising the loading of the puppets into half a dozen assorted vans and trucks.

"Make sure the skeletons' legs don't get tangled in the witches' hair," she was explaining to one of the Bailey guys who had helped carry Dale yesterday. She was still wearing Monty's shirt, now under an orange kimono that flapped in the wind as she waved her arms. She looked like one of her own puppets, sweeping from truck to truck, but when she saw me she juddered to a stop as if one of her strings had been cut.

She *knew*. And she knew that I knew.

"Noelle," she cried. "Take over for me, will you? Make sure the children are all settled for their journey."

I bristled at the word *children*. While I'd been lying in an adoption home she'd been attending to her *children*. But I held my tongue until we were alone in the barn.

"You found your birth certificate, didn't you?" Sunny said. "I can see by your aura—"

"Fuck my aura, Sunny, you knew Amy Birnbach, didn't you?"

Sunny sighed. "Poor Amy, she wasn't well—"

"Did you know she had a baby?"

"It's you, isn't it? I thought you had a bit of Amy's energy."

"Do I have Monty's energy, too? Because that's who Amy named as my father."

Sunny turned as pale as her shirt. "I know she said it was Monty, but Amy was . . . *unstable*. She said a lot of things that summer. She said she was related to Sarah Bernhardt and that her father knew J. D. Salinger. She said she saw ghosts in the house and that they told her she was destined to be the lady of Riven House."

"How do you know she *didn't* see ghosts?" I demanded.

"She said she saw the ghost of Zelda Fitzgerald dancing the Charleston with Janice Joplin. She wanted attention. Poor Monty was sorry he'd ever invited her to Riven House."

"Poor Monty! She was twenty-two years old when she had me—she was his student!"

"She wasn't actually. She'd graduated the year before."

"She'd been his student and he was twice her age! Did he know about the baby?"

Sunny shook her head. "He'd gone on sabbatical to Nepal by the time she found out. I told her she should write to him but she said there was no need because she was going to have an abortion . . . I'm sorry, Clare. I know that must be hard to hear."

"I don't blame her. She was twenty-two and alone. Why did she decide not to?"

"She said she had a dream in which the ghost of Riven House came to her and told her not to. She canceled the appointment. I tried to do everything I could to help her but she became more withdrawn as the year went on. It gets lonely here in the winter—you'll see. Then just before Christmas I found her in the bathtub—the same tub where my Anya had died—with her wrists slit. You can imagine what that was like for me. I had to get her out of Riven House. I took her to the hospital and when she told the doctors that the ghosts had told her to take her life so that she and her unborn baby would be with them forever they did a psych evaluation. Her mother came up. It was a bit of a shock to meet her because Amy had told all these stories about her mother being a fashion model who traveled the world—and then she turned out to be a bookkeeper in the Garment District. And a single mother. She had no idea what to do for Amy, so when the doctors suggested she go into the Hudson Mental Hospital she agreed. She thought it was the best place for her until the baby came and she convinced Amy to put it—*you*—up for adoption. I know it must seem harsh to you, but believe me, growing up with Amy Birnbach for a mother wouldn't have been easy."

It couldn't have been harder than growing up with Trudy Jackson, I wanted to snap, but instead I asked, "What happened to her?"

"Amy? I'm not sure. She went back to Long Island. We kept in touch for a little while but remember, there was no internet then. I imagine you could look her up . . ."

Sunny was looking at me quizzically. I had no idea if I wanted to look up Amy Birnbach. Nothing that Sunny had told me so far made me want to meet her, but then I only had Sunny's version to go on and Sunny, I guessed, had her own reasons for not liking Amy.

"And what about Monty? Did anyone tell Monty that he had fathered a child when he came back from his sabbatical?"

"Amy said she didn't want him to know. She told the social worker at St. Anne's that she'd been mistaken when she named him on the birth certificate. She said she wasn't sure who the father was."

"But why wouldn't she want him to know?" I asked.

Sunny's face reddened. "It's not a very . . . *honorable* reason."

I wondered what could be worse than everything she had told me about Amy Birnbach so far. "I want to know."

"She wanted him to write her a recommendation for graduate school and she was afraid that if he knew about the . . . about *you* he wouldn't."

I stared at Sunny. The thought that my existence had been kept from the man who was possibly my father for the sake of a grad school recommendation had left me speechless. Finally, I asked, "And you went along with that?"

"I understand why you're angry, Clare, but remember, Monty wasn't interested in having children. I doubt the outcome would have been different if he had known."

"Well, we'll never know, will we? But at least I can find out his reaction now—"

"You're going to tell him?"

"Why wouldn't I?"

"It's just . . ." She took a step closer to me and touched her fingers to my arm. "You might want to wait. He's still very upset about Dale. His heart is none too strong."

"You think that finding out I'm his daughter would give him a heart attack?"

"It's not like that, Clare. He's very fond of you. He told me last night how much he's enjoying working on the apple blossom girl book with you. He couldn't feel closer to you if you were his biological daughter. In fact, knowing you're Amy's daughter will only complicate his feelings for you. And coming from you now, while you're so emotional, will only upset him. At least wait until after the parade tomorrow. He's planning to ride in the float with me. Let him enjoy that. You can tell him afterward—when you're calmer."

I guessed that Sunny wanted Monty focused on her for the parade, but I also recognized that it might be a good idea to wait, if only to process the information better myself. "All right," I said, "but I'm telling him after the parade."

Relief swept over her face and she held her arms out to embrace me. "Maybe *this* is what the ghost wanted you to know."

I evaded her embrace and stepped back, sure that even if the ghost of Riven House wanted me to know who my father was, Sunny hadn't.

I LEFT MY car at the fork and walked the rest of the way to the house, trying to sort the warring images in my head—Amy Birnbach lying in a bathtub full of blood, just as Minnie had before her and poor little Anya . . . only there hadn't been blood with Anya, just a tiny life snuffed out, as if the house had drained the life out of her . . .

. . . *the ghosts had told her to take her life so she and her unborn baby would be with them forever* . . .

I stumbled to a stop and looked up at the house, standing like a sentinel on the hill, its windows flashing back light. I remembered what Monty had said about the octagonal structure mirroring the human brain, but what if it were a diseased brain? What if the consciousness that had gotten inside Riven House was insane?

As I kicked off my boots in the mudroom I heard the click clack of typewriter keys coming from Monty's apartment. I thought of going down to see if he was okay, but then realized I'd never gone downstairs into Monty's apartment. He'd never said not to and it had never been necessary because he was usually in the library in the morning. But since Sunny had spent the night there, it felt as though the basement apartment was off-limits. Besides, that steady clack of typewriter keys clearly indicated that he was writing and the unspoken rule of Riven House was that we did not disturb each other when we were writing.

I slipped into a pair of Monty's monogrammed slippers and scuffed through the hallway to the library, thinking I'd pick up the last pages I'd given Monty. He wouldn't have had a chance to read them yet and I'd thought of a change I wanted to make before he did.

I was surprised to find the doors closed. Monty only closed them when he was working to let us know not to disturb him, but he was downstairs in his apartment. I paused outside the double pocket doors, my hand resting on the faded pattern of apple blossoms, and listened for any noise coming from inside. After a minute I heard a faint rustling, like wind blowing through autumn leaves—or pages being turned. I pictured the pages of my book lying on Monty's desk and someone riffling through them.

The ghost of Mary Foley reading what I'd written about her? Or the ghost of Minnie Montague ripping the pages to shreds? Or the two of them together. A wave of nausea coursed through me. Amy Birnbach had said the ghosts wanted her and her unborn baby. Ghosts, plural. As if the two of them—Minnie and Mary—had made some unholy pact to prey on the mothers and children of Riven House.

I slid the doors open, my heart thudding, and saw Jess sitting at the octagonal desk, one leg propped up on a pillowed hassock. He looked up, pen in hand, and stared at me as though he'd never seen me before.

"Oh!" I said. "I didn't know who was in here. Are you—"

"Working," he said. "Monty told me to work in here since I can't manage the stairs."

I was amazed that Monty had ceded his desk to Jess but I only said, "I'm sorry I interrupted you," and started to close the doors.

"Don't go," he called out, trying to get to his feet but grimacing when he put weight on his ankle.

"You'll hurt yourself." I hurried across the room to keep him from getting up and he slumped back in Monty's chair. I picked up the pillow that had fallen, put it back on the hassock, and knelt to help him get his foot back on it. When I looked up I saw he was watching me, his eyes soft.

"I'm sorry about what I said to you before," he said. "You

were right. I *was* jealous that you've been working with Monty. Your story . . . it's *good*. Better than the drivel I'm working on." He gestured toward the pile of typescript pages scattered over the top of Monty's desk. They were covered with red inked corrections—Jess always used red pens to make his corrections. *Lest I forget*, he always said, *it's my own blood I'm spilling when I cross out a word*. It looked like he'd spilled a couple of pints across these pages.

"You know that's not true. It's only what you think when you're rewriting. I could never be the writer you are. My story . . ." I stopped, the words echoing in my head. *My story.* The pieces of what I'd learned today clicked into place. I stared at Jess, remembering that I'd promised Sunny that I'd wait to tell Monty I was his daughter, but I hadn't said I wouldn't tell Jess. And Jess was the one I had to tell first. I was the daughter of the man who, as far as Jess was concerned, had ruined his career. It might be the one thing he wouldn't be able to live with. It might mean the end between us. But he deserved to know first.

"I found out something today," I said, my mouth dry. "I went to look for my adoption papers at St. Anne's . . ." I paused, waiting to see if he'd ask me why. I hated to admit that it was because Sunny had asked so she could do my chart, but now that I was committed to telling the truth I wouldn't have lied.

But instead he said, "Good. I always thought you should."

It was true. The first time I told him that I was adopted he had said I should find out who my birth parents were. It was at dawn. We had stayed up all night talking after a student reading, wandering around the campus, telling each other about the novels we wanted to write, trading the names of our favorite authors like baseball cards.

Tolstoy, he'd say.

Dickens, I'd counter.

Charlotte Brontë, I'd offer.

Emily Brontë, he'd amend.

Conrad, we both said together, although later we argued over which was his best work: *Heart of Darkness* or *Nostromo*.

It had felt like I'd found my other half. At dawn we'd sat on the roof of the library watching the sun come up and I told him my biggest secret, the one I hadn't told anyone, not even Dunstan. I told him all the things I'd seen and heard over the years—Great-Granny Jackson thump-dragging her leg across the attic, her shadow on my wall telling me I didn't belong. I told him that my birth mother had been in a mental hospital when I was born and that my biggest fear was that I was crazy.

"You're not crazy," he said, his face bathed in the glow of the rising sun. "You're a writer."

Now Jess's face was glowing in the light of the setting sun coming in through the glass doors. It kindled a light in his eyes I hadn't seen for a long time and I remembered what it had felt like to be seen by Jess. To have my true self seen by him. I hadn't seen that look for so long because I hadn't let him see my true self for so long. I took a deep breath and spoke in a rush, spilling out the whole story, how I'd found out that I was Monty's daughter.

When I was finished he didn't say anything. He was facing me with the sun at his back so I couldn't see his expression. The silence seemed to swell around us. "That's not all," I said. "I think Monty was really Mary Foley's child, which means—"

Jess leaned forward and I saw that the light in his eyes had expanded to a warm glow that enveloped me. When he touched my hand all my anger at the things he'd said melted and longing for him flared in its place. "It means," he said, "that you're Mary's granddaughter. And so her story *is* your story."

Then he kissed me. His lips were dry and feverish. I pulled away from him and laid my hand flat on his chest. "I'm still mad at you. You said awful things to me."

"It was the Vicodin." His expression was so innocent I burst out laughing.

He grinned and struggled to his feet. "Come on, help me upstairs and I'll make it up to you."

I fully meant to keep my distance until we'd talked through everything, but he needed me to help him up the stairs and having him close like that made it hard to stay angry at him. He'd always been good at disarming my anger. It wasn't so much that he made it go away as he turned it into something else. When I got him to our room, he fell heavily into bed and pulled me with him. I was still angry with him, but the anger felt like an extra charge that made my blood fizz when he kissed me. I kissed him back, hard, and felt him flinch when I bit his lip. He didn't pull away, though, just kissed me harder, his lips tasting like blood, our skin sparking where we touched, as though we were igniting a fire that would burn through all that had gone wrong between us—if it didn't burn down Riven House first.

Chapter Eighteen

Afterward, we lay in bed and I told Jess everything that I'd learned in Elizabeth Foley's diary. Jess was a good listener when he liked a story and he liked this one. He was quiet through the part about Mary giving the baby to her sister and then the part where Elizabeth gave the baby to Bayard, but when I mentioned that Bayard's shirt cuffs were damp and pink he shouted out, "The smoking gun! Obviously the babies were switched."

It was the same conclusion I'd come to but I challenged it now. "We don't know that for sure."

"No," he admitted, "but it's not really that important. What's important is that you've found out who *your* parents are. Why did you finally decide to go looking for your adoption papers?"

I told him that finding out what had happened to Mary's baby had made me want to find out who my parents were. As I said it, leaving out the conversations I'd had with Sunny and Katrine, it *felt* true.

"Of course," Jess said, pulling me closer to him, "why should Monty learn who his mother was and not you?"

"Yes," I said, grateful that he got what I hadn't even understood at the time. "I was lucky that clerk at St. Anne's was willing to show me the file."

"Ah, the threshold helper. Was she old and wrinkled like Yoda?"

"No," I laughed, "but she did have silvery hair and was dressed all in purple."

"In your book give her cat earrings," he suggested.

"She *did* have cat earrings," I cried, leaning up on my elbow. "How did you know?"

"Because I know how stories work," he said, smiling. "Go on . . ."

So I told him about finding Monty's name on the certificate and driving home and confronting Sunny. I realized when I got to this part that having left out my earlier conversation with Sunny it might not make sense that I went to Sunny with the information, but once again Jess came to my rescue and filled in the plot hole.

"Of course! Sunny was living here in 1978; she'd have known your mother."

When I told Jess about Amy I was afraid he'd make fun of her pretentions and fantasies, but instead he said, "Poor kid, just the kind of impressionable young student to fall under Monty's spell."

"Yes!" I agreed, glad Jess got it. No one who hadn't sat through Monty's classes at Bailey would understand the spell he cast. *What's so special about the guy?* Dunstan had asked once when I was going on about Monty. "She must have been crushed when Monty left. No wonder she started . . ." I was going to say *seeing ghosts,* but amended it to "coming unhinged."

"That's why she gave you up," Jess said gently, stroking my hair. "If Monty had been here . . ."

"Sunny says that he wouldn't have wanted me anyway," I said, biting my lip to keep from crying.

"I'm sure that's what Sunny wanted to believe. After all,

Monty had refused to have children with her and she lost her daughter through her own negligence. She was jealous of Amy—just like she's jealous of you now. That's why she doesn't want you to tell Monty."

"She says she's afraid for his heart."

Jess snorted. "It will be *good* for his heart. He's going to be thrilled to find out you're his daughter. He already acts like you are."

I looked at Jess warily for signs of his previous jealousy over Monty's attention to me, but they seemed to have vanished. Maybe it was easier for Jess to think that Monty valued me as a daughter rather than as a writer—and after all, he would now be Monty's son-in-law.

"I hope he'll be pleased, but still it'll be a shock. We should think about the best way to tell him."

"I say we slap the birth certificate down by his breakfast Muesli and say 'Good morning, Pops!' first thing tomorrow morning."

I laughed but said, "No, Sunny's right. We should wait until after the parade."

"Sunny just wants a few more hours as the *chosen one*," Jess said, but at the sight of me frowning he tightened his grip around my shoulder. "But if that's what you want, Lady Montague, that's what we'll do. You *are* the lady of the house. Your wish is my command . . . Hey, I just thought of something!"

"What?" I asked wriggling down into the crook below his shoulder.

"It's a good thing you didn't marry Dusty. Doesn't this, like, mean you two are cousins?"

I AWOKE IN the middle of the night to the sound of my childhood nightmares. *Thump-drag, thump-drag, thump-drag.* Great-

Granny Jackson had found me and was coming to wrap her bony hands around my neck. *Intruder! Bastard spawn! You don't belong here.*

But I did belong here, I could tell her now. I'd finally found where I belonged.

That realization brought me fully awake. I was in my bed in Riven House—alone. The sound I was hearing was Jess limping around the rotunda, heading toward Minnie's Mourning Room. He must have woken up with an idea and gone to write it down. Riven House was good for him and now I'd be able to make sure he could stay here. Once Monty knew I was his daughter he'd want us to stay for good. And someday, when Monty was gone . . .

I squelched the thought. Even if Monty was thrilled that I was his daughter it didn't mean he was going to give me Riven House. I wasn't even sure I'd want it. The house was probably encumbered by debts and liens . . . or whatever old houses were encumbered by. Riven House had the feel of a place that was *encumbered* with more than just financial losses.

There was enough moonlight coming through the window that I didn't have to turn the bedside lamp on to find my way to the bathroom. I wouldn't need to even if there were no moon, I thought, because I *knew* this house. Knew the feel of the hardwood floors under my bare feet and the wavy patterns the moonlight made streaming through the cockled glass windows. I knew how the rotunda would look lit up in the moonlight and how the painted apple blossoms on the library doors would be shimmering in the silver light. Moonlight was spilling through the house, cleaning it of the bloodstains, making the house whole again. My being here would make it whole again.

In the bathroom I stopped and looked out the window over the lawn and toward the pond. The grass was covered by a rime of frost that glittered like spun sugar—like those Christmas decorations Elizabeth Foley had written about in her diary. Poor Elizabeth! Had she figured out that Alden Montague was her sister's son? Or did she die thinking she'd handed her sister's child over to his murderer? As I turned away from the window I saw her handing the baby over to Bayard, his hands bloody . . .

There was something red lying in the tub: a dark spatter on the gleaming white enamel that I knew I'd scrubbed clean last night. I crossed the few feet to the tub, the bathroom tiles icy under my feet, and peered over the rim. No, not blood. The dark splatter was a piece of patterned cloth. I picked it up and held it under the moonlight. It was a handkerchief embroidered with flowers and the initials MNM. Minerva Noyes Montague. Minnie's handkerchief here in the tub where she had miscarried and then years later bled to death. It wasn't embroidered with flowers; it was stained with blood.

IN THE MORNING I saw that the handkerchief wasn't stained with blood but with some kind of red ink. I was tempted to show it to Sunny to see what she thought it meant, but she was in a frenzy getting ready for the parade and I was no longer sure that she was an unbiased witness. She might use it as a reason not to tell Monty he was my father.

So I hid the handkerchief in my dresser and got ready to go to the parade. Jess said he'd stay home. He told Monty that his ankle was bothering him, but I guessed he was too annoyed with Sunny to want to see her reveling in her success.

She did, indeed, revel. I watched the parade from the front porch of the library with CJ Brennan, who provided a running commentary of the participants. "Here's the 4-H club," she announced. "That's my niece Sadie leading her alpaca, Pippa. And here are the volunteer firemen carrying Sunny's skeletons."

The loose-jointed skeletons strutted down the street in front of each dark-clothed fireman. It was a brilliant juxtaposition of brawny men—and a few sturdy women—in their red fireman caps and the white-boned, grinning skeleton puppets. Although I'd seen the puppets hanging in Sunny's barn, it was something else to see them in action. Witches swooped over the heads of the crowd on their broomsticks, piloted by women in flowing dresses. I recognized my eighth grade English teacher, the clerk from the Village Hall, and a philosophy professor from Bailey.

The witches were followed by a horse-drawn wagon filled with bins of apples, pumpkins, and squash. A white-garbed figure floated over the wagon. I thought I recognized the witch puppet Sunny had called Griselda, only she had changed since I saw her last. She wore a wreath of apples and apple blossoms and her cheeks were rouged with bright red circles. A woman dressed in white and wearing the same kind of wreath rode in front of the wagon, waving to the crowd like a beauty pageant queen. A white-haired man, also dressed in white and a straw hat, sat beside her. With a start, I recognized Monty—and the wreathed woman beside him as Sunny.

"Is she supposed to be—"

"The Apple Blossom Queen," CJ said. "I wondered if you had told her about your research, but she told me that she got the idea from Monty. She said she wanted to turn a figure of . . . let me see if I can get this right . . . *patriarchal objectification of women into an archetype of female empowerment*. And look . . ." CJ pointed to the crowd bringing up the rear of the parade. "They're giving out apples!"

A dozen little girls dressed in long white dresses and wearing apple wreaths were carrying baskets full of apples that they were giving out to the crowds. One came running up the steps of the library to hand an apple to CJ.

"Look at me, Auntie Cee, I'm an apple princess!"

The girl turned to me and I shuddered. Her cheeks had been rouged the same red as the apple in her hand and her eyes made up to look like a child beauty contestant's. I took an apple from her, forcing a smile. I felt suddenly ill. I muttered a hurried excuse to CJ and fled, pushing my way through the crowds, toward the municipal lot where my car was parked. The crowd swept forward, though, and I found myself trailing the apple cart. I could see the back of Sunny's head. She was leaning toward Monty, whispering something that made Monty laugh. The little apple blossom girls rode in the cart, their rouged cheeks and made-up eyes making them look like dolls—

They were dolls—or puppets rather—papier-mâché facsimiles of the apple blossom girl. Sunny had reduced the figure of Mary Foley—my grandmother—into a meaningless grinning dummy. Sunny making herself the Apple Blossom Queen and Monty her king was a grotesque parody of Bayard Montague's abduction of Mary Foley. My ears were buzzing with the noise of the crowd and I broke into a cold sweat as I tried to break free. If I didn't get some air I would drown. I stumbled and started to go under—I would be trampled underfoot, a sacrifice to the great pagan goddess—

Someone grabbed my arm and yanked me up and out of the stream of people. I looked up and saw Dunstan. He led me to a bench next to the municipal lot, sat me down, and made me put my head between my knees.

"Breathe, Clare," he said, just as he had when I got panic attacks at pep rallies and Fourth of July parades. I never had done well with crowds.

When the ringing in my ears stopped I sat up and Dunstan handed me a water bottle. "Okay?" he asked after I had taken a long gulp.

I nodded. "It was just the crowd and those dreadful puppets."

Dunstan laughed. "Yeah, Sunny kind of went off the deep end this year. She asked Corbett's to donate the apples, which we were happy to do, but when I saw my niece got up in that outfit . . . well, it seemed kind of wrong."

"I'm sure Sunny thinks she's celebrating the harvest, but given what happened to Mary Foley—"

"It's like she's celebrating statutory rape."

I looked up at him, grateful that he understood. No wonder he had always guessed my moods so well—we were related! "I'm sorry about yesterday. About what Jess said to you."

"Hey," he said, "if I were in his place I'd be jealous too— wait, I *was* in his place and I expressed myself in manure."

I laughed. "Still, he shouldn't have said those things. He was in pain and on Vicodin—"

"Ah." Dunstan nodded. "No wonder he didn't want to take the blood test. I shouldn't have come down so hard on him. It was just . . ."

He looked away. "When I heard there'd been an accident at Riven House my first thought was that it had been you. And if it were you . . ." He looked back at me, the look in his eyes far from cousinly. "If I thought for a minute he had done anything to hurt you, Clary, I'd kill him."

Chapter Nineteen

Dunstan offered to drive me back to Riven House but I convinced him I was all right to drive. I wasn't, but I knew that if Jess saw me arriving in Dunstan's police car it would set him off again. I clenched the steering wheel and took deep breaths to steady myself but when I turned onto River Road and saw the apple cart in front of me I broke out in a cold sweat. I had to follow behind it all the way to the Riven House gate, watching Monty and Sunny waving at cars passing in the opposite direction that honked at them as though they were cheering on a newlywed couple. It took all my willpower not to bump them with the Subaru's fender, but the thought of those papier-mâché dolls rolling off the back of the pickup made me nauseous.

I followed them as far as the fork in the drive and then drove up to the house. I knew there'd be a celebration at the barn but I was in no mood for it. In no mood, either, for the delivery van from Hudson Gourmet parked under the apple tree beside the boot hall door.

"You're in the wrong place," I told the delivery boy—a gawky teenager who had the hawk nose and close-set eyes of the Brennans. "The party's down at the barn."

"Mr. Monty said up at the big house," the boy said, jerking his chin at Riven House.

Mr. Monty? The big house? I was about to ask him what century he thought we were living in when my cell phone pinged for a text message. Who could it be? I wondered. I hadn't gotten a text in months.

I took the phone out and was amazed to see it came from Monty's cell, which he hardly ever used and certainly never texted on.

Put the champagne on ice! Big celebration tonight!

"What the hell?" My sentiments were echoed by Jess, who'd appeared at the boot hall door holding up his cell phone.

"Someone must have shown him how—" I began. Both our phones pinged again. Another text from Monty, this one containing a picture of a champagne bottle.

"An emoji?" Jess asked, dumbfounded.

"One of Sunny's helpers must be texting for him." I looked back at the delivery boy. "Let me guess, you have some champagne for us?"

"A case," he said, reaching into the van. "Dom Pérignon. And food. Where do you want me to put it all?"

Jess helped him bring the boxes through the boot hall and into the kitchen while I unpacked. There were roast squabs, quiches, salads, and a cake from the fancy French bakery in Rhinebeck.

"And caviar!" Jess exclaimed. "The really expensive stuff!"

"I guess Monty is throwing Sunny a party to celebrate the parade."

"Nah, this is something else. I think Sunny must've told him that you're his daughter and he wants to celebrate. That's why he got all this prepared food, so you wouldn't have to cook for your own celebration."

"I don't know," I said doubtfully. "Why would Sunny tell him?"

"So she could confess that she kept you from him thirty-five years ago before you told him. That's why she wanted to wait until after the parade."

I thought of Monty leaning his head down and Sunny whispering in his ear. Had she been telling him, then spinning a story that excused her lying to him thirty-five years ago? I could imagine her finding a way to use her grief over Anya as an excuse for keeping another child out of Riven House.

". . . the important thing," Jess was saying, "is that all this shows how thrilled Monty is that you're his daughter."

"I suppose," I said, trying to repress the smile tugging at my mouth. "I guess I should set the table and get this all laid out."

"No way," Jess said, "I'll do that. You go up and get dressed. Put on that green dress that you wore to my KGB reading last year. The one that shimmies over your hips." He grabbed me by the hips and pulled me to him. I gaped at Jess, equally amazed that he was offering to set a table and that he recalled an item from my wardrobe.

"Are you sure?" I asked. "I could help you and still have time to dress."

"I've got this," he said, giving me a little push to send me on my way, his hands lingering on my hips. "Take your time. Have a good long bath."

I'D AVOIDED THE bathtub since I'd found it full of bloody water, but the idea of a long soak sounded good. My muscles were sore from the tension I'd felt in the parade. *You carry your anger in your shoulders,* a chiropractor had once told me reprovingly, as if I might have carried it in some chiropractor-approved er-gonomic handbag instead.

I rinsed out the tub, scrutinizing the enamel for any traces of blood, then turned on the hot water tap. The hot water would run out before it filled and end up just warm enough by the time it was full—if Sunny hadn't used up too much hot water this morning. If there were going to be four of us living here I should talk to Monty about getting a new hot water heater. He seemed to have enough money to splurge on champagne and caviar.

But then maybe he would think me asking for home im-provements now was presuming on our new relationship. I didn't want him to think I expected money from him because he was my biological father.

I poured bath salts in the tub and swirled them around to make them dissolve, breathing in the crisp scent of rosemary and mint—better than the cloying smell of apple blossoms for covering the metallic tang of blood. I'd hang rosemary and mint in all the closets, I thought as I stepped into the tub, and sew sachets for the drawers. In the spring I'd air out the whole house and talk to Monty about repairing the broken windows in the attic and having the skylight cleaned. Riven House would be like new again. Even houses should have second chances, just as Jess and I were getting a second chance.

I soaked until the water cooled and the light coming in through the window turned violet. Then I got out and toweled off, wishing the rosemary-mint scent would stay with me. On a whim, I rinsed out my nightgown—a delicate batiste chemise I'd found in a trunk and bleached new—in the bath salts and hung it over the shower ring. I opened the window so that the breeze would dry it out. By bedtime it would be dry and still smell of rosemary and mint. Jess would love it.

I put on the green dress that Jess liked. It did shimmy over my hips. I felt like water spilling down the steps of the rotunda as I came down the stairs, the marble cool through the thin soles of my ballet flats. I wasn't holding my anger anymore, I was letting it spill out of me.

Someone—Jess? Or Sunny, more likely—had lit votive candles in the niches around the ground floor of the rotunda. I followed the sound of voices into the library. A table had been set in front of the fireplace. I really should talk to Monty about renovating the dining room . . .

"Ah, here she is, the real apple blossom girl!" Monty cried. He was seated at the table, his chair angled to be closer to the fire, but he stood as I came in—and so did Jess. Only Sunny remained seated, in a chair close to Monty's, the firelight limning her hair so that she looked like a pre-Raphaelite sibyl. "You gave me the idea for the parade float. I told Sunny"—he turned toward her and smiled—"that if the apple blossom girl could be restored to Riven House she should be restored to village."

I smiled uneasily. He was waiting for my reaction, swaying slightly, the glow of firelight on his white suit making him seem frail and insubstantial. If I told him how much I had hated the float he'd be crushed.

"It was something!" I said, too brightly, turning to Sunny. "What a lot of work you must have done to make all those dolls and costumes!"

She smiled, her eyes shining in the firelight. "Doing the work of the muse is never a toil."

Out of the corner of my eye I caught Jess rolling his eyes. "No, I imagine not. Was it the muse who inspired you to dress up as the apple blossom girl yourself?"

"Yes, at first I thought I was too old for the part, but then I realized that if you think of the apple blossom girl as a fertility symbol, then she is young in the spring, but on Samhain she assumes the face of the winter goddess——"

"Is that what you are now?" Jess asked. "The winter goddess?"

I frowned at Jess. He had a half-full glass of champagne in his hand. Mixing alcohol with Vicodin had apparently sharpened his tongue. But Sunny seemed unoffended.

"Quite right," Sunny replied with a tight smile. "Only I prefer *crone*. Monty, dear, you should sit. You know what your doctor said about standing in one place."

"That I'd grow roots or some such nonsense! I'll sit when I'm dead. Right now I'm going to make a toast."

He poured a glass of champagne for me and motioned for Jess and Sunny to raise their glasses. "To all the goddesses in the room, of spring and youth," he toasted me. "And winter and the silver years." He tilted his glass toward Sunny. "And to the lucky bastards who get to enjoy their company." He pointed his glass at Jess. "God knows I reveled in the former in my salad days and now as I approach the twilight of my years I count myself lucky to be surrounded by beauty of both varieties. I probably don't deserve it . . ." He paused and I noticed that his eyes were shining in the firelight. I was alarmed to think he might cry. I wanted to tell him that I forgave him for not saving me from the Jacksons all those years ago, but I had to wait until he acknowledged me. "But hell, what man ever does deserve the love of a good woman, eh, Jess? And this good woman"—he swung his glass around to Sunny, champagne sloshing over its rim—"has conceded to me not once, but twice. In short, Sunny and I have decided to renew our vows and take up where we left off."

"*Renew* your vows?" Jess asked.

Sunny laughed. "You've confused them, Alden. They don't know we're already married."

"Already married?" I asked. "But when? You didn't say . . ." *When I told you I was Monty's daughter,* I almost said.

"Oh, way back in '79," Monty answered for her.

"It was '78," Sunny corrected.

The year I was born. No wonder Sunny hadn't wanted to tell Monty about Amy's baby.

"I was going to be deported otherwise."

"You make it sound so businesslike. We were a couple, of course, only I didn't really believe in marriage back then. We were still hippies! But Sunny had lost her visa . . . Well, that doesn't matter. What matters is that we've come together again now. And that I have a whole family around me." He raised his champagne glass again. His hand was trembling. Sunny was right. It wasn't good for him to stand so long. I moved toward him to help him into his chair.

"Yes, here's to your reunited family," Jess said, holding up his glass. "It's not every man who gets a wife and a daughter in the same day."

Monty's eyebrows drew together. "Daughter?"

So Sunny hadn't told him.

"Maybe this isn't the best time." I glared at Jess.

"What better time?" Jess asked. "We've got champagne, we're all here. Why, I even have the birth certificate!" He retrieved the folded Xeroxed sheet from his vest pocket and shook it out like a magician turning an ordinary handkerchief into a bouquet of roses. Presto! Clare Jackson becomes Clare Montague! Monty put down his glass and took the sheet of paper, patting his jacket for his reading glasses.

"Maybe you should sit," I said, putting my hand on Monty's elbow. Beneath the worn linen of his jacket his arm felt skeletal.

"Yes, Alden, I wanted to tell you about this when you would have a chance to absorb the news—"

"You knew?" The eyes he lifted from the paper were no longer the weak watery eyes of an old man but the piercing ice blue daggers I remembered from class when someone said something foolish. "It says here that Amy Birnbach had a baby and that *I* was the father." He shook the paper in Sunny's face. "Did you know?"

"I . . . I . . ." Sunny stammered. "Amy didn't want you to know."

All the color drained from Monty's face and beads of sweat broke out on his brow. Wasn't that a sign of a heart attack? Sunny had been right. Learning that he was my father was giving Monty a heart attack. He couldn't even look at me. All he seemed to care about was that he had been lied to, betrayed by a woman. I felt something squeezing my own heart, as though in sympathy with Monty's, and cold sweat prickling my skin as if my veins had been suddenly filled with ice water.

"So it's true?" Monty asked, still looking at Sunny.

"True she had a baby, but I didn't know if it was yours. It could have been anyone's."

Monty turned to me. "And when did you find out about this, Clare?"

"Just yesterday," Jess answered for me. I couldn't speak. Jess got up and put his arm around me but I could hardly feel it. I had turned to ice. "She got the birth certificate from St. Anne's. Sunny asked her to wait until after the parade to tell you. When I saw the champagne I thought she'd told you—that all this was a celebration for Clare."

Monty looked at the table set with champagne and caviar on toast points and laughed—a harsh bark like something breaking. I felt something wet streak down my face. I looked at Sunny and saw that her face was wet too, but not with tears. Tears wouldn't have soaked her hair and streaked her face with red. She looked up—we all did—to the ceiling. A long crack branched across the ceiling like an accusing finger pointing at Sunny, rust-colored water dripping from its fingertip.

Not rust. Blood.

Sunny screamed.

"It's the bath," I said, meaning to reassure her. "I must have left it on—"

But she was already running from the room, into the rotunda and up the stairs. Monty took a step to follow her but stumbled. He was patting his hand against his chest. "Pills," he gasped.

Jess understood more quickly than me. He reached inside Monty's jacket and retrieved a small bottle.

"Stay with him," I cried and went to follow Sunny. I ran up the marble steps, which felt slippery under my smooth soles, as if they were coated with ice. I must have left the bath on when I rinsed out my nightgown, I thought. That was all it was. The ghosts were gone.

But when I got to the bathroom and saw Sunny's face I knew they weren't. She had slid to the floor, her white dress soaked, weeping. I stepped through the red water and looked into the tub. Floating beneath the surface was the body of a little girl, her dress swirling around her—

I blinked and the "body" resolved into a length of cloth eddying in the water.

"It's just my nightgown," I said, dredging up the wet cloth. "It must have fallen in the tub after I hung it up to dry."

But at the sight of the dripping cloth Sunny moaned and bolted from the room. I stayed behind only long enough to turn off the taps and throw the wet nightgown over the shower ring . . . and to fish out another piece of cloth from the tub. It was the handkerchief I had found—Minnie's handkerchief.

The red dye spreading in the water was what had turned the bath red. I wrung it out and put it over the bathroom ring too.

Then I turned to follow Sunny. By the time I got downstairs she wasn't in the rotunda. I went into the library and found Jess sitting beside Monty. He'd wrapped an afghan around him and given him a glass of water. He still looked pale, but some color was returning to his cheeks.

"Did you see where Sunny went?" I asked Jess.

"I think she went out through the boot hall," he said. "I heard the door slam."

"I'd better go after her—" But before I could go Monty grabbed my arm, his grip surprisingly strong.

"Leave her," he rasped. "I want to talk to you."

I sat on the hassock by his side. "You don't have to say anything right now, Monty. I didn't want you to find out this way . . . I know it's a lot to take in."

"It's the best news I could ever get," he said, squeezing my hand so hard I had to grit my teeth to keep from crying out. "To find out you're my daughter . . ." His eyes welled up.

"We don't even know for sure. Amy could have lied—"

"No! I know it's true. I think I've always known . . ." He grimaced and I looked up anxiously at Jess.

"Did you call 911?"

"He didn't want me to. I called his cardiologist. He's on his way."

One of the perks of being a Montague, I found myself thinking before reminding myself that *I* was a Montague now.

I tried to convince Monty to go down to his apartment and get into bed, but he refused. We stayed by the fire until the doctor came and he had listened to Monty's heart.

"I think it was just a touch of angina," he told us. "No sense dragging him out on such a cold night. Keep him warm and comfortable and bring him into my office tomorrow for an EKG." He gave Monty a sedative and left.

Jess helped Monty down to his apartment while I made some hot tea with plenty of milk and sugar. *For shock,* Sunny would say.

Staring out the kitchen windows over the north lawn I tried to make out the light of Sunny's barn through the trees but an icy rain was falling, obscuring the view. The doctor had been right—it was too cold a night to be out. I hoped that Sunny was warm inside her barn, finding solace with her *children.* In the morning I'd talk to Monty and convince him to forgive her for keeping my birth a secret. Riven House was big enough for both of us.

I ran into Jess in the boot hall. "He's already asleep," Jess told me, taking the tray from me. "Besides, I don't think he'd like you to see the apartment. 'Clare will be disappointed at what a messy old bachelor I am,'" Jess said, mimicking Monty's fussy quaver down to a tee. "And it really is like some groovy bachelor digs circa 1978. The most modern piece of equipment is a fax machine. Honestly, who faxes anymore?"

We drank the tea in the library by the dying fire and then went up to bed where we huddled together under the comforters listening to the icy rain lashing against the windows and roof. I fell asleep thinking of roof tiles and furnaces. In my dreams I heard a bell ringing but when I went looking for it I found it was the sound of water leaking through the oculus and striking the marble steps. I roamed the house checking for leaks and putting pails under drips. But there was still water everywhere. It was rising from the pond, I realized, so I went down the hill, floating over the ice-rimed lawn on a flying carpet of fog. The water wasn't rising from the pond, I saw, it was coming from the barn. I could hear someone weeping there, their tears, like Alice's in Wonderland, flooding the barn and the surrounding woods. I floated over the floodwaters and into the barn where I saw that it was the apple blossom girl puppets who were weeping, crying because their dresses had gotten soaked.

I hung them all up from the rafters so they would dry. I hung them in a circle facing each other so they wouldn't be alone and then I drifted back up to the house, which was warm and dry and light . . .

I woke up with the sun in my eyes, alone in my bed. I was wearing the batiste nightgown that I'd rinsed out the night before, only it was still damp. No wonder I'd dreamed of floods! I grabbed one of Jess's flannel shirts to put on as I crossed to the window and looked outside, half expecting to see a wasteland of water where Sunny's barn stood, but there was only the sun shining on a thin glaze of ice and a figure running up the hill, slipping on the ice . . .

It was Noelle, yelling something as she ran.

I pulled on jeans and a sweater and ran down the stairs. I heard a door open and voices out on the lawn—Jess and Noelle and Monty. I caught up with them halfway down the hill, Monty leaning heavily on Jess's arm and slipping on the ice. The sensation of sliding down the hill was like it was in my dream, only when we got to the barn there was no flood, only puppets hanging in a circle, their painted faces all pointed toward a puppet hanging in the center. A horrible puppet with a bloated lopsided head and a blue face. Only it wasn't a puppet. It was Sunny.

Chapter Twenty

We waited outside the barn for the police to come. I would have liked to take Monty back to the house, but he insisted on standing outside in the cold and damp in his bedroom slippers and dressing gown. It was a silk burgundy robe with gold braid piping and a crest over the chest pocket with his monogram. There were tears along the shoulder seams and the cuffs were unraveling. Dark stains spread across the chest and hem. With his white hair standing up all over his head he looked like Ebenezer Scrooge visited by the Ghost of Christmas Past. Or like a ghost himself. The cheerful man who'd ridden in the parade float yesterday was gone.

We waited in silence, the only sound the foghorns of passing ships on the river, until the Concord Police patrol car pulled up. Then, as if the sight of Dunstan Corbett getting out of the cruiser had woken him, Monty grasped my hand and whispered hoarsely, "Let me do the talking."

As if there were some question of what had happened and Monty didn't trust Jess or me with the story. I could see why he might not want Jess, who was already bristling at the sight of Dunstan, to take the lead, but what was he afraid of me saying?

Monty straightened up and pulled the lapels of his robe together as if it were a suit jacket and not a shabby dressing gown. "Thank you for coming so quickly, Officer," he said, reaching out his hand to shake Dunstan's.

Dunstan hesitated, his eyes cutting toward me. I could read his thoughts clearly. Monty was acting as if he were the lord of the manor welcoming the local constable to a charity picnic. The old Dunstan would have said something cutting, but he grasped Monty's hand in his and replied, "We always respond quickly to a suspicious death. Is the body in here? Are you sure she's dead?"

"I'm afraid so," Monty said, blocking the entrance to the barn. "And I'm afraid there's no suspicion about it. Poor Sunny. If I'd known she meant to do herself harm I would have insisted she stay at the house last night after dinner."

"Is that the last time you saw her?" Dunstan put his hands on his hips, his eyes glued to the barn door. He didn't like being kept from the body, but he also wasn't about to push a frail old man out of the way.

"Yes. We had a celebration for her success at the parade. Did you see the parade, Officer?"

"Yes, I did. Everyone seemed to love it. Was Miss Gruenwald unhappy about anything to do with it—or about anything else last night? Anything that might have led her to take her own life?"

"Ah," Monty sighed. "That's the thing. She was *ecstatic* over her success—flying high!"

"Then why—" Dunstan began, his jaw clenching with frustration.

"You see," Monty said, laying his hand on Dunstan's shoulder, "what nonartists don't understand is that sometimes success can be as emotionally difficult as failure. It raises one's expectations, lifts one up into the clouds. The drop can be . . ." Monty's voice trembled as he looked toward the barn. ". . . precipitous."

I saw Dunstan's face harden just as it had when I told him he didn't understand what the big deal was about Monty's class because he wasn't a writer.

"I suppose I'll just have to do my best evaluating the situation as a *nonartist*." As Dunstan moved toward the barn, Monty stepped backward, tottering dangerously. I grabbed his arm to steady him.

"You don't have to go back in there," I said. Another police car had arrived, followed by a white van, which I supposed would take Sunny away after the police had examined the barn. "Why don't we go up to the house and wait," I suggested. But Monty shook his head and, leaning heavily on my arm, steered us through the barn door.

The second police officer was taking pictures of Sunny from every angle. Dunstan stood just below Sunny, hands on hips, staring up at her. I looked away from Sunny's horribly bloated face, but looking at the puppets was not much better. Nor was Dunstan's face when my gaze caught his.

"Were the puppets like this when Miss Gruenwald left the barn yesterday afternoon?"

I shook my head. "You'd have to ask Noelle or one of the other volunteers. I wasn't here."

Dunstan narrowed his eyes at me. *I can always tell when you're lying,* he'd said. I wasn't lying about not being down here yesterday, but I was remembering the dream of floating down to the barn, hanging up the puppets to keep them out of the water . . . my ears ringing as if *I* were the one under water . . .

"Officer Ryan, talk to the volunteers who worked here yesterday while I take Ms. Martin's statement." Then Dunstan had his hand on my arm and was piloting me out of the barn toward his squad car, saying something about his notepad being in the car. I looked back and saw Jess stepping forward to say something and Monty holding him back, a worried expression on his face. What was he afraid I would say? That Sunny had killed herself because they fought . . . ? Then I knew what it was. Dunstan had called Sunny *Miss Gruenwald*. He didn't know that she and Monty were married. Didn't they always say that the husband is the first suspect in a wife's murder? Was Monty afraid that he would be accused of killing Sunny? Perhaps to avoid Sunny demanding her share of his estate? Of course that was absurd. Monty was too old and frail to have strung Sunny up on those rafters—

Unless he had help.

And who would help him but his caretaker—Jess.

But what possible motive would Jess have to help Monty kill Sunny—unless it was because his wife had just found out that she was Monty's daughter and would inherit Riven House after Monty's death—*unless Monty had a wife who would inherit instead.*

I broke out in an icy sweat and would have stumbled if Dunstan hadn't been holding my arm. I shook the thought away. I was letting my imagination run away with me—letting it *use* me. Dunstan didn't know that Sunny and Monty were married or that I was Monty's daughter.

At least not yet.

He opened the passenger door for me, pushed me inside, and closed the door. While he walked around to the driver's side I took a deep breath and rubbed my hands on my jeans to dry them off. I had to think. Should I tell Dunstan that Sunny was Monty's wife and that I was his daughter? Dunstan would find out sooner or later. Sunny and Monty's marriage would show up in her records. That woman who showed me my adoption records at St. Anne's might tell someone. As Dunstan had said, Concord was a small town. If he found out from someone else and knew I had deliberately withheld the information from him he would be suspicious.

"At least you didn't throw me in the back with handcuffs," I said when Dunstan got in the car. "So I suppose you're not arresting me."

"Not yet," he said without smiling. He turned and fixed me with those blue Corbett eyes. "But that can change real quick, Clary. I can tell you're not telling the truth about something. And I know that Montague, with his whole lord-of-the-manor act, is leaving something out."

"He is, but only because he's embarrassed. You see, it turns out Monty and Sunny are married—did you know that?— and they'd just gotten back together after Dale's accident . . ." I told the whole story. Dunstan only broke his silence when I got to the part about finding Monty's name on my birth certificate.

"That bastard! Getting his student pregnant—"

"That's why he left it out," I said quickly. "He's embarrassed—as he should be."

By the end I'd told everything but the part about the overflowing tub and Sunny screaming at the sight of my nightgown. I'd told him about Anya, though, and how I thought the apple blossom dolls were a kind of tribute to her and that me turning out to be Amy Birnbach's daughter had brought it all back for her.

"I feel like it's all my fault," I said toward the end. "Sunny thought she was getting a second chance with Monty, but when Monty found out she'd kept my birth from him he was angry. I'm sure he would have gotten over it, but she must have thought he didn't need her since he'd found me. I'm afraid she was jealous of me—"

Dunstan's harsh laugh stopped me. "She wouldn't be the first."

"What do you mean?"

He snorted. "Come on, Clary. For a smart girl you can be awfully dumb sometimes. Half the girls in high school were jealous of you—for your looks, your brains, your . . ."

"For my hunky boyfriend?" I suggested, smiling for the first time this morning. The icy glare of Dunstan's gaze softened into a summery blue. He believed me. And why shouldn't he? I'd only told him the truth.

"Yeah, that too," he said, his voice hoarse. He shook his head. "You need to be careful, Clary. This damned house—"

He was cut off by a sharp rap against the glass. His eyes flicked past me to my window. For a moment I had the horrible thought that when I turned I would be looking into the bloated face of Sunny's ghost—but it was only Jess. He was leaning down, his face blurry through the glass. I lowered the window.

"If you're done with my wife, Officer, Mr. Montague is having chest pains and he wants Clare to go to the hospital with us."

A skeptical look crossed Dunstan's face, but then, perhaps remembering that Monty was my father, he only said, "Yeah, I'm done with her."

MONTY ASSURED ME in the car that he wasn't really having chest pains. "I only wanted to get you away from that police officer. Was he badgering you? What did you tell him?"

When I admitted I'd told Dunstan that Sunny and Monty were married Jess groaned.

"No, it's fine, Jess," Monty said. "Clare did the right thing. He'd have found out anyway. Better it come from a pretty girl." Monty grinned. "What did he say, Clare?"

He said half the girls in high school were jealous of me, I thought. *He said to be careful.*

"Nothing much," I answered. "I don't think he suspects anything."

"It wouldn't matter if he did," Jess said. "We were all in the house last night. We can all attest to that."

We rode the rest of the way in silence. Perhaps Monty and Jess were thinking that they couldn't really attest to the others' whereabouts in the middle of the night, but I was thinking about what Dunstan had said about half the girls in high school being jealous of me. How was that possible, I wondered, when I was jealous of *all* of them? And not just the girls. I was jealous of all the kids whose parents came to the games and plays and concerts beaming with pride at their progeny. Even the kids with drunks and meth-heads for parents. Even Charity Jane with her big chaotic family and hand-me-down clothes and her naked ambition to be the best. At least when Charity Jane burst into tears when I got the Bailey scholarship her mother was there to hug her. Trudy hadn't even come to the assembly. I told myself that it didn't matter, that I was the one going to Bailey in the fall. I already suspected that the kids at Bailey wouldn't care if their parents showed up at Honors Assembly.

And they didn't. The Bailey students acted like they didn't *have* families—or they acted like they despised them. But there were a host of other things they cared about that I knew nothing about: obscure foreign films, the best single malt scotch labels, the best New York City vegan bakeries, where to ski, where to intern, the post-grad programs to get you a job in publishing (never mind that they cost more than I made in a

year working at the farm stand)—a whole new host of reasons
to be jealous. But even there I'd used that jealousy to do better.
I was the one who got into Monty's senior seminar, and the one
who got a job at Broadway Books right out of college, and the
one who married Jess Martin, who sold his first novel only a
year after we graduated.

But even after I married Jess and we were living in the loft
in Williamsburg, going to readings and book launches, I realized
that what we thought of as a lot of money was nothing compared
to what our classmates had in trust funds and inheritances. They
might make a big deal of not *living* on their families' money, but
when they lost a job or didn't get the next freelance assignment,
they had something to fall back on. We didn't. It was when our
debts were piling up that I was most beset with envy—of the
young mothers I saw lingering over coffee at the Williamsburg
cafés, the interns clothed in boho chic Anthropologie dresses
I could no longer afford, at our friends flying to Costa Rica for
Christmas—a corrosive jealousy because there was no exam to
take or scholarship to win to get what they had—the ease of
being born into money. And that was the worst thing to envy: the
warm circle of family protection when you were standing outside
in the cold. Poor Sunny. That's how she must have felt when she
fled the house last night.

I dropped Jess and Monty off at the front of the hospital.
Watching Jess help Monty through the door I felt a surge of
gratitude—and then guilt that I got to have a family while
Sunny lay cold and dead in a medical examiner's morgue. I
supposed that guilt was the flip side of jealousy.

When I was asking how to get to the cardiology department
I realized that there was something I could do for Sunny.

"Can you tell me what room Dale Cartwright is in?" I asked.

Sunny and Dale had been close. I owed it to Dale to tell him what had happened to Sunny before he heard it from someone else. Monty would be fine with Jess—in fact, it was a good idea for them to spend more time together.

When I got to Dale's room I found out that I was too late. A woman in a long mauve tunic was sitting on the edge of Dale's bed, weeping. Dale looked pale and stricken.

"Is it true?" he asked. "Did Sunny hang herself?"

"It is," I said, "but how . . . ?"

The woman in the mauve tunic turned and I was startled to see it was the woman from St. Anne's.

"I heard from my cousin Garnette just now. She was one of Sunny's volunteers. The police called up all the volunteers to ask how the puppets were left yesterday. She said . . ." She shuddered, her enamel cat earrings jingling like wind chimes. ". . . that the puppets were arranged in a circle around her. But that's not how they were when Garnette left for the day. Sunny must have arranged them like that . . ." She lowered her voice to a hoarse whisper meant to convey horror but that instead ended up sounding as if she were *relishing* the details. ". . . like for an audience."

"And what if she did?" Dale demanded angrily. "She looked on those puppets like they were family. If only I'd been there . . ." He flapped his bandaged arm like an injured wing and grimaced.

"You mustn't blame yourself," I said.

"I don't!" Dale spit out between gritted teeth. "I blame that goddamned house. It doesn't want anyone to be happy—it made old Mrs. Montague shoot her husband and kill herself. It made Jess fall on me and made me cut myself with my own chain saw. And now it's taken Sunny. As soon as I get out of here I'm moving to Florida. If I were you"—he fixed me with a bloodshot eye—"I'd get out of there before that house tears you into little pieces."

Chapter Twenty-One

We buried Sunny a week later in the Montague family plot of the Rhinebeck Cemetery. It took that long for the police to declare her death "self-inflicted" and release her body. Each day we had to wait seemed to age Monty a year. By the time of the funeral he could barely stand at the graveside without Jess and me on either side holding him up. I could feel him trembling through his heavy wool coat and hear the wheeze of his lungs.

"He has congestive heart failure," Jess had told me when we came back from the hospital. "He has to take those nitro-glycerin tablets whenever he has pain and he's supposed to avoid stress and extreme temperatures."

The last thing he should be doing was standing in the cold and damp listening to one of Sunny's "coven" (as Jess referred to the dozen hearty women who had descended on Riven House to "usher Sunny to the beyond") chant the seven verses of the Abhidhamma. But he had insisted he was well enough to stand through the graveside ceremony, just as he had insisted on having Sunny buried in the family plot.

I looked around at the gravestones of Montagues dating back to the eighteenth century. They were mostly a long-lived clan, except for Minnie and Bayard, who had died in their twenties within six months of each other. I'd been surprised, passing their gravestones, to see them buried side by side. *Beloved husband and father,* Bayard's stone read. No hint that Minnie had shot her *beloved husband. Beloved wife and mother,* her stone read. No hint that she hadn't been a mother—not *really,* since her own child had died in premature childbirth. She'd suffered delusions that Monty wasn't hers. And she had been right. What everyone had thought was postpartum depression (although no one called it that then) was really grief over losing her own baby and anger at being saddled with her husband's mistress's baby. No wonder she'd gone out of her mind. And no wonder Monty had grown up feeling unloved. We'd both been raised by strangers.

I put my arm around Monty and glared at the woman who was ringing a Tibetan mourning bell. I made eye contact with the minister and he nodded at the men waiting to lower Sunny's coffin into the ground. The bell continued to peal as the coffin was lowered, muffling the sound of the electronic gears as the fog muffled the edges of the gravestones around us, both the fog and the chime of the bells drawing a circle around us mourners.

Like Sunny's circle of puppets.

And now Sunny was surrounded for eternity by Montagues. As someday I would be, I realized, as we turned to leave the grave, my eyes coming to rest on Minnie's gravestone. Would she see me as an intruder?

But she's the intruder, I thought, gripping Monty's arm to keep him from stumbling on the uneven, icy ground. *I'm a Montague. I belong here.*

I found myself, though, thinking of Minnie often in the weeks that followed the funeral. There wasn't much else to do. An icy fog had settled over the valley, rising from the river, creeping up the lawn, erasing pond and garden, and even stealing into the house itself, where it settled into the rotunda, dim now under the iced-shut oculus, like an animal curling up in its winter den.

"Does winter always come so suddenly up here?" Jess asked miserably.

"I suppose," I said. "I never really noticed. There was apple picking season and then winter. I was mostly glad when all the crops were in and the farm stand closed because I had more time to read. It's kind of cozy."

Jess snorted. He was even more confined than Monty and me because his ankle still bothered him and made navigating the ice outside difficult. The lack of exercise made him restless. During the day he wondered aloud why we hadn't moved someplace *fucking warmer*. At night I heard him walking in circles around the rotunda gallery, thump-dragging his injured foot. He reminded me of an animal scratching a hollow in its den. I remembered what Sunny had said about how lonely the house became in winter. It was enough to drive a person crazy.

I could chart the progress of Minnie's mental deterioration in her scrapbooks. The first one I looked through was ordinary enough, even banal. She'd started keeping them the year she came out—the year she met Bayard Montague. It was full of dance cards and invitations to teas and pressed flowers and bits of ribbons and feathers from her favorite dresses and hats. She'd cut out the newspaper notice of her debutante ball at the Sherry-Netherland and every clipping thereafter of her appearances in society. She'd pasted a photograph of herself in her coming-out ball gown and one of her and Bayard in beaver coats and muffs skating on Wollman Rink in Central Park. Looking at these made me realize that Bayard had been "courting" Minnie Noyes before he ran off with Mary Foley. On one whimsical page she had cut out Bayard's head and mounted it on a drawing of a great stuffed grizzly bear and attached her own head to a drawing of a long-necked ostrich. *Minnie and Bay go to the zoo!* she'd written in loopy childish handwriting. The last page of the book was dedicated to her wedding in June of 1929—only a month after Bayard had run off with Mary. When I turned to that page I gasped aloud at the sight of Minnie in her wedding dress. In her white dress and flower wreath she looked like Mary Foley in her apple blossom wreath.

But Minnie wasn't nearly as pretty, and her wreath was made of hothouse orange blossoms. "The bride wore crepe de chine and orange blossoms," the notice in the *Times* read. "After a whirlwind romance, Mr. Alden Bayard Montague and Miss Minerva Delano Noyes were wed at St. Bartholomew's Church. The couple will reside at the Montague estate in Concord, New York, after a honeymoon on the Continent."

They'd moved to River House in the fall of 1929. Minnie started her next scrapbook with a collage of pine branches and pinecones surrounding a postcard of River House. The next page was dedicated to apple picking and featured photographs of Bayard and Minnie riding in an apple cart. Minnie had drawn an arrow pointing to her flat stomach and pasted a flying cupid shooting an arrow toward it. So she'd been pregnant by September—and still happy. She hadn't known there was another girl bearing Bayard's child living not a mile down the road. Had Minnie glimpsed her picking apples in her new husband's orchards? Had she heard whispers of what had happened at the last apple blossom festival?

October went by without any mention of the stock market crash. Minnie cut out pictures of roast turkeys and harvest cornucopias. There was a photograph of a servant dressed in a long black dress and white apron carrying a large platter, only Minnie had pasted a cutout of an apple over the servant's face. It seemed cruel, but she hadn't been much kinder to Bayard, over whose face she had pasted a pilgrim's head. She had made herself into an Indian wielding an axe. A little repressed hostility there? I wondered. Had strains appeared in the marriage? Was Minnie feeling lonely and isolated up here in the country while Bayard stayed in the city, scrambling to save their dwindling fortune?

I thought of her as I walked through the house, peering out the fog-bound windows at the gray and gloomy landscape. The house felt both bigger and more desolate and also smaller and more crowded with the cold bearing down on it. As if it were gathering up its energy for the long winter like an animal stores up fat.

Our own Thanksgiving was a subdued affair. I roasted a turkey and made all the sides, but sitting down to such a huge feast with only the three of us felt gloomy. I'd cleaned out the dining room, polished the old table, and found three chairs that had been finished enough to sit on. I'd pushed the other chairs to the sides of the room, thinking I'd take a class in furniture restoration in the spring and learn how to fix them myself. The empty chairs surrounding us made our dinner seem lonelier, as if they were waiting for guests who hadn't come. Even the champagne failed to lighten the mood, perhaps because it was the Dom Pérignon meant to celebrate Monty and Sunny's renewed vows. Monty grimaced at each sip as if it reminded him of Sunny. Jess drank too much. When I reminded him that he shouldn't mix alcohol and pain pills he said it was a time-honored tradition among writers to experiment until they found the right cocktail for their muse. This observation led to a lugubrious discussion of the various "cocktails" employed by famous writers from Coleridge's opium to Hemingway's martinis and Byron's fondness for laudanum.

"And what was laudanum after all," Jess said, "but alcohol and opiates combined? Wasn't that what Lily Bart drank in *The House of Mirth*?"

"And died of it," I pointed out.

"Don't be so literal, Clare," Jess said, waving a glass of champagne. "Lily Bart died of society's indifference to the plight of the intelligent woman, right, Monty? Isn't that what you taught us in your class?"

"Did I?" Monty asked, gazing into his unfinished glass of champagne. In the firelight the bubbles glowed like gold, like the cockled glass windows of Riven House in the autumn light. Would that sunlight ever return? I wondered. "Minnie drank laudanum. My aunts said she'd hurt her back while giving birth to me and started taking it for the pain, but now I wonder . . ."

"If she drank it because she'd lost her baby," I said, following Monty's thought.

Jess looked from Monty to me. "Is that what you two are writing in that book of yours? That Minnie went mad because she lost her baby and had a stranger's child foisted on her?"

"Jess," I hissed warningly.

"Sorry, Monty. I forget sometimes that it's *your* story. Hearing Clare talk about it I think it's something she made up."

"It's Clare's story too," Monty said. "And as I always said in class, 'We talk about the story, not the storyteller.'"

"Of course," Jess said, pouring himself another glass of champagne and holding up his glass in a toast. "Here's to all the storytellers—and whatever they need to drink to get their stories told."

I'd begun to worry that Jess was getting more drinking done

than storytelling. The sound of Monty's typewriter had begun to drive him crazy, he said, and since he couldn't take his long walks anymore he would drive into town "to find someplace quiet to write goddamnit!" When he came back, though, his breath smelled of beer and cigarettes and I suspected that his someplace quiet was one of the local bars. I worried about him driving on the icy, foggy roads and worried about him giving up on his book. Maybe Riven House was only good for him in the summer and fall. Maybe Riven House wasn't good for anyone once winter set in.

It certainly wasn't good for Minnie. Her scrapbooks grew stranger through the fall. She'd found the picture of Bayard crowning the Apple Blossom Queen and pasted an apple over Mary Foley's face. In another one she drew Bayard biting into an apple, drool dripping from his mouth, his face voracious as a cannibal's. Clearly she had found out about his fling with Mary Foley and had come unhinged by jealousy. In her Christmas collage she'd pasted multiple photos of her and Bayard's heads on a huge Christmas tree. In another the same black-garbed housekeeper—again with an apple pasted over her face— carried a platter with the baby Jesus on it. As if she were serving it to *eat*.

After the explosion of Christmas collages there was a rather subdued New Year's collage of champagne labels. When I turned to the next page I thought that the glue had come undone and loosed all the carefully cut-out magazine clippings and photographs into a chaotic mélange. Jumbled together on the page were magazine pictures of babies and nursery objects—baby bottles, cribs, stuffed toys and dolls, fanciful animals decked out in circus costumes . . . Looking from the book to the walls I saw that they were the circus animals from the wallpaper. Minnie must have saved a sheet of the wallpaper to use in her scrapbooks. In fact, as I picked at the layers of pictures—all covered with a layer of glue as thick as shellac—I made out the wallpaper underneath all the other pictures. She'd meant to use it as the background but then in her pain and grief over losing her own baby she had piled on dozens of baby pictures, as if she were looking for her own baby in the pages of all these magazines.

The idea made me feel so ill I had to close the scrapbook. Looking up was no relief. The circus animals parading around the room looked suddenly sinister, their anthropomorphized faces leering at me as they must have leered at Minnie when she came in here to nurse her baby—who *wasn't* her baby, but an imposter. And when she told her nursemaid that the baby wasn't hers they thought she was crazy and took her away to the mental hospital to keep her away from the baby. Which had only made her crazier . . .

The room suddenly seemed to be spinning, the circus animals going round and round like a carousel ride. I had to get out. I got to my feet, but stumbled. The room spun vertiginously. I lurched toward the door but the floor seemed to tilt like a fun house ride. I found myself leaning against the door frame, my fingers digging into the wall as if to the wreckage of a boat in a storm. When the room righted I was horrified to see that I'd torn long gouges in the wallpaper. I tried to smooth the torn paper back over the wall—and noticed something. Beneath the layer of wallpaper I'd torn was *another* layer of wallpaper. That wasn't so unusual. Lots of people papered over old wallpaper rather than take the first layer off. It was a lot of trouble to steam old paper off—as I'd discovered helping my mother do it when we'd repapered my childhood bedroom. We'd peeled off layers of paper, from some hideous fifties-era clowns to delicate Victorian florals. But what was strange here was that the paper seemed to be the same pale yellow with the same white dots and—I had to rip a little more to see—yes, the same border of circus animals. Why paper over the *same* paper?

My fingers itched to tear off more of the wallpaper to see the layer underneath but I heard Trudy's voice in my head telling me not to. "Why are you always *picking* at everything," she'd admonished me when she found the patch of shredded wallpaper behind my bed. As if I'd been caught picking at a scab.

I pulled my hand away from the wall as if it had been slapped—and heard another voice. This one was coming from downstairs. I opened the nursery door and listened. There were two voices: Jess's and Monty's. So Jess had come back from his drive. I looked at my watch and saw it was almost dinnertime. I'd lost hours poring over Minnie's scrapbooks. It wasn't healthy. I needed to get out of this room.

I smoothed the wallpaper back over the tear—I'd find some paste and fix it later—and headed downstairs to join Jess and Monty. But first I stopped in my bathroom to splash water on my face. It was a good thing I did. I'd somehow managed to get glue all over my hands and face. I looked as though I'd been crawling *behind* the wallpaper, like that poor deranged woman in that story we'd read in Monty's class.

Chapter Twenty-Two

As I came down the stairs in the rotunda I noticed that there was a third voice in the library—another man—and I wished that I'd changed into something more presentable than the grubby jeans, thermal shirt, and ratty old cardigan I was wearing. I'd become sloppy spending my days writing in the house with only Monty and Jess for company. No wonder Jess was hanging out at the local bars with a wife who'd started looking like a deranged spinster librarian.

I was turning around to go upstairs and change when I heard Monty's voice call from the library. "Is that you, Clare?"

Who else would it be? I almost snapped back. For a big house with thick walls, sound traveled easily (something to do with its octagonal shape, I supposed). If Monty heard me on the stairs he often called out *Is that you, Clare?* which meant he wanted me to fetch him a cup of tea or come in and listen to an idea he had for the book, or adjust the pillow at his back, or stoke the fire. Sometimes I wished I could float soundlessly through the house like I had in my dream the night Sunny died. But I only called, "Yes, Monty, was there something you needed?" as I came into the library.

I was doubly sorry I hadn't gone upstairs to change when I

saw the man seated with Monty in front of the fireplace. He was wearing a suit and tie and polished brogues. A mirage of Wall Street come to visit Riven House and just the kind of "suit" Jess despised. I turned toward Jess to see what kind of withering look he was giving our visitor but was surprised to find Jess clean-shaven and dressed in a pressed button-down shirt, sitting upright with a cup of coffee in his hand, regarding the stranger with polite attention.

"Ah, Clare, there you are," Monty said. "I was about to send Jess for you."

I expected at least a grimace at "send Jess" but Jess only smiled and held out his hand for me. "I told Monty that we shouldn't disturb your writing until we had to."

"Oh," I said, moving closer to Jess's chair, "I would have come down right away if I'd known we had a guest." I scraped away a scrap of glue from my hands, guiltily thinking that I hadn't exactly been writing. "I'd have made coffee."

"You see," Monty said to the man in the suit, "she thinks of nothing but my comfort. How lucky I am to have found a daughter like Clare in my dotage—and a son-in-law like Jess, of course."

"Lucky indeed," the man said, holding his hand out to me. "It's a pleasure to meet you, Mrs. Martin. Mr. Montague has told me so much about you—and of course I've come to feel I know you while drawing up the papers."

"Drawing up the papers?" I asked, feeling a sudden draft in the room. I thought of Minnie coming down to this room and finding a contingent of doctors and Montague cousins banded together to tell her she needed a rest away from the baby, at a good hospital . . .

"My will, dear," Monty said gently. "This is my lawyer, Cortland Montague—a second cousin, or is it third?"

Cortland shrugged. "Who's counting? The important relationship here is the one between you and Mrs. Martin." He turned to me. "Our investigations at the firm have confirmed that you are indeed the biological child of Amy Birnbach and that Miss Birnbach did indeed name Mr. Montague as the father. We could do DNA testing, of course, but Mr. Montague has *insisted* that won't be necessary." He smiled at me but I saw a muscle twitch in his jaw. He must have tried to talk Monty into the DNA testing. Any lawyer would—and a lawyer who was related to Monty and might stand to inherit some part of the estate most certainly would have.

"Could I submit to a DNA test voluntarily?" I asked.

"That isn't necessary—" Monty began at the same time that Cortland said, "Yes, of course you could. It's an excellent idea. After all, you might have children yourself one day and you would want them to have the benefit of a full medical history—"

"Or you could be using this as a means of holding up the new will Monty has asked you to draw up naming Clare as his beneficiary."

I stared at Jess. So he had known about this? Why hadn't he said anything to me? My face went hot as I had the dreadful thought that he had asked Monty to put me in his will.

"Why in the world would I care?" Cortland asked. "The previous will gives the estate to the college. I'm certainly happier to see it go to a family member."

"How about this," Monty said, sitting forward, fisted hands leaning on his knees. "We go ahead and sign the damned papers now and then we can get our blood tested if Clare wants. Frankly, I don't care if it comes back showing we're both Martians. This house belongs to Clare and Jess."

Cortland looked as though he wanted to argue, but under

Monty's glare he unbuckled his leather briefcase and drew out a thick sheaf of papers. "We'll need two witnesses—"

"You and Jess make two," Monty said.

"It's a bit irregular to have the spouse of a beneficiary witness the will—" Cortland began.

"That's why I called an impartial witness," Jess said. "I think that's her now."

I followed Jess's gaze to the glass doors—and drew in a sharp breath. A shawled figure stood behind the fogged-over glass, looking for all the world like poor Mary Foley standing on the terrace. As if she had come to witness her child inherit Riven House.

But when Jess opened the door the figure came in, unwrapping a lavender angora scarf from her blond head.

"I thought Katrine would make the perfect witness," Jess said, turning to me. "After all, she brought us here."

AFTER MONTY HAD signed the new will and Cortland and Katrine had witnessed it, Jess went to the "cellar" (by which he meant the boot hall) to get a bottle of champagne. I went to the kitchen to throw together some hors d'oeuvres from the ill-fated caviar, crackers, cheese, and the last of the season's Northern Spys sliced up. When I came back in Jess was already pouring a glass of champagne for Katrine, who was laughing and flirting with Cortland Montague, who, now that his official duties were over, had loosened his tie and was smiling appreciatively at Katrine. Again I was sorry I hadn't changed as I watched Katrine cross her long silky legs. She was wearing a low-cut royal blue velvet dress with silvery stockings and shiny black patent-leather boots. I caught Jess staring at her cleavage when she leaned forward to take a cracker from the tray I held. In my dowdy cardigan I felt less like the new heiress to Riven

House than the spinster aunt always counted on to put out sherry and biscuits for the guests.

I took a glass of champagne from Jess and sat down on the hassock beside Monty's chair. Cortland was explaining to Katrine how he was related to Monty's side of the family. "We're the Connecticut Montagues. My great-grandfather Maunsell was Monty's grandfather Birdsill Montague's brother."

"Ah," said Katrine, "didn't Maunsell marry an Astor?"

"He did indeed. You know your genealogy, Miss Vanderberg."

Katrine dimpled prettily. "You pick it up selling real estate in the valley. My New York City buyers love to know who owned their houses before them. An Astor or a Montague can boost property values by ten percent."

"It's good to know the family name is worth *something*," Monty said, taking a sip of champagne. His face was a hectic pink and he seemed to be enjoying himself. Still, I made a mental note of where his nitroglycerin tablets were. I could see the slight bulge in his left breast shirt pocket under his cardigan.

"Oh, it is!" Katrine enthused, leaning forward again for no good reason. "But what they all like best is a ghost."

"Even if one was ridiculous enough to believe such things," Cortland said, "you'd think it would be a deterrent rather than an attraction."

"It depends on the buyer," Katrine said. "I can usually tell. I had two men relocating from Brooklyn last week who specifically wanted a haunted house."

"And were you able to accommodate them?" Jess asked. The mocking tone he'd used with Katrine during our house hunting had crept back into his voice, but his gaze on her legs wasn't mocking at all. I leaned forward to rearrange the crackers, blocking a little of his view.

"Yes, in fact I showed them the old Jackson farmhouse—isn't that where you grew up, Clare?"

"Didn't two Bailey professors buy it?" I asked, making a daisy pattern with the crackers and apple slices.

"Yes, but they're retiring to Florida. I told the couple from Park Slope—two sweet men who want to raise goats and make artisanal cheeses—the apple blossom girl story."

"But she doesn't haunt the farm," I said. "She haunts Riven House."

There was such a long silence that I looked up from the plate I was rearranging. Everyone was looking at me. I guess I'd found a way of getting their attention without showing off my legs or my tits.

"Have you, er, seen a ghost here?" Cortland asked with a nervous smile.

I looked at Jess. He was clenching his jaw the way he did when he was tense. If I carried my anger in my shoulders, Jess carried his tension in his jaw. I was pretty sure I knew why he was so tense. The last time I'd "seen a ghost" I'd wound up in the hospital for a month. I knew I should tell them I'd been kidding and make a joke of the idea of a ghost, but something in the way they were all looking at me made me want to shock them a little.

"I've seen her four times," I said, and then proceeded to tell of each sighting, from the first day by the pond to the last time from the terrace after Dale's accident. They listened spellbound. "So you see," I concluded, "she came to tell me that Monty was her child and that I was Monty's. Now that she's done that I don't think she'll haunt Riven House any longer."

When I finished there was only the sound of the fire crackling and the wind rattling the glass doors. Then Monty said, "What a lovely story, Clare, and how fitting, as Henry James would say, to have a strange tale in an old house at Christmas-time."

"Oh, I see," Cortland said, looking relieved. "It's a story. Ha ha. You writers must spend all your time spinning tales for each other."

"When we're not sharpening our quills," Jess said, "or dashing off our novels."

"And good thing for us," Katrine said, putting down her half-full glass. "I'm going to use that story with my buyers, if you don't mind, Clare. They're sure to like the idea of a ghost roaming their apple orchard."

"A ghost with a baby," Jess said, draining his glass. "Two ghosts for the price of one."

"Absolutely—and speaking of buyers, I have two to pick up at the Rhinecliff Station. I hope the snow holds off until I can show them a few houses."

Cortland got up and helped Katrine on with her coat.

"Is it supposed to snow tonight?" I asked, watching Katrine wrap her fluffy lavender scarf around her throat. The color brought out the blue in her eyes.

Katrine and Cortland both looked surprised at my question. "My goodness gracious, you writers really do live in a little bubble!" Katrine exclaimed. "The blizzard's all anyone's talking about *out there*. They're saying we could get up to two feet."

"Aaah." Cortland waved his hand dismissively. "You can't trust these forecasts. It's all to boost television ratings."

"You always were a skeptic, Cort." Monty clapped the younger man on the shoulder. "I suppose it's why you went into the law."

"With a name like Cortland how could I not," he quipped. Then with a graver look he added, "It's dealing with people that's made me a skeptic."

I thought his gaze lingered on me for an extra moment, but then he smiled and shook my hand and congratulated me on "landing in my rightful place."

"Make sure you get out a little," he said, waving an admonishing finger, "lest you start seeing any more ghosts."

Everyone laughed at that—except Jess. He walked Katrine and Cortland out through the boot hall because it had already begun to snow and the terrace steps would be slippery. Monty sat down heavily when they'd gone. He looked pale and I realized that the afternoon had taken a lot out of him.

"I'm going to clean up and start dinner," I said. "You might want to . . ." I was going to suggest he take a nap, but knowing how much he hated to be treated as an invalid, amended it to "Get a little work done. I bet you haven't had a chance with all this business on your mind."

He looked at me gratefully. "No, I haven't, but I wanted this out of the way. I'd hated leaving it to Bailey after how they treated me, but I didn't want it to go to those money-grubbing *Connecticut Montagues*. I'm happier knowing it will go to you."

"You know it wasn't necessary, Monty. I'm . . . well . . . *thank you*. It means a lot that you've acknowledged me."

He looked up at me, his eyes gleaming. "I know it doesn't begin to make up for the time we missed, Clare. When I think of you growing up not a mile down the road—"

"It's okay, Monty. The important thing is we've found each other now."

He clasped my hand and then asked if I wouldn't mind handing him his notebook and pen from the desk and then his reading glasses and then a book. I left him with all his writing supplies, but I knew that he would most likely doze off in a few minutes, as he usually did now in the late afternoons. I brought the plates and glasses into the kitchen and washed them, scrubbing at the burgundy stain of Katrine's lipstick on the rim of her champagne glass. She'd hardly drunk any. Perhaps she was watching her weight—or she liked to keep a sharp head for her buyers. Clever of her to tell ghost stories to the hipster Brooklynites. Just like she'd known what to say to draw Jess and me to Riven House. And clever to stay in touch. I remember what she had said that day about having someone on the inside when the house went up for sale. How well it had worked out for her that I would inherit the house. I supposed she thought Jess and I would sell. After all, we probably wouldn't be able to afford the upkeep.

I threw together a quick stew of chicken, diced sweet potatoes, and the apples leftover from the cheese tray, added curry and chicken stock, and put it on the stove to simmer. I heard Jess come back in and head upstairs. He must have walked Katrine and Cortland to their cars, but why had he taken so long? Had they been talking about the will? Or about the ghost story I'd told? I shouldn't have told it. Look at what had happened when Minnie told everyone she'd seen a ghost. And Amy Birnbach. Both of them had ended up at the Hudson River Mental Hospital. It was not a place I ever wanted to see again.

I'd be more careful next time. Any ghost story I told I'd make sure I said it was fictional. And I'd get out more like Cortland said. Being stuck in this old house with two writers would drive anyone a little batty. I'd go into Rhinebeck to do some shopping, buy Christmas presents for Jess and Monty, buy a new dress—maybe a velvet one like the one Katrine had worn, only in emerald green for the holidays. I couldn't blame Jess for ogling Katrine if I let myself go.

I'd start now by taking a bath and changing into the green dress for dinner—the one Jess said shimmied over my hips. In the rotunda I paused on the bottom steps to listen to the house.

I could hear Monty snoring in the library. I could hear the wind blowing, rattling the old glass windows in their frames—we'd probably save a mint in heating if they were all recaulked—and a dry, sandy pattering coming from above me. I looked up and saw that the oculus was coated with a layer of snow. The house had that hushed feeling that comes when it's snowing outside, every tiny noise magnified. I could make out the sound of paper crackling coming from Jess's study on the south side of the rotunda. Jess must be in there writing.

I climbed the stairs as quietly as I could but when I reached the top the door to Jess's study opened.

"There you are," Jess said. "I wanted to talk to you before dinner."

"Talk to me while I take a bath," I said.

He followed me into our bedroom and sat on the edge of the bed while I rinsed out the tub—Jess always forgot to after he took a bath—and started the water. I peeled off my cardigan and thermal shirt and old jeans and turned to see that Jess was watching me.

"Want to join me?" I asked, sitting on the rim of the tub.

"How long have you been seeing ghosts?" he asked.

Feeling suddenly cold—and not a little ridiculous—I reached for my robe.

"It was just a story." I belted the robe loosely and sat down on the bed next to him. "You know I like ghost stories. So did you once."

"That's the kind of thing you like in college. I lost my taste for them when my girlfriend started seeing the ghost of her miscarried baby."

"*Our* baby." I wrapped the robe tighter around me. "And I never said I saw her, only that I *heard* her."

Jess made a nasty sound. "Christ, Clare, you wound up in

the loony bin for a month. You scared the fuck out of me. And then last winter . . . I just don't know if I could go through that again."

"You won't have to," I said. "I'm fine. I've just been really into this story I'm working on. Don't you ever get so wrapped up in what you're writing that you believe in it?"

"Not so much that I see things. Are you seeing things, Clare? Did you really see a ghost all those times?"

"It was foggy or raining each time," I said. "It's easy to see shapes in the fog or the rain. And that time on the terrace, it was really my reflection."

"Jesus, Clare, Cortland was right. You've been spending too much time holed up in this place."

"Cortland's just jealous he's not inheriting Riven House. Besides, we came here so you could write."

"It's not worth it if the place is driving you crazy."

"I'm not crazy!" It came out shriller and louder than I'd meant it to. "And there's nothing wrong with Riven House. Not now—"

"You mean now that the ghost of Mary Foley has instated you as heir?"

I bristled at his mocking tone. "You're the one who knew all about that before me. Did you ask Monty to redo his will?"

"Don't change the subject—"

"*You* brought up the inheritance—and *you* called Katrine Vanderberg to come witness the will. And she's the one who brought up ghosts and the one who's been using my family tragedy as a marketing gimmick, which you might have noticed was rude if you hadn't been ogling her tits."

Jess stared at me and then in a calm, cold voice said, "The last time you started losing it you accused me of fucking every girl in a ten-mile radius. The doctors said the paranoia was one

of the symptoms of your psychotic mania—along with delusions and hallucinations—so I am not going to get angry at
you for that nasty comment. I *am* going to insist you talk to
a psychologist about these hallucinations you've been having.
Maybe if you start medication we can head off a full episode.
If the hallucinations don't stop I think we should leave here."

"And go where? We don't have any money. We don't even
have insurance. If I'd kept my job at Broadway—"

"Yeah, I know it's all my fault, as you're always ready to
remind me. But now that you're an heiress maybe your daddy
will help us out a little. I'm sure Monty won't want you to stay
here if it's driving you crazy. And at least when he's gone we
can sell this rotting pile."

"Is that what your girlfriend Katrine wants?" The words
were out of my mouth before I could stop them. Jess was right.
I was acting paranoid. I started to tell him that I was sorry,
but he had already gotten up, crossed the room, and gone out,
slamming the door behind him, before I could even begin to
think of how to say that.

Chapter Twenty-Three

Monty and I had our dinner by the fire in the library that night. Jess didn't come down. I told Monty that he had an idea that he wanted to keep working on. The last thing Monty needed was to worry about Jess and me fighting. We discussed, instead, the house.

"You don't realize how relieved I am to know it will go to someone who loves it. Cortland and all those vultures down in New York City have just been waiting to get their hands on it to turn it into a museum or luxury hotel or some such nonsense. They've never thought I could manage the estate properly because I'm a writer and not a goddamned lawyer, but the trouble with lawyers is they have no imagination. Think of the novels you and Jess will write here! I believe that's what this house was meant for, that it's designed to channel creative energy. The problem is that for many years the energy had gone stale. But now with you and Jess here writing I can feel it tingling from my synapses to my fingertips."

Monty splayed out his liver-spotted hands, his long arthritic fingers palpating the air as though striking invisible typewriter keys. His face looked hectic in the firelight, two red spots blooming on his veined cheeks, his eyes gleaming feverishly. I

thought of him crouched over his typewriter down in the basement like a spider feeding off the currents of inspiration Jess
and I transmitted through the filaments of cobwebs hanging
through the house. Then I shook the image away.

"Jess thinks maybe I've gotten a little carried away with the
ghost story," I said tentatively.

Monty made a dismissive sound. "I didn't expect Cortland
to understand, but Jess ought to have. I can't tell you how often
I've been working here in this room and thought I heard voices
in the house or looked up from my desk to see *her* standing
out there on the terrace looking in. A true writer gets so lost in
the fictive dream he comes to believe it. That's all those sightings were. Jess . . ." Monty looked around the library, his eyes
lingering for a moment on the glass doors as if he expected
Jess to be there. He leaned forward, grasped my hand, and
continued in a hoarse stage whisper. "Jess is a fine craftsman,
but he doesn't have the imagination that you do, Clare. That's
what I was trying to say in that review. He doesn't empathize
with his characters and so they don't come alive on the page.
But you, Clare, you have the gift of empathy. You feel things
more than other people and that raw talent comes through in
your writing. You're the real talent in the family. It wouldn't be
surprising if Jess were jealous of you."

My face burned from the guilty pleasure of Monty's praise
combined with a dread of what Jess would think if he heard
what Monty had said. I listened to the house for a moment, for
any movement from Jess's study, but I only heard the crackle of
the fire and the furtive patter of the falling snow.

"I think Jess is just worried about me. I had a bad stretch
last year. He wants me to talk to a psychologist."

"Nonsense," Monty said, patting my hand and sitting back.

"You don't need a shrink; you need to keep writing—and a good night's sleep so we can both get an early start in the morning."

I took this as an indication that he was tired and ready to retire. I walked with him to the head of the stairs to his apartment and offered to help him downstairs but he waved me off. "I'm not a complete invalid yet that you have to be my nursemaid."

I had a feeling that he liked preserving the privacy of his apartment. Jess had said it had the air of dreary bachelor digs circa 1978. Still, I stood at the top of the stairs until I heard him get to the bottom. How long would he be able to manage those stairs by himself? What would we do when he couldn't anymore? Could we convert one of the first-floor rooms into a bedroom? I pictured hospital beds and walkers and those awful bedside commodes that looked like crouching spiders. Monty would hate it.

I cleaned up our dinner dishes and took the trash out to the outdoor bins. The ground was covered with five or six inches of snow. I stood for a moment in the shelter of the old apple tree hugging my cardigan around me, looking down over the lawns and garden, all indistinct and muffled in the falling snow. In the distance I heard a foghorn and the low mournful whistle of the southbound Amtrak train. I pictured the snow falling on the black water of the pond and the river. Before long the pond would freeze and then the river. My father had told me that when his father was a boy he went skating on the river like Hans Brinker in *The Silver Skates*. I stood until my hands and toes were frozen and my hair was coated with snow, but nothing emerged out of the swirling gusts of snow and darkness. No ghosts. Monty was right. Writing had driven them away.

As I walked up the stairs of the rotunda, though, I heard a bell ringing. I froze on the stairs, listening for it to ring again, imagining Minnie ringing the servant's bell at the dumbwaiter to summon the bad fairy who had stolen her baby. But instead of another bell I heard a soft murmuring. I stopped on the second-floor gallery and listened, my eyes resting on Bayard Montague's pale face. It was coming from Minnie's Mourning Room, a voice talking to itself, as Minnie must have in her delirium and grief after her baby died. Looking at Bayard's face I imagined how he would have dismissed her grief as ravings. After all, he had given her a live baby. What did she have to carry on about?

I crept softly to the door and put my ear on the old, thick wood. The voice was Jess's. The bell must have been his phone ringing, but who was he talking to? Who did Jess still talk to from our life in the city? He'd alienated most of his friends through one argument or another—this one because he'd said something dismissive about his writing, that one because he'd sold out and gone commercial, another because he'd been offended at a review Jess had written. I didn't think he'd talked to Abe and Yuriko since Yuriko told me about his turning down the Brooklyn College job. Could he be talking to Ansel? Telling him how the work was going?

The thought that the only person Jess had to talk to late at night in this big lonely house was his agent made me so sad I had to rest my forehead against the cold wood door to keep from crying . . . and then I heard my name.

Why was Jess talking to Ansel about me?

I pressed my ear to the door and heard my name again—but that was all I could make out. Murmur murmur murmur *Clare*. As if he said my name louder and clearer than anything else—or because every time he said my name he spit out the word with anger. My tears of pity for Jess turned into ones of grief for us. How had I made him so angry?

Then I made out another word: *Crazy.*

He was telling someone—somehow I doubted now that it was Ansel—that I was crazy. The thought that he was talking to a doctor struck me cold. He had called a doctor and was demanding that I be put away because I was seeing ghosts—

But that *was* crazy. What doctor could he possibly reach at this time of night? He was talking to some friend—or maybe one of my friends.

I realized with a guilty pang how long it had been since I'd been in touch with Marika. Come to think of it, I hadn't even gotten work from her in over a month. I'd told her in October that I was too busy working on my own writing to take on any copyediting. Maybe she'd been hurt that I hadn't called after that. If Jess was telling her that I was losing it up here she'd have no reason to disbelieve his word.

A flicker of fear kindled in my gut. I had cut myself off from my life in the city. I was isolated in this big old house at the mercy of whatever Jess told people about me. I wrapped my arms around my chest and looked up at the oculus, which, covered with snow, stared back at me unseeingly like a blind eye. Monty had said that the house channeled energy, but what if that energy was crazy?

A sound from inside Jess's study startled me out of my thoughts. I mustn't let Jess catch me eavesdropping. I hurried around the gallery and went into the nursery because it was the first door I came to and because I knew Jess wouldn't follow me inside. Not if he thought I was writing. I could shut myself in here for days and neither Monty nor Jess would bother me if they thought I was writing. I leaned my back against the door and pressed my hand over my mouth to keep from laughing out loud. *Writers!* Talk about crazy.

I sat down at my desk to catch my breath. I turned on the

lamp, which cast a warm yellow light on the desk, and opened the window. Cold air swirled in a dusting of snow that glittered in the lamplight like pixie dust. I straightened notebooks, pens, and piles of typescript and then sat back, breathing easier now. In the morning I'd call Marika. I wouldn't ask if Jess had called her but I'd be able to tell if he had. I'd make a date to come into the city and have lunch with her. Cortland had been right; I needed to get out more. Maybe Jess and I just needed a little time apart. Everything would be all right when we'd both finished our books.

I leaned forward to turn off the desk lamp and noticed that with the light shining directly on the wall I could make out a shadowy pattern beneath the frieze of circus animals. Perhaps it was just the pattern of the bottom layer of paper slightly out of line with the top layer. I got up and ran my hand over the paper that I'd torn earlier. It had loosened since before dinner, as if the moisture in the air from the snow had gotten in under the paper and melted the old paste. A long strip fell away under my hand, peeling off like sunburned skin.

Stop picking at it, I heard Trudy's voice say in my head.

But I'd seen a glimpse of something in the frieze that caught my interest. I pulled a little harder and uncovered a foot-long swath of the circus animal parade.

Only they weren't circus animals anymore. Minnie had pasted photographs over the heads of the animals and clowns. I knelt to look closer. Over the face of one of the clowns in the pony car she had pasted a photograph of Bayard. It was harder to make out the face over the second clown. It looked like it had been cut out of a newspaper instead of a photograph and Minnie's gluey fingers had smudged the newsprint. It was only from her wreath that I was able to recognize Mary Foley. As for the circus animals, each one had been given the face of a human baby. That would have been grotesque enough even if Minnie hadn't scratched out all their eyes.

My hand shaking, I peeled away another strip of paper. Minnie had pasted over the entire frieze, making it into a parade of dead babies.

WHEN I WOKE up the next day and looked out my bedroom window I saw a world transformed by snow. A fresh, clean slate. As if the weather had pasted a new layer of wallpaper over the mistakes of the past, just as Bayard had pasted over Minnie's crazy collage in the nursery. When Jess came into the bedroom to dress (he'd spent the whole night in his study) I told him that I would make an appointment with a psychologist. "You're right," I said. "I've been so wrapped up in the writing that I've gotten isolated. I was thinking I'd ask Marika for a recommendation and go have lunch with her in the city."

He seemed to flinch at Marika's name—perhaps it *had* been her he'd been talking to last night—but he quickly recovered. "No need to go so far," he said, sitting down beside me on the bed. "Katrine gave me the name of a psychologist at Northern Dutchess."

Blood rushed to my face. "You talked to Katrine about me needing a psychologist?"

"I didn't need to, Clare. She brought it up after you told that ghost story. She was worried about you. She feels responsible because she brought us here in the first place."

I bit back a nasty comment about what Katrine could do with her concern when I caught the exhausted look on Jess's face. He looked like he'd been up all night. Katrine wasn't the only one who felt responsible for bringing us here. After all, if Jess had taken the job at Brooklyn College we wouldn't have come to Riven House.

Chapter Twenty-Four

It would have taken me a month to get into a Manhattan psychiatrist but Dr. Schermer was able to take me the day before Christmas. After thirty minutes in his office I saw why his calendar was so open. He had spent the time reading questions off a clipboard and scribbling down my answers without once looking up and making eye contact. Only after we'd established my age, sibling order, age of parents, medical history, marital status, and that I was not having suicidal thoughts, did he ask in the same bored monotone what had brought me here today.

My husband thinks I'm crazy because I'm seeing ghosts.

"I've experienced a lot of changes lately and as a result have been feeling some stress," I said. "My husband noticed and suggested I come talk to someone."

"What kind of changes?" he asked, still not looking up.

I folded my hands and was careful not to play with my wedding ring, which according to a novel I once copyedited was a sure sign of marital unhappiness. Not that Dr. Schermer would have noticed.

"My husband, Jess, and I moved up here from the city in September. We'd been having some financial challenges so we took a job as caretakers at the house of our former professor." I paused, pleased with how reasonable it all sounded.

"And how has that been going?" Dr. Schermer asked while stealing a glance at his watch. Did he think because he wasn't looking at me I wasn't looking at him?

"Fine—at first. My husband has been writing again and I've started writing too—"

"You listed your profession as freelance editor," he interrupted. I thought psychologists weren't supposed to interrupt. The one I'd seen in the hospital had been able to spend hours *not* talking.

"Yes, but I've always wanted to write and since I've been up here staying at Riven House I have been."

"Riven House?"

"The estate where we're caretakers," I said, thinking that for a psychologist he wasn't a very good listener, "it used to be called River House—but the locals started calling it Riven House after Minnie Montague shot her husband, Bayard. Then they started calling it the widow's house. . . . In fact, that's what I'm writing about."

I paused to give him a chance to react to that bit of information, but he was scribbling busily now and merely waved his hand for me to go on.

"You see, it turns out that I'm really the granddaughter of Bayard Montague and the Apple Blossom Queen, Mary Foley." As I said it out loud I realized how crazy it sounded. I clenched my hands more firmly to keep the laughter from bubbling up my throat. "I realize that sounds improbable, but in fact it's true. You see, I found out that Monty—Alden Montague—the professor we're staying with, is really my father and he turns out to really be Mary Foley's son because his father switched the babies at birth. I know, it sounds like one of those dreadful daytime soap operas that my mother used to watch—my adoptive mother, that is, Trudy . . . but it's all true. I got my birth certificate from St. Anne's"—I waved my hand toward the window in the direction of St. Anne's Services across the parking lot—"and my biological mother named Monty as my father. He hadn't known because he'd been on sabbatical, but since he's found out he's been wonderful. He wrote me into his will even before we had DNA testing, but his lawyer thought it was a good idea in case I ever have children so we came here two days ago to have our blood drawn." I waved my hand in the other direction, back toward the hospital and, I vaguely thought, the genetics department where Monty and I had gone. I wished I hadn't started moving my hands around. If I put them back in my lap now it would look like I was trying to rein them in. Why wasn't he interrupting me now? I hadn't meant to tell him the story about Minnie and Mary and Bayard and about Monty being my father.

After a few minutes of consulting his clipboard Dr. Schermer asked, "Did you fantasize about finding your birth parents growing up?"

I groaned. "This is not a fantasy. Monty has named me in his will."

"And how did that make you feel?"

"Good! I mean, it's not so much about the money—although God knows we needed it and it's a huge relief after Jess not writing his second novel and all our financial problems—but really, it's about the acknowledgment."

"You feel you've attained your father's approval?"

"I guess you could put it like that. It's not just that he's my father, he's also a teacher and writer I've always respected. It means a lot to me that he values my writing—" I choked to a halt, my throat tight. To my horror and embarrassment I realized I was on the edge of tears.

"Do you feel that your husband doesn't value your writing?" Dr. Schermer nudged a box of Kleenex toward me without looking up.

"Of course he does! That was part of the reason we came up here—" Only it wasn't. I'd imagined *that*. "Or at least, I think he used to, but when I stopped writing I think Jess gave up on me . . ." I plucked a Kleenex from the box and wiped my eyes. "I mean, how can I blame him. If I couldn't believe in myself why should he? But now that I *am* writing he seems . . . well, he doesn't seem happy with that either." I blew my nose and sat up straighter. "To tell you the truth, I think he's jealous. That's what Monty thinks. Monty says I have a stronger imagination than Jess and that's why Jess doesn't understand about seeing—"

I cut myself off before saying *ghosts* but Dr. Schermer was onto me.

"Seeing what?" he snapped, scribbling more furiously. "Are you experiencing hallucinations?"

I almost laughed at the question—one that had struck me as funny in the hospital. If I were really crazy and seeing hallucinations how would I *know* they were hallucinations?

"No," I said firmly. "What I meant was that Jess doesn't understand that when I'm writing I *see* what I'm writing about in my mind. John Gardner called it 'the fictive dream.'"

"But you don't see these 'fictive dream images' out in the real world?"

"No, of course not," I lied.

"And you've never experienced hallucinations?"

"No," I said, clasping my hands together.

"Are you sure?" he asked, flipping a page on his clipboard. "Because according to your records from your hospitalization in May of 2000 you reported aural hallucinations of a baby crying and visual hallucinations of blood and in the records of your hospitalization last winter you reported hallucinations of a woman following you—"

"Of a woman following my husband. And they weren't hallucinations . . . wait . . . how do you have those records?" I asked, the blood rushing in a hot wave to my face. "Those are confidential."

Dr. Schermer raised his eyes from his clipboard and made eye contact with me for the first time since I'd entered the office.

"When you made your appointment you faxed a waiver releasing all your previous records to our office—"

"I did no such thing!" I cried.

"Here's the waiver." Dr. Schermer passed the clipboard to me with what I could have sworn was a smug look. I took it with shaking hands and looked down at the blurry fax. Who faxed anymore? But then I remembered that Monty had a fax machine down in his apartment. The short typed letter gave Hudson River Mental Hospital and Bellevue Hospital permission to release my records to Dr. Schermer. It was signed by me—or by someone who was very good at forging my signature—and the only person I knew who could do that was Jess.

I LEFT WITH a prescription for Zoloft and Xanax and an appointment for next week with Dr. Schermer. I was lucky I was able to leave at all. I'd maintained that I'd forgotten about faxing the form. Saying that my husband had forged it sounded paranoid and I didn't need to add paranoid to delusional.

But was it paranoid? I sat in the parking lot staring at the filthy rutted snow melting under a dreary rain, willing my hands to stop shaking and my heart to stop pounding enough that I could drive home and ask Jess if he'd forged my signature. And what if he said he hadn't? What if he said I'd done it and didn't remember? He'd be furious at me for accusing him of forging my signature. As furious as he'd been when I said I'd seen the tattooed barista from Sweetleaf's hanging around the apartment. That had led to him checking me into Bellevue—the "hospitalization last winter" Dr. Schermer had referred to. Which made it sound much worse than it was. I'd only stayed the weekend—and only to reassure Jess that I was all right. I'd made him promise not to tell anyone. So who else could have typed that release letter?

I stared out the steamed-over window. White curdled fog was rising from the melting snow like smoke. So much for the clean slate of this morning's snow, I thought. I turned on the car and put on the defrost, as if clearing the windshield would clear my mind. As the windows defogged I made out a figure in a violet cocoon coat topped with a matching knit pillbox hat trimmed with lime green and muffled in a lavender scarf. She looked like a giant petit four. She looked . . . *familiar.* I wiped at the windows and peered through the streaky swipes. It was the cat-earring lady from St. Anne's. Going home, I supposed. I watched her approach a lime green Ford Focus, aiming her key fob at it, but then she turned and looked behind her. Someone had called her name and was approaching from the opposite side of the parking lot—a tall slim woman in a black coat and a lavender scarf identical to the one cat-earring lady was wearing.

That's where I'd seen that scarf before. It was the same one Katrine had been wearing when she came to witness Monty's will. And here was Katrine now waving at cat-earring lady and calling her name—

I rolled down the window in time to hear Katrine's voice call out "Aunt Jeanne!"

"Trina!" Jeanne called back. I watched as the two hugged each other. Katrine presented her aunt with a red and gold gift bag tied with red and green ribbons. Jeanne opened the gift right there in the parking lot, riffling through layers of red tissue paper to pull out what I could tell even from a distance was a candle. Jeanne hugged her niece and then opened the hatchback of her Focus and pulled out a decorative tin—one of many stacked in the back. The whole scene was like a pantomime in a play. *The happy townspeople exchange Christmas presents in the town square.* So why was my face wet with tears? And why did I feel a mounting queasy unease? So the cat-earring lady who showed me my adoption file was Katrine's Aunt Jeanne. *It was a small town.*

Katrine and her aunt embraced once more and then Katrine walked smartly across the parking lot, her high-heeled patent-leather boots smoothly navigating runnels of water from the melting snow, to her bright yellow Suburban. When I saw her red brake light go on something kindled inside me.

I pictured myself signing forms in Katrine's real estate office. "Just a formality," she'd said. "We're supposed to have you fill these out before showing you any properties." I'd signed because Jess had been outside smoking a cigarette. How easy would it be to make a Xerox of my signature and transpose it onto a fax releasing my records? But why?

Katrine's Suburban pulled out and headed to the hospital exit and I followed. She turned left onto Route 9 and drove north, back toward Concord. Even if she saw me there was nothing remarkable in me driving that way. Still, I hung back, letting a silver Honda make a right out of the diner parking lot in front of me. It was easy to see Katrine's bright yellow car up ahead. *Obnoxious gas guzzler,* Jess had whispered in my ear when we'd gotten in Katrine's car last summer. And then he'd mocked her all day.

She made a left onto 9G instead of taking 9 straight into Concord. So she wasn't going to her office. Maybe she was showing a house—or maybe she was going home. I didn't know where she lived. I didn't really know much of anything about her, considering she was a local girl. What had she said that first day?

You wouldn't remember me. I was a year behind you and not in honors classes like you were.

No, I didn't remember her, but apparently she had remembered me.

At the intersection of 199 Katrine turned left toward the Kingston-Rhinecliff Bridge. If she was going to Kingston to do her last-minute Christmas shopping at the mall I'd stop following her—

But she turned right before the bridge onto River Road. The prickle of unease in my stomach bloomed into an acid ache. She was going to Riven House . . . but then she turned right onto Apple Ring Road. I slowed down. There were only two houses on Apple Ring Road—the Corbett farm and the Jackson farm, my old house. If I went up the road she'd know I was following her. But I knew that the road curved around the orchard and came back down to River Road. If I took the next turn I would come around from the opposite direction. If I passed Katrine I could always say I'd been going to see my old house. It was funny, really, that I hadn't gone back sooner.

I didn't pass Katrine driving up the hill, nor did I see her car parked at the Corbett farm. The orchards began at the top of the hill, the now-bare apple trees standing like gaunt sentinels in knee-deep fog. A quarter mile below the top of the hill was a turnoff where we used to park the tractor during picking season. I pulled in here and parked in the rutted grooves between two sycamores, exactly where Dunstan and I used to park when he drove me back home and we wanted a little more time together. Through the leafless trees I could see the back of my old house and Katrine's yellow Suburban parked in the driveway. She wasn't inside the car, so I assumed she'd gone inside. She was probably meeting buyers here and had arrived early to better "stage" the house—turn up the heat, switch on lamps, open windows to banish the stale smell old houses got in the winter. On a dreary day like today it would be a challenge to make the old place look cheerful. Even with a new coat of paint and fresh trim on the shutters, the house would look dark on a day like today. People from the city might romanticize these old farmhouses, but they usually had small rooms, low ceilings, and small windows—all to conserve precious heat. The eyebrow window in my second floor bedroom, which I could see now through the trees, was too small for me to squeeze out of and my ceiling was so low that Dunstan hadn't been able to stand in my room. The barn was a cheerier red than it had been in my day, but I remembered getting up at 5 A.M. to feed our chickens and milk the cows and spending weekends mucking out the soiled hay. I could almost smell the manure now even though the Bailey professors probably used the barn to keep their matching Volvos instead of livestock.

I can't wait to get away, I would tell Dunstan when we sat here in his old pickup, huddled together for warmth under his denim jacket.

It would be different for us, Clary, he'd say. *You only hate it because of how your folks treat you. A place is good or bad because of the people in it.*

But I'd been afraid. I'd seen how the mean, cramped space of our house and the unrelenting toil of farmwork had turned Trudy into a bitter, carping shrew—seen how she cringed at the sight of my father's muddy boots on her clean linoleum floor, seen how she pressed herself against the narrow hallway when he walked past her, heard her muffled complaints when he got too close to her in bed.

I hadn't wanted that. I'd wanted to go away, find a different sort of life, a life I thought Jess would take me to. So I'd broken up with Dunstan in my senior year of college and moved to New York with Jess. And for a while it seemed that I'd gotten the life I'd dreamed about in that low-ceilinged room behind the eyebrow window. Jess and I had been good together before the money troubles, but when things got tight even our spacious loft had come to feel claustrophobic—and haunted. I *had* told the doctor at Bellevue that there was a woman trying to get into the loft to take my husband away from me. I'd said that she was covered with tattoos of Jess's novels—the parts that described Rachel Bartley, the character based on me. *Don't you see,* I had told the doctor at Bellevue, *she's trying to take my place.* That was when Jess suggested we move and start over again. That's why we'd come to Riven House. But maybe Dunstan had been right. A place was only as good as the people in it. And maybe that's why I'd seen ghosts in Riven House—Jess and I had poisoned it.

I wiped my eyes. When I opened them I saw that another car had pulled into the drive behind Katrine's. A small sports car. Her city buyers? But only one man got out, a man who glanced at the mean little farmhouse with such disdain it was hard to believe he'd ever said he'd be willing to live in a shack. Jess turned the collar of his black leather jacket up around his neck, ground a cigarette out in the mud, and went inside as if he owned the place.

Chapter Twenty-Five

I sat in the car staring at the mute face of my childhood home trying to think of innocent reasons for Jess and Katrine meeting there. Jess had decided we needed to get out of Riven House for my mental health and was planning to rent the Jackson farm for us to live in. He was just checking it out . . .

But with every minute that passed that likelihood melted just as surely as the snow leached into the gray air. What did I think they were doing in there? Checking to see if the basement was dry? Measuring the windows for curtains? Only a woman naïve enough to believe that her husband moved to the country so they could have a second chance together would believe that. I wasn't that woman anymore.

I wasn't really sure *who* I was. Was I the girl who had grown up in that cramped room listening to noises in the dark and dreaming of a way out? Or the girl who'd broken Dunstan Corbett's heart here on this hill? Or the woman who'd married Jess Martin? The woman who had believed he still loved her despite all evidence to the contrary? The woman whose husband was cheating on her with Katrine Vanderberg?

But he'd made fun of her!

Of course he had, a voice inside my head replied, *so you wouldn't suspect. Stupid girl!*

It was the voice of Great-Granny Jackson, the voice that had told me throughout my childhood that I was stupid, ugly, *wrong.*

And here it turned out she had been right all along. How exultant she would be to see my husband cheating on me under her own roof.

Because, really, what else could be happening in there?

It must have been an hour before they reappeared. The gray afternoon was deepening to dusk by then and the rain had changed to sleet. They were two indistinct shapes in the gloaming, but it was clear enough how they clung together on the slippery path. They didn't kiss, but then Jess had never been one for good-bye kisses. I waited until both their cars pulled out of the driveway and watched until their taillights were swallowed up by the fog like embers extinguished in ash. Then I started the Subaru. I'd been sitting in the car without heat for so long that my hands were frozen through. They felt like someone else's hands as I fumbled with the ignition and the gearshift and clutched the steering wheel as though it were a life preserver.

Where was I even going? Back to Riven House where Jess would be sitting by the fire with Monty, smiling at me as if nothing had changed at all?

I turned left onto Apple Ring Road, onto the steep decline down to my old house. The sudden dip made my stomach lurch. I was going to be sick. I couldn't be sick in Monty's car. I turned the wheel to the right to pull over, but the car kept going down the hill. *It doesn't matter which way you try to turn,* Great-Granny Jackson's voice mocked, *the only way you're going is down.*

"Fuck you, old lady!" I cried aloud, wrenching the wheel again and hitting the brakes. The rear tires fishtailed and the car began to revolve in a slow, lazy pirouette. I was sliding down the hill sideways. Another voice spoke in my head—Dunstan's. *Black ice,* he said, but it was too late.

The Subaru careened into the oak tree at the end of my old driveway. I heard metal crunch, glass shatter, and my own scream. Eyes closed, I braced for the concussion of an air bag—or worse: the steering rod through my heart, windshield glass in my face, head smashed against the ceiling—all the horrors Dunstan had described to me the summer he worked as an EMT, all leading to a bloody, violent death—

Just what Jess and Katrine wanted—me out of the way and Riven House for themselves.

As if the thought had suspended time, everything stopped. The sudden silence was shocking after the screech of metal and shattering of glass. I thought I must be dead. Slowly, I became aware of a pattering sound, like mice in the attic, and I wondered if I was back in my childhood bedroom listening to noises over my head. What a hell that would be! Like Dale going back to Vietnam when he got hurt. But then something wet and cold hit my face, shocking me awake. I opened my eyes.

The world had turned upside down and splintered into a million pieces.

Of course it had. Jess was cheating on me.

I blinked away ice water mixed with hot tears. I was look-ing through my shattered windshield at upside-down apple trees, bony branches hanging from the clouds. I recalled a picture from a children's book of Norse myths of the world tree Yggdrasil growing in the center of the earth. I'd gone to Norse Hel.

At least I wasn't in my childhood bedroom listening to Great-Granny Jackson thump-dragging her leg—

I looked down—or up rather—toward my legs, but the interior of the car was too dark to make out anything. I didn't seem to be in pain, though, so they must be all right.

Then again, I didn't feel much of anything at all. All the blood had rushed to my head because I was hanging upside down, held by my seat belt. I fumbled for the catch, my hands so numb I could barely feel them. Was I paralyzed? But when I pressed the seat belt button I fell headfirst onto the roof with a painful thud and stab in my left hip as it hit the steering wheel. I used my hands to pull myself forward along the roof toward the passenger side door, which looked like it had been pleated into a fan. What if I couldn't get out? What if I were trapped here all night on a road where nobody came, in the cold and dark? Would Jess come looking for me? And if he found me—injured and alone— would he help me?

The thought I'd had in the skid came back to me: this was what Jess and Katrine wanted, me out of the way.

But no, that was too awful. Jess might not love me anymore, he might be cheating, but want me dead? I was being paranoid. This accident hadn't been Jess's fault. Still . . . I couldn't wait for him to come find me here.

I crawled toward the door over broken glass, wishing I was wearing gloves. It was so disorienting to be upside down it took me forever to find the door handle and when I did the door didn't move. I was trapped here. I would freeze to death. When they found me in the morning they would wonder what I had been doing on this lonely road outside my old childhood house.

She was coming from a psychologist's appointment, Jess would say. *She hasn't been herself lately.*

And what would Dr. Schermer say? That I'd been depressed, delusional, paranoid. Little wonder if I'd run my car off the road into a tree—

I always knew you'd come to a bad end, Great-Granny Jackson said in my head, *crazy and alone.*

I slammed my hands against the car door and it swung open so suddenly I slid out into the icy mud. The fall knocked the wind out of me. I lay there for a moment looking up into the darkening sky, catching my breath, wondering if I could walk.

I cannot die here.

This time the voice inside my head was my own. *Good.* It was time I started listening to myself and not all the others. They were liars. Great-Granny Jackson, Trudy, Jess—Jess worst of all. Pretending to make fun of Katrine while he was fucking her!

I rolled to my side and scrambled onto my hands and knees, then sat back on my heels. The Subaru was hanging over the edge of the road, upside down, the front end accordioned around the old oak. Thank God it was a sturdy old car or I'd be dead. I planted one foot on the ground, braced my hands on my knees, and got to my feet. I felt a sharp pain in my left hip where I'd hit it against the steering wheel but otherwise my legs seemed okay. I was okay. I was going to walk away from this—and I'd have to walk unless I wanted to get back in the car. My cell phone had been in my purse in the backseat of the car.

Who would I even call? Not Jess. He'd know then that I'd been spying on him and Katrine. No, I had to think first before I saw him. Should I call Dunstan? And explain to him that I'd been spying on the cheating husband I'd left him for?

No. I couldn't talk to anyone until I figured this out. Riven House wasn't far.

A mile down the road, Monty had said.

Monty. I had to tell Monty. He would believe me. He had believed me when I told him I'd seen Mary Foley. He hadn't thought I was crazy.

I started toward the road but then I remembered the black ice. Sleet was still coming down. In the few minutes I'd been standing here my hair had become icy. The footing on the steep road would be treacherous. I'd be better off in the orchard and I knew a shortcut that was quicker than the road. I turned and walked toward the trees.

This part of the orchard, the part originally owned by the Jacksons until the Corbetts bought them out in the Depression, lay in a gentle incline between the hill and River Road, sheltered from the winds and the worst cold. But even here the icy rain was coating the branches of the apple trees. I touched one of the gnarled old branches—a Sommerfeld—and felt a slick coating of ice. In their draperies of ice the apple trees looked like girls in white dresses holding up their arms to the sky. Beautiful! But if the icy rain kept up, their branches would become so heavy they would break under their burden.

But that wasn't my problem anymore. My problem was getting back to Riven House and figuring out what I would say to Jess. I wrapped my scarf over my head and I walked on, my feet crunching in the newly formed ice, my head bowed against the driving sleet, playing out all the opening gambits in this scenario.

I know you're having an affair with Katrine Vanderberg!

How long has this been going on?

I want a divorce!

Lines from some horrible soap opera like the kind Trudy used to watch. I saw myself as the shrill, hysterical wife, throwing a vase at Jess's head, then collapsing in tears as he left—

But could I even throw him out of Monty's house? I had to talk to Monty first. Surely he would be on my side.

Not that Monty had ever been a paragon of monogamy and fidelity. And he had asked Jess and me here. Riven House was still his—

I stopped and looked up. I'd come to the stone wall that bordered the road directly across from the gate of Riven House. I remembered Jess standing at that gate, looking covetously at the house, beautiful and golden in the summer sunlight, and Katrine slyly suggesting the idea of Jess and me becoming the caretakers so she'd have an "in" on the ground when the house came up for sale.

Had Jess been sleeping with Katrine then? Or had it started later? I thought back to how we'd found Katrine in the first place. It had been Jess's idea that we needed a change of scene after my hospitalization, but hadn't it been my idea to look for houses upstate?

Yes, but it had been Jess's idea to look around Concord because he'd always liked the countryside around the college. He'd lived off campus his junior year in one of those old falling-down houses in town—in fact, he remembered the name of a real estate company just around the corner. Van something.

Vanderberg's? I'd asked.

Yeah, that was it. Do you want me to call them?

Sure, I'd said, relieved that he still wanted to be with me after my second breakdown, *why don't you set up an appointment for next weekend?*

And then Katrine had showed us all those awful split-levels and modular homes. Jess mocking her accent, whispering little asides in my ear. When she said she'd gone to SUNY Potsdam Jess had remarked *SUNY Pothead* in my ear.

Didn't you date a girl who went there? I'd asked, but he'd shushed me. Because, I thought, he didn't want Katrine to hear us making fun of her.

Or because Katrine was the girl that Jess had dated in college before me. He'd dated a girl who'd gone away to one of the SUNYs . . .

Katrine had been one year behind me in high school. She'd gone to Dutchess Community for two years. That would have been Jess's and my sophomore and junior years. Then she went away to SUNY Potsdam. Leaving Jess alone . . . to meet me.

When Jess and I argued about Dunstan he told me he'd broken up with the girl in Potsdam for me. Had he ever said her name?

Tina? Hadn't it been Tina?

Or had it been *Trina?* Which is what her aunt had called Katrine in the parking lot.

I sat down on the wall. I could feel the ice seeping through my wool coat, but I didn't care. I was frozen straight through now. Katrine was the local girl Jess had dated before me. How she must have hated me when Jess broke up with her. But then they'd started seeing each other again—but when?

I thought of the last year we'd spent in Brooklyn—Jess always going out in search of his muse, out for hours, with that tattooed barista I'd thought, but what if he had been seeing Katrine?

I go in to the city all the time. I have a friend who's got an apartment she lets me use.

I got up and crossed the road, heading for the gate. As I walked up the drive I pictured Jess and Katrine meeting at the friend's apartment. *Fucking* in the friend's apartment. Jess saying how he'd made a mistake, he shouldn't have broken up with her for that crazy girl.

What could I do? She got pregnant and then after she miscarried she wound up in the mental hospital—

Everyone in high school said she was crazy. No one would blame you now for leaving—

I'd feel bad leaving her with no money, alone in the city. If we moved back to Concord—

She'd be back in her hometown. Still, it would be better for everyone if there were more money—

They must have come up with the idea of Riven House together. Get Jess and me up here at the house as caretakers, then when Monty found out I was his daughter . . .

But how would Katrine know I was Monty's heir?

Because her Aunt Jeanne worked at St. Anne's and had seen my birth certificate.

I had come to the fork in the road between the drive to the house and the one to the cottage. I stopped and stared up at the house. *The color of old money,* Jess had said. Katrine had told him that I was Monty's daughter and together they had planned for me to inherit Riven House. Had they counted on me remembering the apple blossom girl story and following the leads in it to my birth certificate at St. Anne's? Hadn't it been Jess who asked Monty to give me back my old notebook with the story in it? And then I had seen the ghost of Mary Foley—

A chill worse than the pelting sleet coursed through me. Jess and Katrine couldn't have planned that—

Unless the ghost hadn't been real.

As cold as I was and as warm as the lights of Riven House looked, I took the lower drive toward the pond and gardens. To where I'd seen the ghost of Mary Foley. Once in driving rain like today and the second time in the fog. Both times it had been hard to see her closely. What had I really seen but a woman cloaked in a shawl—

As Katrine had been when she came to the house a few

weeks ago. Could it have been Katrine pretending to be the ghost? So that I would follow Mary Foley's story to the story of my own birth? And so that once I'd inherited Riven House Jess could have me shut away in a mental hospital?

After all, who saw ghosts but a crazy person?

I walked across the field, paying no more heed to the sleet that fell on me than the trees standing beside the pond noticed the ice building up on their branches. I must have looked like them, a figure bowed down by the weight of water, limbs growing heavier and heavier until they broke. I expected I would crack in two as I stood staring at the pond.

A scum of ice clung to the surface, not hard enough to stand on yet, but if the temperature kept dropping it would be frozen solid by the morning. I pictured Mary's body frozen beneath the ice. I looked up at the bridge over the weir and remembered the figure I had seen there and how that last time she had vanished behind it—

But Mary hadn't vanished behind the weir; she had stepped forward into the pond. Why would her ghost do something she hadn't? And how, if she hadn't been a ghost, had she vanished? I walked around the edge of the pond, my boots crunching over the frozen mud, until I came to the bridge. I climbed up the steps and looked over. The stream had partly frozen over the rock wall, water moving slowly beneath ribbed channels of ice. Without the spray of water I could see that the stone weir wasn't solid all the way back. There was a gap between the staggered stone steps and the rock face below the bridge. I walked down the steps and picked my way across the rutted, frozen mud to the weir. Yes, there was a gap beneath the steps, narrow, but large enough for a slender woman to squeeze in.

I crouched down and crawled in, my knees sinking into the mud. It was warmer in here, like a fox's den burrowed under the snow. For the first time since I'd seen Jess walk out of my old house I felt a kindling of warmth. I could hear the trickle of water above my head, wending its slow course to the river. I felt like I had burrowed into the heart of the estate, into the river itself. I wrapped my arms around my knees and looked up. In the little bit of purple dusk that seeped in through the narrow opening I made out icicles hanging from the upper rocks. It was as if I'd stumbled into the crystal cave where Merlin had been shut away by the sorceress Nimue. A violet crystal cave, I thought, reaching up to pluck a pale purple icicle. It broke with a brittle chime and fell into my hands. When I brought it closer I saw what gave it color was a tuft of wool frozen inside. A bit of yarn the same lavender as Katrine Vanderberg's scarf.

Chapter Twenty-Six

Katrine was the ghost.

Of course she's the ghost, I thought, *she's the* thing *haunting my marriage, the specter hanging over Jess and me.*

Jess knew that I'd believe in the ghost because I'd seen one before. That he must have shared that with Katrine hurt worse than the thought of him sleeping with her. He must have told her how I'd been after the miscarriage, how I'd heard a baby crying in the night.

Katrine had laughed when I told her I thought I heard a baby crying at night.

Foxes, she'd said.

Only it had been her playing a tape, using it to lead me to the pond on a foggy night, letting me see her on the weir and then hiding down here, laughing at me. Later she and Jess would meet at my childhood home and laugh some more. Their plan was working beautifully. I'd started obsessing over the apple blossom girl story. Looking her up in the library and the Village Hall . . . and then, in case I didn't think of it myself, Katrine had brought up the idea of me looking for my birth certificate at St. Anne's, where Aunt Jeanne conveniently let me see my records. And then I'd run back here to tell Sunny—

Sunny. They hadn't planned on Sunny, had they? I remembered Jess's shock when he heard that Sunny and Monty were married. Sunny could have ruined everything.

A tremor moved through me, so hard that I thought the ground was moving beneath me. The icicles seemed to tremble over my head. If Sunny had lived I might not have inherited Riven House. Their plan would have been ruined. And so Sunny had to die.

I was shaking uncontrollably now, feeling the cold because I was thawing out. But I didn't have time to thaw out. I had to think about this coldly.

I crawled out from the cave. The frigid air hit my skin and turned the layer of sweat and mud to ice. As I stood I heard my hair, frozen into long icy dreadlocks, rattle in the wind. I pulled my scarf back over my head and started walking up the hill, picturing as I went Sunny hanging from the rafters of the barn surrounded by her puppets. Was it possible Jess and Katrine were responsible for that? Had they murdered Sunny so I would inherit Riven House? And if they had murdered Sunny, what wouldn't they do to achieve their plan? Why stop at having me declared crazy? Why not kill me? Jess would inherit Riven House, Katrine would sell it for them, and they could retire to someplace *fucking warmer*.

I was walking fast now, the sound of my boots cracking through the ice like gunshots, my frozen hair clattering like tribal war rattles. My face and hands were tight with frozen mud and tears. I was a golem risen from the mud. This is what Jess and Katrine had made me into with their plans—a monster.

But what they hadn't made me into yet was the owner of Riven House. I paused at the crest of the hill and looked up at the house. It rose above me like a medieval tower, the light in the library glass doors a beacon. Monty would be there sitting by the fire, waiting for me to come bring him his evening cocktail. Monty—my father and still owner of Riven House. What good did it do Jess and Katrine to have me committed—or *dead*—if Monty still owned the house? Monty had to die first for me to inherit the house.

Had they planned to wait until he died? He wasn't well. According to Jess, his doctor said his heart was failing. A shock could kill him. A shock Jess and Katrine could easily manufacture themselves. For all I knew they had done it already. Monty could be lying dead by the fire.

I began to run. I had to get to Monty and tell him what was happening. It would break his heart to learn that Jess would plot against him. Perhaps he wouldn't believe it at first, but I'd convince him and then we'd confront Jess together. Monty would demand that he leave. We might have to call the police. I would call Dunstan—

At the thought of Dunstan I reflexively reached into my coat pocket, but I didn't have my phone. It was lying in the wreck of my car. I should have gone back for it. I should have called Dunstan right away. I was going into a house alone with a man who was plotting to kill me, blundering in—

I skidded to a stop at the steps to the terrace. Jess could be in the library with Monty. If I burst in, covered with mud and ice, blathering about murder plots, Monty would think I was crazy and Jess . . . what would Jess do when he knew I'd discovered his plans? Tearfully confess? Or kill me and Monty?

No, it was stupid to rush into the library. I had to get to a phone before I saw Jess and call Dunstan, then try to talk to Monty. I'd go in through the boot hall and straight down to Monty's apartment. Maybe Monty was even there, typing or napping, but if he wasn't I could at least use his phone.

I skirted the terrace, passing under the old apple tree that, weighted by ice, hung lower than usual over the window to Monty's apartment. I looked in through the window. I could see a bit of Monty's desk with the old manual typewriter and stacks of paper. But no Monty. I went in through the boot hall, not stopping to shuck off my muddy boots for once, and straight down to Monty's apartment. The door was closed, but not locked. He was too trusting by half, letting all sorts of people live on his property, taking Jess and me in—I hated to think what it would do to him to learn what Jess was trying to do. I opened the door as quietly as I could and stood for a moment listening to the house, but I couldn't hear anything. That must be why Monty liked it down here; it was quiet.

There certainly had to be some reason why he holed up down here when he had a whole beautiful house above him. It certainly couldn't be the aesthetics of the apartment. Jess had described it as faded bachelor digs circa 1978 but that had been generous. Crazy-ass hoarder was more like it. The little room was lined with shelves that were double stacked with books, manuscript boxes, file folders, and old newspapers. More stacks of books, file boxes, and newspapers stood on the floor and tumbled out of a monstrous Victorian wardrobe. The only surface in the room that was remotely clear was the desk. There the old manual typewriter crouched like a shiny black beetle under a circle of lamplight. Monty must have just been here. A gurgle of pipes came from the next room. He must be in the bathroom. He'd be embarrassed to come out and find me here but that couldn't be helped.

I moved closer to the desk, instinctively drawn to that circle of light. Here there was order. Pens lined up, folders aligned neatly with a stack of manuscript pages beside the typewriter, just as I kept my things on my desk. Was there anything more satisfying, I thought, letting my hand rest on the top page, than a thick stack of completed pages growing beside a typewriter or laptop?

Monty *had* been productive. He must have over three hundred pages here. Nearly a completed book. I looked down, unable to resist, and read the header in the left-hand corner of the top page.

"*The Apples of Discord,*" it read. "A. Montague."

It was the title of the story I had written for Monty's class. Was he using it for his memoir? Had he forgotten it was *my* title? Surely he wouldn't use it if he did remember. Should I tell him . . . ?

And then I remembered I had more important things to tell him. It really didn't matter if he'd used my title. After all, he'd given me a house . . .

Still . . .

I picked up the page on top of the stack and read.

> Every year when the apple blossoms bloom the town council of Discord selects a Queen of the Apple Blossom Festival.

It was exactly how *my* book started. I looked at the next page—and the next—and the next—pages sliding to the floor as I riffled through them—all my words. The pages I'd given Monty to read, the ones he'd been critiquing—

I opened the folder on the other side of the typewriter. There were the pages I'd last given him. And there on the typewriter was a page typed directly from my pages only with his name on the header. Monty was retyping the pages I gave him. He was stealing my book.

A door creaked open and I looked up. Monty stood in the

doorway, one hand gripping his cane, the other tugging at his trousers, his eyes down on the floor. *Why, he's just a sad old man,* I thought, swiftly followed by: *the fucking bastard.*

His eyes flicked up as if he'd heard my thought and widened comically. *Never use clichés,* Monty always told us in class. *Never let me catch you writing "He stopped dead in his tracks or his mouth dropped open or his eyes widened in surprise."*

But that's just what he did. He stopped dead in his tracks, his mouth dropped open, and his eyes widened in surprise. And then he did the most cliché thing of all—he clutched his chest.

"Oh, come on," I said. "You're going to have a heart attack? I'm the one who just found out her husband is trying to kill her and her father is stealing her book."

"Clare?" He croaked my name. Like he was only now recognizing me. I looked back at the window behind me, at my reflection. The scarf wrapped around my head was covered with dripping icicles, my face was streaked with mud frozen to pasty gray, my sweater and skirt covered with the same chalky rime. I looked like the ghost of Mary Foley newly risen from the frozen pond come to wreak vengeance on the man who'd stolen her story.

To wreak vengeance on her own son. My father.

I stepped forward, relenting, pushing back my scarf, but Monty backed away into an overstacked shelf. Papers slithered off a pile. He clutched at the shelf, but the books slid under his fingers. His knees buckled under him. One hand patted his shirt pocket as he slid down. It was like watching one of Sunny's puppets crumple to the floor.

I rushed toward him, reaching for the bottle of pills at the same time as he fumbled them out of his pocket. His eyes met mine as my fingers grazed the plastic vial, the jaundiced whites rolling back as though he were afraid of me. As if he thought I was trying to take the pills away from him when I was only trying to get the bottle from him so I could open it and give him the nitroglycerin tablet more quickly. *I'm not the one trying to kill you,* I wanted to say, *Jess is!*

But he jerked the bottle away from me and the motion made him drop it.

I heard it fall to the floor with a clatter. I cursed and dropped to the floor and saw the bottle roll under the Victorian wardrobe. I crawled after it and stuck my hand under the wardrobe . . . felt nothing. I stretched out on the floor and looked under the wardrobe, past dust and dead stink bugs and paper clips and wads of paper. I saw the bottle but it was too far back for me to reach. I needed something to fish it out. Or to find out if Monty had another bottle of nitroglycerin tablets.

"Monty," I said, scrambling up and turning to him. "Do you have—?"

I stopped when I saw Monty's face. His skin was the color of old newspaper. Beads of sweat coursed down the deeply carved creases. His bloodshot eyes stared at the ceiling. "Monty! Do you know where you have more pills?"

His eyes rolled in their sockets toward me but didn't register my presence. As if I were invisible. As if I were a ghost.

"I'm going to call 911," I shouted, more to myself than to Monty. I lurched to my feet and stumbled to the desk. There'd been a phone there, hadn't there? Yes, an avocado green push-button model circa late seventies like everything else in this room. I lifted the grimy receiver but heard only static. It was broken or the lines were down, pulled down by the ice—

At the thought I heard a crack and the lamp on the desk flickered. Outside the sleet was hardening on the trees and power lines. We were in the middle of an ice storm. Any minute now we could lose power.

Another creak drew my attention but this one came from the doorway to the stairs. I looked up and saw Jess staring at me. "My God, Clare, what happened to you? I came down to see if Monty had heard from you—" He stopped when he saw Monty slumped on the floor. "Monty! What's—"

"He's had a heart attack. I was trying to call 911 but the phone's dead. Do you have your cell?"

"It's upstairs in my study," he said, kneeling beside Monty. He laid his fingers on his neck. "Shit, I can't feel a pulse. Do you know how to do CPR?"

I did. I'd taken the class with Dunstan the summer before college, but I'd never used it.

"Lay him down flat and put something under his neck," I barked.

Jess did what I told him to. I had the idea that if I just kept talking to Jess in this voice I could get him to do anything I wanted him to. *Stop fucking Katrine. Stop plotting my murder. Love me again.*

I could have as soon commanded Monty's heart to start beating and his lungs to draw breath. Pumping my folded hands over his heart didn't work, nor blowing my breath into his parched, sour-smelling mouth.

"Don't just sit there," I screamed at Jess. "Go get your phone and call for an ambulance."

Jess flinched. "Clare, I don't think it will matter. He's gone."

I sat back on my heels and looked down at Monty. His eyes were staring sightlessly at the acoustic tiles of the drop ceiling. He shouldn't have died staring at those, I thought, he should have at least died in one of the better rooms.

I looked up at Jess. He looked almost as pale as Monty. "Of course you want me to stop. You want him dead."

He flinched as though I'd struck him. I wondered suddenly what he'd do if I did hit him.

"I'm going to ignore that because of how upset I know you are. I'll go call 911 and you go clean yourself up. I doubt you want your boyfriend Dusty to see you looking like that. What the hell happened to you, anyway? I've been going out of my mind worrying."

"You mean after you came home from screwing Katrine at my old house?" I asked, getting to my feet.

"I *was* at your old house," he said slowly, as if talking to a child. "How did you know that? Have you been following me?"

Typical Jess move to make the argument about my behavior. He'd been doing it for years, turning every question I asked into a sign of irrational jealousy.

"No," I replied coolly. "I was following your girlfriend back from the hospital. Where I learned, by the way, that you forged my consent to have my records sent to Dr. Schermer. Part of your plan to have me committed, I suppose."

"Clare, do you realize how crazy you sound?"

"That's what you keep telling me. I made it easy for you, telling Cortland about the ghosts, didn't I? But when everyone learns that Katrine was posing as the ghost I don't think that tack will work so well."

Jess laughed. Then shook and dropped his head and startled at the sight of Monty as if he'd forgotten he was there. "Christ, Clare, you've really gone round the bend now. Yes, I sent the consent form to Dr. Schermer. I knew the appointment wouldn't do any good unless he knew your background; you're too damned good at telling a story. And yes, I was at your house with Katrine. I thought we might rent it to get you out of here before this house drove you nuts, but I can see I'm too late."

"You took an hour to look at the house?"

"You were watching the house for an hour?" He got to his feet. "I'm sorry, Clare, but I don't think I can do this anymore. I thought you'd be better up here in the country, in your home-town, but according to Trina you never really fit in here either. She said you never had many friends."

"That's what you and *Trina* were talking about for an hour?" I asked, seething at the idea of Katrine telling Jess I didn't have friends growing up. Who had time for friends with all the chores I had to do?

"Yes," Jess said, "but she can tell you herself. I called her before to see if she'd heard from you. She said she'd come over to wait with me for news. There's her car now."

I turned, following Jess's gaze to the window. Headlights strobed across the glass and then went out. I crossed behind the desk and looked out. Yes, there was Katrine's yellow Sub-urban. The car door opened, lighting up the frozen branches of the old apple tree and silhouetting Katrine against the lit interior of the car. I had a glimpse of her grim, determined face. I don't think I'd ever seen her before without a smile on her face. I realized that everything I'd seen before was an act—the brittle façade of a saleswoman. She had cajoled and maneuvered me into this place. I remembered now the hint of bitterness in her voice when she'd said on that first day that I probably didn't remember her. But she had remembered me. She'd been jealous that I was the one who'd gotten Jess. She'd hatched a plan to get him back and to ruin my life in the process.

She glanced at herself in her rearview mirror, adjusted her scarf over her head, and stepped out of the car.

Bitch, I muttered under my breath.

She looked up as if she heard me—or perhaps because she heard the creaking of the apple tree branches over her head. A wind was blowing off the river, rattling the ice-covered branches like dry bones. She shivered and then swung shut the car door with a sharp crack that seemed to echo and reverberate through my body, plunging the scene into darkness. I was staring in the now-dark window at the reflection of myself and the room behind me and of Jess coming toward me, his arms out as if to strangle me. Then the whole world shattered and turned black.

Chapter Twenty-Seven

I thought I'd been struck unconscious—that Jess had struck me. There'd been an enormous crack and then the lights had gone out. I lifted my hand to my head. There was still ice in my hair—no, not ice—glass. The window had broken. Had Jess hurled something at me and broken the window? Something cold and sharp brushed against my face—a long bony hand wrapping itself in my hair. I screamed and flailed my arms to escape its grasp and the fingers snapped back and slapped my face. Then I smelled it. Sap and resin and the faint breath of rotting apples. It was the old apple tree. The ice had brought it down and it had crashed through the window and taken down the electric cables to the house.

"Clare?"

I froze. It was Jess's voice, on the other side of the desk.

"Clare, are you all right? I think a tree crashed through the window."

Yes, the tree had crashed through the window, but before that I'd seen Jess coming at me, arms stretched out to throttle me. He'd been about to strangle me when the tree came through the window.

"Clare?"

"Jess?"

The voice came from outside. Katrine. So she hadn't been killed by the falling tree. She was outside the window.

"Jess? Are you all right? Is Clare?"

She'd seen me at the window. She must think the tree hit me and killed me. *Well, it hadn't, bitch.*

But how easy it would be to say that it had.

My wife was giving CPR to Mr. Montague when the tree crashed through the window, Officer. She died a hero. Yes, after *Mr. Montague so she died his heir.*

"I don't know. She isn't talking," Jess called back. "Do you have a flashlight?"

"In my glove compartment," Katrine said. "I'll go get it."

I suddenly thought of Katrine's faux country getup that day she'd shown us houses—jacket, Wellies . . . *All she needs is a hunting rifle to look like she strode out of Downton Abbey.* What if she kept a gun in her car?

I couldn't wait to find out. I could hear Jess crawling over the broken glass toward me. The tree was between us. Behind me I felt glass and twigs but nothing large impeding my way. I tried to remember the layout of the room—what lay between me and the door to the stairs. No furniture, I thought, but there were stacks of books and newspapers everywhere—

A hand touched my leg and closed down on my ankle. I jumped up at the touch, kicking out to free myself of Jess's grip, and sprung away, feet crunching on broken glass. I ran with my arms out, searching for the doorway. I tripped—damn all these books!—and landed on something soft.

Monty. I'd landed on Monty's dead body.

I swallowed the scream rising in my throat and scrambled over him, but something pulled me back. Jess's hands on me. I kicked free of him and crawled forward, groping for the opening to the stairway. My outstretched hands smacked into a bookshelf. Books skittered under my fingers. I heard Jess's step right behind me. My hand tightened on a thick spine—an enormous lexicon of some obscure language no doubt—and I hurled the book in Jess's direction. It made a satisfying *thunk* when it struck Jess but what was even more satisfying was Jess's cry of surprise. I'd done something he didn't expect. It felt good. But I didn't think it was going to improve our relationship any. I groped my way up the bookshelf and to the doorway and then I was running up the stairs into the octagon.

BUT FIRST I had to get through the boot hall—pitch black and cluttered with decades' worth of cracked Wellies and split-heeled Weejuns. Why hadn't I ever cleaned in here? But if I had to get through it, so did they. I kicked shoes and boots into the middle of the hallway, dragged coats and jackets off the hooks and swept stacks of newspaper behind me. I ran through to the kitchen where a pale gray rectangle over the sink cast a little more light. I went straight to the knife drawer and drew out the sharpest carving knife, the one I used to debone chickens. Would I really use it on Jess?

I pictured Jess's face in the reflection in the window—enraged, ready to strangle me. What had I done to make him that angry? And how had I been so blind not to know?

You writers really do live in a little bubble, Katrine had said, mocking me for not knowing that she was sleeping with my husband. I realized I was shaking all over, whether from rage or grief I wasn't sure. I didn't have time for either. I gripped the knife harder and listened. I heard muffled thumps coming from the boot hall. I couldn't stay in here—but where should I go? I could flee through the library doors out onto the terrace but then what? I didn't have a car. The nearest house was a

mile away. Over ice, in the dark. If they tracked me down outside it would be easy to make my death look like an accident.
Poor deranged Clare Jackson out wandering in an ice storm
just like her grandmother Mary Foley. No, I wouldn't die like
that. I had to reach someone and tell them what was happening. If only I hadn't left my phone in the car—

But Jess's phone was upstairs in his study. If I could get to
it before he did—

The voices in the boot hall were coming closer. I had to
choose.

I bolted from the kitchen into the rotunda—into a well of
light. The storm had passed and the moon was shining straight
through the oculus, spilling moonlight down the marble steps
like a frozen waterfall. Beautiful, but deadly. I would be completely exposed. I sprinted up the stairs as fast as I could, taking
two steps at a time, glad for the solid marble that didn't creak
like the wooden floors. Even Bayard's fish-white face seemed
welcoming. This was my house now, I realized as I reached the
top gallery. I'd be damned if I would let Jess and Katrine wrest
it from me.

Or keep me from any of its rooms. I felt a thrill of owner-
ship turning the doorknob to Jess's study. I hadn't been in it
since Jess had taken possession of it. I wasn't supposed to go
into his *writing* space. But here I was, trespassing in the inner
sanctum, going straight for his desk, where his cell phone lay
in a wedge of moonlight from the window. I pulled it out of its
charger, checked to see it had power, and dialed 911. A NO SER-
VICE message flashed on the screen. Jess had complained that
the service was spotty in his study but I'd thought it was just
an excuse not to use the phone. I'd have to find a place to get a
signal. I could hear Jess and Katrine downstairs searching the
first floor for me. I still had a little time, but not much.

As I slid the phone into my back pocket next to the knife, my eyes strayed across the desk. There was no manuscript stack here as there had been on Monty's desk, only Jess's closed laptop and a few loose pages shining in the moonlight. I couldn't help glancing at them and then, seeing my own name typed on top, couldn't help reading them.

It was Dr. Schermer's report on my visit that afternoon, faxed from the hospital to Monty's number. That must have been what Katrine was doing at the hospital today. She'd gotten access to my confidential files—after all, *she* had recommended Dr. Schermer—and faxed them to Jess. If I'd needed any more proof of their plan I now had it. They wouldn't have had any trouble convincing anyone that I was unstable with this.

Patient exhibits signs of paranoia . . . patient became defensive when confronted with past psychiatric history . . . denied having signed release forms . . . obsessed with fictional family history . . . delusional . . . possible suicide risk.

How convenient. I wouldn't be surprised to learn that Katrine had bribed Dr. Schermer. With this report my death would look like a suicide. Which meant that was what they were planning. Not just to put me away, but kill me. It should have devastated me, but instead I felt a cold joy. I had proof that Katrine and Jess were plotting to do away with me. I just had to live long enough to get it into the right hands.

I folded the fax in quarters and stuck it in my pocket. I listened but the house had gone quiet. Where were they? Had they come upstairs? How long before they found me? I had to find a hiding spot with cell phone reception.

I was turning from the desk when I thought of Jess's laptop. What more evidence might be on it? I scooped it up just as I heard a creak on the wooden floor outside. They were in the gallery. Then I heard Katrine's voice. "She's not in her study, but you should see what she's done with the wallpaper in there. She really *is* crazy."

Bitch. Calling me crazy when she was the one plotting to kill me. It was a good thing they'd checked my study, though. They wouldn't check it again so soon. And I was pretty sure that they didn't know about the adjoining closets.

I hurried to the closet and opened the door as quietly as I could, slipped inside, and closed the door behind me. My heart was pounding as I listened for any sign they'd heard me. But I heard instead their footsteps receding to the other side of the gallery, into my bedroom.

I crouched down in the dark and opened Jess's laptop to give myself enough light to see. I hadn't been in the closet since I had been getting Minnie's Mourning Room ready for Jess. *What a good little wifey I'd been, fixing everything nice for her husband.* I'd piled all Minnie's belongings into trunks and boxes and pushed them to the back of the triangular closet. And I'd noticed the door. It was only three feet high, but wide enough to crawl through into the nursery. I crawled through it now, into my study, still clutching Jess's laptop. I put it down on the floor and, leaning against the wall, tried the phone again—this time I had service, but I was afraid that if I talked Jess and Katrine would hear me. I put the phone on mute and tapped in Dunstan's number, which I'd memorized from the card he'd given me weeks ago, and texted him a message. In trouble at Riven House. Please come!

Would he think it was a joke? I wondered. I really should call 911 as soon as I was someplace I could talk.

I listened again and heard Jess's and Katrine's voices coming from the gallery. Even though they'd checked this room they could check it again. I looked desperately for someplace to hide—and saw the closet on the opposite side of the room—

and remembered the dumbwaiter inside the closet—unused for decades, papered over because Minnie had developed paranoid fantasies that her baby had been secreted away through the dumbwaiter on the night she gave birth. The nurse had caught her putting baby Monty in the dumbwaiter because she said he was a changeling and she had to give him back to the fairies to get her own baby back. I remembered the faint peal of a bell coming from behind the wall and that Minnie believed that if she rang the bell the fairies would come to take their own child back. I remembered the sound of crying I thought I heard from behind the wall.

Mice, I told myself now, or the groan of old pipes. There were no ghosts in Riven House, only the two would-be killers searching for me. I could use the dumbwaiter to get downstairs to the kitchen instead of taking the stairs in the rotunda.

I hurried into the closet, opening and closing the door as quietly as I could, and crouched down in the dark to find the door to the dumbwaiter. I opened Jess's laptop to light the wall and saw the bulge where the door had been papered over. It looked like it had grown since I had seen it last, like this was the cancer eating away at the house . . . or as if something—or someone—was trying to crawl out from behind the walls.

I shoved the thought away and attacked the wall with my hands, tearing at paper and plaster, searching for the door. The paper was thick and lumpy, as if someone had slapped on handfuls of glue and paper, hurriedly trying to cover something up. It felt like one of Sunny's papier-mâché puppets after it had been water damaged, its features lumpy and disfigured . . . I could almost imagine the outline of a face—a broken nose, an empty eye socket—

I drew back my hand, covering my mouth to keep from screaming. There *was* a face in the plaster. I could see the skull in the light of the laptop—its hard, smooth bones jutting out of the rotting paper and glue, an empty eye socket staring at me—and then the laptop screen went black and I was alone in the dark with the entombed child.

I wanted to bolt from the closet but even if I could have moved I'd have run right into Jess and Katrine. Instead I forced myself to reach out and tap the track pad to bring the screen back to life.

I almost wished I hadn't. The face stuck in the plaster was even worse than my first glimpse of it. A cracked cheekbone, a staring blue eye, a tiny bone-white hand reaching out for me. A *doll,* I told myself, a broken china doll that Minnie had shoved into the wet plaster. They had given her a doll when she kept trying to stick her baby in the dumbwaiter and then she had torn it limb from limb and shoved it into the wall. Swallowing back the bile that had risen to my throat I plunged both hands into the wall and pulled out handfuls of crumbling plaster and doll parts—a knobby knee, a blue glass eye, a dis-membered foot—and also the dismantled bell that Minnie had rung to summon the servants, and later, the fairies who had stolen her baby. I uncovered a slatted door here, only about three feet high. Would I even be able to fit inside? I uncovered the bottom edge, gripped it with my torn and pasty fingers, and pulled. The door rolled up like a rolltop desk with a clatter that sounded horribly loud in the enclosed space. I listened for any sign that Jess and Katrine had heard me but detected nothing. Dank, stale air trapped for decades in the dumbwaiter chute wafted against my face.

I shone the laptop down into the chute and made out two ropes hanging on either side. Looking down I saw a wooden shelf. Looking up I could see a large metal wheel—the pulley. I put the laptop down and grasped one of the ropes. It felt smooth, worn down by decades of servants hauling up nursery dinners and tea trays. I pulled on it and felt the resistance of weight and heard a faint creak from below. Hardly a sound at all.

The Silent Servant. That was the other name for a dumbwaiter. And weren't all good servants silent, moving on well-oiled hinges behind the walls? I bet that's what they taught them at St. Anne's. *Be quiet. Don't make a fuss. Even when the lord of the manor gets you pregnant and leaves you for another.* The dumbwaiter rose smoothly up the shaft, a three-sided wooden box open on the side facing me. There was something in it. I reached for it, my hand shaking, bile in my throat, imagining the decaying corpse of a baby—

But no, Monty was the baby all grown up and he lay two stories below, a dead old man—

Somehow that didn't make it any easier to touch the moldering cloth and pull it out of the dumbwaiter. The cloth fell apart as I touched it. In the light of the laptop I saw embroidered apple blossoms crumbling into dust. It was the blanket that Mary Foley had made for her baby, but what was it doing here?

The cloth disintegrated under my hands and something fell out of it. Not bones. Only a book—another of Minnie's scrapbooks. She must have hidden it in here before the dumbwaiter was papered over, maybe the last time she'd put the baby in here. But I didn't have time for it now. I laid it aside along with the remnants of the blanket and then wrapped the rope around a hook on the side of the wall to steady the frame. I checked the ropes for frays and then the wooden frame. It felt solid, but then I weighed more than a tea tray.

I reached for Jess's laptop and started to close it but stopped when a line of print snagged my eye. *The thing I loved first and best about my wife,* I read, *was her imagination.*

Was this Jess's novel? I wondered, feeling a prurient thrill at reading the forbidden work in progress. But Jess never wrote in the first person (*Too easy!* he said) and he hadn't mentioned changing for this book. I didn't have time for this, but still, curiosity compelled me to read on.

> I loved the way she told a story, whether it was about one of the crazy old families who lived in the river mansions or growing up the unloved changeling in that cold farmhouse and turning her own frightened heartbeats into the footsteps of a vengeful ghost. It wasn't until she started telling stories about me that I saw the danger in an imagination like hers. *You aren't in love with me anymore, You're seeing someone else, You're going to leave me.* She spun these stories so well, inventing seductive sirens out of chance acquaintances—the barista at the café where I wrote! a middle-aged fan at a reading!—that it was hard not to believe them. Why not sleep with the tattooed barista if she already thought I was? Maybe I didn't love her anymore. Maybe I was tired of trying to correct her version of reality like a punctilious copyeditor marking over her inspired scrawls with a cool blue pencil. Maybe I was tired of finding my wife bleeding on the bathroom floor or driving her to the hospital to have her stomach pumped.
>
> But perhaps her most effective feat, the story I really fell for, was the one about us starting over. We'd move to the country for a new start! We'd go back to where it had all begun and finally get things right. I'd really bought into that one. Sold everything, packed the moving van, moved up here to

the godforsaken sticks. And for what? To watch her mind slowly unravel, seeing ghosts, casting herself the heroine of some Gothic romance? How tempting to play the part she's cast for me—the Byronic villain plotting to put his wife away—

A sound from the room outside the closet drew my attention away from the nightmare screed I was reading. Was this really how Jess saw me? Was it some exaggerated fictional version of me—or had Jess finally turned to that last resort of the failing imagination—the memoir. I didn't have time to find out. I closed the laptop and stashed it in one of the boxes. With its light out, darkness enveloped the closet and chute, a darkness that felt like the inside of my brain. *Maybe I didn't love her anymore.* I'd thought I'd faced the worst already but reading Jess's damning—and false!—description of me felt like having my skin flayed off and my bones dismantled—like the poor doll that lay in parts all around me. Climbing into the dark box felt like crawling into a coffin. The wooden frame creaked under my weight with a noise that sounded like a baby crying. Maybe that's what I'd heard at night, I thought, but then the thought of the dumbwaiter moving up and down on its own nearly made me bolt. I took a deep breath . . . and smelled the oil from the pulley, a smell that brought back memories of tractors and threshers, cold metal tools that could flay flesh. I grabbed the rope to unhook it—but froze at the sound of voices on the other side of the closet door.

"I told you I checked in here." Katrine's voice.

"I know but she's got to be somewhere and this is where she would hide. This is where she'd feel safe."

Katrine laughed. "In this creepy room? See? Look at what she's done to the wallpaper."

Katrine's voice was close—just on the other side of the closet door. I could smell her perfume—something citrusy and outdoorsy. I had to dig my nails into the rope to keep from wrenching the door open and tackling her. That would wipe the smug smile off her face.

"I think Minnie did that," Jess said, his voice not as close. "Clare just uncovered it. She's writing about Minnie . . . Wow! She's got over a hundred thousand words!"

He was on my laptop, looking through my files! The sense of violation shocked me (even though I'd just been reading his laptop), but then he said, "Whoa, she's really gotten into this character," and I felt a pang at the admiration in his voice.

"No wonder she's gone off the deep end," Katrine said.

"Yeah . . . but some of this looks really good . . ."

"Huh . . ." Katrine said, unimpressed by Jess's approbation. "I didn't notice this closet before . . ."

I released the rope at the same moment the door opened. I had a glimpse of Katrine's startled face—I must have looked strange crouched and hunched over in the back of the closet, like the changeling of Minnie's nightmares—and then I was hurtling downward. I tried to let the rope out slowly, hand over hand, but my own weight was too much for me to control. The rope sped through my hands, ripping skin off my palms. The wooden box crashed to a bone-rattling halt that I felt from my tailbone to my teeth. I tasted blood, then the acid wash of fear. They would be coming for me. I wrenched open the door and fell out onto the kitchen floor. I rolled up to my feet and bolted through to the library, toward the terrace doors, but my legs were so numb I lost control of them halfway there and tripped and fell. I was lying on the rug in front of the fireplace. I'd tripped over the fire tools.

I heard voices coming from the rotunda. *Clare, is that you?*

Monty would call when I came down the stairs. I understood now why he always heard me. The rotunda with its spiraling stairs was like a giant seashell magnifying every sound. I could hear Katrine's voice shouting, "She's in the library!"

I got up, braced my hand on Monty's desk, and started for the terrace door—when I remembered the gun in the desk drawer.

I find a loaded gun focuses the mind.

Was it really loaded? I'd always meant to check and unload it but I'd never gotten around to it. I opened the desk drawer just as I heard Jess say, "Clare, we don't want to hurt you."

I looked up. The only light in the room came from a glimmer of moonlight filtering in through the terrace doors. I could just make out Jess's silhouette—and then Katrine edging around him.

"That's right, Clare. We want to get you help." And then I saw the gleam of steel in her hands.

I gripped Monty's pistol, raised it, and aimed it at Katrine. "Don't come any closer," I said.

"Clare," Jess said, the warmth in his voice nearly distracting me from the metallic click. Nearly. I knew what a gun safety being released sounded like. I fired. I heard Katrine's scream and the impact of her body falling over the desk and the sound of something metal falling to the floor. As Jess reached for her he moved into the moonlight and looked up at me, his face, for the very first time since I'd known him, empty of all thought. For once he didn't have a thing to say.

Neither did I.

I turned and ran, gripping the gun and banging out of the glass doors so fast they shattered in my wake.

Chapter Twenty-Eight

The sound of breaking glass ushered me into a world made of glass. It was so beautiful I nearly stopped to admire the view. The moon hung over the frozen river, turning the world silver and pearl. It looked like the enchanted fairy land Elizabeth Foley had described the night she followed Mary to the weir—

But I couldn't stop to admire the night. Jess was right behind me. I heard his step crunch in the glass on the terrace. He would have picked up Katrine's gun. I ran, down the hill and toward the road. If Dunstan had gotten my text he might be on the drive by now.

But he wasn't. And as soon as I stepped in the road I realized how vulnerable the open space made me. I looked back and saw Jess scrambling down the hill, slipping in the ice. If I stayed on the drive he would run me down. I had to find someplace to hide while I was waiting for Dunstan.

I sprinted across the road and scrambled over a downed tree branch. The lower drive was a maze of broken branches. Let him try to follow me in here. I'd grown up climbing trees while he'd hung out at the mall on Long Island. I stuck the gun in my pocket, first making sure the safety was on, and scrambled through the fallen pines. It wasn't so different from climbing apple trees. Hand over hand, fitting my feet into the crooks of branches. I wished I had gloves, though. My palms were still raw from the dumbwaiter rope. I pulled the cell phone out of my pocket, but my hands were so covered with sap I couldn't get the touch screen to work.

I couldn't stand here out in the open. I needed someplace warm and hidden until help came. I looked around and saw the roof of the old barn over the trees. I'd go there. At least I could clean my hands enough to use the phone and if I climbed up into the loft and pulled up the ladder Jess couldn't get up there. I tucked the phone back into my pocket and started toward the barn, sliding over the ice. It was thick where the Saw Kill had flooded in the fall, so thick my boots didn't break through. Jess wouldn't be able to track me.

I hadn't been to the barn since Sunny died. Monty had given Sunny's volunteers permission to use it for a memorial project for Sunny and I'd seen a few of the "coven" and the Bailey students coming and going along the drive. Maybe there'd be a crowd of volunteers sitting around a circle sewing costumes and sipping herbal tea, celebrating the winter solstice. But when I reached the barn it loomed dark and quiet over the moonlit ice, like a ghost ship.

The truth was that I'd been avoiding the barn, guilty that I'd been responsible for Sunny's suicide and afraid that her vengeful spirit might still be lingering there. That Sunny's death might not be a suicide gave me no relief now. If Jess and Katrine had killed her to keep her from getting in the way of my inheriting Riven House, her death was even more my fault. Sunny's ghost would have all the more reason to haunt me.

But the ghosts hadn't been real, I reminded myself as I opened the barn door, I didn't have to be afraid of them any-

more. And indeed, the barn was empty. The volunteers had
cleared all the puppets away and even swept up the scraps of
cloth and paper that usually littered the wide plank floors. It
felt empty . . . and sad. All trace of Sunny's creative energy was
gone. I had thought she was pathetic for calling her puppets
her children but how much more deluded I'd been imagining
myself part of a happy family with Monty and Jess. Now my
father was dead and my husband was trying to kill me.

Remembering Jess, I hurried across the long yawning space
to the loft ladder. I climbed up quickly, then turned and pulled
up the ladder behind me and laid it down along the ledge. Then
I turned, looking for something to use to wipe my hands, and
looked into two staring blue eyes.

I nearly fell backward off the loft. The thing staring back
at me was as white faced as a corpse, its blue eyes as sightless
as Monty's had been at the end. My first thought was that the
coven had dug up Sunny's body from the Montague plot and
brought her here for some ghoulish ritual; my second that I'd
been fooled once again by Sunny's puppet. It was the witch
puppet that Sunny had transformed into the apple blossom girl
for the parade. She was one of the puppets that had been hanging beside Sunny when she died. In fact, the rope from which
she'd hung still attached her to a hook in the ceiling. Maybe
the police had shoved her up here and Sunny's volunteers had
forgotten about her. Maybe she was just too gruesome for
anyone to want.

I could use her dress, though, to wipe my hands clean. I
scrubbed at my hands, avoiding the puppet's reproachful gaze,
then tried the phone again. Finally a signal, and the touch
screen worked. I called 911. When a woman answered I realized I had no idea how to explain all that had happened. *I'm
hiding from my husband in a barn loft because he's trying to kill*

me sounded like a prank call, so I said instead: "This is Clare Martin at Riven House. I'm hiding from an intruder in the barn. I think he's armed."

"Are you at the barn or the house, ma'am?" the woman asked.

"The barn. Please send someone quickly."

"Are you safe where you are, ma'am?"

I wished she would stop calling me ma'am. It made me feel like an old woman who'd fallen and broken her hip.

"I think so—for the time being . . ."

"Then stay put and we'll send an officer right away. Keep your phone on."

I laid the phone down on the floor, its light comforting, and leaned against the wall in the corner below a triangle-shaped window. I could feel the cold pressing through the slats but I could also watch the gate where I would see the patrol car when it arrived. I pushed the puppet away from me, closer to the ledge, so I wouldn't have to look into her reproachful eyes. I drew my knees up to my chest and wrapped my arms around them, trying to still the shivering that had taken hold of me. It was the cold, I told myself, now that you're not running the cold has caught up with you . . . but then I was sobbing and I knew it wasn't just the cold that had caught up with me. It was the grief and the horror . . . and the *shame*.

I hadn't even been able to tell the 911 operator the truth, that my own husband—*Jess!*—was prowling the frozen night, hunting me down as if I were an animal. What had I done to make him hate me so much?

It's because he never wanted to marry you in the first place.

I thought it was Great-Granny Jackson's voice at first, but it wasn't. It was my own voice, telling the truth for once. I'd trapped Jess, first by getting pregnant, then by falling apart after the miscarriage. How could he leave me then? I'd known he wouldn't leave me the moment I felt the cramps and the blood running between my legs—or had I known a moment *before* the cramps started and the blood began?

I won't be blackmailed into marriage, Jess had screamed at me and I had run down the hall and locked myself in the bathroom. And I'd thought *If only I wasn't pregnant* and the cramps had started—

But you couldn't make yourself have a miscarriage by *wishing* for one.

Still—I *had* wished for the baby to be gone and for Jess to forgive me and take care of me and marry me.

And that's what I'd gotten—just like I'd gotten the highest grade point average in high school, and the Bailey scholarship, and entrance into Monty's seminar, and Jess, and, now, Riven House.

Clare always gets what she wants.

So, really, hadn't I driven Jess to this?

"Clare?"

The voice was so soft, so tender, I thought it was inside my own head. Surely Jess would never say my name so sweetly again—but it *was* Jess.

"Clare? I can hear you crying, Clare."

He was below me in the barn. I slid down and crept across the floor to the ledge to look down. He was standing at the door of the barn looking down at a trail of silvery footprints that led across the old plank floors straight to the loft. My own icy footprints left like a trail of breadcrumbs to lead him to me. As if I'd wanted him to find me.

"I've called the police!" I screamed.

"Good," he said, taking a slow step inside. He was wearing his leather jacket, which was way too light for this cold, his hands in his pockets. The moonlight made his hair look silver and his face white. How he'd aged from that first day when he'd stood in the gold light at the gate! "When the police come we can explain that Katrine came in through Monty's apartment. That's what gave him the heart attack. Then she'd gone looking in his desk upstairs for his will. We heard her and came downstairs. We thought she was an intruder. I shot her with Monty's gun. I'll say it was me, Clare. No one needs to know it was you."

"That's very generous of you, Jess. How long will you wait then to kill *me*?"

"Why should I, Clare? We can sell Riven House and go our separate ways . . . or . . ." He looked up at the loft. His gaze fell a couple feet to my right. He was looking at the puppet, whose head was just visible above the ledge. The look he directed at her was as full of emotion as if he were gazing into my eyes. ". . . or we could go someplace together and give it another try. Back to Brooklyn—or someplace new. Without money troubles hanging over our heads we could be good together again."

"And I'm supposed to forget that you were screwing Katrine and plotting to kill me?"

"I wasn't doing either of those things, Clare, I swear." He moved a few more steps into the barn, his eyes still on the puppet's head. "Yeah, Katrine was the girl I dated before you. I didn't tell you because I knew you'd be jealous. You know how jealous you've been in the past, how it made you—" He stopped himself as if he'd just realized that calling me crazy probably wasn't the best tactic right now. "How it *upset* you. So when Katrine got in touch with me because she'd learned through her aunt that you were Monty's daughter, I thought it made sense to come up here. I knew once Monty spent time with you again he'd fall in love with you. He always thought you were the better writer."

This time he couldn't quite disguise the envious look that crossed his face, but it was soon replaced by a smile. "Heck, I see now he was right. That stuff on your laptop is the real thing, Clare."

I didn't think he was faking the look of naked admiration on his face. I'd seen him in workshop too many times—he was incapable of pretending to like something he didn't. I'd only seen this look once before—when I'd read my story out loud that first day of class and I'd looked up to see Jess Martin—campus legend!—looking at me as if I were something remarkable. *The thing I loved first and best about my wife was her imagination.* The intervening years fell away and we were staring at each other across the oak conference table, the scent of cut hay and ripening apples in the air. Only Jess wasn't looking at me right now, he was looking at Sunny's gruesome puppet.

"Come on, Clare, let's get out of here together. We'll go someplace *fucking warm* and rake in the royalty checks from your *debut* novel. What do you say, Clare? Are you going to stay here with Dusty? Do you think he'll understand how *good* you are?"

No. Because the truth was I wasn't *good*. I was the girl who wished CJ Brennan to fail her English exam, who wished her own baby dead. Maybe I *did* belong with Jess. If only I could be sure . . .

As he moved closer, his gaze still fixed to the puppet, I could see the right side of his face. His jaw was clenched, the muscle twitching. His right hand rested in his pocket, which hung a little lower than the left pocket. He had Katrine's gun. Did he plan to use it when I came down? There was only one way to tell—

I pushed the puppet over the ledge. She swung down on the rope straight toward Jess. He raised his arm and silver flashed in the moonlight but before he could fire the puppet hit him in a burst of sawdust and papier-mâché. The apple blossom puppet swept Jess off his feet and knocked the gun from his hand. I grabbed the rope and swung down from the loft, hitting the floor a few feet from the gun. I didn't have time to grab it so I kicked it out of Jess's reach. The gun skittered across the barn floor and into the shadows beneath the loft. "Clare!" I heard Jess call for me. I had Monty's gun, but I couldn't shoot him. And if I tried to hold him at gunpoint till the police came he might overpower me and use it on me. So I ran. Out the barn door and across the ice, expecting any moment to feel a bullet in my back.

He'd been about to shoot the puppet, which he'd thought was me. There really wasn't any question of what Jess intended to do to me. I didn't think he was even worried anymore about how my death would look. He'd claim I was deranged, that I'd already killed Katrine and he was afraid I'd kill him.

I ran blindly, only realizing after a few minutes that I was going in the wrong direction, toward the gardens and the pond instead of the gate. At least I *thought* I was running toward the pond. While I'd been in the barn a ground fog had risen, a white mist seeping out of the ice. The temperature must have gone up since the storm and the melting ice was condensing in the air. I couldn't even see my feet, only feel frozen grass under them and the uneven rutted ground—

Then suddenly I was skidding over slick ice. I'd found the pond, all right. I was on it. It spread out in the moonlight, pure, perfect, not a crack in sight.

Of course there are cracks you can see and those you can't.

I started to turn back but then I heard his footstep behind me. I had no choice. I had to go forward. I stepped onto the ice, planting my feet wide apart to distribute my weight, listening for the sound of something breaking—

How had I not seen this coming? How had I not known what Jess was planning? I should have seen the signs months ago—his eagerness to move up here, his pretended mocking of Katrine, even all the times he made it up after we'd fought—when had he ever done that before? Of course I could see it now; he couldn't let us break up before I'd become the heir to Riven House and he could claim I'd gone crazy—

I almost turned around to face him—to ask him if that's all he wanted—to put me away. Or did he always know it would come to this? Pursuing me across the frozen pond, tracking me down to my death.

Wisps of fog were rising up off the ice. Because it was melting? Or because *she* was here? This is where I saw her first—on the bridge above the weir. I could see it only a few feet in front of me. I was almost there. But I could also see the cracks spreading out before me, a pattern like the neurons in a mind gone mad. I had to follow them to the end . . . I stepped onto the bridge . . . but then I felt the touch of a hand on my arm. It felt *gentle*, loving—

I turned around, the fog seeming to wrap itself around me like an embrace, but then I heard the click of metal and was blinded by the light. I couldn't see his face, or tell if he had the gun, but he must or he wouldn't have ambushed me like this.

"Clare, listen to me," he said. "It's not what you think it is. You've concocted this whole story. It's such a good story I've been using it myself. It's what my novel is about—a man plotting to drive his wife insane and take over the house she's inherited—but that's all it is: a story. I would never hurt you. This is all your imagination."

In other words, he was saying I was crazy, a tool of my over-wrought imagination.

I could feel the anger rising up in me as steady as the fog

rising off the ice, the heat of my ire curdling in the air around us, taking vengeful shape. I could almost see it—almost hear it—

Jess heard it too—cracks on the ice behind him like the sound of footsteps coming toward him. He half turned, his eyes widening in horror at something in the mist.

Then a louder crack as the ice beneath his feet split open and he shot down into the water.

I fell to my knees and reached for him. His hand flailed at the edge of the broken ice. I slid across the ice on my belly and grabbed his hand. His eyes met mine, frantic, pleading . . .

Looking at me as he had that first day of Monty's class. As if he were really seeing me for the first time.

And then Jess's hand was ripped from mine and he vanished into the water as if something had reached up from beneath the ice and yanked him straight down to the bottom.

Chapter Twenty-Nine

I was never sure later how long I lay on the ice before Dunstan found me and carried me up the hill and into the library and laid me on the couch.

"Too long," he said, guilty that he hadn't seen my text, that he hadn't gotten there sooner, that he'd gone to the barn first and then to the house and only then to the pond when he looked down from the terrace and saw me lying on the ice. "You could have died of hypothermia."

Hypothermia explained why I drifted in and out of consciousness as I lay on the couch and Dunstan chafed my hands and feet and wrapped me in blankets while we waited for the ambulance. And why I rambled, telling him about the ghost on the ice who had appeared behind Jess.

"The only sensible thing you told me was where to find Jess's laptop."

I remembered lying on the couch staring at Katrine, who lay across the desk, blood seeping over all Monty's research folders, and thinking, now he won't be able to write his book. Then the room was filled with flashing red lights and Dunstan was back barking orders, carrying me out to the ambulance so the EMTs wouldn't contaminate the crime scene. The last thing

I remembered was looking back at the library, at how the red lights filled the room the way the light from the sunsets had, as if those evenings that Jess and Monty and I sat on the terrace watching the sunset had been distilled into one magic elixir and that if that light could just be bottled and examined the truth would be known. Fortunately, there was another version of the truth waiting on Jess's laptop that explained everything.

"The bastard wrote it all down," Dunstan told me when I came to in the hospital. "The arrogant prick. The whole plot. As if it were a novel! So you don't have to worry, Clary. The whole story is there—how he plotted with Katrine to have you recognized as Monty's heir and then make it look like you were crazy by posing as the ghost."

"And to kill me?" I asked, grasping at that last straw.

A flicker of impatience crossed Dunstan's face, quickly replaced by a look of compassion. "Yes, only the husband in the novel is driven to it because his wife is crazy. I think in his twisted way it was how he justified himself."

I knew he meant to reassure me that my story would be believed and I wouldn't be accused of murdering Jess and Katrine even though Katrine's gun wasn't found when the police dredged the pond. "It must have gone over the weir and down the Saw Kill to the river. It'll be buried in the Hudson by now."

But what I'd read of Jess's novel hadn't absolved me of guilt as far as I was concerned. *It's the story she started,* he'd written. *I am only playing my part.* What if it *had* all started out as an idea for a novel? He wouldn't be the first writer to work out his hostilities toward his spouse by killing her in prose.

"What about Katrine?"

"We have cell phone records of their communications. They're cryptic, but they constitute evidence of a conspiracy. When you're able to give a full statement I think we'll see a correlation between those calls and your "ghost sightings." We found more fibers from her scarf under the weir and an old white dress and a shawl in Katrine's closet that looks like what she wore when she was posing as Mary Foley. Katrine was up to her eyebrows in credit card debt and yet she'd been pricing condos in Sarasota, Florida. She was clearly expecting a windfall. Maybe she hadn't planned to kill you, but that's what happens when you start down this trail. You have no idea how many times I've heard grown men weeping that they didn't *mean* to kill the clerk at the liquor store they were holding up, they just needed the money. Put your mind at rest on that count, Clare. When those two set out to deceive and steal from you they sealed their own fate."

I knew that Dunstan was trying to reassure me because he understood that I would feel responsible. That's how well he knew me. As well as a second cousin? Had he figured out that connection yet? Did it matter to him? I wasn't sure. The kisses he planted on my forehead were chaste enough, but that could be out of respect for my newly widowed state and the appropriate distance of an investigating law enforcer. I figured there was time enough to talk about our "relationship" when I got out of the hospital and the investigation was completed.

I was released from the hospital a few days after Christmas. Marika came up to drive me home. She wanted to take me back to the city, but I pointed out that I had to be close by for the police investigation. Then she suggested that she book us rooms at the Beekman Arms in Rhinebeck, but I told her that was ridiculous when Riven House stood empty a few miles away.

"I don't know how you can stay there," she said when she drove me back in her rental.

"It's not the house's fault," I told her as we parked next to the toppled apple tree. I'd have to call Devon Corbett's tree removal company to come remove it. Luckily the only damage that had been done was to Monty's apartment in the addition and I was beginning to think that I might get rid of that.

"Are you sure?" Marika asked, looking warily up at the house. "The place looks haunted."

"It isn't," I told her, adding to myself, *at least not anymore.*

Marika stayed a few days but I could tell that she was uneasy in the house and anxious to get back to the city and Duma for New Year's. I placated her by returning with her to the city and spending New Year's Eve and Day at their apartment in Park Slope. They had a little party on New Year's Day with lots of prosecco and organic lentil and kale dishes and vegan cupcakes and a few dozen friends, many of whom I knew from my days in publishing. They all hugged me and told me how sorry they'd been to hear about Jess and tried to pretend they weren't dying to hear all the gory details. A few asked me if I was going to write about what had happened.

"I haven't thought about it yet," I said. "First I'm going to finish the novel I started this fall."

"About the apple blossom girl?" Yuriko asked me. "That story you told at your apartment last summer?"

"The night the table cracked?" Abe asked.

"Yes, I suppose that was an omen."

There was a surprised gasp of laughter from a few guests. Yes, I had that story to tell too, I thought, noticing that Ansel was looking at me. Before he left he told me that he'd love to see what I'd written. I told him I'd be in touch.

I took the train upstate the next day against Marika's protests. Dunstan met me at the station and drove me back to Riven House, arguing about my staying at the house the whole way. "I've got a separate apartment at my place," he told me when we pulled up in front of the house. "I used to rent it out to Bailey students but I got tired of their noise and their attitude. You could stay there. I wouldn't . . . it wouldn't mean . . ."

I cupped my hand around his face and kissed him. His mouth was so much wider than Jess's that it felt strange for a moment and then when his lips pressed back against mine it didn't feel strange at all. We could have been nineteen, making out in his old pickup parked under the apple trees. When we separated I was looking straight into his eyes—eyes the blue of summer sky glimpsed through apple branches.

"Come on in if you're so worried about the house," I told him. "You can give it your professional going over to make sure it's . . . *secure*."

He came in with me, but we didn't spend much time going over the house. We didn't even make it past the boot hall.

Before he left, though, he went around checking windows and doors and complaining that none of the locks worked. The next time he came back with his toolbox and put locks on all the windows and on the boot hall door. We spent our third "date" replacing the library glass doors. It felt good to work with my hands—and to watch Dunstan's large capable hands moving over the surfaces of the house, recaulking clattering window panes, tightening loose washers, scraping old paint off rotting window frames, replacing broken light fixtures. The house seemed to sigh with contentment at his ministrations. This was what Riven House needed. To be mended.

In the second week of January we drove into town, stopped at Cassie's for coffee, and walked over to the police station, where I gave a full account of the "hauntings" to a young police officer. Luckily I'd written down each "sighting" in my notebooks. Dunstan had been right that the sightings often correlated to a communication between Jess and Katrine. On the day Jess and

I moved into the caretaker's cottage, Jess had called Katrine, no doubt giving her the signal to don her shawl and stand on the weir in the rain and drop down behind it to hide underneath the weir. He'd called her on the night I'd awoken to the sound of crying and went to find its source.

"She must have spent a lot of nights standing out there in the cold while you were warm in bed," the nice young officer, whose name was Andrew Brennan and who turned out to be CJ's brother-in-law, helpfully pointed out.

Warm in bed beside my lying, cheating husband.

But I smiled at Andrew Brennan, unable to explain how particularly galling it was to find all this damning evidence on Jess's cell phone when he couldn't ever be bothered to pick up the phone when *I* called. Perhaps Officer Brennan sensed my growing discomfort because he took down the rest of my statement without providing the corresponding texts or emails, maintaining the polite silence of a lab technician taking scans that would be "read" later by an expert. And it did feel like I was pouring out all the symptoms of a long disease—the scratches on the wall, the overflowing bath, the blood on the handkerchief.

I saw poor Andrew Brennan furrow his brow at that one and I told him that it wasn't really blood—only ink.

"Of course," he said, looking embarrassed. "None of it was real, was it?"

"No," I said, feeling like I was the one reassuring him. "None of it was real."

DUNSTAN DROVE ME home after the interview.

"You did good," he said, reaching across the car seat to squeeze my hand.

"How do you know?" I asked.

"I was watching the whole thing on the remote and following along with my own transcript of the texts . . . What's wrong?"

"I just didn't realize you were watching," I said, reviewing all I'd said now for anything I might not have wanted Dunstan to hear. Dunstan was quiet, but I could feel his gaze on me as I looked out the window. It had begun to snow, but only flurries. The local radio station, which I'd started leaving on in the kitchen so the house wouldn't be so quiet, didn't predict any significant accumulation. The flakes danced in the air, weightless as apple blossoms. When we pulled up at the back of the house he put his arm over the seat and turned to me.

"I'm sorry, Clare. I should have told you. I should have realized that after all you've been through it would feel creepy to have someone watching you."

"Not when it's you," I said, cupping his clean-shaven jaw in my hand. "And I'm glad you think I did all right."

He smiled, blue eyes vibrant in the pale wintery light. "We should always have writers for witnesses. You had a record of every incident we found on the cells and then some."

"And then some?" I asked.

He shrugged. I could feel his jaw tense under my hand. "All the 'ghost' sighting were accompanied by a call or text from Jess to Katrine, but some of the minor incidents you mentioned—the scratches in the plaster, the flooded tub, and the stained handkerchief, the bell in the dumbwaiter—have no corresponding record. But that makes sense. The scratches could have been made at any time, they could have left a time-delayed tape recorder in the dumbwaiter, and Jess could have gone upstairs and turned on the tub."

I tried to remember where Jess had been the two times the tub overflowed. "He could have done the first, but not the second—"

"No, that would have been Katrine. Maybe she came up with it on her own. Only . . ."

"Only what?"

"After that incident Jess texted Katrine 'bath?' and she texted back three question marks. Jess responded with the initials PG."

"PG? What does that stand for?"

"I think," Dunstan said, taking my hand off his face and holding it in both of his, "that it means poltergeist. Jess writes about it in his supposed novel. The husband character has this idea that his wife has the power to make things move or break—tree branches, cups, tables—"

"Tables?"

"Yeah, he's got this preposterous scene in which their dining room table cracks in two because the wife's mad at something."

"Oh," I said, wondering if I should tell Dunstan about the Bend Becker, but then that had happened before we got to Riven House—

"Maybe I shouldn't have told you about it, Clary. I think it just shows how jealous he was of you—to invest you with so much power."

"Able to bend iron bars with the raw power of my mind," I joked. "If the whole writing thing doesn't work out maybe I can go on *Amazing Psychics*."

"Yeah." Dunstan smiled, relieved that I wasn't upset. "That's my Clary. I can be your sidekick. Shall I come by later to practice our act?"

I told him I'd like that and kissed him good-bye. As I was getting out of the car he said, "Just remember what Andy said."

"What was that?" I asked, leaning down to look back at him.

"None of it was real."

Chapter Thirty

I let myself into the boot hall and locked the door behind me, took off my winter boots, slipped into the sheepskin slippers I'd left there, and shuffled into the rotunda.

"None of it was real," I said aloud, and then listened for any contradictory echoes. Any bells ringing or babies crying. But there was nothing. Even the snow gathering on the oculus was the quiet kind. There was only the sound of my own padded footsteps as I walked into the kitchen to put the kettle on for tea and then my own footsteps as I took my tea into the library to sit at the octagonal desk. Since Dunstan and I had fixed the glass doors I'd taken to spending my afternoons in the library. It had the best light. I'd thought I might have to get rid of the desk because of the blood, but Katrine had bled out on an ancient leather blotter that had soaked up all her blood. When the forensics lab removed it, there wasn't a spot of blood on the desk. All I'd had to do was polish it with a little Old English lemon oil and the desk gleamed in the late afternoon light— even on a snowy day like today. I put my teacup down next to my laptop and leaned back in Monty's old chair to look out the glass doors. The river was a deep slate gray. The mountains across the river were indigo fading to pale blue to white where it was snowing more heavily, the light the color of old tarnished silver.

"None of it was real," I told the river and the mountains, which looked back at me placidly as if to say, *But we are.*

"But that's just the problem, isn't it?" I said aloud again. I wondered what Dr. Schermer would make of me talking to myself. But I wouldn't be seeing Dr. Schermer anymore, nor would anyone else—at least not in a professional capacity. His license was being revoked for leaking a confidential file to his cousin, Katrine Vanderberg. I wouldn't have been likely to go back to him at any rate, but still it would have been good to have had someone to talk this out with.

"You see," I said aloud again (after all, there was no one here to report back that I'd taken to talking to myself), "that's the problem. None of it was real. But what does that make of my life? When did my life *stop* being real? From the day I met Jess? Was that look of awe he'd given me when I read my story aloud real? Or what about Jess sitting beside me in the hospital holding my hand? Or the day he got the first copies of his novel and he showed me that he'd dedicated it to me. 'To Clare, who makes all things clear.' Hadn't that been real? So when had things *stopped* being real?"

I took out the notebooks I'd brought to the station and laid them on the desk, aligning their edges with the edge of the pile of typescript that sat beside the laptop. *The Apples of Discord*, the novel I'd started to write in September, was nearly done. I'd sent it to Ansel last week and he'd been as excited as it was seemly to be in front of a newly widowed author whose husband had tried to kill her. He was already getting interest from editors—the word having spread from Marika's New Year's Day party.

"The truth is that even if it weren't a great piece of writing it would sell because of all the publicity surrounding Jess's death. But it *is* a great novel, Clare. You should be proud of it. You did what artists have always done—salvage something beautiful out of something godawful."

I'd thanked Ansel and gotten off the phone then before he started to cry. Learning about Jess's duplicity had been a tough blow for him and I suspected that he felt that representing my book would provide a way of working through his own feelings of betrayal. *Good,* I'd thought, but I didn't need to hear him weeping on the phone. And I didn't need him to tell me how good the book was. Monty's theft had accomplished that. He wouldn't have stolen it if it weren't good. Still, when I laid my hand on the pile of typescript all I could think was *None of it was real.*

So instead of turning to my book now, I turned to Minnie's book. The last one that I'd found in the dumbwaiter. Although it was in a scrapbook album it didn't contain any more of Minnie's crazy collages. It was a diary of her last months, part confession, part suicide note. In it she explained, most rationally, how she had "come unmoored" after giving birth and how she had arrived at the decision to kill her husband. Most disturbing was her account of being *haunted* in the months after she killed Bayard. I'd read it several times now, but still there was something about it that nagged at me, something that Jess's poltergeist theory had reminded me of. I opened it and read it again now, my chair angled so I could see out the window when I looked up and watch the snow falling.

On the night of January 11, I began having labor pains even though the baby was not due for another six weeks. Dr. Melchior was summoned but he was delayed because of the icy roads. Fortunately our housekeeper was here and she and my husband, Bayard, were able to deliver the baby safely. I quickly lost consciousness due to exhaustion from the labor. I awoke sometime in the night to the sound of a baby crying. The sound seemed to be coming from the dumbwaiter in the closet. I got up and listened to the sounds of the poor piteous infant, wondering why they did not bring it to me. I went in search of the child, first in the closet, where I listened at the dumb-waiter chute, but then creeping down the circular stairs of the rotunda quiet as a mouse into the library, where my husband stood at the doors to the terrace and an apparition in white handed to him a child in swaddling clothes. Of course I had heard the rumors, heard the kitchen maids and the parlor maids whispering when they thought I couldn't hear them about my husband's dalliance with the girl from the apple farm down the road—and here she was giving him her child! But where was my baby? The crying I had heard before had stopped. I had to find him. But when I tried to go back up the stairs I found I was too weak. The stairs were slippery with blood—my blood! The last thing I recalled was Bayard leaning over me and behind him our housekeeper, her face screwed up like a wrinkled old apple.

"Take care of it!" Bayard shouted, handing something to her. Something wrapped in a pink blanket. Which was strange, I thought, because I had purchased only yellow for our baby . . . but then I thought no more. I must have fainted.

When I came to it was morning. I was in my bed, in a clean nightgown, and the baby was beside me

in the lovely yellow bassinet Mama had sent me from
B. Altman's. But when I looked at it I knew it was
not my baby because if it were my baby then I would
have loved it right away and I didn't. It belonged to
that farm girl down the road. Later I heard the maids
whispering that her baby had been found on the steps
of our house frozen to death, but I knew that wasn't
true. I knew that Bayard had put our own child out to
die so he could raise that whore's child as his own. Be-
cause he loved her more than he loved me. But no one
would listen to me. When I told them I saw the girl's
ghost standing on the terrace they thought I was crazy.

Of course they did, I thought for not the first time reading over the sad account. And as I always did when I got to this point, I lifted my head to look out the doors—

And saw a figure standing on the terrace.

But it was a male figure, one I instantly recognized from the expensive cut of his suit as Cortland Montague.

"I'm sorry if I startled you," Cortland said when I opened the door for him.

"You didn't," I said, not wanting to give him the satisfaction. I had picked up a distinctly suspicious vibe from Cortland since Monty's death—a result, I guessed, of him having to hand over a huge family estate to a complete stranger. Also, I think he was genuinely disappointed that pretty, leggy Katrine was gone. All in all, I didn't blame him for resenting me, but I didn't have to like it either. "But in the future you can come in through the boot hall. I've had the doorbell fixed there."

His smile barely hid the twitch in his jaw muscle. The same tic that had given Jess away in the barn. He should learn to control it.

"I did mention that no repairs or home improvements begun before the final settlement of the estate would be reimbursed should the estate revert back to—"

"Yes, you did," I said, cutting short the long legalese explanation he was about to embark on. "And I told you I was happy to pay for these repairs out of my own pocket should the estate revert back to . . . who exactly? Oh, to you, right? Is that what you've come to tell me? Are you the new owner of Riven House? Because if you are, I should go over with you some peculiarities in the wiring."

"That won't be necessary," he said, not bothering this time to mask the twitch in his jaw with a smile. "Although it will take another few weeks to go through probate, there should be no problem with Monty's most recent will being upheld."

"Not even with one of the witnesses hoping to profit from my inheritance by killing me?" I asked.

"No," he answered my facetious question bluntly. "Ms. Vanderberg's criminal intentions are immaterial here. Clearly it was Monty's wish for you to inherit Riven House and the police have cleared you in any wrongdoing with respect to his death. And"—he opened his briefcase—"as it turns out, you *are* his biological daughter."

He took a sheet of paper out of his briefcase and handed it to me. I recognized the letterhead of the genetics lab Monty and I had gone to at the hospital. Remembering that day— Monty's flirting with the young lab technician, the discovery that we were both "difficult sticks" due to our narrow veins, my eyes filled up.

"I wish he had lived long enough to know," I said.

"I don't think it would have mattered to Uncle Monty. He told me he considered you his daughter and heir no matter what the blood tests showed. He never cared about all that 'blue blood nonsense' as he called it. Which might explain why he was so unconcerned at the idea that he was Mary Foley's child and not Minnie's."

I looked up from the page at Cortland, but he had leaned back in the deep wing-backed chair and his face was in shadow so I couldn't read his expression. "Should he have been . . . *concerned*?"

"Yes," Cortland answered. "If he was the illegitimate son of Alden Bayard Montague he would not have been entitled to inherit River House."

"Who would have inherited it?" I asked.

"My grandfather." Cortland's teeth gleamed in the shadows.

"I see," I said, feeling the first prickling of unease. My bravado at taking on the costs of the repairs had been a bluff. And now Cortland had called me on it. "But there's no real proof—" My hand strayed to Minnie's diary. "Only the belief of a deranged woman." I felt a pang of guilt consigning Minnie once again to the nut house, but if that's what it took—

"No, Minnie's testimony that her baby was snatched by fairies and replaced by an illegitimate changeling would not hold up in court. But a DNA test would." He took out a folder from the briefcase, the same genetics lab insignia on it.

"But you'd have to have Minnie's DNA," I said, my voice rising so high in the still room that I thought I heard the glass in the new doors chiming. "You'd have to—"

"Have Minnie's body exhumed from the family crypt? Easy enough since my family has been paying the fees on the plot for the last thirty years. Just another one of those boring family details Monty didn't care to bother with. Too busy writing, I suppose, better to leave those details to the unimaginative lawyers in the family." He laid the pale blue folder on the desk, right on top of Minnie's scrapbook, his blunt, carefully manicured fingernails gently drumming over the folder as if he were typing a secret code out on it. As if he were rewriting the family *history*.

None of it was real.

For a moment my vision swam, the room in the fitful silvery light seeming to run like liquid mercury. What would be left when it was gone? Would I melt along with it? Or was I just a construct of Monty's fantasies?

". . . another of Monty's fantasies," Cortland was saying, his voice coming to me as though under water. "Really, what you writers come up with! Babies swapped at birth! Ghosts of girls coming back to reinstate their long lost children! A good story, but alas, just that—a story."

Cortland smiled ruefully and shook his head. "You had me going there. But facts are facts." He knocked his knuckles against the folder, the sound blunted by Minnie's scrapbook beneath it. "According to DNA testing Alden Montague was the son of Minerva Noyes Montague."

"But what happened to Mary's baby?" I cried.

Cortland shrugged. "I suppose it died and Bayard put it on the steps to be discovered by the maid or . . ." Here he met my eye. "I'd hate to think he killed it himself. That he worried that his legitimate son's position might be compromised by the product of a youthful dalliance. At any rate, there's no way to prove it one way or the other. If I were you I wouldn't dwell on it. Not here alone in this big old house . . ." He looked around and shuddered. ". . . which does belong to you—or will in a matter of weeks. I wish you luck with it."

He slapped his knees—much as Monty had when he was finished with a story—and got to his feet. "I hope you'll make a better go of it here than Monty did. You can use the money from your books to fix up the place. You seem like a practical girl. That's what Katrine said about you that day when we were walking down to the weir—"

"Walking down to the weir?" I repeated, more interested in this detail than in what Katrine had thought of me.

"Yes. Jess wanted to show us the work he'd done on it. He was particularly proud of the stonework. He showed us how you could actually walk under the stone steps—"

"Did you?"

"What? Not me. I didn't want to ruin my shoes. But Katrine went in to have a look. I had the feeling she was humoring Jess, although I didn't know then—" He had the grace to look embarrassed then at what he must think was further proof of my husband's affair with Katrine Vanderberg. "At any rate, when I expressed concern about your 'ghost sightings' Katrine said, 'Don't worry about Clare; she always lands on her feet.' And so you have." He held out his hand for me to shake. I put my hand in his but I barely felt his grip. "But for God's sake, invest in a new furnace. Your hands are like ice."

He turned and let himself out the terrace doors, letting in a chill draft that ruffled the pages on the desk. *None of it was real,* they whispered silkily. Except—

I opened Minnie's scrapbook and reread the description of waking up in the night. *The sound was coming from the dumbwaiter in the closet.* She'd thought it was her own baby crying but what if it was Mary's baby crying . . . But no, she'd gone downstairs after and seen Elizabeth delivering the baby to Bayard so it couldn't have been Mary's baby crying in the dumbwaiter and besides, Bayard had carried her up the stairs when she fainted—

But only after he had handed over a bundle wrapped in pink to the housekeeper. The bundle wrapped in pink was Mary's baby. And the housekeeper—

I grabbed one of the scrapbooks I had stacked on the desk, flipping through the pages. There was the stern figure of the housekeeper in a high-necked black dress and white apron, always with an apple pasted over her face because Minnie thought her face looked like a wrinkled old apple. A little joke at her servant's expense. I stared at the figure and noticed for the first time the cant of her shoulders, the left higher than the right, and remembered a line from Elizabeth's diary. *She's a spiteful old shrew. Working in those big houses has made her think she's better than everyone else.*

And then I remembered my mother saying that working in the big river mansions had made my father's grandmother a bitter old woman.

The housekeeper at Riven House was Mildred Jackson—Great-Granny Jackson who had haunted my childhood because I was an intruder.

But the real intruder was Mary's baby, who she would have foisted on her son Ernst. What had she thought when Bayard put the baby in her hands? When she recognized the pink blanket her daughter-in-law had knitted? Did she think Bayard would raise the baby as his own? Or give him back to Mary and Ernst to raise? A bastard child growing up to inherit *her* farm. Great-Granny Jackson wouldn't have liked that. She would rather lay the child on the doorstep to freeze to death—

No, she couldn't take the chance that Bayard would hear the baby's cries. She would have taken him someplace quiet. To her kitchen where she laid him inside the dumbwaiter—the silent core of the house—so no one would hear his cries while she smothered him in the blanket his mother had made for him.

Only Minnie *had* heard his cries and they drove her mad. Not that she'd had that far to go.

I turned to the page I had been reading when Cortland interrupted me, fingering the pink ribbon—the one remnant of the pink blanket—that marked my place.

When I told them I saw the girl's ghost standing on the terrace they thought I was crazy just as Mama had when I told her about the things I saw and heard. Nanny had always believed me, though. She said I had what they called back in Ireland "the sight," which was why I knew when Mama's train was going to be late and what letters would say before they were open, and how I saw old Grandpa Noyes on the day he died even though he was in Hyde Park when it happened and I saw him in the house in the city. I could even sometimes make things happen, like the time I wanted a new dress and the parlor maid spilled tea all over my wretched old one or when I wanted Bayard Montague to be my escort at the Ogilvies' ball and Louisa Marsden, whom he was supposed to escort, came down with the measles. It wasn't that I wanted the parlor maid to be let go or poor Louisa Marsden's face to be ruined for the rest of her life, but I knew that my wanting something very badly could have unintended consequences so I should have known when I wanted not to be pregnant anymore—only so Bay would look at me again and put his hands around my slim waist again—that it would make the baby come early. And if I thought in the throes of pain "Oh, I wish this baby would die!" I didn't really mean it. I didn't mean for him to put it in the dumbwaiter to die.

But the baby doesn't know that. It cries and cries and cries—it won't ever let me forget that it's my fault

*it's dead until I make things right. That's why I had
to shoot Bayard. He had to die for killing our baby. I
thought the baby would stop crying then, but it never
has, even when they took the other woman's baby from
me. I still hear my baby crying. It wants me to come
to him. And I will. It's only right because, after all, it
was all my fault.*

I sat staring at Minnie's last words for so long they grew
faint as the room grew dim.

I could even sometimes make things happen.

These were the words that had struck a chill in my heart
the first time I'd read them because I might have written them
myself. It didn't make me feel any better now to tell myself that
they were part of Minnie's delusion, because didn't that mean
I'd inherited the same delusion myself?

I was Minnie's granddaughter.

But I wasn't crazy. The ghosts had all been tricks played by
Jess and Katrine to make me think I was crazy. And I wasn't
paranoid. My husband and his girlfriend *had* plotted against
me. So what did it matter that Great-Granny Jackson had
killed Mary's baby and haunted my childhood or that I was
Minnie's granddaughter and not Mary's. I hadn't inherited her
insanity—

Only her ability to make things happen.

Like Ryan Moser falling on the playground after he called
me a name and Charity Jane's pencil snapping during her
English final.

It didn't mean I'd driven Jess into another woman's arms—
even though I'd envisioned it so many times—or made him

stop loving me—even though I'd *imagined* that he didn't love me anymore. Even if that was what he had written in the novel he'd been working on.

How tempting to play the part she's cast for me—the Byronic villain plotting to put his wife away, I'd read that night in the dumbwaiter. Only later had I finished the passage. *Sometimes I feel as if I'm being used by her imagination, that I've become a character in a plot she's cooked up. But I won't let myself become what she imagines me. I won't be a stock character out of some silly Victorian melodrama. I will remain myself—a man who loves his wife precisely because she has the power to make real what she imagines.*

I could only assume that Katrine had convinced him otherwise. I certainly hadn't made him try to kill me. Even I hadn't imagined *that*. And all those ghost sightings (I pictured Katrine going under the weir that day, her scarf snagging on the rocks, but that didn't mean she hadn't been there before), Katrine had made those happen—

Except of course for the last one. The figure that had appeared out of the fog behind Jess on the pond, the one that dragged him down under the ice—that hadn't been Katrine. Katrine had already been dead.

That one came out of my imagination.

You have a powerful imagination, Jess always said. *If you don't use it—*

I would *not* use it to imagine that I had made Jess fall out of love with me, that I had made up the story of him trying to kill me, that it hadn't been a gun in his hand that night, only a flashlight, because if I began to imagine those things, I truly would go mad.

I closed Minnie's scrapbook and rubbed my arms to banish the gooseflesh that had risen on my skin. Cortland was right.

I should invest in a new furnace. For now, though, I'd make a fire. Dunstan (who wasn't my cousin after all!) was coming over later. I'd go upstairs and take a bath and put on the new burgundy velvet dress I'd bought in town last week. It would look beautiful in the firelight.

As I got up I saw someone standing on the terrace, a girl in white, the cold wind whipping her dress as she stood looking in at the warm, bright room. I could feel her longing through the panes of glass, her cold and loneliness and, most of all, her terrible, aching anger—and then she was gone. There was only a gust of snow beating against the glass as though it wanted to come in. I bolted the doors, drew the drapes against the cold, and then turned away from the night into the warmth of my house.

Acknowledgments

Thank you to my inestimable agent, Robin Rue, for finding the perfect home for this book, and to Beth Miller and Genevieve Gagne-Hawes at Writers House for working on its early drafts with me. I am grateful to have found an editor as gracious and insightful as Margaux Weisman.

I am forever grateful to my circle of first readers: Wendy Gold Rossi, Lauren Lipton, Scott Silverman, Lee Slonimsky, and Nora Slonimsky.

I owe a special debt of gratitude to Purcell Palmer and The Catwalk Foundation for providing me with the space and time to work on a revision of the present book.

And as always, I am thankful to my family, Lee, Maggie and Nora, for their love and support.

About the author

About the book

Insights,
Interviews
& More...

Meet Carol Goodman

CAROL GOODMAN grew up on Long Island, attended public school, and started writing at age nine, when her fourth-grade teacher introduced the topic of "Creative Writing." She wrote a ninety-page, crayon-illustrated epic entitled "The Adventures of the Magical Herd" in which a girl named Carol lives with a herd of magical horses. She knew from that moment that she wanted to be a writer.

During her teens Goodman wrote poetry and was named Young Poet of Long Island by Long Island University at the age of seventeen. She took a break from writing to major in Latin at Vassar College, never realizing that her first published novel would be about a Latin teacher. After college, she worked in publishing and then in a series of less demanding office jobs while writing short stories at night. Then she went back to school (to the University of Texas at Austin) to become a high school teacher, rediscovered Latin, and wrote a master's report on young adult fantasy literature. She taught Latin for three years in the Austin Independent School District until her daughter, Maggie, was born.

A few years (and two unpublished novels) later, Goodman came back to Long Island. She started writing poetry and short stories again and completed her MFA at the New School. She published poems and short stories in literary journals, including *The Greensboro Review, Literal Latte, The Midwest Quarterly, The New York Quarterly,* and *Other Voices.* A year after she finished her MFA, Goodman picked up a short story she had written about a Latin teacher at a boarding school in upstate New York (called "Girl, Declined") and started to write her bestselling and critically acclaimed debut novel, *The Lake of Dead Languages.*

Since its publication, Goodman has been writing full time (*The Seduction of Water, The Drowning Tree, The Ghost Orchid*) and teaching at the New School and SUNY New Paltz. Goodman's books have been nominated for the IMPAC award twice, the Simon & Schuster/Mary Higgins Clark Award, and the Nero Award; *The Seduction of Water* won the Hammett Prize in 2003. She lives in the Hudson Valley with her family. ❧

A Field Guide to Haunted Houses

When I moved to the Hudson Valley I found myself driving down country roads and village streets gazing covetously at stately Victorians and riverfront mansions. My house-buying budget ran closer to the Red Hook faux Colonial that Jess turns his nose up at, but I could still dream about living in one of those grand old houses. It seemed to me that if I could just find the right angle, the right moment at dusk, I might catch a glimpse of those long-gone inhabitants, just as Clare thinks she might hear "the sound of glasses clinking and laughter from a long-ago summer party" in the wind chimes hanging from the gatehouse of Riven House. It wasn't long before I began to imagine a ghost story and the house it might take place in. I've long been a fan of ghost stories and haunted house tales, whether the ghosts were real or imagined, whether the houses were haunted by the living or the dead. After all, what's a ghost without a house to haunt and what's a house without a whiff of the past to breathe life into its empty frame? Here are a few of my favorite haunted houses that I hope you will enjoy visiting—just don't expect a good night's sleep in any of them.

Although not strictly a haunted house, Thornfield Hall in *Jane Eyre* by Charlotte Brontë is where I fell in love with the gothic. *Someone* or *something* is up in the attic, setting fire to bed curtains and rending bridal veils, and whether the madwoman in the attic is flesh or represents Governess Jane's secret desires and alter ego, you won't look at your attic steps in quite the same way ever again.

Another governess haunts the halls of Bly, the country estate in Henry James's *The Turn of the Screw*. Or perhaps there are two governesses, the current nameless one and her predecessor, Miss Jessel. Or perhaps the ghosts are all in the governess's head. Henry James isn't telling in this masterpiece of ambiguity, but really, what's scarier: that the ghosts are real or that the woman in charge of your children is crazy?

We might doubt the sanity of Eleanor Vance, the heroine of *The Haunting of Hill House*, but there's no question of the house's sanity. "Hill House," Shirley Jackson tells us right off the bat, is "not sane." Doors don't stay closed and none of the angles are right, either. Oh, and just in case you were ▶

wondering, "whatever walked there, walked alone." Because that's the really scary thing about the haunted house: sooner or later, you're going to end up there alone.

No one is quite as lonely as the unnamed wife in Daphne du Maurier's *Rebecca*. Sure, she's married handsome millionaire Maxim de Winter and come to live in beautiful Manderley on the Cornish Coast, but all anyone can talk about is Maxim's dead wife, Rebecca, who haunts the house and the narrator's marriage. Is there any peskier ghost than an ex? Here's another case where the ghost might not be literal, but the house is haunted just the same. In fact, it's the house itself that continues to haunt the narrator as she tells us in the very first line, "Last night I dreamt I went to Manderley again."

The house itself is the culprit in Anne Rivers Siddons's *The House Next Door*, a tale of gentrification and construction gone wrong. If you've ever had your view ruined by an ugly monstrosity you'll feel for Colquitt and Walter Kennedy when modern architecture intrudes on their peaceful suburban backyard.

Haunted houses aren't only in the country. Jan Bryant Bartell encountered a haunting in the cozy rent-controlled West Village apartment she calls home in *Spindrift: Spray from a Psychic Sea*. This nonfiction book chilled me when an office-mate passed me a used copy in the early eighties. I used to walk by the townhouse where it took place and wonder whether I'd give up a rent-controlled apartment in the Village even if it *were* haunted. I recently ordered a used copy of the book to replace the one I'd lost and felt more haunted by nostalgia for my salad days in the city than by the bangs and knocks Bartell reports. But what *is* chilling is that the author died before the book's publication and, according to Internet lore, copies of the book mysteriously disappear. Sure enough, though I bought a copy less than six months ago, I can't find it anywhere.

I've had to reorder my copy of *The Uninvited* by Dorothy Macardle again, too, even though I could swear I've owned three over the years. The Cornish cottage where a brother and sister settle is haunted by the scent of mimosa. This is a gentle ghost story with a happy ending. Read it to regain your equilibrium after you read *The Little Stranger* by Sarah Waters. The ghost that haunts Hundreds Hall, an English country manor falling into genteel postwar decline, may be class consciousness and the Labour government, but that doesn't mean it's not just as terrifying.

Why are we so afraid of haunted houses? Perhaps it's what we see when we look at them. "There are many houses whose fronts suggest faces," John Langan writes in his chilling *House of Windows*, "but Belvedere House was the only residence I've seen whose front suggested a face hiding amongst its windows and angles, just out of view." Whose face *just out of view* are we afraid to see when we look through the windows of our haunted houses?

The predecessor who did our job better? The late wife who's more beloved than us? The raging alcoholic father of Stephen King's *The Shining*? Or is the face we're most afraid to see when we look in the windows our own reflection? As Monty says, quoting Orson Squire Fowler, "Just as men's skulls correspond to their characters, so men's habitations correspond to their intellect." In which case, the scariest haunted house may be the one in which we see ourselves. Red Hook faux Colonial, *c'est moi.* ༄

Reading Group Guide

1. What are your first impressions of Clare and Jess's relationship? What clues and subtext does the author include to paint the landscape of their marriage early on?

2. How did the author use themes and motifs from gothic tradition and classic literature to richen the novel? What were some that you were able to identify?

3. Both the house and the town have a very vivid atmosphere. In what ways did sense of place contribute to the narrative?

4. In your opinion, what was the significance of the various strange discoveries that Clare made: the handkerchief in the bath, the illustrations beneath the wallpaper, the collage? How do each of these speak to existing fears and questions in her own life?

5. Were you surprised when the villain was revealed? Why or why not?

6. After reading this novel, how have your views on marriage changed? Is it possible to have a marriage without any secrets?

7. Did you feel bad for Jess after hearing his side of the story (that he felt trapped by the miscarriage)? Why or why not? How could he have handled things differently? ∼